The Plaza was a torture chamber of memories. Think about business, she exhorted herself. Supposedly that's why she was here, though most of the details of her anticipated second corporation were in place. From Harry, she thought involuntarily, she had learned the fine points of running a business. Today's conference was a triumph for her.

When she first awoke the day was gray and cold. But by the time the conference was over, it had brightened. Sunlight washed the city. Empty hours loomed ahead of her. She could shop, go to a museum, she considered—but she was in the mood for neither. Nor was she ready to go to lunch. On impulse she decided to go to a beauty salon for a facial. That was a relaxing way to push away an hour. Maybe a facial would relieve some of her tenseness. Then she'd have lunch. The beauty salon at B. Altman, she decided, then lunch at the Charleston Gardens.

At the beauty salon Katie flipped through a supply of magazines, chose a recent edition of *Town & Country*. Hardly absorbing what she saw—the magazine lying across her lap—until a familiar face jumped at her from the pages. Her heart pounding, she gripped the magazine and brought it closer to her eyes. It was just someone with a startling resemblance to Harry, she told herself.

She read the caption beneath the photograph of the man who so resembled Harry. A man with a tall young blonde. "Mr. and Mrs. Harry Newhouse at an embassy party." *Harry had remarried.*

Why did she feel betrayed? Harry wasn't her husband any longer. She had driven him out of her life. Why did she keep playing this ridiculous game? There would be no tomorrow for Harry and her, Katie knew.

If only she could believe it . . .

THE BEST IN HISTORICAL ROMANCES

TIME-KEPT PROMISES   (2422, $3.95)
by Constance O'Day Flannery

Sean O'Mara froze when he saw his wife Christina standing before him. She had vanished and the news had been written about in all of the papers—he had even been charged with her murder! But now he had living proof of his innocence, and Sean was not about to let her get away. No matter that the woman was claiming to be someone named Kristine; she still caused his blood to boil.

PASSION'S PRISONER   (2573, $3.95)
by Casey Stewart

When Cassandra Lansing put on men's clothing and entered the Rawlings saloon she didn't expect to lose anything—in fact she was sure that she would win back her prized horse Rapscallion that her grandfather lost in a card game. She almost got a smug satisfaction at the thought of fooling the gamblers into believing that she was a man. But once she caught a glimpse of the virile Josh Rawlings, Cassandra wanted to be the woman in his embrace!

ANGEL HEART   (2426, $3.95)
by Victoria Thompson

Ever since Angelica's father died, Harlan Snyder had been angling to get his hands on her ranch, the Diamond R. And now, just when she had an important government contract to fulfill, she couldn't find a single cowhand to hire—all because of Snyder's threats. It was only a matter of time before the legendary gunfighter Kid Collins turned up on her doorstep, badly wounded. Angelica assessed his firmly muscled physique and stared into his startling blue eyes. Beneath all that blood and dirt he was the handsomest man she had ever seen, and the one person who could help beat Snyder at his own game.

Available wherever paperbacks are sold, or order direct from the Publisher. Send cover price plus 50¢ per copy for mailing and handling to Zebra Books, Dept. 3592, 475 Park Avenue South, New York, N.Y. 10016. Residents of New York, New Jersey and Pennsylvania must include sales tax. DO NOT SEND CASH.

JULIE ELLIS

NO GREATER LOVE

ZEBRA BOOKS
KENSINGTON PUBLISHING CORP.

For Barbara Sichel,
Barry Cohen, Merna Zinnershine,
and Marsha Mattus

ZEBRA BOOKS

are published by

Kensington Publishing Corp.
475 Park Avenue South
New York, NY 10016

First Zebra Books printing: December, 1991

Printed in the United States of America

Cover photo by Karen Knaver

Part One

Chapter One

HER LUSH, honey-colored hair bobbed as decreed by fashion in this late June of 1923, her blue-green eyes announcing her rapture at the prospect of spending today with Harry Newhouse, sixteen-year-old Katie Freeman hurried down the dark, dreary stairs of the Rivington Street tenement. Emerging into the humid heat of the late morning, the street noisy with Sunday shoppers in search of Lower East Side bargains and children at play, she felt herself suffused by a glorious sense of escape.

With Harry she dared to venture—admittedly an onlooker rather than a participant—into the uptown world of the Plaza and the Waldorf-Astoria, Saks Fifth Avenue and Tiffany, the Palais Royal and the Trocadero. Once she had roamed with Harry about Manhattan until dawn so they might savor the excitement of early breakfast at the deluxe Child's at Fifty-ninth Street and Fifth—as favored by New York society.

For the past five Sundays Harry had been "showing the city" to settlement-house volunteer Michelle Goncourt—at her imperious request. But this Sunday was *hers*, Katie told herself in triumph. She was to meet Harry in front of the deli, where they'd buy picnic makings. Then they'd go up to Central Park, Katie's favorite spot in all Manhattan.

Born and raised in New Orleans, Michelle attended some fancy finishing school uptown. She was beautiful and wore dramatic clothes that came from such awesome stores as Saks and Bergdorf and Best. How could Harry refuse when their French teacher specifically asked him to take Michelle to the Statue of Liberty and the Aquarium and the Metropolitan Museum on Sunday afternoons?

From the first week of this school year—when they'd met in their French class at night school—Katie and Harry had been close friends. She didn't dare allow herself to think of their relationship as anything else. She knew Harry was determined to go on to City College in the fall and then to law school. She, too, meant to go to college.

But since the first evening when Harry asked her to have coffee with him at the Garden Cafeteria after class, she had wanted to believe that he would be forever part of her life. He was so handsome, so smart, so full of big dreams. And there were moments when Harry looked at her, when they accidentally touched—that she was sure he shared her feelings.

Her father had died when she was seven—because he had lost the will to live after an accident sentenced him to a wheelchair, her mother always said. Her mother died in the terrible flu epidemic of 1918—the same epidemic that had robbed Harry of his whole family.

Dying, her mother had turned over her savings to a neighbor with a plea to take in Katie and see her through high school. The money that was supposed to be their key to a new life in the West Bronx—"in a flat with elevators and parquet floors and French doors." Her mother was to open a shop in the Bronx. "All the neighborhood ladies will come to buy from me, Katie!"

Her mother died, and Katie moved into a closet-sized bedroom with Ruth and Abe Kornfeld's sullen daughter Celia. At the end of the school year Mrs. Kornfeld sent her out to work as a cash girl in Hearn's Department Store up on Fourteenth Street.

8

"You won't be goin' back to school," Mrs. Kornfeld said bluntly. *"Your Mama left just a little money."* Not true, Katie railed inwardly, but went to work six days a week and to school at night. Each week she brought her pay envelope home to Mrs. Kornfeld, who gave her money for carfare and a tiny allowance "for little things."

For the last three years—ever since Mrs. Kornfeld admitted her husband was "not quite right in the head anymore"—Celia insisted they keep their bedroom door locked at all times. "Papa don't mean nuthin', but he wanders through any open door."

Even in good times—like now—Celia couldn't hold a job for more than a few weeks at a time. Abe Kornfeld hadn't worked for years. Katie understood that Mrs. Kornfeld had a hard time supporting the family on the piecework sewing she did at home, but she felt justified in concealing her promotion seven months ago from cash girl to clerk. The extra money in her pay envelope each week went into a secret bank account that would help her get settled in a room of her own when she graduated from night school. Mama wouldn't expect her to stay with the Kornfelds once she had her diploma.

Now, stopping at the corner for traffic, Katie suddenly realized she had forgotten to take her vanity and Woolworth-bought lipstick. She turned around and hurried back toward the house. Makeup was an important part of appearing a fashionable young lady. That and the chemise she had bought in Klein's basement on Union Square at one tenth of its price in an uptown department store were her passport to the fantasy life she and Harry wove for themselves.

She fumbled with her key at the door to the flat, impatient to be on her way to meet Harry. She pushed the door open, darted across the kitchen, past the tiny living room to the bedroom she shared with Celia. Behind the closed door of the other bedroom the phonograph blared an old Caruso recording of *"Vesti la giubba."*

Katie unlocked her door, crossed to the chest she

shared with Celia, reached into a drawer for her lipstick and vanity. If she walked fast, she consoled herself, she wouldn't keep Harry waiting.

"Ruth—" Katie whirled about with a start at the sound of Abe Kornfeld's voice. "Why you keep runnin' away from me all the time?"

"Mr. Kornfeld, I'm K-Katie," she stammered. *Where was Mrs. Kornfeld?* She never left him alone in the house. Either she or Celia was always with him. "Katie," she reiterated uneasily as he walked into the room with his shuffling gait. A small, obese man with wispy graying hair and faded brown eyes that wore a constant air of bewilderment.

"Ruth, why do we have to wait until the dark to get under the sheet? I like when we do it in the daytime, too."

"I'm Katie," she said again in panic as his hairy arms reached for her. "Mrs. Kornfeld will be home soon. Go listen to the music and wait for her," she cajoled. Mrs. Kornfeld thought she had left for the day, Katie realized.

"I wanna do it now." Abe pulled her roughly against his flabby body, one hand fumbling at her breast. "Sometimes you're mean to me," he accused.

Katie was unnerved by the hard mass prodding against her small, slender body as a hand reached to lift the hem of her short skirt.

"Mr. Kornfeld, no!" she protested, struggling to free herself. "Let me go! Abe, no!"

"Abe!" Ruth Kornfeld's voice crackled with command. "Take your hands off her. This minute, Abe!"

Reluctantly, comprehension slowly taking hold of him, Abe released Katie and turned to Ruth.

"I—I thought she was you." He stuttered in childlike terror. "Honest, Ruth."

"Go to our room, Abe," she ordered, gentle now. "Go listen to the music. I'll be there in a minute." She waited for Abe to leave them, then turned to Katie. "He didn't mean nuthin', Katie. He just gets mixed-up sometimes.

He didn't mean no harm. You forget about this," she said with sudden, menacing strength. "You don't tell Celia. You don't tell nobody."

"No, ma'am." *If his wife hadn't come back, he'd have raped her. How could she forget that?*

"You goin' out with that Harry Newhouse again?" Casual now, almost contemptuous. "That Harry, always givin' himself airs."

"We're going up to Central Park," Katie told her, still cold and trembling from the encounter with Abe.

"Well, go on." Mrs. Kornfeld gestured arrogantly, but Katie understood she had been unnerved by Abe's actions. "And lock up behind you." Katie could read Mrs. Kornfeld's mind. *"You left your door open—you asked for it."* And all at once she understood Celia's sullenness, her dislike for men, her insistence on their bedroom door being locked. *How was she going to live in this flat after today?*

Her mind in turmoil, Katie left the flat and walked down the stairs with compulsive haste. *Why did she keep shaking this way? Nothing happened.* But if Mrs. Kornfeld had come in a few minutes later, Abe would have had her across the bed.

She knew what happened between a man and a woman in bed. The girls in the store, at school, talked about it in self-conscious whispers. The new cashier in their department bragged about carrying "protection" in her vanity so she wouldn't "get caught" if she did that with a boy.

Katie shuddered, remembering the ugly moment when Abe had pressed himself against her that way. She'd felt outraged and terrified and helpless.

Harry reached into the closet for his blue flannel jacket—which had elevated eyebrows in the flat when he had brought it home from Brooks Brothers eight months ago—and dropped it across his arm. None of the men in his cousin's family had ever even walked inside Brooks Brothers. When one of the men wore a jacket, it was because of the need for warmth. But his Brooks Brothers jacket—which cost him what he earned in a month—gave Harry the confidence to rub shoulders with those whose incomes far exceeded his own.

He frowned as he inspected his reflection in the mottled mirror that hung over the dresser between his bed and Izzy's. The young man in the mirror might appear casual and self-assured. Inwardly Harry was shaken by the events of the past forty-eight hours.

Mr. Ryan had *promised* him the next opening for a clerk in his office. The old bastard told everybody in the office that "Harry Newhouse has the most phenomenal memory I've ever come across." It would mean a lot toward helping him get into law school—once he was through City College—if he was clerking in a law office.

He'd learned to drive so he could chauffeur Ryan to the cheap hotels where he met his string of floozies and then drive him back to the office. But Ryan had given the job to the nephew of a client, and *he* was still the office boy.

"Hey, Harry . . ." Izzy hovered in the doorway with a self-conscious grin. "You gonna be away the rest of the day?"

"Probably . . ."

"The rest of the family's gone off to Coney Island," Izzy told him. "Don't come back before eight. I'm bringin' up Dolly. We wanna play house." He winked knowingly.

"I won't be back before eight," Harry promised. "And be careful." He tried for a playful note. "You said you didn't want to get married before you're thirty."

"Hell, no," Izzy shot back. "Not with all those flappers out there dying to give it away."

"See you later." Harry sauntered from the room and out of the flat.

Walking down the stairs, he allowed his mind to relinquish the somber realization that he had been bypassed for the long-coveted promotion. Instead, he focused on his humiliating discovery at the settlement house that Michelle had left for New Orleans without a word of farewell to him.

"She graduated from her school," Miss Fenwick told him. "She went home to announce her engagement. She's getting married in October."

"To who?" he demanded. *All the time they'd been together, she'd been engaged to somebody else.*

"To whom," Miss Fenwick automatically corrected. "I don't know. Some student at Princeton. She came up here to school so she could be near him."

She came up to New York to be near some student from Princeton, but the first night she'd been at the settlement house, she'd asked *him*—and Miss Fenwick had encouraged it—to show her the sights on Sundays. The first Sunday he'd taken her out to the Statue of Liberty. On the boat coming back to the city she'd invited him up to the apartment she shared with her aunt, who wrote stories for the ladies' magazines. But her aunt had left for Europe the night before.

"She left a full refrigerator," Michelle said airily, and her eyes sent him a blatant invitation. "We can have dinner." She giggled. "I hope you know how to make coffee."

"I'll make the coffee," Harry promised, suddenly tingling with anticipation. And apprehension. Would she guess he'd never slept with anybody before? he asked himself in agonizing embarrassment. He was glad now that Izzy bragged so much about his "sexy broads" and what they did together. All at once he couldn't wait to be with Michelle.

Michelle's aunt lived in an apartment in an elegant townhouse off lower Fifth Avenue. Harry marveled at the beautiful antiques, the lush draperies. In the kitchen Harry encountered his first refrigerator.

"You put up the coffee," Michelle ordered. Her melodic southern accent, he thought giddily, was like the voice of a modern Circe, luring him into her power.

"Your wish is my command," he said with an amorous smile. Trying to envision how John Barrymore would play a scene like this.

"You mean that?" she challenged, pausing before the open refrigerator.

"Try me," he said, his heart pounding.

"Take me into the bedroom and make love to me," she commanded. "Afterward we'll have dinner."

"Point me in the right direction," he drawled, and blushed when she stared down at his bulging crotch.

"You're in the right direction, Harry," she laughed, and lifted her face to his.

She kissed differently from the few girls he'd kissed in dark hallways. He remembered what Izzy had said and opened his mouth to probe hers.

"Oh wow," she murmured when they paused for breath. "I figured you'd be hot." She reached for his hand and walked with him from the kitchen down the hall to one of the two bedrooms. "Do you have a condom?" she asked at the door.

He stared at her for a painful instant.

"Not with me," he stammered. Remembering that Izzy always carried one in his wallet.

"Never mind," she soothed. "I have a package hidden away."

With exhilarating swiftness they stripped and fell across the bed. Harry was euphorically aware of the discarded satin teddy, an exotic perfume, and silken sheets.

"Let me," she whispered when he seemed awkward with the condom. "Oh, sugar, I can't wait!"

He'd thought about this many times. Izzy bragged he'd been doing it since he was fourteen. *He'd* had "wet dreams." But now he was here in bed with Michelle Goncourt, and he didn't want this ever to end.

"Honey, take it easy," Michelle protested breathlessly

while he thrust himself within her with ecstatic frenzy, but he knew she was pleased.

Every Sunday for the past five weeks they'd gone back to Michelle's apartment after hours of sight-seeing, and they'd done it again. And on the intervening days he sleepwalked, waiting greedily for Sunday with Michelle. Even the triumph of receiving his high school diploma last week had seemed minor in comparison with those hours each week with Michelle, who was a willing and adept teacher in the fine points of making love. And then she'd gone away without even saying goodbye. Because he wasn't some rich Princeton student, he taunted himself.

Harry Newhouse from the Lower East Side was somebody she'd talk about with her girlfriends back home. He felt his face redden as he imagined Michelle talking about them in their most intimate moments. Izzy said women talked about everything among themselves. *"Harry, they're worse than men."*

Now—his jacket over one arm—he charged toward the deli where he was to meet Katie. He hadn't had a chance to tell her that old man Ryan hadn't given him the promotion. She'd be angry for him, he thought tenderly. She was so pretty and so sweet. And she was smart, he thought with pride.

What happened between Michelle and him had nothing to do with how he felt about Katie, he told himself, and was startled that he was suddenly assaulted by visions of Katie in bed with him. But Katie was a lady. Michelle was a slut in silk and lace.

He slowed his pace as he approached the deli. Katie wasn't here yet. Most times she was the first to arrive. He reached into his pocket for two cents and bought a *Daily News*. He tried to focus on the front-page news stories, but today his mind was in too much turmoil for this. He needed to talk to Katie—she always understood, was always sympathetic.

Turning the corner, Katie spied Harry standing in front of the deli, reading a morning tabloid. She understood why Michelle had wanted Harry to spend Sundays with her. Every girl in their French class looked up when Harry walked into the room.

As though feeling the weight of her gaze, Harry turned in her direction. His dark eyes lighted. Subconsciously he ran one hand through his unruly near-black hair. His smile was mesmerizing. All at once—in the comfort of Harry's presence—Katie felt her shaky hold on composure evaporating.

"Katie, you're so pale," he said solicitously. "What's happened?"

She told him in short, jagged sentences. Fighting tears. Feeling his rage and his sympathy.

"The bastard!" Harry's face flushed. She had never heard him use such language. "Katie, did he—" He halted, unable to bring himself to say the words.

"No," she managed, and color flooded her high cheekbones. "Mrs. Kornfeld came back in time."

"You're not going back to that flat," Harry told her, dropping an arm about her waist.

"Harry, where can I go?" She had some money in her secret bank account, she remembered. But it was so hard to find a vacant room. Everybody talked about the housing crisis in the city.

"We'll figure that out later. You won't go back to the Kornfelds." He made a show of dismissing for now the grim reality of the past few moments, strived for a casual air. "Let's buy some salami and potato salad here, then walk to Ratner's for onion rolls. You wouldn't let us have a picnic without Ratner's onion rolls, would you?"

For now Katie allowed Harry to sweep her up into their usual convivial Sunday mood. They shopped for picnic makings, took the "El" uptown, walked across to Central Park. Yet, shaken as she was by her encounter with Abe Kornfeld, Katie sensed an unfamiliar depression in Harry that penetrated his efforts at banter. She waited until they were in their favorite, private corner of the park—with their picnic spread before them—to probe.

"I didn't get the promotion," Harry blurted out. "After everything Ryan told me! He gave it to the nephew of one of his clients." Harry's eyes blazed in fresh rage. "Katie, I was the office boy, not his chauffeur! And remember how often I used to drive him on my own time—because I was working for that promotion. I never made excuses."

"You can find a better job, Harry," Katie encouraged him. "Times are good now."

"Another job as an office boy." His voice was caustic. "I'd be starting all over again." He paused, seeming to be involved in some inner debate. "I have to change my life, Katie. There has to be something better for us than working at rotten jobs and living in tenements. So once a week we walk through the lobby of some fancy hotel and pretend we're somebody we'll never be if we don't break out now."

"You're going to City College in the fall," she reminded. Unnerved by his sudden show of restlessness. They had their lives all planned. Both of them were going to night college. One day he would be a lawyer, and she'd be a social worker. "When you have a college degree, you'll—"

"I don't want to wait!" He radiated a determination that was contagious. "I've been reading about Texas. People go out there and become rich in six months. The newspapers and magazines are full of stories about how people from all over the country are running out there and striking oil. Katie, it could happen to us!"

"We can't just p-pick up and go to Texas," Katie stammered.

His face softened.

"We'll get married, Katie. Together we can do any-

17

thing. We'll give a week's notice, be married, and head for Texas."

"Just like that?" A surge of conflicting emotions threatened to suffocate her. *Harry wanted to marry her*. But how could they go thousands of miles away—with no jobs out there and little cash between them? *What about college?* Did they have night college in Texas? Harry always bragged that New York was special in having free colleges. "It'll cost a lot of money to take a train all the way to Texas. . . ." *But Harry talked about their getting married.*

"We won't take a train," he plotted with newfound confidence. "Old man Ryan is selling his car. He wants to buy a new Franklin. He feels guilty about screwing me on the job—he'll sell it to me cheap. We'll buy a tent and camp out across the country. Katie, I'm glad he didn't give me that promotion. Now we'll do what we should be doing. And you won't go back to the Kornfelds," he said gently. "I'll tell my cousin what happened, and she'll let you sleep on the sofa in the parlor till we leave town." Unexpectedly he chuckled. "She'll be glad I'm finally moving out, so Izzy can have his own room."

"Harry, you're sure about this?" Katie was ambivalent—joyous at the prospect of marrying Harry, yet terrified of so uncertain a future.

"I'm sure." He reached for her shoulders and brought her face close to his. "I guess it's all right to kiss my future wife."

"I think it's all right," she teased, and lifted her mouth to his. All at once impatient for this first kiss. It wasn't ugly when you did *that* with your husband, she told herself. It would be beautiful then.

Whatever happened, she'd be with Harry, Katie told herself. That was all that really mattered.

Chapter Two

CRINGING AT the necessity to return to the Kornfeld flat—even with Harry at her side—Katie packed her few belongings into the suitcase she and Harry had bought at a pushcart for this purpose. She had haltingly explained to Ruth Kornfeld that she would be staying with Harry's cousins until her marriage. Now—in a surge of sentiment—she collected her mother's cherished pot of geraniums, which survived year after year under Katie's solicitous care.

She was welcomed by Harry's cousins with a warmth that almost brought her to tears. Mama had been like this. But lying on her improvised bed on the sofa—too excited to sleep—she was tormented by doubts. Mama had wanted her to graduate from high school—it was Mama's dream. And what about her own dream to become a social worker? The social workers at the settlement house—so eager to be useful to others—were her idols. Someday, she had promised herself, she'd go out into the world and make life easier for the poor and the troubled.

And what about Harry's dream of college and law school? Could he just walk away from that? Would he hate her someday, blame her because he'd given up college and law school to go with her to Texas? What would happen to them out there, two thousand miles from everything that was familiar? Were they making an awful mistake?

At Sophie Hirsch's insistence, they abandoned their first thought of being married at City Hall.

"Your families would expect you to be married by a

rabbi," she insisted. "A very small wedding here in the flat. We will arrange everything." She ignored her husband's stare of consternation. "Can we do less?" she demanded dramatically.

On Monday morning Katie and Harry went to work, knowing that they would give notice today. That same evening Harry came home to tell Katie he'd bought Mr. Ryan's six-year-old Ford.

"I bought it cheap, like I told you." He was jubilant. "The old boy was glad to get it off his hands before his wife got her hands on it. She wants to learn to drive." He shook his head in gentle derision. Katie forced herself to be silent. Why shouldn't Mrs. Ryan learn to drive? During the war women drove ambulances and Red Cross trucks. Now they weren't supposed to be able to drive. Men didn't want to admit that times were changing. "Think of it, Katie! A week from today we'll climb into the car—*our* car—and start on the road to Texas."

"I can't wait," Katie said effervescently. Yet in a secret corner of her mind she asked herself if she and Harry were crazy to do this. Dallas was so far away. If they didn't like it, they couldn't just turn around and come back. This was forever. In a strange way, she thought, it was as though she were removing herself from the memory of Mama by leaving behind the world they had shared.

"Tomorrow night we'll go over to the camping store," Harry pursued. "We'll buy ourselves a tent and a cookstove—the kind people take on camping trips—and some vacuum bottles."

"Harry," Katie asked in sudden trepidation. "How will you know where to drive?"

"I've got our route all worked out already," he said with satisfaction, and she thought, How smart Harry is! "There are two million, eight hundred thousand miles of highway in this country, crossing from one ocean to the other. I know exactly which roads to take."

"How long will it take us?" she asked, excitement battling fear.

"Maybe two or three weeks. We'll see." Harry shrugged. "Anyhow, we'll be seeing most of the country. It'll be something to remember all our lives."

The next few days sped past. On Sunday afternoon Katie dressed for her wedding in the Hirsches' bathroom. She could hear the sound of voices in the tiny parlor, where Harry's male cousins were practicing to hold up the *chuppa* provided by the rabbi. Even here in the bathroom—while she inspected her reflection in the mirror, telling herself she was *about to be married*—she could smell the pungent scent of the carnations that Izzy had brought home at his mother's behest, and which blended incongruously with the aromas of brisket simmering on the kitchen stove and rugelach baking in the oven.

Then Harry was knocking on the door to tell her the rabbi was waiting to marry them. The details of the ceremony had been planned with poignant solemnity. Izzy's father escorted Harry to the *chuppa*. His mother walked with Katie in the absence of her own mother. The four young male cousins held up the *chuppa*. Izzy's only sister—who had provided the bridal bouquet of pink rosebuds—was the maid of honor.

Since there had been no wedding rehearsal, the rabbi instructed the bride and groom as he performed the ceremony. In the torpid heat of the Sunday afternoon Katie felt her turquoise shift clinging between her shoulder blades. Then at last the rabbi said the final words. She and Harry were husband and wife.

"Kiss her!" Izzy ordered Harry. "Then it's my turn."

"So young to be married," Sophie said sentimentally, kissing first Harry, then Katie. "But you're both smart and willing to work. Life's going to be good to you," she predicted.

"Mama, bring on the food," her husband ordered in

mock reproach. "And don't forget the bottle of schnapps."

"All right, all right," she clucked, and headed for the kitchen.

"You gonna tell us where you're spendin' the wedding night?" Izzy prodded with a grin. "I promise not to break down the door."

"We have a room at the Plaza," Harry said self-consciously, while Katie lowered her eyes, less from bridal reticence than to hide her amusement at the response—shocked silence—that she correctly anticipated.

Izzy's eyes seemed to double in size.

"You're spendin' the night at the Plaza Hotel?" Izzy derided them after a leaden moment.

"Unless it burns down and we have to get out." Harry was enjoying the excitement he'd created.

"Hey, one night at the Plaza costs more than you make in a week," Izzy protested.

"How many times do I get married?" Harry challenged. She, too, had been shocked by Harry's decision, Katie admitted to herself. But she understood. "So it'll make a dent in the bankroll. But we're starting off first class."

"You really gonna drive all the way to Texas?" Izzy's youngest brother asked, radiating envy.

"Everybody's driving these days," Harry drawled. "Every town's setting up campsites for travelers to stay overnight."

"Here's a class act," Izzy chuckled as his mother walked into the parlor with a tray of food. Slabs of succulent brisket smothered in onions. Pastrami in thick slices. Pickles from a barrel at its peak, and rye fresh from the oven. And a bottle of schnapps for toasting the bride and groom. Later, with glasses of hot tea, there would be rugelach.

Two hours later Katie and Harry were being ushered into their room at the Plaza—the smallest, least expensive room in the hotel, but it *was* the Plaza. Never on those Sundays when she and Harry had mingled with the guests in the lobby had Katie imagined she'd ever be spending the night in one of these rooms. She gazed admiringly—fighting against revealing her awe—at the elegant furniture, the lush drapes at the windows, the fine carpeting.

She was startled when she saw the lavish tip Harry gave to the bellhop who had brought up their two small, inexpensive valises. Then, for an agonizing moment, she was caught up in embarrassment. Had she imagined it or did the bellhop look disgusted? Had he expected more?

"Katie, we're on our way!" Harry pulled her close in exultation. "We did it!"

"I'm a little scared," Katie confessed.

"At traveling to Texas or being married?" Harry joshed.

"At leaving home," she told him, her eyes lighted with laughter. "I'm not afraid of being married."

"You modern girls," he scolded tenderly. "Nothing scares you."

Katie was surprised by the surge of excitement she felt low within her. At the same time she felt a sudden self-consciousness in Harry.

"It's early," he said without looking at her. He dropped his hands to his side. "The sun is just going down."

Did he mean it was shameless to make love when it wasn't night yet? They'd pull down the shades and pretend it was night. She was Harry's wife—they didn't have to stop at soft kisses. Erin at the store had told them all about her wedding night. While the other girls giggled, she vowed it was beautiful. *"It just hurt for a minute, and then—zowie!"* It wasn't wrong to do *that* when you were married.

"Can we see the park from here?" she asked.

"No." He was apologetic. "Those rooms cost lots more." He hesitated. "You know what we should do, Katie? We should go out and say good-bye to the city.

We'll be leaving first thing in the morning." For the first time she felt her own trepidation reflected in Harry.

"All right," she agreed, waiting for his lead.

"Let's take the E1 downtown," he plotted. "We'll walk to the middle of the Brooklyn Bridge. Nobody else will be walking," he predicted. "Everybody will be driving or riding the street cars. That's the place to say good-bye to the city."

They left the hotel hand in hand and traveled downtown to the bridge. They arrived as sunset descended on New York. They followed the pedestrian walk to the middle of the bridge. Cars, streetcars rushed past, but they were the sole foot travelers. The rose-tinted sunset bathed everything in view, lending a touching beauty and softness.

Katie and Harry stood in the wondrous solitude of the pedestrian walk and watched in silence—her hand in his—while the sunset gave way to dusk. Then millions of lights, it seemed, were switched on. The endless strings of lights that outlined the bridge. The lights in the myriad apartments and offices that rose into the night sky.

"Good-bye, New York," Harry said softly. "When we stand here again, we'll be rich!"

"Good-bye, New York," Katie said with a mixture of wistfulness and bravado. "We'll come back someday."

Only for a moment did Katie feel uneasy when she walked out of the Plaza bathroom into their bedroom—where Harry waited for her in bed. Her white chiffon nightgown was a going-away present from the girls at the store. Her unease evaporated when she saw the luminescence of his eyes as they traveled over her.

"Katie, you're beautiful," he whispered, and tossed aside the sheet. "My beautiful bride."

"My handsome husband," she murmured with an air of levity, feeling as though she were a character in a movie. She didn't feel shy, she told herself exultantly. Modern girls enjoyed their wedding night. "Oh, Harry, I can't believe everything that's happened."

"There's more," he laughed. "Kiddo, you ain't seen nuthin' yet!"

He was a warm and tender lover, and Katie reveled in their shared pleasure.

"Oh, Katie, Katie." He held her with a strength that was almost painful as they finally moved into the ultimate moment of shared ecstasy. "I didn't know it would be so great."

Had he slept with a lot of other girls? Katie asked herself in sweet torment. But that didn't matter, she comforted herself. Now he was her husband. Erin said every man had slept with girls before he married. But she had pleased Harry, she remembered with pride. He was surprised—but *pleased*—that she enjoyed making love. Erin said a lot of women just put up with it.

She slept in Harry's arms, their legs entangled, sheet discarded. She awoke with a start as a phone rang close by, immediately conscious of being in a strange room, of Harry's closeness. She knew it was morning because a sliver of golden sunlight lay across the foot of the bed.

"It's all right," Harry soothed, and reached across her to pick up the phone. "I left word for a six o'clock wake-up call."

Katie listened while Harry spoke briefly with the switchboard operator. He was so smart about everything. She would never have known about asking for a "wake-up call."

"We'll check out, have breakfast at the Automat, and go find the car," he said, reaching to pull her close.

"Harry," she reminded him as his mouth reached for hers, "you said we have to be on the road by seven. . . ."

"So we'll cheat a little," he teased.

She hadn't thought married people made love in broad daylight, Katie mused while Harry's hands slid away the straps of her nightgown, but she offered no protest. At this moment nothing was so important as being with Harry this way. If it seemed a little wicked, that just added something special.

By 7:30 A.M. Katie and Harry were driving toward the ferry that would take them and the car to New Jersey.

"Harry, I've never been in another state," Katie marveled. She'd never been further from Rivington Street than Coney Island.

"You're going to be in a bunch of states," he boasted. "We'll just pretend we're a pair of tourists seeing the country."

Katie was conscious of a tingle of alarm as they boarded the ferry. Her eyes clung to the retreating shore while the ferry chugged toward its destination. They were leaving behind their whole lives, everything that was familiar. But then a defiant smile lighted her face. She didn't have to be afraid. She was with Harry—her husband.

In New Jersey Harry sought out the Lincoln Highway. He made a show of confidence, but she sensed his tension.

"There it is," he said with relief, and pointed to the red, white, and blue marker. "We stay on this highway all the way to Chicago."

Katie was mesmerized by the passing scenery. Tall, lush trees, enormous stretches of open land. *She had never seen so much land!*

"Harry, I can't believe all this open space," she said in awe. "And we lived in miserable little boxes piled one on top of another!"

"Not all flats in New York are like ours," he pointed out. "Uptown people live in apartments that take up a whole floor, sometimes two floors. That's for the rich." She sensed his envy that they had never lived in such opulence.

"With open land like this around us, *we're* rich." She leaned forward, drinking in the view. "Harry, will we own land someday?"

"You bet we will." One hand left the wheel to fondle hers. "Our own oil well, maybe, and a ranch with thousands of acres. It's out there for the taking, Katie."

But they were going to Texas with so little money, she reminded herself. Why couldn't she feel the way Harry did? That they'd be rich so fast they'd be dizzy. But whatever, she was with Harry. And they were escaping from the Lower East Side.

They drove through the town of Princeton, which Katie found quaint and charming.

"They've got a fancy college here," Harry told Katie with an air of contempt. "Princeton College. One of the Ivy League schools."

Katie was somber for a moment. Was Harry already regretting giving up college and law school?

They followed the Lincoln Highway through Trenton into Philadelphia.

"Except for New York, Philadelphia, and Pittsburgh, the Lincoln Highway goes right around the big cities," Harry boasted when they had gone through Philadelphia and were searching for a place to pull off the road and have lunch. "We save a lot of time that way."

After sixteen years of living in the overcrowded, grubby Lower East Side, Katie was enthralled by this new version of American life. For miles they saw only fertile fields, forests, an occasional farmhouse. Katie was developing a passionate love for the hills and valleys of farm country, for the fragrant, clean air.

"Harry, I can't believe all this land!"

"Believe it." He grinned in youthful anticipation. "And we're going to carve out a chunk of it for ourselves."

Harry's primary concern was to maintain the forty miles an hour he had set for themselves. Refusing to admit he was tired—though Katie knew he was exhausted—Harry insisted on driving until near-sunset, when Katie ordered him to stop so she could prepare a makeshift supper.

"Wouldn't you rather we camp in the woods than in

27

one of the town campsites?" Harry asked persuasively. "I read somewhere—I think it was in the *Literary Digest*—that travelers are complaining that a lot of camps are unsanitary."

"I'd much rather camp in the woods," Katie agreed enthusiastically—like Harry, appreciating the benefit to their tight budget. "It'll be our private little house for the night."

"On nights that it's raining," Harry told her, "we'll go to one of those new tourist homes. I won't have you sleeping in a tent in the rain," he said tenderly. Tourist homes were less expensive than hotels.

On this first night of their long journey they set up their tent in a wooded area fifty feet from the highway. Exhilarated by the knowledge that this was the first supper she was preparing for her husband, Katie cooked on the small cookstove designed for travelers. They sat on a blanket and watched dusk give way to night. The sky was splashed with stars. Katie and Harry pretended their Campbell's canned soup and the frankfurters provided a gourmet fare such as they might have shared at the dining room of the Ritz or the St. Regis back in New York. Before they slept, they made love in the exquisite solitude of the tent, the air aromatic with the scent of pines and summer wildflowers.

Each day followed a similar pattern except for the occasional night when rain drove them into a tourist home. Katie and Harry tried to avoid this new institution. Though some were clean and comfortable, a middle-aged couple they encountered at a service station told them many were not.

"Watch out for those dirty rings in the community bathtub," the woman warned. "And never walk around in your bare feet—you don't know what they're gonna meet."

"Place we stayed last night," her husband complained, "we couldn't get a half hour of uninterrupted sleep. The fella across the hall snored straight through."

Every third or fourth day they treated themselves to a cheap meal in a small-town restaurant or bought hot dogs and ice cream from a roadside stand. They found clear brooks in which to bathe. On one particularly exhausting day they left the highway to seek out a movie theater and—for twenty-five cents each—saw a new Gloria Swanson film.

At the approach to Chicago they left the Lincoln Highway to follow the Jefferson Highway. Now they drove south into Kansas, past sweeping fields of wheat and corn. Katie was ever mesmerized by the beauty of the land. She gazed endlessly at the growing wheat waving in the wind. It was so beautiful, she thought—swaying with the grace of a million Isadora Duncans. The corn was head-high now, and reaching toward the sky.

"That's winter wheat," Harry told her. "It's planted in the fall before the cold weather starts. It stops growing during the winter, and begins again in the spring. See, they're harvesting it now."

Katie was proud of the way Harry had spent long hours in the settlement-house library reading up on all the states they'd be passing through. For both of them books were the road to knowledge.

Propelled by an impatience to be in their new home, Harry drove the three hundred miles to Kansas City in one day. A long stretch, he conceded, but they were young and strong.

"Tomorrow will be easier," Harry promised as they settled themselves in their tent for the night. "It's only a hundred thirty-four miles to Emporia."

"Harry, what will we do when we arrive in Texas?" Now that their destination was close, she battled with alarm.

"We'll find a place to stay," he said calmly. "Then we'll go out to look for jobs." He was silent for a moment. "In Texas the bosses pay big money to men who work in the oil fields. I won't work in a law office," he said with a new contempt. "I'll work where the money is. We'll save and buy land of our own. With luck we'll strike oil. We'll have to learn a lot," he conceded. "But we'll read and listen to people. We'll be sharp, Katie."

Both Katie and Harry felt a tumultuous sense of adventure when—at last—they drove across the state line into Texas. Here was cotton country. The sprawling fields that flanked the highways were lush with head-high cotton plants that would be ripe for picking, a service-station attendant told them, within another two or three weeks.

"Cotton is king in Texas," he said.

A few miles down the road Harry had to ask at a service station about the roads to take to Dallas. The sun burned bright and strong, making the Ford a kind of oven. The Texas summer, they realized, could be murderous. Twice they took the wrong road and had to backtrack. Hot and tired, Harry cursed at this delay. By nightfall he meant for them to be on the outskirts of Dallas, where they'd find a tourist home along a roadside.

"I can't wait to get into a bathtub," he admitted with a grin while perspiration dampened his hair, trickled down his throat, and made his shirt cling to his back. "I've washed in enough brooks to last a lifetime."

"Could we stop at that stand just ahead?" Katie asked. "I'm so thirsty."

"Sure." He took one hand from the wheel to reach into his pocket. "Let's have some soda pop."

"We'll split a bottle," Katie decreed. "Then we can have another later."

"I think the old jalopy can stand a little rest, too." All at once Harry seemed apprehensive. "It keeps overheating."

They were forty some-odd miles out of Dallas when the Ford wheezed, rattled, and came to a halt.

"What's the matter?" Katie asked, unnerved by the Ford's rebellion. They'd had some trouble along the road, but it had never just stopped dead this way.

"I don't know." Harry frowned. He was upset—as she was—at the prospect of having to hand over a portion of their precious cash to get the car moving again. "Maybe it's just this lousy heat." He made a show of nonchalance. "I should give it some water."

"You could ask at that farmhouse there," Katie said.

The small white clapboard house sat close to the road. Potted geraniums lined the porch, and curtains fluttered at the open windows, but dirty curls of paint hung from the walls, and one side of the porch sagged. Corn grew tall behind the house as far as they could see. Now a tall, lean woman in a gingham dress appeared on the porch. Her arms crossed, she watched as they deliberated.

"It ain't gonna start up less you give it some water," the woman called. "Bring a can and fill it up in the kitchen. We got runnin' water," she said with a proud smile.

"Thanks." Harry reached for the car door, and Katie opened the door on her side to go with him. Not many farmers they'd encountered along the road were this friendly. Maybe the woman was lonely, Katie thought with sudden compassion. The last house they'd passed was two miles back.

"You look hot, too," the woman said as they approached. She was an older woman, Katie judged. Her skin was weathered from the sun of Texas summers, her hands heavily veined and rough. "Set down on the porch and I'll bring you some lemonade."

They quickly learned that their hostess was Amelia Stone, widowed three years ago and trying to run the farm with the help of a pair of hired men who had defected only that morning.

"They all wanna work in the city," she grumbled. "They make more money there. Costs 'em more to live, but they don't think about that till later. It don't mean nuthin' to them they're leavin' me with corn out there needin' to be harvested."

Katie sat with Amelia Stone while Harry went back to

the car and tried to start it up again. After a vain struggle he returned to the porch.

"I don't know what's wrong with it," he admitted. "Unless it's this heat." Katie knew he was trying to hide his alarm.

"You interested in a job?" Amelia asked after a moment. "It don't pay much, but you can have a room of your own and all you can eat. Farmers around here are all having rough times. It's a real fight to hang on to your land with the way crops are bringin' so little and everything else costs so much. We pay double the taxes we paid before the war. And the banks charge farmers eight percent interest when folks in the city pay only five percent. That's a sin, but what can we do? Well?" she demanded. "You want the job or not?"

Katie and Harry glanced at each other in eager exchange. Mrs. Stone knew they were stranded, but she wasn't asking them to work for nothing. On the other hand, Katie reasoned, she hadn't said how much she'd pay them.

"What would I do?" Harry asked tentatively.

"The two of you can work in the fields," she said. "It ain't hard. From the looks of you, I suspect you don't know nuthin' about the land, but you'll learn fast enough. I'll be workin' right along with you." She hesitated. "I can give you each a dollar a day in cash." She seemed simultaneously apologetic and defiant. "That and room and board."

"We're grateful to you," Harry accepted.

"Bring in your suitcases, and I'll show you where you'll sleep," Amelia said briskly. "Then we'll go out and try to make up for what those two loafers didn't do today."

Katie understood. Harry meant for them to stay here awhile and catch their breath. He'd find out about getting the car fixed, and then they'd move on.

Chapter Three

KATIE WAS impressed to learn that the Stone family farm consisted of almost three hundred acres. Small compared to neighboring farms—Mrs. Stone talked about a nearby farm of over a hundred thousand acres—but huge in Katie's eyes. Amelia was proud that she had water piped into the house and gas and electric. Only one farm family in ten had gas and electric and running water, she told them.

"The year Pa died, we put in the telephone." Later they learned that over sixty percent of farms were without phones. "We were doin' right well just after the war. Then the same year he died—late in 1919—everything seemed to be goin' downhill. Workers askin' for five dollars a day. Fertilizer, fencin', machinery—everythin' costin' twice what it had before the war. But prices for farm products keep goin' down."

Amelia's furniture was forty years old but showed loving care. The crocheted doilies on the backs of the faded late Victorian, maroon-upholstered sofa and armchair were immaculate. Worn segments of upholstery neatly darned. The hooked rug, too, was faded but clean.

Katie and Harry slept in the sparsely furnished bedroom that had been shared by Amelia's two daughters. The sheets and pillowcases showed their many washings through the years. Samplers made by Amelia as a young girl decorated the walls. Katie kept her mother's geranium on a shelf Harry improvised beneath the windowsill—where the morning sun encouraged it to bloom.

The kitchen was the largest and friendliest of the four rooms. A brightly printed oilcloth covered the kitchen table, the roses repeated in the curtains at the windows. The iron cookstove gleamed. Small hooked scatter rugs added additional color. On a shelf above the sink Amelia still displayed her late husband's favorite pair of pipes. Katie knew that—when she thought she was alone—Amelia talked to those pipes.

Harry managed to push the car into one of the outbuildings and worked on it when he wasn't in the fields or baling hay for the few hogs Amelia was raising. Like many farm families, the Stones had never bought a car.

Though unaccustomed to physical labor, Katie and Harry enjoyed the first weeks on the farm. They agreed this was a waiting period—a time to grow accustomed to life away from New York. Both were drunk on the beauty of the land, the marvelous quiet, the miracle of the rich black earth that brought forth such an abundant crop. Each day they discovered some new delight—the taste of a cucumber plucked from the dirt, corn on the cob only minutes from the field.

Amelia Stone was an embittered woman but kindly. She was frank to admit she had been lonely before they arrived. She talked wistfully about the day when one of her two daughters—both born and raised here—might return to the farm with her family.

"I know a lot of folks think it's easier workin' in the city, with wages comin' every week. Not havin' to worry about not enough rain or too much rain, about whether the price of corn or wheat is goin' up or down. But on the farm we don't have to answer to nobody but ourselves. Last year a couple we know for thirty years—farmers like us—lost their farm and had to move into the city and look for jobs. Dear Lord, they were unhappy off the farm." But the prospect of bankruptcy hovered over most farmers, Katie knew from reading the farm journals that came to the house. The farm bankruptcy rate was rising fearfully.

Katie and Harry were in the fields from sunup to sundown. They enjoyed each sunrise, each sunset, with the ardor of big-city expatriates. And they agreed they couldn't leave Amelia alone with the harvest. When the corn was picked, Harry said, they'd hire a mechanic to put the Ford into working order again and move on to Dallas.

In late September, still reeling from the low prices of corn on the market, Amelia received her new tax bill.

"My children are grown up and livin' down in Houston," she railed. "Why do I have to pay for schools for somebody else's kids? I paid for mine already."

The following morning—over the customary heavy farm breakfast—Amelia Stone offered Katie and Harry a deal.

"You two are young—you love the land, the way I used to. But I'm too old and tired to fight anymore. Buy the farm from me and run it," she told them.

They stared at her in shock. Did Amelia think they were rich? Katie asked herself.

"Oh, don't look at me like that," she grumbled. "All I'm askin' you to do is give me train fare to Houston, plus half of what the farm brings in—after bills—every year for the next ten years. With the farm in your names you can get a short-term bank loan against next year's harvest. We'll get everything written legallike, and I'll take you down and introduce you to the folks at the bank. There's a livin' to be had here, and land you'll own forever."

Katie turned to Harry. They had enough cash to buy a railroad ticket to Houston. Never mind there wouldn't be much left if they did. Her eyes pleaded with him to accept—even though his heart was set on going into the oil-fields. *Had they ever dreamed of becoming landowners only weeks after leaving Rivington Street?*

"We don't know anything about running a farm," Harry said, yet Katie knew he shared her excitement at the prospect. "You've spent all your life farming."

"It ain't that hard," Amelia pursued. "I'll explain what you have to do now that the harvest is in and how you go about preparin' for the next harvest. When you got questions, call up Jim Crane. Folks in Texas are real neighborly," she said with pride. But Katie was sure that Mr. Crane—friendly as he was toward them—wouldn't believe they could run a farm by themselves. *Could they?*

"But we have so little cash," Harry protested. "You've got that tax bill to pay—and there won't be any more money coming in until another harvest. And that'll cost."

"Harry, listen to me. It's like I told you. I'll introduce you at the bank, explain you own the farm now." Already, Katie sensed, Amelia was conscious of a sense of loss, even while she was determined to give up the fight and go to live with her daughter. "They'll give you a loan."

"If the bank will give us credit, we'll be glad to take over the farm," Harry told Amelia gravely, and Katie was suffused with joy. Somehow, they would manage.

"I'll call Jim Crane at the farm below us," Amelia said. Jim Crane was always helpful when Amelia was in a bad spot. But from cryptic remarks she'd made, Katie knew Amelia disliked their neighbors on the other side. Amelia told them the original owners had died off, and a son and his "flighty wife" had come back just a year ago to work the farm. "He'll take us into town in the morning. And then," she said with satisfaction, "we'll go over to the railroad depot and buy me that ticket to Houston."

As Amelia anticipated, Jim Crane came over with his truck to drive them into Dallas the following morning. Katie and Harry had dressed in their best for this first visit to the city.

"Your timing was just right, Amelia," the ruddy-faced, lanky farmer said while Harry helped Katie into the back of the truck and Amelia took her place up front. "I need to go into town to buy supplies."

She didn't feel like a married woman who would soon own a farm, Katie thought as she sat on the floor of the truck and held tightly to Harry's hand. She was just a little scared that they would have to hand over most of their cash to buy Amelia's ticket to Houston. But Amelia was sure they could get a loan to cover taxes now and putting in a new crop later. And they'd have all they could eat from the vegetable garden Amelia kept for that purpose plus a roof over their heads.

"I'll talk to Mr. Crane about the car," Harry told her with fresh confidence. They weren't just "passing through"—they belonged here now. "Amelia says he's handy with all kinds of equipment. He'll know how we can get it running again."

Katie felt a fresh excitement as the truck approached the city, its skyline marked by a dozen skyscrapers.

"Dallas is not some hick town," Harry said with respect. "It has over a quarter-million people. Not as big as New York," he teased, "but I think we can make do."

Now Amelia called out to them at intervals from the front, to point out the thirty-one story Magnolia Petroleum Building—impressive even to ex-New Yorkers, the German baroque Hotel Adolphus—built by the Busch brewing family, and—catercornered from it on Commerce Street—the pleasant, stone-block Baker Hotel. She talked with pride about the Cotton Bowl stadium, which could seat forty-six thousand spectators.

"And right ahead, Katie"—Amelia's arm emerged to indicate direction—"is Neiman-Marcus, the most elegant store you can find in this country. I can't say we can afford the prices, but it's sure fun to look in the windows and peek inside."

Katie felt a sudden surge of homesickness as she inspected the windows of the most elegant store in the Southwest. She remembered lingering before the windows of Bergdorf, Saks Fifth Avenue, Best, Bonwit Teller—and further downtown, those of Lord & Taylor and B. Altman. But she and Harry hadn't lived in that New York, she told herself realistically—they just passed through it for a few hours on Sundays.

Jim Crane deposited them at the building where Amelia's longtime lawyer had a modest office. She'd phoned the day before to explain the situation, and he was ready with the necessary papers.

"I think you're wise in going to stay with your daughter," he comforted her, because he knew—as did Katie and Harry—that it was a traumatic experience to hand over the farm that had been her home since she was a bride forty-two years earlier. "And I'm sure these young people will carry on just fine." But Katie sensed his doubts, his apprehension at their youth and inexperience.

From the lawyer's office Amelia took them to the bank. Katie was all at once frightened at the prospect of the debts they would incur when the planting season arrived. She remembered how Mama always said, *"You buy what you can pay for—I don't like running up bills."* But to operate a farm, you had to borrow, she reasoned, yet was uneasy that the bank would control their lives.

The three emerged from the bank into an October sunlight that pushed the temperature close to 80 degrees. Each was conscious of the impact of the morning's transactions. Katie understood that for Amelia this was a bittersweet occasion. She looked forward to living with one daughter, the other daughter just a few miles away—but she was leaving behind the long life she had shared with her husband. For Harry and her, Katie told herself, this was the most wonderful moment in their lives.

"We'll take ourselves over to Union Station now," Amelia said with forced jubilation. "I can't wait to get down to Houston and spoil my grandchildren." But Katie felt her pain.

With her railroad ticket bought, Amelia took off for a brief visit with former neighbors who'd moved into Dallas. Like others unable to cope with the farm crisis of the past four years, they'd lost their land.

"Remember, we meet in front of the Adolphus at noon

for the ride home," Amelia called as she hurried to catch a trolley. "Don't keep Jim waitin'. A few hours in the city and he's rarin' to get back to the farm."

Caught up in the miracle that happened for them, Katie and Harry walked about the streets of Dallas.

"Maybe we haven't got ourselves a chunk of all that oil money," Harry admitted, his face triumphant, "but would anybody back home believe we've just bought ourselves a house and almost three hundred acres?"

"It'll be ours when we pay for it," Katie pointed out. Instinct—and what she read in the *Dallas Morning News*—warned her this wouldn't be easy. Folks might claim the farm crisis was over, but farmers were hurting. Not just Amelia Stone—lots of them.

Katie and Harry liked what they saw of Dallas. They felt the air of optimism that permeated the fast-growing city. Harry pointed out that Texas had been a state only since 1845—before that it had been a republic for almost ten years.

"It's kind of different from the rest of the country," Harry said with relish. "It's a city full of dreams. People here are proud of their town—they fight to make it bigger and better. Some of the richest people in the world call Dallas home. And you know, Katie," he said reverently, "one of these days we'll be among them."

Katie and Harry were conscious of a soaring exultation in these first days of being alone on the farm. They remembered Amelia's instructions. "You turn the hogs into the corn and let 'em hog it off. Then you sell the hogs." With their few hogs taken off to market—and Katie was upset by the prospect of their future—they focused on preparing the fields for a cover crop of alfalfa.

On a glorious Sunday morning in early October Katie and Harry settled themselves in a pair of Boston rockers on their porch with slabs of bread just out of the oven and fragrant cups of coffee. For the first time since they had arrived in Texas, they were both conscious of an unsettling sense of isolation.

"We ought to do something about getting the car fixed," Harry said somberly. Mr. Crane had admitted he was good with farm equipment—not with Fords.

"It might cost a lot," Katie hedged, ever conscious of their precarious cash situation.

"We can't walk into town," Harry reminded her. Without a car they were prisoners. "And we can't phone up Mr. Crane every time we have to go into Dallas for something." It was Katie—usually so frugal—who'd insisted on keeping the phone when Amelia Stone left.

"Harry, look." Katie's voice was electric. A vintage Ford was slowing as it approached the house. "Are they stopping here?" Katie inspected the young couple on the front seat with avid interest.

"I don't think they're breaking down here," Harry chuckled, remembering their own arrival. But he sat upright in anticipation. Katie sensed an excitement in him that matched her own. They had not seen another human being since Amelia left for Houston.

"Hello there . . ." A slim, vivacious young woman in a fashionably short dress stepped down from the car's running board. She appeared to be in her early twenties. Attractive rather than pretty.

"Hello . . ." Katie leapt to her feet, her smile brilliant.

"We're from the next farm," said the young woman, walking toward the porch. "I'm Maura Warren." The "flighty" young wife of the son of Amelia's neighbor, Katie mentally placed her. "He's Jeff." Maura waved a hand toward the tall, sandy-haired young man emerging from behind the wheel of the car. "We heard down at the bank that Mrs. Stone had sold to a couple from the city."

"That's us," said Harry, on his feet and an arm about Katie's shoulders. "We're from New York."

"The Automat still selling the best cup of coffee in New York?" Jeff asked ebulliently as he and Maura reached the porch steps and laughed at Katie and Harry's startled stares.

"We both lived in New York for close to three years," Maura explained. "Jeff was born on our farm down the road. I'm from upstate New York. Albany."

"Would you like some coffee?" Katie asked eagerly. She admired Maura on sight—her casual charm, the aura of city sophistication that clothed her.

"I'll bet that's hot bread straight out of the oven." Jeff sniffed in appreciation as he gazed at the uneaten segment on Katie's plate.

"Sure is," Harry said. "Katie bakes real good. Why don't we all go out to the kitchen and have some?"

The Warrens went into the house with Katie and Harry. The two young men settled themselves about the table and reminisced about their mutual favorites—the baked beans, the mashed sweet potatoes, and the beef potpies—at the Automats back in New York. While Katie sliced the second loaf of hot bread, Maura—at Katie's instructions—brought out the crock of freshly churned butter and a bottle of Amelia's homemade strawberry preserves from the aging icebox. The sunlit kitchen ricocheted with the mutual pleasure of the four young people.

Jeff was somewhat reticent, but Maura spilled over with background information.

"Oh, I was sure I was going to be the next Katharine Cornell or Ethel Barrymore," Maura mocked herself. "After high school I clerked in Woolworth and took tap dancing at the Irving Dance Studio in Albany, and then I headed down to the big city. I think I could have been very good, but I didn't know how to play the game. I'd work a while to save up money to live on, then 'make rounds.' That means looking for a part in a play. But I did everything wrong. Then—when Jeff's father died a year and a half ago and his sisters didn't want the farm—we got married and came out here. Mrs. Stone hated me." Maura chuckled.

"She never even met us," Jeff picked up, "but the word spread around that our hogs didn't get fed till eight because Maura refused to get out of bed before seven."

Maura shrugged good-humoredly. "They learned to wait. After all, where were they going?"

"To the bacon counter," Jeff said, and Katie winced.

"I've practically become a vegetarian since we came out here," Maura confided. "How can I eat pork when I've been eyeball-to-eyeball with a pig? I cried for an hour when Jeff killed our first chicken. I remembered when it was a furry little ball."

Over tall cups of coffee and chunks of butter-lathered hot bread they discussed New York with some nostalgia. Maura and Jeff had lived near Greenwich Village rather than the Lower East Side, but they shared memories of picnics in Central Park, walks on the boardwalk at Coney Island, seeing an occasional Broadway play from cheap seats high in the second balcony.

"Jeff's a writer," Maura said with defiant pride. "A good one. I told him he doesn't have to be in New York to write a novel. He can write in Texas. And I couldn't stand living in that rotten hall bedroom on West Twenty-second Street and sharing a bathroom with a bunch of screwy old ladies. Then Jeff's old man died, and he inherited the farm. It made sense for us to come out here. It's not an easy life," she admitted. "Sometimes we cuss a lot and swear we wish we were back in New York—but not for long. We're our own bosses on the farm. Nobody to tell us what we have to do. We've got a place to live and enough to eat."

"My family's been on that farm for four generations," Jeff reminisced. "None of them could understand why I wanted to go off to live in New York City."

"Your sisters got married and took off," Maura

pointed out. "They're both living out in Los Angeles now," she told the other two.

"My grandfather had five sons to work the farm," Jeff said. "That's the way it should be. No need to pay workers every week. That's the way a farm family survives. My father had my two sisters and me—and none of us wanted to work the land. But you know," he pointed out, "all those years in New York there were many times I wanted so bad to come home. Just too stubborn to admit it to Pop. I couldn't bring myself to admit I'd made a mistake. But he'd be glad to know we're here."

Harry brushed aside Jeff's gentle banter about Katie's and his youthfulness. Maura was twenty-one, Jeff twenty-two. They considered themselves far more mature than Katie and Harry.

"We're not kids—you grow up fast when you're left alone in the world and thrown out into work. I was fourteen," Harry said grimly. "Katie was twelve."

When Maura and Jeff finally left, Katie knew she and Harry had acquired real friends in Texas. Texans were friendly, she conceded, but they were four outsiders—even Jeff, born here—who'd found one another. She stood on the porch, arm in arm with Harry, and watched them drive away. She was feeling richer because they knew the Warrens.

Chapter Four

TWO DAYS after their first meeting Katie and Harry were pleased to see the Warrens' beat-up Ford turn into their driveway. The Newhouses hurried out to welcome them.

"I baked a lemon-meringue pie," Maura said as she

emerged from the car with an effervescent smile. "I figured you'd have coffee on the stove anyway."

"Lemon meringue's Maura's main baking accomplishment," Jeff teased. "Most of the time it's corn pone, corn bread, corn pudding."

"Corn goes a long way to feeding us when the cash is low," Maura told Katie. "I'll teach you."

"We'll have popcorn all winter," guessed Harry, enjoying the presence of the Warrens.

"Hell, you'll even use corn for fuel when the coal runs out," Jeff told him.

"You were down in the city today?" Harry asked. They'd approached from that direction.

"Yeah, we needed to buy some stuff at the feed store." The two young men settled at the kitchen table while Katie and Maura busied themselves with the small domestic task of serving pie and coffee. "I was talking to some people there." All at once Jeff was somber. "I hear the KKK is bragging they've got almost thirteen thousand members in the Dallas chapter now. Chapter Number Sixty-six—the biggest in Texas."

Katie's mouth opened wide in shock. She knew about the KKK, of course. She'd read about them in the *New York Tribune* and the *Herald*. But they had always seemed far removed from her own life. Now Jeff talked about thirteen thousand members right in the Dallas area.

"I don't like to think about them." Maura grimaced. "They don't like Catholics or Jews. Not to mention Negroes." Now she managed a gamine grin. "Jeff's the only one here that'll pass their test."

"They don't do anything except parade and make a lot of noise," Jeff said guardedly. But Katie intercepted the uneasy glance between him and Harry.

"Jeff, pull your head out of the sand," Maura scolded. "Last year Mayor Aldredge—who came right out and said he was against the Klan—lost for reelection almost three to one, along with the rest of his ticket. He lost because he said the Klan in Dallas should disband. He argued all over Dallas against the Klan. Now"—she turned to the other two—"practically every city and county office is held by somebody who belongs to the Klan or made a deal with them."

"So we have a Klan chapter in Dallas, and they've caused some problems. In a city of close to a quarter-million, they don't amount to anything. And they're being fought by the Dallas Citizens' League, the Texas Bar Association, and some branches of the American Legion." Jeff chuckled reminiscently. "Would you believe, ninety percent of Dallas bootleggers are Klansmen?"

"They're running this city!" Maura shot back. "Even a lot of Protestant clergymen approve of the Klan. They see it as an enemy of the 'Roman Catholic menace,'" she said scathingly.

"Maura, get off the soapbox," Jeff scolded. "That's my little Irish firebrand."

After Maura and Jeff left, Katie tried futilely to push the disturbing conversation about the KKK out of her mind. On Thanksgiving Eve of 1915, Maura said, the Ku Klux Klan—dead since the end of the Reconstruction period in the South—was resurrected on Stone Mountain near Atlanta, Georgia. No longer just a threat to those in the South, Katie understood, the KKK had become a nationwide menace.

Katie's sleep that night was invaded by ominous visions of men in white hooded robes. For the next few days Maura's talk about the Klan darted across her mind at unwary intervals. She remembered her mother's terrifying stories about the pogroms in Russia that had sent her grandmother and grandfather—both had died when Katie was a baby—fleeing to America.

Katie and Harry were grateful when Jeff offered advice about daily problems that arose on the farm. Jeff had farming skills bred in him from early childhood. He read every article on farming that he could find—and now he passed them on to Harry. Katie and Harry were impatient with their own lack of knowledge.

"Look, my folks have been doing this for four generations," Jeff comforted them when Katie chastised herself for believing they could harvest corn in late summer, then plant winter wheat for a spring harvest. "That's how you pick up things."

"I don't want to wait for our great-grandchildren to tell us what to do." Katie sighed. "Why do we have to plant a crop that's going to be chopped up and allowed to go back into the earth?"

"Because we have a responsibility to take care of the land," Jeff told her. "Every year we lose a little topsoil. When we plow back a crop into the earth, we're nurturing it."

Katie and Harry listened absorbedly to Jeff's current words of wisdom, nodding at intervals in comprehension. Then talk turned to cars, and Jeff promised to help Harry get the Ford moving again.

"Come over for Sunday dinner," Maura invited.

A lapsed Catholic, Maura talked vaguely about going to church in the morning, but Jeff derided this.

"Maura, you talk but you don't go." Jeff declared himself an agnostic. "I observe Christmas and Easter to be sociable."

At Sunday dinner Katie and Harry listened in shock to Jeff's account of the coming Klan rally in Dallas.

"They figure on anywhere from two-hundred-thousand to two-hundred-fifty-thousand Klansmen being in the city on Wednesday—coming from all over the South. It'll be the biggest KKK gathering ever in the southern half of the country."

"Let's go into the city to see it," Maura said, her eyes defiant. "This is one Irish Catholic who would like to spit in their faces."

"We'll go," Jeff agreed, and grinned. "But no spitting.

What about you two?" He turned to Katie and Harry. "Go with us?"

"Yes," Katie said instantly, and smiled at Harry's stare of astonishment. "I know—it's a time to avoid the city. But I want to see what kind of people join the KKK."

"They'll probably be hiding behind masks," Maura warned.

"Some yes, some no," Jeff countered. "They'll feel safe and triumphant. Dallas is controlled by the Klan."

"You two"—Jeff's eyes swung from Maura to Harry—"you both remember to keep your opinions to yourselves. I don't want to see Katie and me having to bail you out of jail."

Late Wednesday morning the four of them arrived in Dallas in the Warrens' Ford. Klansmen in the thousands were already flooding the streets. The imperial wizard of all the Klans had arrived the night before. Since dawn other members had been pouring into the city.

Katie clung to Harry's hand as they moved through the throngs—some of the men in hoods and robes, others in civilian garb. They filled the restaurants and hotel lobbies and the shops.

"I hate phony patriotism," Maura hissed. "Look at all those little red 'one hundred percent American' buttons. They're traitors to everything this country stands for."

"They look as though they're ready for a costume ball," Katie said with distaste, inspecting the elaborate robes of gold, royal purple, or scarlet that some of the men wore.

"The fancier the outfit, the higher the rank in the Klan," Jeff explained.

"What do you think, Jeff?" Harry challenged. "As many KKK members here as they expected?"

"Harry, they're all over the place!" Maura protested.

"There are a lot less than the quarter of a million they bragged about," Jeff said with a glint in his eyes. "Maybe this is the downturn."

At noon—after an hour of circulating among the visiting horde—the two couples returned to the car and drove out to the State Fair Grounds to have a picnic lunch under the warm autumn sun. It seemed to be a festive occasion—but not for one moment did the Newhouses and the Warrens forget that this was a Klan rally, proclaiming an ugly message abhorred by decent-thinking people. The major feature of the day for the Klan was the speech at the fairgrounds by the imperial wizard Hiram W. Evans—scheduled for 1:00 P.M.

Now people surged into the fairgrounds. Most of them Klan members, but there were the curious, too. The KKK brass bands began to assault their ears. Maura grunted in rage when a band struck up the familiar old hymn—"Onward, Christian Soldiers"—which the KKK had adopted as its own.

"How many people here?" Harry challenged again as they stood at the fringe while others pressed toward the stand.

"No more than ten thousand," Jeff surmised, inspecting the sea of faces that extended over the expansive acreage. "I would have expected a hell of a lot more. That son of a bitch Evans used to be a Dallas dentist, until he was 'enthroned' in Atlanta. You'd think that alone would be enough to bring out half of Dallas."

They remained at the edge of the crowd while the loudspeaker apparatus was tested. Katie fought against an instinct to flee. She gazed at the faces around her and recoiled from the fanatical zeal she saw there, from the bigotry and hatred these people wanted to fan across the country.

"Sure you want to stay, Katie?" Harry asked gently.

"Yes." Her eyes were bright with contempt.

At 1:00 P.M. the imperial wizard appeared on the stand to join the other chief officials.

"That guy never stops smiling," Maura commented. "I don't trust a man like that."

George K. Butcher, the cyclops of Dallas, introduced

the wizard now, praising him as the most "one-hundred-percent American in these United States." There were a few moments of cheering. Katie exchanged a glance of surprise with Harry. She'd expected a tumultuous welcome. The wizard began to read his speech. Katie listened, gritting her teeth to keep back the accusations that she longed to scream at him.

"The usual hogwash," Harry whispered.

It was the Klan's contention that neither Jews, Roman Catholics, nor Negroes could ever be "100 percent Americans," and the imperial wizard was expounding on this theory.

"Jews are alien and unable to be assimilated," he wound up his first diatribe finally. "They're mercenary-minded and money mad."

He condemned Roman Catholics as putting church before country. He ranted about the dangers of parochial schools. His references to Jews and Catholics received some mild applause; but when he attacked the Negroes, there was a loud outburst. He concluded with the familiar statement that Jews, Catholics, and Negroes "do now and forever will, defy every fundamental requirement of assimilation."

"Let's get out of here." Swearing under his breath, Harry reached for Katie's arm. "I'd like to plough through the crowd and kill that bastard."

In the evening, they learned, the Klan would hold a public initiation at the racetrack—five thousand men would take the oath and two thousand women would be initiated into the women's order. Then—at 11:00 P.M.—the KKK would parade through the city. By official order all traffic would stop.

"The KKK are losing their grip in Dallas," Jeff said with pleased conviction when they were back in the car. "This was not the kind of turnout they expected."

"Maybe," Harry conceded. "But they'll be a power in the '24 election. The situation might get worse before it gets better."

The following day Katie and Harry heard that downtown Dallas had been blacked out the previous night so the KKK could march in the darkness.

"What else would you expect?" Maura countered when Katie reported this over the phone. "The Klan still dominates Dallas. It controls big business. Of course the electric company turned off the lights."

Katie and Harry had Thanksgiving dinner in early afternoon at the Warrens' house. Work on the farm had come to a near-standstill. Katie and Harry were somberly anticipating the coming spring planting season—and the loans they'd have to take out at the bank. Over the roast wild turkey Jeff had killed two days earlier, Harry confided that he was thinking about looking for a job for the winter.

Katie gaped at him—first in consternation, then accusingly. He hadn't said a word about that to her.

"It's been running about in my head for a while," he told Katie, his eyes apologetic. He'd read her mind, she thought. They were so close that often happened. "Business is good down in Dallas. I could drive into town and pick up some extra bucks to make things easier for us. Maybe keep our loans down." He knew how she worried over being in debt to the bank.

"It's a terribly long drive into the city—I mean, to make that trip every day. Twice a day." But Katie knew from the glint in his eyes that he was already counting the money he could earn.

"I can make it in an hour and a half each way," he surmised. "Providing the old jalopy holds up. There're jobs for the asking in Dallas."

"It might be smart for me to do the same," Jeff said after a moment. "Prices keep going up on everything else, but we get less and less for our crops."

"You're writing," Maura reminded Jeff. Suddenly she appeared tense. "We agreed. We can make it through till the next crop." She turned to Katie and Harry. "All spring and summer and into the fall he never had a minute to write. He just fell into bed at night after sixteen hours in the field. I want him to finish his book."

"How about our going into the city next week to see that new Colleen Moore movie?" Harry derailed the conversation. "Our big extravagance for the next month. We'll eat corn all week."

On Monday morning Jeff dropped Maura off to visit with Katie while he and Harry drove into Dallas, Jeff to buy parts for farm machinery, Harry to look for a job.

"I brought along my secondhand copies of *Vogue*," Maura said ebulliently when she and Katie were alone. "Let's choose ourselves a spiffy wardrobe."

"I have coffee on the stove," Katie said, her face tense. Maura lifted an eyebrow in question, and Katie forced herself to continue. "I wouldn't say anything to Harry about it—he'd get all upset—but I just can't forget about the KKK. Have they—have they hurt anybody around here?" She felt self-conscious at asking this, yet she was determined to know the truth.

"Right in Dallas last year at least sixty-eight men were beat up—most of them at what folks are calling the Klan whipping meadow. Down on the bottom of the Trinity River. A couple of years ago nine colored men were burned, shot, or hanged. And nobody got arrested," she added grimly. "People are sure the police commissioner is a Klansman—and most of the police officers. Even the sheriff. They're scared to belong to the Klan—and scared not to."

"You're Catholic, and I'm Jewish," Katie said softly. "Should we be afraid of the Klan?"

"Out here in Texas they go after gamblers and abortionists and husbands and wives who play on the side. And any Negro they suspect is too friendly with a white woman. It doesn't have to be true—just that they think so. Over in Houston they castrated a Negro dentist for supposedly associating with a white woman. In Tenaha they kidnapped a girl from her hotel room—they thought she might be a bigamist—then stripped her to the waist, beat and tarred and feathered her."

"Maura, they're animals!"

"They're scum." Maura grimaced in disgust. "But no, Katie," she managed a wry smile, "neither you nor I personally have to worry about the KKK—at least, not yet."

"You and Jeff keep saying that lots of people in Texas are fighting the KKK," Katie probed.

"You bet." Maura nodded emphatically. "Both the *Dallas Morning News* and the *Dispatch* are after their hides. Not long ago the KKK chapter in San Antonio tried to keep Fritz Kreisler from playing a concert in town, but local people prevented that. We have a lot of anti-Klan groups in Texas, and they're fighting mad. But the worst—to me—are the Klanswomen. Last June about fifteen-hundred of them—masked and robed—marched in a parade in Fort Worth. Women ought to be against that crazy violence. But enough talking about the KKK," Maura ordered. "Let's have our coffee."

Shortly past seven—in apparent high spirits—Harry and Jeff returned from Dallas. Maura rose immediately to her feet from the sofa and collected her copies of *Vogue*.

"Don't sit down and get comfortable, Jeff," she warned him. "We're going home for supper. If we don't finish up last night's stew, I'll have to throw it out."

Katie understood Maura's insistence. Maura knew she was anxious to hear how Harry made out with his job search.

"You must be starving," Katie sympathized as she walked with Harry into the kitchen. "All you took with you was one sandwich. I'll get supper on the table." When he was ready, he'd tell her about the day in Dallas.

"I know business is good in Dallas, but I didn't expect

to find a job on the first try." All at once Harry was grinning. "But I did."

"Oh, Harry, that's wonderful!" Katie hugged him exuberantly, forgetting her earlier concern about the heavy driving. "I knew you wouldn't have any trouble."

"I didn't get the one I was after," he admitted. "I said I was twenty-three, a City College graduate, and that I'd worked two years as a law clerk." He sighed. "I guess they didn't believe me." His smile combined frustration and apology. "I'm an office boy at Wilson Brokerage, Inc. Starting tomorrow."

"Do they know you can work only till planting time?" Katie asked.

"That'll be a surprise," Harry conceded. "Katie, you don't tell a boss you'll be there only as long as it suits you. Nobody will hire you. Anyhow, they're underpaying because they guessed I needed the job bad. 'All the way from New York and unemployed,' was the way the boss put it. But the money will help," he said seriously.

"I hope the car holds up." Katie worried about the Ford. "You'll have to do a lot of driving."

"The car will be all right," Harry reassured her. "Jeff and I've put a lot of work into it."

"Harry—" She hesitated, not sure of his reaction. "As long as you're driving into the city every day, maybe I could find a job, too."

"No." Harry bristled defensively. "The wife takes care of the house. The husband goes out to work."

"But that's so old-fashioned," Katie protested. "I can take care of the house and still work."

"No," Harry repeated. "We'll manage fine now that I'll be bringing home a pay envelope." His face softened. "Katie, I need to know you're here at the house. I need to come home and find you fixing supper for us. That's the way it should be." He reached for her hand. "Now feed your starving husband."

Chapter Five

EACH WORKDAY morning Katie and Harry were up before daybreak. Katie prepared breakfast for the two of them, then made two sandwiches for Harry to take with him into Dallas. Each evening after supper—even when they discovered that Dallas's blistering summers were followed by bone-chilling winters—they walked about their acreage, relishing the knowledge that this was their private realm.

Katie quickly realized that Harry enjoyed his daily excursions into Dallas. He railed regularly—bitterly—against an employer who took advantage of his anxiety for work to hire him at a lower salary than his predecessor, but not even the long drive into the city each day eroded the adventure of being part of an exciting, growing city. And Harry admitted to being fascinated by what he was learning about the brokerage field. Often too stimulated to sleep, he would lie in bed far beyond their normal bedtime to talk about his daytime activities.

"Katie, I listen to what's going on all day in the office—you wouldn't believe the money that changes hands every day in the brokerage business. Anybody with a nest egg to play the market can be rich in six months!"

"It's gambling," Katie pointed out, calm because she knew Harry was in no position to participate. "People can lose everything they own."

"Not these days," Harry insisted. "Not if they're smart. It makes me so mad, Katie. Everybody talks about the good times in this country, but the farmers don't see it."

Katie suspected at times that he regretted their being involved in farming. "Anyhow," he said, striving to be philosophical, "we're saving up money toward the planting. Every dollar we don't have to borrow from the bank is money we don't pay interest on."

With the approach of Chanukah and Christmas Katie persuaded Harry to let her go into Dallas with him with the hope of finding a job in one of the shops.

"Just for the holidays," she wheedled. "It'll be fun."

"It won't be fun spending three hours a day on the hard seat of the Ford and another ten hours standing on your feet in a store," Harry argued. While U.S. Steel had just reduced its workday from twelve hours to eight, this was not the norm.

"Harry, it'll be that much less we have to borrow at the bank," she reminded him. She would never feel comfortable owing money, she told herself.

Harry wavered a moment.

"All right. For the holidays. Provided you can find a job."

Dallas—like all America—was experiencing a boom in business. New products such as radios and electric refrigerators were pouring into the market. The automotive industry was touting faster cars. Kitchen appliances, bathroom fixtures, were being offered in fancier styles. The impressive growth of chain stores and the increasingly popular installment buying were powerful stimuli to business. The economy was spiraling. Income was up for most Americans—but not for the farmers.

Katie was too in awe to approach the likes of Neiman-Marcus, but she was hired by a small women's wear shop to work until Christmas Eve. Usually she slept in the car during the long drive into Dallas and home again in the evening. Refusing to admit to her exhaustion, triumphant in bringing in additional money.

Katie decided in a surge of holiday high spirits that she and Harry would invite Maura and Jeff to share with them the night of Chanukah that fell on Sunday. In turn they would go to the Warrens' house for Christmas dinner. Maura confessed to being homesick at most major holidays.

"I couldn't go home if we were back East," Maura admitted while they lingered at the table over coffee and cake on this Chanukah eve—after the traditional potato *latkes* and applesauce. Katie had just explained that Chanukah celebrated the victory of the Jews in Judea after a three-year struggle against the Syrian tyrant Antiochus. "I can't ever go home," Maura added with a fatalistic calm. "My family disowned me when I said I wanted to be an actress."

"But you're not," Harry pointed out.

"In their eyes I'm forever sullied. I did a couple of bit parts in plays down at the Provincetown Playhouse. To them, all actresses are immoral. They kiss men onstage." Maura managed a wry smile. "You don't know my folks. They sent me to a parochial school because they were sure public-school teachers taught disrespect for the pope."

"And here you are," Jeff joshed, "with best friends who're Jewish." Now he turned to Katie with a teasing smile. "Is your rabbi going to punish you for sharing our Christmas tree?"

"We don't have a rabbi," Katie admitted. "Unless you count the one who married Harry and me."

"We'd tell him it's a Chanukah bush," Harry laughed. "What's the difference? We're all members of the human race. We all believe in God."

"I have reservations," Jeff chuckled. "Questions. Don't frown like that, Maura. I won't go to hell for asking questions."

"I don't think it matters whether you worship in a church or a synagogue or a mosque," Katie said softly. "I think what's important is how you treat other people."

"This is supposed to be a party," Maura clucked. "Let's put the dishes in the sink and go into the parlor."

"You three go into the parlor," said Katie, pushing back her chair. "I'll do the dishes."

"Let them sit," Maura told her.

"Harry hates dirty dishes in the sink," Katie pointed out.

"Then let Harry wash 'em," Maura decreed. "There's no law saying men can't wash dishes."

"This is what happened when women got the vote," Harry said with a grin. "Next thing you know, they'll want us to share the cooking." But Katie understood; it was all right—tonight—to let the dishes sit in the sink.

"We brought over our Victrola," Maura reminded them while she and Katie cleared the table. "I wish we could afford some new records. I'd kill for a Paul Whiteman record of 'Tea for Two.'"

"Did you bring wine?" Katie asked. With the popular disrespect for the Eighteenth Amendment, Jeff made wine in their cellar.

"Harry wouldn't have let me in the house without the bottle." They never had wine with a meal. Afterward, Maura insisted, because then she felt as though they were in a speak-easy.

Katie and Maura walked down the narrow hall to the parlor, where Jeff had set up the Victrola. The wine bottle was on prominent display. Already the strains of "Blue Moon" were filling the air—somewhat scratchily because the record had been played often.

"Hey, let's pretend we're at a tea dance at the Plaza," Maura said effervescently, holding her arms out to Jeff.

"Make it a dime-a-dance palace on Times Square, and you girls are hostesses," Jeff ordered, pulling Maura close. Self-consciously Harry reached to draw Katie into his arms. They had attended just a few ballroom-dancing classes at the settlement house. "Harry, you ever go to one of those joints?"

"No." Harry seemed almost defensive.

"I did a couple of times when I was so damn lonely in

57

the city. It's weird," Jeff mused, "how with millions of people around me, I used to wander into a cafeteria for a cup of coffee, just to talk with a busboy. I could be alone on the farm for days and not feel lonely."

"I worked one night in a dance hall," Maura recalled.

"You never told me," Jeff scolded.

"You never asked," she retorted. "I earned four cents a dance, I remember."

"Customers paid ten cents to two for a quarter," Jeff recalled, "and you had to buy tickets for at least six dances—which lasted about forty seconds each—just to get in the place."

"The big spenders put out about five bucks," Maura said. "For forty-second cheap feels. I had the same tired feet when I waitressed, and no hands all over me."

Before nine o'clock Maura insisted that Jeff and she go home.

"It's early," Jeff protested, and Harry nodded in emphatic agreement.

"You and Katie have to be in the car in the morning before sunrise," Maura told Harry. "Not to mention that it'll take forty minutes to get our bedroom warm enough for me to take off my clothes."

"Not tonight, baby," Jeff crooned. "I'm horny as hell. I'll warm you up fast."

"Talk about city boys," Maura laughed. "This farm boy sure talks dirty."

A few days after Christmas—her city job over—Katie kept the kitchen warm with baking. Maura was driving over for their regular afternoon "coffee klatch." Katie's face brightened as she heard the car pull up in front of the house. She hurried down the cold hall to the front door.

"I hate men," Maura called as she scurried through the bitter outdoor cold to the door.

"Again?" Katie laughed. Regularly—after a battle with Jeff—Maura made this pronouncement.

"Pour me some coffee so I can thaw out and talk."

Over coffee and kuchen Maura reported on her morning's battle with Jeff. He was ever self-conscious that he was not working in the city when there was little to do on the farm and their finances were so stringent.

"He feels guilty that he's not working when Harry is. I keep reminding him that writing's work, but all he sees is that he isn't bringing money home."

"Harry hates his job," Katie admitted. "At first all he thought about was the money he was making, then he was excited about being part of a brokerage office. Now he hates being just an office boy. The big deal is a promise to let him start making quotation prices on the display board soon. And by that time he'll probably have to quit so we can put in our corn."

"You've heard me mention the Muellers about six miles down the road," Maura said. "They have a thousand-acre farm, and they're doing all right, even in these bad times for farmers. They own their place free and clear. And they saved during the good years, Mrs. Mueller once told me. They're not suckered by the banks into paying high interest rates. Nice older couple, always willing to help out neighbors. Now Mrs. Mueller has to go into the hospital for some serious surgery. They want somebody to come to clean the house and make meals for Mr. Mueller and the hired man, and then for the three of them when she comes home from the hospital. It's a job for about a month," Maura gauged, "and they're willing to pay good. But that screwy husband of mine said, 'No, you can't go out and be a servant when I'm sitting on my ass and doing nothing.'" Maura was incensed. "I could pick up a chunk of money."

"Maybe he'll change his mind," Katie said.

"No chance." Maura was emphatic. Katie's mind leapt into action. Would Harry let *her* take the job? It was for just a month. "And why does the husband always have to make the final decision? If we're smart enough to vote for the president of the United States, aren't we smart enough to decide other things?"

Katie hesitated a moment.

"What about Sundays?"

"That would be my day off. I'd make a big pot of spaghetti or a heavy soup or whatever on Saturday and put it in the icebox to be warmed up the next day. I would," she said grimly, "if Jeff wasn't so bullheaded."

"Would you mind if I tried to get the job?" Katie asked. "I mean, if Mr. Mueller is willing to provide transportation."

"I'll be your chauffeur," Maura offered with a grin. "Let's call Mr. Mueller and talk to him. He's awful anxious to know somebody will be there to take care of the house."

Katie knew she ought to talk about it with Harry first, but she was afraid the job might be grabbed up by somebody else. A lot of farm families would welcome the extra money. Katie listened while Maura talked to Mr. Mueller, then took the phone from Maura and talked with him herself.

"My wife's never been sick a day in her life," he said wistfully. "I'm havin' a real hard time getting used to the idea that the doctor is going to cut her open. I want to be sure everything's nice when she comes home from the hospital. She has to go in a week from tomorrow. Can you come in that mornin'—so she'll know somebody's here?"

"Yes," Katie assured him. *Don't let Harry put up a fuss.*

"It'll be the first time in fifty-one years that we spent a night apart," he said, and Katie sensed his fear. "But I'll be drivin' into the city every day to see her."

"I'm sure she's going to be fine," Katie reassured him. "And just tell me what time you want me to come in. I'll be there."

As Katie anticipated, Harry balked at the thought of his wife working as a "servant."

"Harry, I'll be doing just what I do at home. And we can put more money away for planting season. It's just for a month," she cajoled. "I haven't much to do here until we start putting in the corn. I'll be home in plenty of time to clean up the house and put up supper."

"I don't like it, Katie," he grumbled, but she knew she'd won.

"It would be crazy to throw away the money," she said.

"If it gets too hard, you just tell him you can't keep on," Harry stipulated. "It's not like we'll go hungry if you don't work."

As arranged, Katie was at the Mueller house the morning Mr. Mueller drove his wife to the hospital. She was touched by the way Mrs. Mueller tried to comfort her husband. They had no children—only each other and the farm.

"You remember what I said," she told Katie. "Mr. Mueller can't tolerate too much cabbage. And he's got a terrible sweet tooth. I left an apple pie in the icebox, but you make sure he's got somethin' sweet for nighttime before he goes to sleep."

"Yes, ma'am," Katie promised. "My husband's got a sweet tooth, too."

Katie liked Mr. Mueller. She was uncomfortable in the presence of Pete, their hired man, who lived in the house with them. Pete was somewhere in his thirties, arrogant, and often sullen. Katie gathered he was a good worker but that he had trouble with the other hands during the planting and harvesting seasons. She clenched her teeth when he wandered into the house at odd hours and demanded coffee, because his eyes always focused on her breasts and legs as he towered above her.

Mr. Mueller left the farm right after the noonday meal each day to visit his wife in the hospital. His eyesight made night driving difficult for him, so he headed home in midafternoon. Per arrangement Katie left each day at five, after preparing supper for Mr. Mueller and Pete—to be warmed up by Pete when Mr. Mueller arrived.

In the middle of her second week on the job Katie was nervous when Pete lingered at the table after the noonday meal, when Mr. Mueller had already left to drive to the hospital.

"Come on, sit down and have some coffee with me," Pete coaxed while Katie moved about the table clearing away the dishes.

"I've had my coffee," she said, avoiding meeting his eyes. *Why did he keep staring at her that way?*

"If I had myself a pretty little wife like you, I wouldn't send her out to work."

"My husband didn't send me out to work," Katie shot back. "I wanted the job."

"Big-city girl like you got bored on the farm," he joshed. Mr. Mueller must have told him she was from New York.

"I wasn't bored," she said coldly. "Mr. Mueller needed somebody here, and I like making money." She stopped dead as he rose from his chair to block her path to the kitchen. All at once her heart was pounding. "Move, Pete." Despite her alarm she gazed up at him in defiance.

"Sugar, I can show you a high old time—" He reached and took the dishes from her and put them on the table. "It ain't like you never been with a man." He reached to pull her close.

"Take your hands off me!" she blazed, and kicked him in the shins.

"You little whore!" he yelled, stepping back in rage.

"You touch me again—talk to me like that again—I'll tell Mr. Mueller," she warned. "He won't like it one bit."

"You fucking little whore," he shot back at her, and stalked from the kitchen. But Katie was certain he wouldn't try to touch her again. He liked his job here.

Katie said nothing to Harry about the encounter with

Pete, because she was anxious to hold on to the job. If Harry knew, he'd insist she quit. She was tense when she walked into the house the next day, then relaxed a bit when Pete did not wander into the kitchen for his endless cups of coffee. At mealtime he ignored her, talking to Mr. Mueller about the problems on the farm. Pete wouldn't bother her again. Anyhow, she comforted herself, Mrs. Mueller would be home in a week. The doctor said she was doing fine.

On Sunday—while Harry and Jeff were out in the barn working on the Ford—she told Maura what had happened with Pete.

"That's men for you." Maura shrugged. "Especially these days. Ever since women got the vote, bobbed their hair, and shortened their skirts, men think every girl's ready to hop into bed with them. Some do," she conceded. "Some don't. If I'd been smart enough to," she said with a wry smile, "I might be on Broadway today. But all that Catholic schooling cramped my style."

"You should have seen Pete's face when I kicked him." Katie giggled reminiscently. "I kicked him *hard*. He knows I'd tell Mr. Mueller if he tried to get funny again."

"All the same, watch out for Pete," Maura cautioned. "He'll be looking to get back at you."

"Make sure you don't tell Jeff—Harry doesn't know. He'd make me quit the job."

The following morning—the sky still night-dark at just past 5:00 A.M.—Katie and Harry woke up to find the temperature had dropped almost 20 degrees overnight. The wind howled in the vast emptiness of the winter-barren fields, seeming to creep into the house through treacherous crannies. Harry ordered Katie to stay in bed until he got a fire going in the kitchen stove, and the room was warming up.

"After the kind of summer we had, I never thought we'd be freezing like this in the winter," Harry grumbled. "I never thought Texas got so cold. We might even have a blizzard before the day's over."

From a parlor window Katie watched Harry drive off in the cold gray morning, sunrise still almost an hour away this time of winter. If there was to be a blizzard—the first of the season—she hoped it would hold off until night, when Harry would be back home. Now she went back to the kitchen to make sure the coffee was hot. Maura would like a cup when she arrived, before driving her over to the Muellers'.

"Would you believe we're out of coal?" Maura greeted her and rushed into the house. "Jeff's been waiting to buy in hope that the price would drop."

"We can let you have some," Katie offered.

"We're burning corn," Maura said. "With what they're asking for coal, we might as well."

In the cozy warmth of the kitchen—the only room in the house that was not dank and cold—the two young women talked over steaming cups of coffee for a few minutes, then rose to their feet to head for the car.

"Did you ever believe back in New York that it could be this cold in Texas?" Maura sighed. "I hope I don't have trouble restarting the car. I brought along a blanket to cover our legs." She giggled. "Times like this I hate short skirts. I'd wear a pair of Jeff's pants, but he's six inches taller than me."

Katie was delighted to discover she would be alone in the house all day. Both Mr. Mueller and Pete were going into the city within an hour. They had to shop for supplies for the livestock, and Mr. Mueller wanted Pete's advice about some machinery he was about to buy.

"Keep the kitchen fire and the stove in the parlor going all day," Mr. Mueller ordered Katie. "We don't want you catching cold."

Katie put a record on the Victrola before she started to clean the parlor. She'd closed off the bedrooms so the heat circulated between the kitchen, the hallway, and the parlor. Outside, the wind continued to moan in the gray daylight, as it had all through the night. When she finished with the cleaning—before she started baking the bread and making a corn pudding—she'd take all the antimacassars off the parlor furniture and wash them, so they'd be nice and fresh when Mrs. Mueller came home from the hospital.

Late in the afternoon she sat down with a cup of coffee and the remaining portion of last night's pumpkin pie. She was washing her dishes when she heard a car pulling up in front of the house. It must be Maura—Mr. Mueller wouldn't be here for another two hours. She reached for a dish towel. No need to go to the door—it was never locked. She glanced at the clock. Maura was a little early today.

Katie paused, dish towel in one hand. *That wasn't Maura.* Not that heavy thud of boots in the hall.

"Pete?" she called out warily. How did he get home alone?

"It ain't Pete," a voice called out, and suddenly a cluster of white-robed men—their faces masked by white hoods—appeared in the doorway. Five of them, Katie counted in shock.

"Mr. Mueller isn't home," she stammered. They were the Ku Klux Klan, she realized in terror. *Why were they here?* "He's down in Dallas."

"Whore!" one man spit at her and moved forward menacingly. "We know about you and the old man."

"Mrs. Mueller's in the hospital. I'm the housekeeper while she's sick." Katie refused to cower.

"Adulteress!" another shouted, and the other four joined him in a chant. "Adulteress! Adulteress! Adulteress!"

"No!" Katie denied. *This wasn't real. This couldn't be happening.* "I'm Katie Newhouse. My husband and I are working the Stone farm." Involuntarily she stepped backward as they advanced into the room.

"You came here when his wife was lyin' sick in the hospital, and you wiggled your ass in front of him. You threw your tits in his face. It wasn't the old man's fault. You seduced him!"

"Spreadin' your legs for him in the bed he slept in with his wife!" another taunted, and imprisoned her wrist.

"No! Let me go!" From the corner of an eye—as she struggled to free herself—she saw the whip in the hands of one of the men. "Let me go!"

"Take her out to the barn," the man who appeared to be the leader ordered. "She won't be lyin' down for no man tonight!"

With clenched fists she pummeled the back of the man who picked her up and threw her over his shoulders. She felt a furtive hand at her rump as they moved out through the back door into the stinging outdoor wind. Her short flannel dress was meager protection against the cold.

"You're all crazy!" she screamed. "Mr. Mueller never touched me. I'd never let him!" She gasped as hands moved beneath her skirt to fondle a thigh. "You'll go to jail for this!" she shrieked. "Every one of you!" Yet in the back of her mind she heard Maura's voice—*"Right in our county last year at least sixty-eight men were beat up. And nobody gets arrested."*

"Shut her up, Joe," one man drawled. "Then let's give the little whore what's comin' to her." In her terror Katie heard the excitement in his voice.

They carried her into the barn and tossed her on the haystrewn floor. She lay there, flinching as she saw the whip rise in the air, crying out in pain as it came down to cut across her shoulders. The four other men goaded the whipper to stronger efforts.

"Harder, Joe! Make the little whore feel the leather!"

"And when you've given her a good lickin'," another chortled, "let's give her somethin' else."

Encased in pain and terror, Katie heard the sound of yet another car pulling up before the house. The men heard it, too.

"Hey, somebody's here!" one man gasped. "Joe, I thought you said Mueller and Pete wouldn't be back till almost six!"

"Let's get the hell out!" There was a concerted rush to the barn door.

Katie was alone. Fighting—futilely—not to lose consciousness.

Chapter Six

"Katie! Oh, my God! Katie—"

Slowly Katie forced her eyes open. Maura had arrived early.

"Oh, Maura, I couldn't believe it," she moaned. "They called me an adulteress. They said I'd been—been in bed with Mr. Mueller." Her voice broke. She felt sick and hurting and humiliated.

"The Ku Klux Klan?" Maura's face was white with rage.

"Yes. Maura, how could they think such a thing?"

"I'll give you one guess," Maura said grimly. "Pete. It was his way of getting back at you. Katie, can you stand up?"

"I think so. . . ."

With Maura's help she rose to her feet, swaying until Maura steadied her.

"I'm driving you to the hospital," Maura told her, flinching at the laid-bare skin visible on one arm.

"No," Katie rejected. "I don't want anybody to know. I feel so shamed—" It was just like Maura had said—they didn't care about the truth. They believed what Pete told them.

"Honey, you need a doctor. We'll go over to Doc Reilly's house. Remember, he's the doctor who looks after most of the families on the farms around here."

"Just help me home," Katie whispered. "I don't want to see anybody."

"We'll pick up Jeff and then we'll go to your house," Maura said gently. "I'll fix supper for the four of us. After I've put something on those welts and the cuts. Have you got some aspirin at the house?" Katie managed a nod. "That'll stop some of the hurting," Maura comforted.

"They put their hands on me," Katie's voice was a painful whisper. "One of them put his hands under my dress."

"And they talk about their being 'custodians of womanly virtue,' " Maura seethed. "They're scum."

Jeff was first solicitous about Katie's condition, then outraged at what had happened. On the brief drive to the Newhouse farm he spoke with conviction about his belief that Katie should go to the newspapers and report what had happened.

"No use going to the police," he conceded. "General Crane—he's one of the anti-Klan leaders—has told Governor Neff that the Dallas police commissioner, the chief of police, and most of the police officers are Klansmen. Even the chief is a Klansman. Nobody's going to lift a finger. But the newspapers are fighting mad."

"Jeff, I don't want to talk about it to anybody," Katie whispered, and she saw Maura glare at him in reproach. "I just want to go home." She couldn't identify one of the men. All she knew was that one of them was named Joe.

An hour later—with Harry home and Katie propped up with pillows in a chair at the supper table, though she made no effort to share the meal—Harry exploded in rage.

"That bastard Pete will pay for this, Katie! I'll break his neck!"

"No, Harry," Maura protested. "I've seen Pete. He's four inches taller and forty pounds heavier than you."

"Harry, we can't prove he set the Klan on me," Katie said quickly, with a fleeting glance of reproach for Maura. "You'd just get in trouble."

"I think it's time for us to clear out of Texas," said Harry, his face set. "I don't like what's happening in this state."

"We can't give up the farm," Katie protested, her stomach churning at the prospect. "We made a deal with Amelia."

"We didn't make a deal for you to get beat up," he shot back.

"Harry, Texas isn't the only place in the world that's infested with the KKK," Jeff pointed out. "They're all over the country. They're—"

"New York outlawed the Klan," Harry said with pride. "Governor Smith signed the bill last May. New York's the first state to stop the KKK."

"*Is* it stopping them?" Maura challenged.

"Harry, we don't want to go back to New York." Never, Katie thought, had she ever defied Harry. But they mustn't leave the farm. This was a giant step upward for them.

"No," Harry concurred. "We won't go back to New York." He recoiled at the vision of taking up life again on the squalid Lower East Side; that was the only New York open to them. "But let's get out of Texas before I kill some bastard KKKs."

"Don't let them drive you out of here," Maura argued. "There are more of us than there are of them. Everybody has to fight to—"

"Katie, we'll go to Florida," Harry said. She knew he hadn't heard a word Maura had said. "Why don't the four of us go down there? Miami," he pinpointed, his face alight with zeal. "People are going down there with practically nothing and become rich in a few weeks. Land that was worth five hundred dollars a few years ago is selling for fifty thousand today!"

"We don't have a pot to piss in between us," Jeff said bluntly. "You don't go to Miami without a nest egg. We'd be sleeping on the streets, starving to death."

"Harry, we're putting in our first crop in a few weeks."

Katie struggled to sound logical. "In the fall we'll have our first harvest. We pay Amelia one half of our profits, and we'll be on our way to owning the farm. We'll never get another chance like this."

"I'll quit the job in town," Harry said after a moment. "I don't want to leave you alone out here."

"No," Katie rejected. "I'll be fine." She would *not* allow the KKK to drive her off her farm. "Just buy a shotgun," she said with bravado, "and teach me how to use it."

Katie and Maura talked much in the next few days about the hated Klan. Katie made a point of not discussing this with Harry because she knew he was consumed by anger and frustration—and humiliated that he had not been able to punish her tormentors.

"Katie, stop stewing," Maura scolded when they sat together in the cozy warmth of the kitchen, the rest of the house closed off to save on burning coal. Most afternoons Maura drove over to spend a while with Katie while Jeff wrestled with his writing. "It doesn't help to worry about what you can't change."

"I want to do something to fight the KKK," Katie said passionately. "I never wanted anything so bad in all my life."

"Lots of people right in Dallas are fighting them," Maura soothed. "In time they'll win."

"But how many others will be hurt before that happens?" Katie challenged.

"There's a new weekly in town," Maura reported. "Jeff brought home a copy when he went into Dallas yesterday. Its sole purpose, the editor says, is to fight the Klan."

"Maura, what do Klan members hate most?" Katie asked. There had to be a way she could get back at them for what they did to her. Not revenge, she thought. *Justice.* "What causes them trouble? Not the police," she acknowledged with newly acquired cynicism.

"What they hate most is having their names made

public," Maura replied. "They take an oath not to give out the names of any members."

"Let's go into Dallas tomorrow and talk to the editor of that weekly." Katie felt a surge of exhilaration. "Let's ask him what we can do to help." Vague possibilities were infiltrating her mind. "If women are becoming members of the Klan, then other women ought to be fighting the Klan."

"Harry would kill you," Maura warned, but Katie sensed she, too, was stimulated by the prospect of being involved in the fight.

"We don't tell Harry," Katie said. "We don't tell Jeff. Just say we're bored to death, and we want to drive into Dallas to go through the stores. That doesn't cost anything," she pointed out conscientiously.

"Gas does," Maura reminded her. "But we don't go into the city often. We'll do it," she resolved, her smile dazzling.

"I'll pay for half the gas," Katie promised. "Harry lets me handle the money." Her own smile was wry. "Harry's only interested in large bills. I count the pennies."

The following afternoon—somewhat shaken by their own daring—they sat in the office of Dan McPherson and talked about their eagerness to help in the campaign against the Klan.

"We heard that the Klan has been organizing women," Maura explained. "We figured if we could pretend to want to be Klanswomen, we could infiltrate the chapter and bring you some useful information."

"They'll probably accept anybody who wants to join." Belatedly Katie worried about initiation dues.

"It's strange that you two walked in just at this time," McPherson said, his voice resonant with pleasure. "We've just learned that a new branch of Klanswomen is being formed. My wife offered to make a show of joining up—but that would be ridiculous because she's well-known by Klan families in town." He gazed first at Katie, then Maura. "You're not from here in town?"

"We're from farms about forty miles out," Maura explained. "Nobody'll know us."

"They're eager to enlarge the membership," he acknowledged, "but they're scared, too, about being identified."

"Everybody knows who they are," Katie protested. "I don't understand the oath of secrecy."

"We don't know them all. What I do know," McPherson chuckled, "is that anytime a newspaper runs the names of people belonging to the Klan, they all scatter. And that's where you two can be helpful. But I must warn you, it could be dangerous." His eyes moved searchingly from Maura to Katie. "They do terrible things."

"I know." Katie's voice was scathing. "That's why we want to be part of the fight." She'd said nothing about being attacked—but Mr. McPherson understood. She could feel his compassion.

"My informants tell me that there's to be a secret meeting on Thursday at the Sandford house." Katie remembered that Mr. Sandford was a big wheel in the local utilities company. "Supposedly it's a masquerade tea, which provides an alibi for the masks. This is an introduction to the new women's chapter. Do you have access to a car?"

"Yes," Maura told him.

"Won't it be difficult to learn who they are?" Katie asked. "I mean, if they're all wearing masks. I suspect they won't be offering names at this first meeting—"

"Jot down the numbers on the license plates of the cars," McPherson told them. "We'll check out the owners, and in the next edition," he said with relish, "I'll run the names on the front pages of the *Dallas Weekly*."

The three spent an absorbed forty minutes working out details for the infiltration of the "masquerade tea."

"There's no way you can pass yourselves off as Texans," McPherson warned good-humoredly. "You talk like Easterners."

"We'll say we're cousins from upstate New York," Katie's quick mind fabricated. "We came out to Texas because we're furious about the Walker Law against the Klan back home."

"Right," Maura agreed. "We think it's just awful that the New York Legislature dared to pass such a bill." She giggled, exchanging a whimsical glance with Katie. "Katie's Jewish and I'm Irish Catholic. But nobody'll know that."

Katie and Maura left the office of the *Dallas Weekly* with a sense of accomplishment. She wasn't just sitting back and doing nothing, Katie comforted herself. She was part of the campaign to save Texas from the Ku Klux Klan.

Walking out into the sharp cold of the day, Katie and Maura debated about taking time out to visit Neiman-Marcus, the high point of any trip into the city.

"I'd rather go straight home today," Katie admitted. "Not just because it's so cold. I have to think about how to handle this whole thing."

"You can't tell Harry," Maura cautioned.

"I know." She'd never kept anything from Harry since the first day they met. "I feel so guilty."

"Look, there are some things you tell husbands—and some things you don't." Maura reached to squeeze her hand. "It's like when I used to go to Confession. There were some things I told the priest—and some things I didn't. Men are a breed apart. They'll probably never accept the fact that they're not a superior race."

"I've never kept anything from Harry before." Katie fought against a surge of desolation.

"Join the club, darling. Now you've grown up."

In the Warrens' vintage Ford—meticulously washed for the occasion—Katie and Maura drove on Thursday afternoon to the house where the Klanswomen's masquerade tea was to be held. The cars parked on the spacious grounds of the elegant colonial house ranged from beat-up jalopies to a beautifully maintained Hispano-Suiza and a Mercedes Benz.

"Oil money," whispered Maura, enviously inspecting the Mercedes.

Adjusting their masks, they made a furtive inspection of license plates and scribbled down numbers until the approach of another ancient Ford stopped the effort.

"All at once I'm scared," Katie admitted, but her eyes were defiant.

"It's like playing a part in a play," Maura effervesced. "We're two cousins from New York who just hate what's happening back home to the poor Klan members."

In the huge, ostentatiously furnished living room of the house—which Katie and Maura knew belonged to one of Dallas's leading families—the masked women sat at attention and listened to the recruitment spiel of the pair of organizers. The atmosphere was supercharged. Circulars that listed the obligations of accepted Klanswomen along with the initiation fee and monthly dues—shockingly high—were distributed. There was no pretense of this being a social tea.

"Ladies, we'll meet here again two weeks from today—at which time you'll all be expected to present your initiation fees and to take the Klanswomen oath," a tall, heavily corseted woman in a fashionable dress Katie remembered seeing in a Neiman-Marcus window instructed. "We will dedicate ourselves to upholding the moral standards that are proper for this nation. We will remember we are white Protestants who believe in the supremacy of the white race. We promise to obey the constitution of the Ku Klux Klan."

The meeting was closed with the Pledge of Allegiance to the flag of the United States. Katie and Maura—both tense and furious—led the exodus to the waiting cars. They were not going directly home. First they would deliver the license numbers of the cars that brought the prospective Klanswomen to the initial meeting of this new chapter. Dan McPherson would track down the names of the owners. They would be made public in the next edition of the *Dallas Weekly*.

Katie and Maura made a pact; they would not tell Harry and Jeff about their activities until Saturday night supper—this week to be shared at the Warren house. On Saturday evening Katie was in the kitchen pressing the dress she meant to wear when Harry arrived home from the office.

"A clean shirt's hanging in the closet," she told him when he had kissed her lightly on the mouth. "And I steamed your good sweater." The temperature had slid downward, and Maura was guarding their supply of wood for the kitchen stove.

"Why do we all have to dress up to have dinner together?" he complained, but she knew he accepted this rule.

"Because that reminds us we're civilized," she scolded. Even in field clothes Harry was so handsome, she thought tenderly. Maura said he looked like a movie star. "Maybe we can't go for supper at the Adolphus Hotel or the Dallas Country Club, but we pretend we can. And we wouldn't go there dressed like we do in the fields."

"One of these days I'll take you for supper at the Adolphus," he promised. "We'll order the most expensive things on the menu."

"Dress and let's go over early. Jeff's going to read us another chapter from his novel."

"Oh, God, do we have to listen to that?" Harry felt uncomfortable when Jeff read to them, Katie knew. Jeff's novel—about the poignant lives of a struggling farm family—was not the kind of fiction he enjoyed. Harry devoured the E. Phillips Oppenheim novels.

"Jeff is good. Someday you'll be proud you know him." Maura said Jeff was upset that he'd have to stop the writing in another eight weeks to start with the planting. He'd be too tired after twelve to fourteen hours a day in the fields to write at night. The book would have to be pushed aside until late fall.

"That book is not going to help pay his taxes this year or buy coal for the stove." Harry reached into the bread box for a cookie, bit into it with approval.

"They're burning wood or corn now," Katie said defensively. She knew Maura was worried that they were behind in their taxes. So many people were losing their farms because they couldn't meet their expenses. But Maura had an antique dealer from the city coming out to look at the Chippendale bed stored out in the barn. She hoped it would bring enough to pay the tax bill.

When Katie and Harry arrived at the Warren house, Jeff was shoving chunks of freshly chopped wood into the cookstove. A bottle of their homemade sherry sat on the table.

"The antique dealer was here," Maura said in triumph. "We've got the tax money."

"I suppose you could always become bootleggers," Harry joshed, while Maura poured wine into the four glasses in readiness on the table. "You've got a great still going out there in the barn."

"Shall we tell them now or wait till after supper?" Maura asked Katie.

"Now," Katie decided.

The two men stared in disbelief while Katie reported on their venture on behalf of Dan McPherson and the *Dallas Weekly*.

"You're both crazy!" Harry exploded. "Katie, didn't you have enough of the KKK?"

"We could do something to help fight the Klan," Katie said, her face incandescent. "That's important. But we knew if we told you, you'd make us stop."

"What do you know, Harry?" Jeff drawled. "Our wives aren't kids anymore. They're women."

"You could have been hurt," Harry worried, yet Katie sensed he was proud of her. "You stay away from that chapter, Katie. You did enough."

"We won't go back," Maura soothed. "But won't those

women be surprised when their names show up in the *Dallas Weekly!*"

Six days later Maura drove over to the house, crunching to a stop with a roughness that alerted Katie to her emotional state. Katie hurried down the hall from the kitchen to the front door.

"When you drive like that, something's happened." She greeted Maura with an anxious smile.

"Mrs. Crane drove over this morning to borrow some sugar. She told me about the *Dallas Weekly* reporting on the 'masquerade tea' out at the Stanton house. Complete with a list of names—"

"Maura, that's wonderful." She was suffused with satisfaction. "When do you suppose we'll see a copy?"

"Not so wonderful." Maura's face tightened. "The *Dallas Weekly* came out yesterday morning. Last night—while Dan was still out delivering the papers—his wife and fourteen-year-old daughter were kidnapped and taken out to the Klan whipping meadow. They didn't whip them," she conceded, her eyes blazing. "They made Mrs. McPherson and her daughter strip to skin before that crowd of nightgowned men, and then they molested them."

"Oh, Maura! Because we supplied Dan with those names," Katie whispered in shock.

"If we hadn't, somebody else would have," Maura insisted. "We shouldn't blame ourselves."

"Has anybody been arrested?" Katie demanded, trembling in recall of her own attack.

"Are you kidding?" Maura scoffed. "Of course, the Klan's saying *they* had nothing to do with it. But the word is that Dan McPherson and his family are leaving town."

"I feel so awful for them." Katie shuddered. Ever since she could remember, she'd wanted to be useful to people—and now she'd been part of hurting Dan McPherson's wife and daughter.

"You're not to feel guilty." Maura was sharp, and Katie

realized this was because she herself felt sullied by what had happened. "This county is not going to sit by and let the Ku Klux Klan take over. I think we're past the worst of it. Too many people are fighting mad."

With the approach of early spring Harry quit his job at Wilson Brokerage. Planting time for corn began about ten days after the final killing frost. Katie and Harry went to the bank in Dallas to arrange for a loan to see them through until harvest-time. With Jeff advising, they spread manure, disked the land, planted corn. Amelia Stone had worked alongside two hired men to put in the crop, but Katie and Harry were determined not to lay out a cent for labor.

They worked from sunup to sundown seven days a week, too exhausted at the end of each day even to consider driving into Dallas for an occasional movie. Their sole diversion was Sunday suppers with Maura and Jeff, engaged in the same battle. The four of them were ever conscious that—in the midst of national plenty—farms were being foreclosed at an escalating rate.

By the Fourth of July the corn was more than knee-high. Three weeks later it was head-high. Katie and Harry worked beneath the broiling Texas sun in wide-brimmed straw hats and as few clothes as possible. By late summer the first harvesting began.

Now at the end of each day—while Katie prepared supper, much of which came from her small vegetable garden—Harry read to her from Henry Wallace's new book on corn growing, or they discussed the coming election. Vice President Coolidge—who had become president when Harding died last year—was running for a full four-year term now.

"Texas won't vote for him," Harry predicted. "Texans always vote Democratic." He paused. "And now we've got Miriam Ferguson running for governor here." He shook his head in disbelief. "*A woman.*"

"Why shouldn't a woman run for governor?" Katie

demanded. "Maybe not this one," she conceded. Everybody understood Miriam Ferguson was a front for her husband, who was barred from holding state office because he had been impeached as governor back in 1917.

"Look, what choice have we got?" Harry reasoned. In truth, neither he nor Katie was old enough to vote in this election. "She's the Democratic candidate. She won against a Klan-backed candidate in the Democratic runoff primary. The Fergusons are anti-Klan, at least."

"Jeff says that in Texas elections the only important points are: Is the candidate backed by the KKK, where does he stand on Prohibition, and will he raise taxes?"

Katie and Harry were anxious about the price this year's corn crop would bring. Predictions were that it would be low—again. As the weeks went by, they realized their profits after paying off the bank loan would be minuscule—and half would have to go to Amelia.

"Katie, you still want to stay on the farm?" Harry asked on a day when he had returned from negotiating a discouraging sale and they sat on the porch in the deceptive beauty of the early dusk.

"Harry, yes." She was unnerved that he could consider anything else. "We're buying ourselves land that will be ours forever." Her eyes searched his anxiously.

"I talked to Mr. Thompson at the brokerage office," he admitted. "They're willing to take me back at the first of November. Their office boy," he said with sardonic humor, "is quitting to go to the University of Texas in Austin."

"I'll find a job in a shop again," Katie said firmly. "We can drive into Dallas together." She tried to make it seem a small adventure.

"I don't want you working," Harry balked.

"Just till Christmas," she cajoled. "We'll have a little extra money on hand."

"Damn it, corn prices should be higher," he raged. "We work our butts off and end up with practically nothing."

"Every day—if the weather's right—we see a wonderful sunrise and sunset," she said softly. "We have a house to live in and plenty to eat. And in nine more harvests we'll own this farm."

"I'm going to talk to Mr. Thompson about moving up in the firm," Harry said, squinting in thought. "I'll tell him we'll be hiring hands to put in the next crop, so I won't be quitting like last spring." His face lighted in a way she hadn't seen in quite a while. "Katie, it's the craziest business you ever saw."

"You'll lie to him?" Katie was shocked.

"That's good business." Harry dismissed the accusation. "Who knows? If I move up fast enough, maybe I *can* hire a hand to work in the fields in my place." He smiled self-consciously as she stared at him.

"You'll have to pay a farmhand more than you make in the brokerage office," Katie protested. She was upset at the prospect of Harry's abandoning the farm. *He loved the land.* He said he felt like a king when he looked over their acreage, which stretched further than the eye could see.

"Katie, you wouldn't believe it if I told you what some people earn in the office," Harry said softly. "I know what Mr. Thompson takes home every week. Why do I have to be an office boy? Why can't I be a commission salesman? The stock market is making people rich practically overnight. Everybody's investing in the market."

"Everybody with money," Katie amended. "And that's not a lot of people."

"Katie, wake up! The farmers are starving to death. But off the farms people never had it so good. Every family's buying refrigerators and cars and washing machines—"

"On time," Katie interrupted grimly. "They miss two payments, and the car or the refrigerator or washing machine is repossessed."

"You're living in the past," Harry reproached. "Everybody—except the farmers—is seeing more money every week than they ever saw in their lives."

"They're adding ten to forty percent to the cost of everything they're buying on installment payments. That's not the way to live. It's all going to blow up in their faces one day."

"Down in Florida people are running a few hundred dollars in 'binder money' into a fortune." Harry's voice deepened in frustration. "That same thing is happening in the stock market. We have a customer who started out seven months ago with a five-hundred-dollar investment. He's worth fifty thousand dollars today. Katie, I want that kind of money for us. *I've got to figure out how to get it.*"

"He's worth fifty thousand dollars on paper," Katie qualified. But she knew Harry wasn't listening.

Chapter Seven

ON NOVEMBER 4 Republican Calvin Coolidge—despite the outcries of both Democrats and Progressives over the scandals of the Harding administration—was elected to serve a full term. Most Americans thought the economy was booming. Not the farmers, the Western lumbermen, the New England textile workers, the coal miners in Pennsylvania and West Virginia, or the Negro sharecroppers in the South. They were hurting badly.

On this late November morning Harry was in high spirits. He was whistling as he waited for Katie to join him on the front seat of the Ford for the long drive into Dallas. For three weeks now he had been working again at Wilson Brokerage. Katie was in her second week of work as a salesgirl at the same women's wear shop where she had worked last year.

His second day on the job Harry had been promoted to posting quotation prices on the office display board. Within a few days he was able to figure mentally—to a fraction—how much a stock rose or fell. Now he made a point of staying late each day, copying closing prices into a notebook, comparing them with the previous day's prices. He realized that the way to make money buying stocks was to be able to analyze each stock's behavior, to detect a pattern. But to buy stocks he needed money.

Then, yesterday, another young office worker at Wilson Brokerage had told him about the "bucket shops" around town and how he hoped his prospective father-in-law would back him into opening one of these.

"Hey, so it's not exactly legal," the clerk conceded. "Neither is gambling, but everybody does it. Once we're married, Alice's old man will probably give me the loot to set up shop."

This morning—as usual—Harry dropped Katie off at her shop and headed toward the brokerage office. But today he took a slight detour, though it meant he'd be late for work. He went to the bank to draw out money from their minuscule savings account. He was praying Katie wouldn't notice the bankbook was missing from the drawer. But with any luck at all, he promised himself, he'd put it back fast—and still have a stake to continue playing in the bucket shops.

On his lunch hour Harry went to a nearby bucket shop—where customers bet on prices while they were being scrawled on the quotation board. If the customer bet on a stock that went up, he won. If it went down, he lost. Often, Harry understood, there was no real buying and selling of stocks here. It was a game.

Harry suspected that with his prodigious memory plus the information he picked up at Wilson and his knack for judging price fluctuations, he ought to be able to make a killing in the "bucket shops." Now he planned to put that suspicion to the test.

He walked into the shop—appearing, he knew, the perfect customer. Young, inexperienced, and eager. Katie would kill him if she found out, he thought involuntarily—but he'd come this far and he wasn't going to backtrack now. With a guileless smile he gave his orders to the fast-talking *bucketeer*. Confident that he would win.

The next day he was able to return his initial stake to the bank account and keep enough cash to play again. Now each day at lunchtime he returned to the bucket shop, winning regularly. At the end of six days the owner refused to allow him to play any longer.

"Go play somewhere else!" he ordered. "I don't wanna see your face in here. Out!"

Harry sought out another bucket shop, where his uncanny skill was unknown, not yet telling Katie of his tremendous luck. His daily small winnings piling up. Again—some days later—the surly owner ejected Harry from his shop. Harry was unperturbed. He'd find other shops.

He waited until Christmas Eve—Katie's last day at work—to tell her of his secret venture. While she pulled a blanket about her against the bitter cold of the night as they headed home in the Ford, he explained about bucket shops and what he had been doing the past four weeks. Quick to explain he had been lucky.

"Harry, those bucket shops are illegal." He could feel her shock that he had gambled their money, had not confided in her.

"The owners run an illegal establishment," he conceded, "but I'm doing just what customers do in a legitimate brokerage office. I'm buying." He removed one hand from the wheel to reach into his pocket. He pulled out a wad of bills and handed them to Katie. "Those are not dollar bills," he said with a chuckle, because he knew she was unable to see in the darkness of the car. "Tens and twenties. That's our stake to play the stock market. We're going to be rich, Katie!"

Two nights later—despite Katie's protests at such extravagance—Harry took her to dinner at the magnificent Adolphus Hotel. She wore a simple black velvet shift that she and Maura had fashioned from a dress Maura had discovered in an old chest. With the shift—that was copied from a photograph in a recent *Vogue*—Katie wore her long strand of Woolworth pearls and gold earrings that had once belonged to Maura's grandmother-in-law.

"I'll carry my coat," Katie decided self-consciously as they approached the dining-room entrance. Folded over her arm, she told herself, it would appear less shabby.

"I'll buy you a new one soon," Harry promised. "From Neiman-Marcus."

They walked into the elegant dining room with the same aplomb that characterized their strolls through such New York City landmarks as the lobbies of the Plaza, the Waldorf-Astoria, and the St. Regis. It was unreal and delicious and faintly intimidating.

"You order whatever you like," Harry insisted when they were seated and alone with the menus. "We're celebrating tonight."

"I can't believe all that money," Katie murmured. She brushed aside the truant wish that Harry would put it into the bank instead of the stock market.

"That's nothing to what we're going to see." His face radiated confidence. Katie was aware of furtive glances in his direction from women diners at nearby tables. She was unaware of the male glances that focused on her. "I'm not leaving the company," he reminded her. "I'll work there for now because I hear tips all day long. I know who's sharp and who's just making guesses. I've learned how to anticipate price fluctuations. My way, it's not a gamble. It's a sure thing."

"It's so much money." Katie wavered. "And all you see for it are pieces of paper."

"You don't understand the stock market," Harry said zealously. "What happens on Wall Street affects the whole world."

"It's gambling," Katie insisted. "It scares me."

"You'll change your mind when we're rolling in money," Harry said confidently, and focused his attention on the menu. "Damn Prohibition. We ought to celebrate with champagne."

Though Jeff always derided the fare in Dallas restaurants—*"You're lucky to find a decent bowl of chili or beef stew"*—Katie was impressed by the gourmet dinner served to them in the Adolphus dining room.

They enjoyed the luxury of dining here. To Harry, Katie understood, it was more than the pleasure of eating fine food. It was being here in luxurious surroundings, amid people who were rich and successful. She wouldn't allow herself to remember what this dinner was costing them.

"Terrific food," Harry conceded, clearly feeling mellow, "but you know, nothing beats the vegetables we pick from your garden in the summer—or the peaches from our tree. If somebody could find a way to lock that flavor in, wow, they'd make a fortune!" Now he gazed into space with that contemplative air Katie had come to recognize. Harry was envisioning some new money-making venture.

"Harry, we can't freeze them in the summer and keep them for winter," she laughed.

"Why not?" he challenged. "I'll bet that one of these days people will pick fruit from the trees and freeze them to eat the rest of the year. Lots of money there—"

"But it would take lots of money to find out if it could be done." But now Katie was thoughtful. "Remember when Jeff was talking about his mother's greenhouse? Maybe we could make one and have fresh vegetables year-round."

"You want a greenhouse, go ahead," he said indulgently. "Right now all I can think about is what stocks I'm going to buy tomorrow. Two weeks ago," he said reverently, "one of the stenographers invested her life savings—three hundred dollars. Two days later she sold her shares for fifteen thousand. If I work at it, consider all the numbers, I can figure out just where the Dow Jones Index and *The New York Times* Industrial Averages are going."

Katie felt as though she were living in a make-believe world in the weeks ahead as Harry came home each night, barely waiting until the supper dishes were removed, to pore over his notebook—where figures had been surreptitiously entered in the course of the workday. She made no pretense of comprehending the facts Harry spouted at her because her mind had erected a wall against such financial maneuverings as "buying on margin" and "selling short."

Her mother had done well—like most Americans—during the war years, had saved for the day when they would move away from the Lower East Side and she would open her shop. "You buy what you can afford," her mother always insisted. But then her mother died tragically young and the money disappeared.

Harry was right, Katie told herself, in saying that it was fine to think of tomorrow but that somewhere along the line they ought to spend a little to enjoy the present. Still, she was uneasy each time Harry took her to the Adolphus dining room for dinner or bought some small gift he knew would please her.

She was upset when they went to the bank again to borrow for the planting season. Paying high interest rates.

"Katie, that's a different business," he exhorted. "I can't use my stock-market stake for the farm."

It worried her, too, that he insisted on hiring a hand to work with her in putting in the harvest—though they must pay the hand more than he was earning at Wilson's. But his winnings on the market were impressive.

"This is high finance," he told her with relish. "You should see the way my broker respects me. Because I'm buying low and selling high. He can't figure out how I do it. He doesn't understand that playing the stock market is a science."

Early in April Katie and the hired hand began the task of putting in the corn. She was wistful at working with a stranger rather than Harry. Much of the joy of planting was gone. She was aware now of physical exhaustion at the end of each day—which she had ignored when Harry worked beside her.

In May Harry told her he was hiring another man to work the farm.

"I don't want you out there breaking your back, Katie. We don't need that anymore. I can take off enough cash to pay the second hand and still be able to operate comfortably."

"What will I do with myself all day?" she challenged.

"Take care of the house and your garden. Cook." He shrugged. "Do what city wives do. *Read*," he pounced. "Educate yourself." He smiled in satisfaction. Here was something he knew she cherished. "Borrow books from Jeff."

That same week Harry bought a new Ford. Katie watched, puzzled, when the salesman drove up behind Harry and parked in front of the house. She watched while a handful of bills passed from Harry's hand to his. In the balmy dusk Harry stood beside Katie on the porch and viewed the new car with pride while the salesman climbed into a third Ford that had followed them.

"Fords have come down to two-hundred-ninety dollars—without a self-starter, but I don't need that," Harry pointed out. The self-starter was a feature that appealed to women. "The first Model T sold for nine hundred fifty dollars. That's progress."

"Let me use the old Ford," said Katie, her heart pounding in anticipation while they walked hand in hand into the house. "Then I can drive over to see Maura sometimes instead of her always having to drive over to see me."

"When will Maura have time to see you during the season?" he hedged. "Except in the evening—when I'm home to drive you over." He still refused to teach her to drive—on the basis that if anything happened to the car, he'd be unable to go in to the office. But now there was a second car.

"Now and then Maura can take an hour off." She was prepared for battle. Maura drove. Why shouldn't she? "At night you're all tied up with your notebook. You wouldn't even know if I left the house for an hour."

"Why do you have to drive?" he asked in irritation.

"Because other women do," she told him, bristling with defiance. "Maura always says she's going to teach me. Now she will."

"We'll see." His mouth was set. He was annoyed. But this time she would fight him.

The following day Maura drove over just at sunset. Once night approached, Katie and the hired man abandoned work in the fields. Maura and Jeff did the same. The two women sat together in the kitchen with oversized cups of coffee.

"All I have to do is heat up last night's stew," Maura said. "Jeff's sitting down at the kitchen table to try to write. If he doesn't fall asleep first," she said wryly.

Now they talked about the hired man who would start to work in Katie's place next week and about the new Ford Harry had bought.

"I'll teach you to drive." Maura was pleased. "I'd rather give up eating than give up my car."

"It's scary," Katie confessed. "Harry's making all this money on the stock market—but except for the car and wages for the hired man and a few little things, it's all going back into stocks. I wish some of it was going into the bank."

"Jeff says Harry's awful smart about stocks."

"Harry keeps saying everybody's playing the market these days." Katie's smile was wistful. "To me it's crazy."

"There's all this talk about people playing the market—but when you get down to facts, Jeff keeps telling me, maybe a million people out of all the millions that make up this country are doing it. Like we read in the newspapers and magazines about speakeasies and bathtub gin and Freud and jazz babies. Most people never see the inside of a speakeasy or ever taste bathtub gin. They don't play mah-jongg, and the only flappers they've ever seen are in the movies. And who knows about Freud except people who read the smart magazines? People in small towns and on the farms live the same kind of lives their parents did. Most of them worry about meeting the payments on the new washing machine or the piano or the car. But that husband of yours—he's somebody special," Maura conceded.

Harry agreed with Katie that it would be wise for her to supervise their two farmhands. He'd accepted her learning to drive.

"Just look out on the hands now and then," he said indulgently. "Let them know you're around. Drive over and spend a little time with Maura in the afternoons," he encouraged. "I know it gets lonely out here."

Katie refrained from reminding Harry that Maura was out in the fields with Jeff. At times she felt guilty that she was having life so much easier than Maura. Still—though she said nothing to Harry about this—she continued to work in the fields for a few hours each day.

The two hired men accomplished far less than Harry and she, but she understood. They were both tired, bitter old men who had lost their own farms in the past. They didn't have the incentive that pushed Harry and her on to work their hardest. They worked so their families could survive.

Late in August—when Texas was fighting a horrendous hot spell—Harry came home with a box from Neiman-Marcus.

"Try it on, Katie," he ordered while she stared in awe at the parcel. "Go on, open the box. The woman at the store said it ought to fit you. I measured one of your dresses last night and gave her the figures."

"Harry, it must have cost so much," she whispered, reaching to open the box.

"Tomorrow night we're having dinner at the Adolphus," he told her. "And the next day we go to Neiman-Marcus to buy you a coat."

"In August?" She laughed shakily.

"They'll have coats in August," Harry insisted. "It's not like Klein's basement." Harry knew that to every woman in Dallas a dress or coat from Neiman-Marcus was something to be cherished.

"Harry—" Katie inspected him with a blend of pride and apprehension. "What have you been up to?"

"I made a killing today. I'm quitting my job. I don't need Wilson anymore. I'll go in to my stockbroker every day, and handle my business. And you, Katie. I want you to travel down to Houston to offer a deal to Amelia."

"What kind of deal? Harry, what are you talking about?"

"I've figured out just about what Amelia can expect from her share of the profits of the next nine harvests. I'm prepared to pay her off right now—" He chuckled at Katie's stare of astonishment. "I told you—I made a killing today. I want the farm to belong to us, free and clear. I'll go to the lawyer and have the papers drawn up. You'll take the night train down to Houston, talk to Amelia. Then have her sign the papers and you'll give her the check. She'll be happy," he predicted. "She won't have to wait nine years for her money."

"You want me to go to Houston alone?" Momentary alarm gave way to anticipation.

"You can handle this." He smiled reassuringly. "First

you write and tell Amelia you'll be in Houston, arriving on the overnight train. She can meet you at the depot. She'll be glad to see you—you'll spend the day together, transact business, and then you take the night train home."

"And then we'll truly own the farm!" Katie's smile was ecstatic.

"I'm putting it in your name," Harry said tenderly. "So you'll always know the farm is yours."

Katie pushed up the shade of the window of her Pullman berth and watched the first gray light of dawn appear in the night sky. The tiny fan was doing nothing to alleviate the sultry heat of the night. She had slept little on this overnight trip to Houston, but the heat was not to blame. Her mind was a kaleidoscope of memories. The parade of nights when she and Harry had made their way cross-country from New York. Those first days on the farm with Amelia. And now they were about to own that farm.

She was touched by Harry's insistence that the farm be in her name. It was his way of reassuring her because every dollar he made went to buy more stocks. In her mind more bits of paper. The only paper she believed in, she thought with a flicker of humor, was that issued by the U.S. Mint.

Soon she struggled to dress within the narrow confines of her lower berth. She would make her way to the women's washroom early, she told herself—before those other, more experienced travelers arrived there. She felt simultaneously sophisticated and self-conscious as she left the berth to move down the aisle to the washroom.

Amelia was at the depot to meet her. She knew Amelia was curious—even a little nervous—about this visit, though she had explained that "Harry's had a little luck on the stock market." They went to a restaurant for breakfast, with Katie insistent that Amelia order more than coffee. Over breakfast Katie explained Harry's offer. She saw Amelia's eyes widen in astonishment. Then the astonishment was replaced by a wary scrutiny.

"Nobody's been diggin' for oil on the farm?" Amelia blushed at this inquiry. "Now I didn't mean that," she said anxiously. "I know you and Harry—you wouldn't cheat me."

"Nobody's digging for oil," Katie assured her. "Though you know every farmer in Texas is always hoping to strike oil. Our little oil well," she said with a chuckle, "is Harry's knack for knowing which stocks will go up and which will fall."

"I got no truck with the stock market," Amelia admitted, "even though you hear such stories about people becomin' rich overnight. Now the farm—that's something you can see."

At Amelia's house her daughter carefully read over the papers Katie had brought along.

"Mama, I think you ought to have a lawyer look over these," she said finally, but Katie knew she was impressed by the check about to change hands.

"I don't need no lawyer with Katie and Harry," Amelia told her. "You don't see nuthin' wrong in the contract, do you?"

The contract was signed. The farm was Katie's. Later in the day Amelia's daughter drove them to the depot. In the morning Harry was at the Dallas depot to meet her.

"You're now a landowner," he greeted her after a warm welcoming kiss. "How does it feel?"

"Wonderful," she said, her face luminous. "But I missed you last night." It was the first night they'd spent apart since their marriage. "I couldn't sleep."

"I couldn't sleep, either," he admitted. "It was terrible."

They held hands under the restaurant table while they waited for breakfast to be served. For the first time Harry took Katie with him when he went to place his orders for the day with his broker. After lunch, he told her, he would give orders to sell certain stocks. Then they'd drive home.

Katie recoiled from the cacophony of shrill voices and the staccato sounds of the array of tickers that lined one wall of the brokerage office. And she stared in astonishment at a pair of women in noisy discussion about the behavior of copper and steel.

"I hear there're brokerage offices in New York and some other large cities that only admit women," Harry told her. "One is all furnished like a speakeasy." Neither Harry nor Katie had ever been inside a speakeasy. "The women sit around on sofas and easy chairs and smoke Turkish cigarettes in those long holders"—he gestured in amusement—"and sip their drinks while they watch girls chalk price quotations on a blackboard. No men there," he emphasized.

"I'll never go to one," she said firmly, and Harry laughed.

Katie was conscious of the side glances directed at Harry and herself as he prodded her about the crowded room. She was astonished by the mixture of envy and respect for Harry she felt in some of the brokerage customers. To them, it was clear, Harry was somebody special.

She stood at one side while Harry transacted business. A couple of men were feverishly making notes as they eavesdropped on Harry's conversation.

"This is my wife," Harry told his broker with a proud smile. "Katie, this is Mr. Maxwell."

"So young and beautiful. But what else should I expect?" The broker nodded sagely. "The two of you—the golden couple. There's no stopping Harry. He's a miracle worker."

Now Harry slipped an arm about her waist and walked with her toward the door.

"I'll be here for the next three hours. . . ." He reached into his pocket for his wallet. "You go over to Neiman-

Marcus and buy yourself something pretty." His eyes caressed her. "Buy one of those negligees or nightgowns that Pola Negri wears in the movies."

After she had washed the supper dishes and put them away, Katie went into the bedroom to prepare for bed. She knew that tonight Harry wouldn't dally long over his nightly routine of studying stock quotations. They were both so conscious of having slept alone last night.

Evening had brought little respite from the August heat. She lingered longer than she had planned in the tepid water of the bathtub, enjoying the fragrant aromas of the Helena Rubenstein bath salts she had bought at a posh Dallas shop. For the first time in her young life she had spent extravagantly without a feeling of guilt.

Out of the tub she patted herself dry and pulled on the sheer black nightgown she had bought at Neiman-Marcus. She hadn't bought the matching negligee—how long would she keep it on? she'd asked herself realistically. Now, with a touch of perfume at her throat and wrists, she walked from the bathroom down the tiny hall to the parlor, where Harry sat hunched over the ledger he used to enter his daily transactions.

"Harry," she said tentatively, her heart all at once pounding. She had never wanted him to make love to her more than tonight.

He turned to look at her. She heard his sharp intake of breath.

"Katie . . ." The word was a caress. "You look like a movie star."

"It was awfully expensive. . . ."

"Nothing's too expensive for my wife," he said, and rose to his feet. "I'll finish my calculations later." His eyes were dark with passion when he suddenly scooped her up into his arms.

"Harry," she scolded, her eyes alight with laughter. "You'll break your back."

"Some weakling's back," he derided, walking with her into the hall and toward the bedroom. "Not Harry Newhouse's back."

They lay tangled together in the darkness, the expensive black nightgown on the floor beside the bed. His mouth moved from hers to her throat with the soft, moist kisses that aroused her. His hands knew her erotic areas, as hers knew his. In bed, she marveled, they were equals.

"You're sensational," he whispered as they moved together. "How'd you learn?" he teased.

"From you." Exhilaration made her bolder than normal.

"Oh God, Katie!"

All at once there was no time for their customary dalliance. Both were breathless with the need to touch totally, to merge into one being. In the humid heat of the night the sounds of their moment of climax was a glorious erotic symphony. They lay still now, bodies wet with perspiration.

"Oh God, Katie," Harry said again, the weight of him heavy on her but both reluctant to move.

"You said that before," she murmured.

"That was when I forgot I wasn't properly dressed for the occasion." Now he sounded uneasy. To be "not properly dressed" meant that he had not bothered to reach for a condom. "Maybe you should go out to the bathroom. . . ."

"Later," she stalled. "Oh, Harry, I love you so much!"

Chapter Eight

By LATE September Katie was admitting to herself that even the three or four hours a day she was spending in the fields was exhausting her. She blamed it on the heat and made a point of soaking in a cool tub before Harry arrived back home from his day in the city.

"Thank God, we'll soon be done with the harvest," she confided to Maura on a Sunday afternoon while they sat on the porch trying to cool off, and Harry and Jeff worked on the old Ford out in the barn. "I'm so tired—and I'm always sleepy."

"You sound just like Mrs. Crane's daughter-in-law, Elvira," commented Maura, her eyes speculative. "How late are you?"

Katie stared in acute, sudden awareness.

"Maura, I lost track." She squinted in thought. "Two weeks—no, three."

"Uh-huh." Maura nodded knowingly.

"Are you saying I'm pregnant?" Her mind charged backward to the one night they'd neglected to take precautions. "Maura, I'm pregnant!" She was assaulted by conflicting emotions. Tenderness and exultation that she was—probably—carrying Harry's baby. Alarm that he would be upset because he thought they were too young to start a family.

"That's what keeps the world going." Maura's smile was tender.

"But we didn't plan . . ." Katie's voice trailed off.

"Famous last words. When are you going to tell Harry?"

"Tonight," Katie said instantly. "The minute you two go home."

"We could go now," Maura offered.

"No," Katie rejected. "I need a little while to get used to the idea."

Still, Maura prodded Jeff into going home at least two hours earlier than normal. Katie realized Maura understood that now she was anxious to tell Harry that—unless the classic symptoms were wrong—they would be parents in another seven months or so.

"What was Maura's rush tonight?" Harry asked while he stood with Katie on the porch and watched the other two drive down the road.

"She knew I wanted to be alone with you," Katie said softly, and Harry raised an eyebrow in mock dismay.

"Wow, you're getting to be a hot little number," he joshed.

"I have news for you." She lifted her face to his, her smile brilliant. "You know that song Eddie Cantor sings? 'We're Having a Baby, My Baby and Me'? Well . . ." She took a deep breath, her smile incandescent. "That's us."

Harry froze, for a moment seeming incapable of speech.

"You're having a baby?"

"It takes two," she reminded him. "*We're* having a baby."

"Oh my God!" He was ashen.

"Harry, you're pious at the craziest moments."

"I'm not sure I want you to have a baby."

"It's a little late to change our minds. . . ." She tried to sound flip. *Didn't Harry want their baby?*

"I'm scared," he confessed, suddenly seeming very young and vulnerable. "You're such a kid."

"Lots of girls have babies when they're younger than me. It's natural. It's not as though we—we can't afford it," she stammered, shaken by his disapproval.

"I don't want to see you go through that." He reached

to pull her close, and she felt his heart pounding. "I remember when my mother had my youngest sister. I was only seven—but I remember all the screaming from the bedroom when Mama had Grace. I don't want you to go through that."

"I'll be all right," Katie said firmly, and laughed. "But I'm not sure about you."

Harry insisted that Katie find a doctor in Dallas, though Maura had assured her there was a competent doctor right in their own area. When she hedged, he consulted acquaintances at the brokerage office where he conducted most of his business. He insisted, too, that his son—he was convinced Katie carried a boy—would be born in a hospital. Katie was touched by his solicitude for the baby and her—and his very real terror for the pain of delivery.

Harry went with Katie to see the doctor, who was clearly affronted by some of his questions.

"For a very young prospective father you ask a lot."

"If I was older," Harry countered, "I might know some of the answers."

Early in November he drove Katie—already grappling with safety pins to cope with her expanding waist-line—into Dallas, presumably to shop for clothes to see her through her pregnancy. Though she had already ordered clothes by mail from Lane Bryant in New York, Harry ordered her to look in Neiman-Marcus for something suitable to wear immediately. It was a ritual now for them to go to the Adolphus Hotel for Sunday evening dinner. He relished the admiring, covert glances sent in her direction in the dining room. He saw no reason for a prospective mother to go into seclusion.

"Harry, you took the wrong turn," Katie scolded as they approached downtown Dallas.

"Uh-uh," he said mysteriously. "I have to show you something first."

"What?" she demanded.

"You'll see." His smug smile told Katie it would be futile to pursue this. He loved coming to her with small surprises. They drove into a charming residential area of well-kept houses and neat lawns outlined by neatly trimmed hedges. Suspecting Harry was taking her to visit a business associate, Katie inspected her attire with some anxiety. Her coat was fine, she consoled herself—but she knew her overblouse only partially masked the tightness of her skirt. Why must Harry always be so impulsive?

Now he pulled up at the curb before a small two-story Tudor house set pleasantly behind a lawn framed by beds of golden and scarlet zinnias.

"Harry, who lives there?" Reproach in her voice.

"You do," he said nonchalantly, and reached into the pocket of his jacket and brought out a key. "I bought it for us, furniture and all." He grinned at her open-mouthed astonishment. "Katie, it's our house." He reached across her to open the car door.

"But we have a house. . . ." All at once she was desolate. *She didn't want to leave the farm.*

"We'll live here during the week," he explained. "I worry about you alone all day out there. And I'm tired of all the driving. Freezing in the winter, roasting in the summer. We'll go out to the farm on Friday evenings, then drive back into the city on Monday mornings. It'll be wonderful, Katie," he encouraged. "Come on, let me show you the house."

They left the car and walked hand in hand up the narrow path to the entrance. Katie forced herself to ask the realistic question.

"Harry, how can we afford a house?" It probably cost three thousand or four thousand dollars. Even more.

"I took out a mortgage. I put some cash down," he acknowledged, "but the rest we pay off in monthly payments."

"What'll happen to the farm?" It was unnerving to consider moving away.

"We'll lease the land to some neighborhood farmer." Harry shrugged. "It won't be much, but it'll pay the taxes."

The following day—because of Harry's eagerness—they took up residence in the new house. Katie tried to share his enthusiasm, but she missed the vast stretch of open land—without another house in view. She knew she'd miss the awesomely beautiful sunrises and sunsets that had been part of life on the farm. She disliked the somber Victorian furniture, the dark walls.

In time, she promised herself, she'd replace the heavy, depressing drapes with sheer curtains that would allow the sunlight into the small, cluttered rooms. She'd move some of the pieces into the attic. Still, she conceded with pride, they'd come a long way in a very short time from tenements on Rivington Street.

Katie realized they were embarking on a whole new lifestyle. At moments this was intimidating. She was proud of Harry's success, their growing affluence—on paper, she constantly reminded herself. Still, the material evidence was impressive. Harry bought himself a lavish wardrobe, a raccoon coat, and a diamond wedding band and a washing machine for her. In a surge of extravagance—after a triumphant day at the brokerage office—he put the new Ford up for sale and bought a Pierce-Arrow.

"The monthly payments are nothing," he soothed Katie.

Now Harry found pleasure in inviting his new friends—most of them twice his age—into the house for small dinner parties. Katie remembered how he'd missed the gatherings in his parents' home after their untimely death. *"Mama loved to cook, and Papa loved to talk. He should have been a politician, the way he worried over everything that happened in the city and the state and the country. From the time I was twelve until the day they died, they talked about how their son would someday be a lawyer."*

At Katie's delicate prodding, Harry allowed her to

refurnish the dining room. He stood at her side in the posh furniture store that was responsible for some of Dallas's finest homes and ordered her to spend whatever she liked. Instinctively he knew she would choose well.

The friends Harry invited to weekly dinner parties were lavish in their admiration for the English Regency table and chairs and the sideboard that were exquisitely simple in comparison to the heavy furniture of the other rooms. With the aid of the stream of women's magazines she brought into the house, Katie planned dinners that were attractive to the eye as well as gastronomic delights, and colored with pleasure when one guest—thirty years her senior—remarked that Socrates said that the first taste of any meal was with the eyes.

The men talked only about the stock market; the women discussed clothes and the problems with servants. She was a cordial, attentive hostess, but Katie was bored and often lonely in this new environment.

Then Maura called to tell Katie—even before she told Jeff—that she was sure she, too, was pregnant. Katie was enthralled that they would be sharing this experience. Instantly she felt less alone.

"Do you suppose it's contagious?" Maura laughed. "Jeff's going to be upset at first." All at once she was anxious. "He'll come out with all that stuff about how it's time to forget the writing and do something sensible. Like earning a living for his family. But he won't stop writing," she said with conviction. "We can survive on the farm—and he has those winter months for writing. You know what, Katie?" Now she was reverting to her earlier mood of levity. "You have a boy and I'll have a girl—or vice versa—and they'll grow up, fall in love, and get married."

"Harry's convinced we'll have a boy. I don't want to see his face if the doctor tells him it's a girl."

"He can't send it back, honey," Maura laughed. "But I know Harry. He'll love it, boy or girl. You'd think he was the first husband to plant a baby."

"He's so sweet, Maura. And so proud. You know how he lost his whole family in the flu epidemic—and now *we're* going to be a family. He'll spoil the baby to death. And then—other times—he's so scared for me. You'd think no other woman ever went through labor."

"We'll be there to hold his hands," Maura promised. "You're due at least two months ahead of me."

Early in her seventh month—explaining she felt self-conscious in late pregnancy—Katie pleaded with Harry to abandon their dinner parties.

"Katie, you look beautiful," he insisted. "But we'll stop having people in until after the baby's born." The baby he was convinced would be a son—to grow up to go to Harvard College and Harvard Law School. "Only Maura and Jeff." They were like family.

Katie cherished their weekends on the farm, but now—with Katie "big as a house," Harry gloated—they abandoned the long, tiring trips to the country. Instead, Maura and Jeff drove in to spend Sundays with them, though Maura warned late in March that they would soon be caught up in the planting season—and she herself was "too far along for all the driving."

In mid-April Katie went into labor. White and frightened, Harry stayed with her until the doctor ordered him from the room.

After a long and difficult labor—while Harry was comforted in the hospital waiting room by Maura and Jeff—Katie delivered her first child.

"It's a boy," the doctor told an exhausted Katie.

"Thank God," she sighed. "Harry would never forgive me if it'd been a girl."

Katie came home from the hospital with her son—named Leo David Newhouse, after her father and Harry's father—the day after he was circumcised in accordance with the teachings of the Jewish faith. Like Harry, she was enthralled by the precious bundle that was their first child. And already—her painful delivery behind her—she was dreaming of a sister for Leo.

She discovered that Harry had arranged for a warm, middle-aged Mexican-American to act as Leo's nurse, and an eager young Mexican-American to be the house-maid.

"You knew I wanted to learn to speak Spanish," Katie teased when Carmen had taken Leo off to the nursery and Rosita hurried off to the kitchen for a pair of glasses so that they could toast Leo's homecoming with a bottle of Jeff's excellent home-brewed peach brandy.

"That's the bonus." Both she and Harry were eager to learn what they considered "almost the second language of Texas." He reached to pull her close. "It was awful, being here alone these last nights without you."

"Harry, you're happy about Leo?" At intervals she remembered his initial reluctance to become a parent. It wasn't enough that Harry accepted parenthood. It must be precious to him.

"Katie, he's wonderful. I never saw such a beautiful baby."

"How many babies have you seen?" But she glowed at his approval.

"Katie, I want you to listen to me." All at once he was stern. "I'm making lots of money. Okay, once in a while I guess wrong—but most of the time I come out way ahead. I want you to enjoy yourself. Mama spent all her life in the kitchen or cleaning our flat. It mustn't be like that for you."

Sometimes it seemed to Katie that they were, indeed, the golden couple. She was learning—at last—to relax in their growing affluence, though it disturbed her that Maura and Jeff were not sharing in this. In the midst of a soaring economy they—like many other farmers—were hurting. Nor would they accept financial aid when it was offered.

"It's Jeff," Maura admitted. "I'm not all that proud. But Jeff comes from a line of people who think it's their duty to suffer," she said humorously, "and by God, we won't break family tradition."

Maura gave birth to a son—at home, attended only by a midwife—on a sultry late June evening while Jeff labored in the fields with the aid of a searchlight because they couldn't afford to hire a hand. Exhilarated by the arrival of George Edward Warren, Maura insisted she would be there in the cornfield within a week or two.

"We did it, Katie," Maura chortled while Katie cradled the day-old "Georgie" in her arms. "We're parents."

The weeks sped past. Each day Harry hurried home to hear the latest tale about Leo's progress. Their world revolved around their son.

But Katie's euphoria was shattered when she discovered on a July weekend at the farm that Harry had embarked on a second occupation. With Jeff's help he was operating a still in the barn, and bootlegging the brandy they made. Jeff's small still was inadequate to operate a business.

"Katie, I need the extra operating capital for the stock market. In six months we'll be millionaires!"

"Harry, it's against the law." Katie was terrified.

"It's a bad law. Everybody knows that. Right here in Texas—soon after the Eighteenth Amendment was passed, they found a still making a hundred-thirty gallons of whiskey a day on Senator Morris Sheppard's farm. He's the guy who wrote the amendment!"

"It's still against the law." Her eyes challenged him to deny this.

"Katie, it's an impossible law to enforce. Everybody knows that."

"But people *are* caught, and they go to jail."

"I'll keep it going for just six months," he soothed. "The market is so ripe for the pickings. And Jeff needs the money," he pointed out cannily. "He has to hire a hand to help in the fields. Maura can't strap Georgie on her back and work out there."

"I don't like it." Katie was trembling. How could Harry

do this? A man who wanted to be a lawyer. "What happens if you get caught?"

"I won't get caught," he said with conviction. "Only stupid people get caught."

When Katie confronted her, Maura was philosophical. Yes, she knew about the still on the farm; but she'd said nothing to Katie.

"Why tell you?" she apologized. "They were determined to go ahead, and you'd just worry."

"Don't you worry?" Katie countered.

"Look, in life you always worry about something. The extra money is terrific."

Katie's life now was tainted by fear. Harry avoided talk about his second occupation, but she always knew when he was involved in some phase of his bootlegging activity. Either he took the Pierce-Arrow from the garage early in the morning—meaning he was going out to the farm—or he left the house with a parcel, a signal that he was making a delivery to a special "client."

On a sunny September morning after an agonizing heat spell, Katie stood at the front door with Leo in her arms to see Harry off for the day. Carmen was busy putting diapers into the washing machine. Rosita was in the kitchen washing the breakfast dishes. For a moment life seemed incredibly peaceful.

Then all at once Katie tensed as her eyes watched an outdoor tableau. Harry was strolling down the street, his parcel in one arm. A pair of men who had appeared to be in casual conversation before a house across the street suddenly abandoned this stance and were walking in Harry's direction. Federal agents, she identified them. *They were trailing him.*

Her heart pounding, Katie swung back into the hall, put Leo in the carriage there, and rushed from the house, pushing the carriage ahead of her. Emboldened by the urgency of the situation, she strode down the street in pursuit of Harry. She saw rather than heard one of the two men swear as she passed them.

"Harry," she called breathlessly—trying to sound carefree—and fell into step beside him. "Don't say anything, just listen to me," she whispered, smiling all the while as though in casual conversation. "And don't turn around. There are two men following you."

"Damn!" He was ashen.

"Walk with me to the children's shop," she told him. "You know the one—around the corner and three blocks down. Go inside with me. I'll buy something, and we'll exchange packages."

"Don't walk too fast," Harry cautioned. "Make this look natural." He sounded calm. Katie knew he was a shambles inside. *Suppose the agents stopped Harry now?*

Katie and Harry pretended to be engrossed in discussing a prospective purchase for Leo, now asleep in the carriage. Katie sighed in relief when the shop was only a few feet ahead. Let them make it into the store. As they turned into the entrance, she noted that the two men slowed down. They were going to wait for Harry to come out, follow him to his destination, and arrest seller and buyer, she surmised.

Inside the shop Katie quickly chose an outfit for Leo, and Harry paid for it. Now—as though interested in another item—she pushed the carriage between two racks of merchandise and gestured to Harry to follow her. While Leo slept, Katie took the bottles of bootleg whiskey and hid them beneath the carriage mattress and thrust her purchase into the bag Harry had been carrying.

"All right, let's get the hell out of here," Harry said with fresh confidence. "Katie, that was fast thinking."

Outside, Harry leaned over the carriage to kiss Leo, exchanged a smile of relief with Katie, and sauntered off. The federal agents would be disappointed when they tried to arrest Harry and his "client."

Chapter Nine

FOR THE remainder of the day Katie fought to cast off the specter of Harry being jailed by federal agents. It hadn't happened, she reminded herself repetitiously—but it might have happened. She couldn't—she *wouldn't*—go through something like that again. She had been raised to believe that the most terrible thing that could befall someone close to her was to be guilty of a crime, to be sentenced to a term in prison.

Harry made a pretense of being in high spirits when he came home, yet she saw the guarded glint in his eyes. He said nothing about the morning's incident, of course, in front of either Carmen or Rosita. Katie said nothing, either. He talked about the Scopes trial down in Tennessee last July and how the Ku Klux Klan membership in Dallas was down from thirteen thousand members the previous year to a little over twelve hundred.

"We've got the KKK on the run, Katie," he said enthusiastically, but he was uneasy in her unfamiliar disinclination to share in the table talk.

Katie waited until after dinner—when both Carmen and Rosita had left for the night—to confront Harry.

"We have to talk," she said quietly as they settled as usual in the living room—presumably to listen to their new radio. She saw Harry tense in anticipation of a battle. "Harry, I have to know that what happened this morning will never happen again."

"Katie, you were terrific," he said with tender pride.

"You could have gone to jail!" Despite her determination to appear calm, her voice was shrill. "All you think about is making money. Unless you swear to me that you'll destroy that still out on the farm, that you'll never sell another bottle of brandy, I'm leaving you. I'm taking Leo and going back to New York." She didn't know if she'd have the courage to do that, but she must make Harry believe she would.

"Katie . . ." He gaped at her in disbelief. "You know that you and Leo are my whole life. I just want to be able to give you both everything that'll make you happy."

"Grow up, Harry!" She had grown up this morning. "You took a chance on going to jail!" The terror she had felt this morning assaulted her again. "I'd be left alone to take care of Leo. How could I pay all our bills? The mortgage on the house. The installment payments on the car, on the furniture. The taxes on the house and the farm. How would Leo and I survive?"

"Katie, listen to me." He reached for her hands, his eyes anguished. "I promise you. I'll always be here to take care of you and Leo."

"Not if you keep on with the bootlegging," she defied.

"As of this minute, no more. I swear it. I don't need it anymore," he emphasized. "I can handle the stock market with the capital I have now. We're living in wonderful times, Katie. And I know what I'm doing."

Katie knew Harry was not lying to her. He was distraught because of her reaction. The still would be moved to Jeff's farm. Jeff would carry on in a small way on his own. He and Maura desperately needed the money the bootlegging brought in.

Within six months Harry decided they'd buy a bigger house, something more suitable to their status in Dallas.

"Look at the Alex Sanger house," he began with the awe that always accompanied discussion of the Sangers, the Marcuses, and the Neimans. He was proud that their Jewish compatriots were so highly regarded by Dallas citizens—though even they were not allowed to join the posh Dallas clubs, and their wives and daughters were denied membership in the Shakespeare Club and Junior League. "That's what I call a house."

"Harry, we can't afford anything like that." On several occasions Harry had driven her past both the huge, wide-verandahed Philip Sanger house—with a double staircase leading to its entrance, attic turrets, and beige wood trellises—and the even more elegant three-storied cream-colored brick masterpiece that housed Alex Sanger's family. Both houses were located in the Cedars, Dallas's longtime prestigious residential area that was only a dozen blocks from downtown.

"If we find the right house," Harry declared, "we'll buy it. We're not jumping this time. We'll look around carefully." Harry would buy it, Katie realized painfully, with a small down payment and huge monthly mortgage payments.

Harry told Katie that this coming summer they would go to the Grand Hotel on Mackinac Island, situated in northern Michigan where Lake Michigan and Lake Huron meet. He knew that for decades the cream of Midwest and Southwest society had been summering at the island—including such Dallas families as the Sangers.

"We'll get Leo away from the awful Dallas heat. Write for reservations for the month of July," he ordered Katie.

When he talked about giving up the Pierce-Arrow for a Cadillac, Katie asked for the old car. The Ford was unpredictable.

"Okay," he agreed, but Katie knew he was annoyed that Maura had taught her to drive. "You won't be happy unless you can do everything a man does."

"Not everything, Harry." Katie's eyes lighted with laughter. She remembered Maura's remark when Jeff uttered this typical male complaint. *I still prefer to sit on the toilet seat.*

Harry took Katie into Neiman-Marcus with exhilarating frequency to buy the latest fashions. For Leo he bought every new toy that came along. And just two weeks before their scheduled departure for Mackinac Island, Harry chose their new house. An elegant three-storied red-brick house that Katie considered a mansion. The papers would be drawn up during their vacation and signed immediately upon their return.

On the first of July Harry proudly escorted Katie—Carmen followed with Leo in her arms—into a suite aboard the northbound Pullman. Sitting in the drawing room of their suite—while Carmen solicitously fanned Leo—Katie remembered the arduous trip from New York City to Dallas just three years ago. Sometimes it seemed they were living in a dream.

While Harry focused on stock quotations, she reached for the novel he had read months ago—F. Scott Fitzgerald's *The Great Gatsby*—and had been urging her to read ever since. While she was an obsessive reader—eager for a new Sinclair Lewis or Edna Ferber or Theodore Dreiser—she had been avoiding the new Fitzgerald because she knew it dealt with the palatial mansions on Long Island, the lavish parties of the ultra-rich. Sometimes Harry's obsession with money and power unnerved her.

Harry felt a surge of pleasure as he stepped with Katie off the ferry at St. Ignace. The view was spectacular from every side. The closest either he or Katie had ever come to a vacation had been a day at Brighton Beach or Coney Island back in New York. Now they were to spend a month in a suite at the Grand Hotel, where three American presidents—Cleveland, Taft, and Roosevelt—had once been in residence.

He didn't have to worry about being away from business all the time they'd be here, he remembered with satisfaction. The Grand had a special room where current stock-market listings and prices were kept on display. He could check on the market every day—as many times a day as he wished—and direct his broker to buy or sell. He could even read *The Wall Street Journal* there.

In truth, the existence of these facilities made their vacation possible.

"Harry, I don't believe this," Katie whispered in delight while he helped her into a Victoria carriage with a top-hatted, red-coated coachman. No cars were allowed on the island. Carriages carried guests up the hill to the sprawling Greek Revival hotel. "I feel like a character in a Hollywood movie." She looked like a movie star, he thought, in her pink two-piece knit traveling dress.

"This is just the beginning for us," he said with serene confidence. "Next summer we'll go to Europe. London and Paris," he stipulated. This made up for those terrible years when he was left alone in the world and shared a grubby closet-sized bedroom with his cousin Izzy.

"Then we'd better start brushing up on our French," Katie laughed.

"Yeah . . ." For a moment he was caught in bitter recall of those last weeks at the settlement-house school, when Michelle Goncourt had taken him into her bed. But she'd gone off without even saying good-bye—to marry some rich bastard from an Ivy League college.

"Oh, Harry, what a beautiful building!" Katie's awestruck voice brought him back to the moment.

The tall nine-columned, white pine structure—on the heights, with a golf course and gardens on one side and a view of the Straits of Mackinac on the other—featured what Harry had read was the world's longest porch, extending for 880 feet. An avenue of pristine white rockers sat on the flower-box-lined porch.

"Did you ever see so many geraniums?" Katie paused in admiration before they went into the magnificent parlor. He saw the tears that filled her eyes, and he knew she was remembering her mother's love for geraniums. God, they'd nursed her mother's pot of geraniums across two thousand miles of America.

Harry was aware of the interested glances they were collecting. They were both obviously very young. Katie was beautiful and elegantly dressed—and Leo, carried by Carmen, was a beguiling toddler. And they knew, Harry told himself with satisfaction, that he had to be successful in business to pay the tab here.

He hadn't written home to his New York cousins since they first arrived in Texas. He'd send a postcard to Izzy and one to Izzy's parents. And maybe a fancy present at Chanukah—to show them how great he was doing. He didn't feel any financial obligation for their having taken him in; he'd paid his own way from the first week.

Once they were settled in their luxurious suite—and he'd spoken at length with his broker in Dallas—he swept Katie off for a walk about the grounds while Carmen coaxed Leo to nap. Leo would grow up knowing only the best, he promised himself as he and Katie strolled through the magnificent public rooms.

"Remember all the Sundays we spent roaming about the lobbies of the Plaza and the Waldorf and the Ritz-Carlton?" Katie reminisced, and he enjoyed her pleasure at being a guest here at the queen of summer hotels.

"When we go to Europe next summer," he plotted, "we'll stop off for a few days in New York. We'll stay at the Ritz-Carlton. We'll have lunch at the Algonquin, supper at the St. Regis, and afterward we'll go up to Connor's in Harlem."

"Would anybody we know back in New York believe we're here?" Katie reached for Harry's hand.

"I'm sending Izzy and his folks a postcard," he said with a hint of laughter in his voice. "And you know what they'll say? 'He must be a busboy in the dining room.'"

Later—scanning the pages of the Detroit newspaper provided for guests—he waited for Katie to emerge from the bedroom and join him in their drawing room. It was almost time for dinner to be served. From the bathroom came the sounds of Leo's laughter as Carmen bathed him. Harry was conscious of a joyous sense of well-being. A line of poetry—a favorite of Ka-

tie's—danced across his brain: "Mornings at seven . . .
All's right with the world!" All was right with their world.

He glanced up with pride when Katie walked into the room. She wore a black georgette dinner dress fringed with a multitude of narrow beaded strips of the same fabric—knee-high and displaying much of her milk-white back. In an era when most women sought to acquire the golden tan that Coco Chanel had made fashionable, Katie's skin was exquisitely fair.

"You look terrific. Of course, you took long enough," he scolded, but his voice was tender.

"Was it worth it?" she challenged.

"It was worth it. Let's go down to the dining room. I'm starving."

They took an elevator downstairs, followed the pillared walkway to the main dining room—sufficiently large to seat all the guests at one sitting. Harry relished the aura of luxury on every side. The guests were all expensively dressed, the women adorned with fine jewelry.

When they were seated and awaiting their first course, Harry gazed about appraisingly. Some of these people were millionaires—even multimillionaires. Katie and he were living like millionaires, he told himself complacently.

All at once his gaze settled on a young woman seated three tables away. Attractive rather than beautiful—with a smile that said she knew her power to draw masculine attention. She looked like a character from *The Great Gatsby*, he thought.

Harry's mouth felt dry as their eyes tangled. Her resemblance to Michelle Goncourt was uncanny. All at once he was back at the settlement house, and Miss Fenwick was telling him Michelle had gone back to New Orleans. *She went home to announce her engagement. She's getting married in October.* After all they'd been to each other, she'd gone off without even saying good-bye.

"They call this smoked Nova Scotia salmon." Katie's amused voice intruded on his reverie. "On Delancey Street it was lox—and too expensive for the likes of us."

"You can afford anything you like now." His voice was unintentionally brusque—because he didn't want to remember the hurt and humiliation Michelle had inflicted on him. Katie lifted an eyebrow in astonishment. "When we're back in Dallas, we'll go over to the jewelry store to buy you a string of pearls." The girl who so resembled Michelle wore pearls. He was sure they were real. "The real thing," he emphasized.

All through their lavish meal—the smoked Nova Scotia followed by chilled banana-strawberry soup, salad, a broiled filet of Mackinac whitefish, and a grand pecan ball—Harry was conscious that the young woman three tables away was scrutinizing him. When Katie and he left the dining room to have a demitasse in the parlor, Harry suspected that Michelle's double would follow them. Her eyes had telegraphed this message.

Her name was Cynthia Ross, she was recently divorced, and she was traveling with her mother, he quickly learned. It had been simple for them to fall into conversation, though Harry suspected her mother disapproved. She was a taciturn, arrogant woman in her late forties, and clearly not happy about her daughter's divorce.

"Call me Cindy," the daughter instructed Katie and Harry. "Everybody does back home in Boston." *Had Katie noticed her strong resemblance to Michelle?* No, he decided, and was oddly relieved.

Cindy was fascinated to learn that Harry and Katie were from Texas.

"Daddy has some business going on down in Texas," she recalled. "Some oil wells that he bought into."

They talked briefly about the new Hemingway—*The Sun Also Rises*—which Katie and Cindy had read but he had not, about the detachment of U.S. Marines sent to

Nicaragua after an outbreak of insurrection there, and about how airmail service had been inaugurated between New York and Boston.

Cindy's mother interrupted to insist that Cindy return with her to their suite.

"We just arrived this morning from Reno, and I'm exhausted."

From a corner of an eye—while he asked Katie if she'd like another demitasse—Harry watched while Cindy and her mother left the drawing room. Instinctively he knew that Cindy would be in pursuit of him. It was of no concern to her that he was married. Not once had he ever been unfaithful to Katie, but he felt an odd exhilaration in realizing that a rich Boston society divorcée was attracted to him.

In the morning—with Katie—Harry went down to breakfast in guilty but eager expectancy. This was just a game he was playing—*nothing was going to happen.* Moments after they were seated, he saw Cindy come into the dining room. She wore a white wraparound skirt, a bright red sweater, and Deauville sandals. She looked, Harry thought with sudden arousal, like one of those models in the fashion magazines Katie loved.

"Let's take a long walk about the grounds," he said to Katie, suspecting she would not want to leave the hotel because Leo had been fretful when he awoke. He was cutting an especially difficult tooth. "Not that I expect you to walk every one of the five hundred acres," he conceded with a chuckle. Cindy was alone. Her mother would have breakfast sent up to their suite, he surmised. *What was the matter with him?* He was acting like a dumb kid.

"You won't mind if I don't walk with you this morning, Harry?" Katie was apologetic. "I should go back upstairs and try to comfort Leo."

"It's too early to call my broker." Harry sent a perfunctory glance at his wristwatch. "I'll walk about an hour, then come back to make the call. And stop worrying about Leo. He's a tough guy—he'll push that tooth through soon."

They ate breakfast more swiftly than they would have if Katie had not been anxious to return to Leo. Both of them enjoyed dining leisurely on such occasions as this. But this morning he, too, was eager to be done with breakfast. Only once did Cindy indicate she was aware of his presence in the dining room, yet he was convinced she was standing by for a private encounter. All at once he was eighteen again, and Michelle Goncourt was in pursuit of him.

"Katie, run on upstairs to Leo," he said indulgently when she sneaked a glance at her watch. "I'll finish up my coffee in a couple of minutes and go for a walk."

He watched Katie hurry from the dining room: small, slender, beautiful, the object of furtive masculine admiration. Katie had style, he thought with pride. And class. Nobody would ever guess she had grown up in a tenement on Rivington Street.

Now he rose from his chair, shot a brilliant smile and a wave of one hand toward Cindy. He knew his impact on women, yet there was always a certain self-doubt in him—implanted by Michelle Goncourt. A sense that he might be found wanting on further acquaintanceship.

As he strode from the dining room, he saw Cindy push back her chair. He'd linger on the porch, wait for her to catch up with him. This had nothing to do with Katie and him, he told himself in a flash of guilt. Katie was his wife. Cindy was a society flapper looking for new thrills. Any man in his position would do the same.

Already he felt a stir of passion. Too bad that cars were not allowed on the island. There were only those stupid bath chairs—brought in, someone said, from the Royal Poinciana down in Palm Beach and operated by "colored men."

He'd enjoy parking a car somewhere with Cindy and climbing into the backseat with her. Not just because she'd probably be a terrific lay. Because in a strange way it would be like getting back at Michelle. He'd been such a dumb bastard in those days.

Not much could happen, he warned himself as he paused on the huge porch, only slightly populated at this hour of the morning. A walk in the woods, some heavy petting if the coast seemed clear. He tensed in heated anticipation. Ever since his marriage he'd been faithful to Katie, he reminded himself again. But what she didn't know couldn't hurt her.

Harry relished the crispness of the morning air after weeks of Dallas heat. He was subconsciously aware of the spectacular view of sweeping lawns and the straits beyond, the water shimmering in the sunlight.

"A sensational day for walking." Cindy's voice was a sensuous invitation.

"My thought, too," he drawled. Instinct ordered him to allow Cindy to make the first approach. And he knew it would not be long in coming.

"I hear there are lots of paths in the woods. And if we get lost"—her eyes were bold with promise—"we'll find our way back eventually."

They made a pretense of casually strolling down the front lawns, then detoured into the woods. Robins flitted among the trees, chirping exuberantly. Harry made the necessary replies to Cindy's casual chatter while he fought an urge to pin her against a tree trunk and thrust himself into that seductive—clearly willing—body.

"Let's see what's over there." Cindy pointed to a tall clump of flowering shrubs. No subterfuge now. They silently agreed on their destination.

"No thorns, I hope," he said humorously when they stood together behind the semiprotective screen of shrubs. There was scarcely an inch between them.

"With me you won't even notice," she promised, and lifted her already parted mouth to his.

The years seemed to rush backward, and he was with Michelle in the bedroom of her aunt's apartment. While their mouths clung and tongues dueled, his hands crept beneath her sweater. As he suspected, she wore nothing beneath it. He grunted in encouragement as her hand moved to his crotch.

"Take off your jacket and spread it on the ground," she ordered as she pulled her mouth from his. "Nobody'll see us here."

"Sorry I couldn't carry a mattress on my back," he said, managing a chuckle, and swept off his jacket. God, this one meant business! The whole enchilada! Too late to turn back, he thought in fleeting discomfort. But Katie would never know.

"What about 'protection'?" she asked while he spread the jacket on the lush green grass.

"You'll take care of that later," he decreed. He'd go out of his mind if she backed out now. In a corner of his mind he remembered how Izzy always carried a condom in his wallet. "Let's get this show on the road." He was practically popping out of his pants. He saw her eyes linger between his thighs. She knew he'd never be more ready than he was this minute. He heard the strangled sound of excitement that escaped her.

"I'll take care of it." In one provocative movement she dropped to the ground.

Before he even lowered himself above her, she had drawn her short skirt above her hips and was already unbuttoning the strip of her teddy that kept them apart.

"This vacation is going to be the cat's meow," Cindy gasped as they moved together. "We'll make whoopee every chance we get!"

Katie scolded herself at intervals for suspecting that Cindy Ross was chasing after Harry. It was natural that they spent a lot of time together here at the hotel. Harry was awfully good-looking—he always attracted women. He was flattered by Cindy's attentions, she considered;

but he wouldn't let anything happen. Yet sometimes she intercepted a look between them, and she was frightened. Cindy was divorced and available.

Katie was relieved when Cindy and her mother left for Boston a week before she and Harry headed home. But on the long trip back to Dallas she found her thoughts dwelling recurrently on what might have happened on Mackinac Island between Harry and Cindy Ross.

Before they left the train, she had made up her mind to have a second child. With a wife and two children, she told herself irrationally, Harry would be too involved with family to think of another woman. He might look—but nothing would happen.

She couldn't stay with a husband who was unfaithful. But how could she survive without Harry? She could not envision a life without him.

Chapter Ten

ON THANKSGIVING EVE—after some heart-wrenching fears that she could not become pregnant again—Katie told Harry that they would have a second child sometime in June. Tears filled her eyes when she saw his joy.

"A little sister for Leo," he said tenderly, drawing her into his arms. "Katie, I can't wait!"

"I'm afraid you'll have to," she laughed. "We've got seven months to go."

"We'll buy a bigger house," he decided.

"Harry, this house is big enough," she objected.

"A bigger house," he insisted, "and in a better neighborhood. And stop worrying," he clucked. "We can afford it. But we won't be able to go to Europe next summer." There was a touch of apology in his voice. "Not with a newborn."

"We'll spend more time at the farm," she consoled him. The months she had carried Leo were the most beautiful months of her life. This pregnancy would be a repetition.

"We'll go the next year," he promised. "We'll stop off in New York for three days. I'd like to take a look at the Stock Exchange—now that I know what it's all about," he jested. She was convinced there was little Harry didn't know about the stock market. At their dinner parties she had heard him referred to by guests double or triple his age as "a young Jesse Livermore." She knew that Livermore was a living legend, who could single-handedly push down stock prices when it suited his purpose.

On Saturday afternoon Harry came home to present her with a string of exquisite pearls.

"Oh, Harry!" She gazed in awe at the necklace that rested on black velvet. She noticed, too, the name on the jeweler's box, which told her these were real pearls. "It's gorgeous."

"You can dump your Woolworth beads now." He grinned in pleasure at her delight. "Back on Mackinac Island I told you I'd buy you the real thing."

"I guess about two of them are paid for," she teased. Harry was addicted to the national mania for installment buying.

"I paid for them outright." He was suddenly serious. "I wanted you to wear them knowing they were all yours. Now ask Carmen if she can stay with Leo tonight. I'm taking you out to dinner at the Adolphus."

Katie knew that Harry was often annoyed by the social structure of Dallas, though he was proud that there were Dallas Jews who were well-regarded in the highest circles. "Token Jews," he sometimes complained. Society in the city was divided into cliques that favored the conservative Idlewild Club—composed of business and professional family men—and the Hesitation Club, whose members held more hedonistic attitudes.

Much of Dallas social life revolved around dinner dances at the brick clubhouse of the Dallas Country Club. Katie and Harry—who were "new money"—cultivated their own small groups: Harry's business acquaintances and their wives—who were delighted to attend dinner parties at the Newhouse home—and Maura and Jeff, whom they saw regularly on weekends. Maura was in high spirits these days because Jeff anticipated finishing the first draft of his novel during the slow months on the farm.

Katie was happy that Maura, too, was pregnant again—though she worried that Jeff was making bootleg wine in the house cellar and selling to a few choice customers.

"Look, Katie, the law's a joke," Maura reminded her. "We've got congressmen in Washington, D.C., making whiskey in their cellars."

"But they're not selling it," Katie pointed out. She was terrified that Jeff would be caught and jailed.

"I can't take care of Georgie, carry another baby, and work in the fields. I know—things are slow on the farm now. But in April we have to put in the new crop. Jeff can't handle it alone. He'll have to hire a hand—and we need money for that. We won't operate on a big scale," Maura cajoled. "We won't get caught. We just want to build up a bankroll to see us through the spring and summer months."

As with her first pregnancy, Katie moved through these months on a cloud of euphoria. She protested only briefly when Harry put their house in town on the market and bought a seventy-five-thousand-dollar two-story brick mansion in the exclusive Highland Park community. She was awed by the splendor of this new house, but threw herself with ebullient enthusiasm into the task of shopping for furniture, decorating. Harry manipulated so that no physical exertion was required of her.

She spent with an abandon that sometimes unnerved her, but Harry insisted she buy only at the finest shops. The domestic staff was enlarged to cope with the demands of the new house. Now there was also a chauffeur to drive her, plus a laundress and part-time gardener.

Despite her advancing pregnancy, she and Harry entertained at least two evenings a week. Harry's guest list grew with his continuing success. Each dinner was planned with a specific purpose in mind. The presumably social evenings with men enjoying the same huge success as he—and who might drop words of wisdom he could use. The evenings when they entertained junior employees of brokerage offices, who were pleased to enjoy the gourmet dinners Katie provided—and could be expected to offer the latest market tips and gossip. The table talk always revolved around the stock market—and the titans he most respected: Jesse Livermore, Joseph Kennedy, and John J. Raskob.

Early in June—just twelve days after Maura was delivered of a daughter, named Willa because Jeff so admired Willa Cather's writing—Katie, too, gave birth to a daughter. Named Joanne for Katie's mother, their tiny daughter was a replica of Katie except for the dark hair she had inherited from her father.

"Harry's out of his mind with joy," Katie confided to Maura in one of their lengthy phone conversations. "He has his son who'll be a lawyer and a daughter to become a schoolteacher."

"That's what he thinks." Maura laughed reminiscently. "My father was convinced I'd be a schoolteacher or a nun."

"What's with Jeff's book?" Katie asked solicitously. He'd finished the final draft only days before planting season began.

"He shipped it off to a publisher three weeks ago. We're waiting and praying."

"Maura, he's good," Katie encouraged.

"That's not always enough." Cynicism crept into Maura's voice. "You have to be at the right publisher at the right time with the right book. Thank God, Jeff's too busy with the crop to mope much."

Nine weeks later Jeff's book came back from the publisher. Maura refused to be depressed; she shipped it off to another the next day. At this moment, Maura conceded to Katie, she and Jeff were concerned about the index of farm prices, which had fallen from 205 at the beginning of 1920 to 116 the following year and continued to creep upward with painful slowness—standing now in 1927 at only 131.

Yet despite the hardship of the farmers—and the miners, the western lumbermen, and the New England textile workers, the country was considered to be enjoying a booming economy. Installment buying moved furiously ahead. The stock market gave no indication of any setbacks.

Katie was pleased that the Dallas Ku Klux Klan membership was dwindling, impressively, as it was throughout the state. Back in March the U.S. Supreme Court had ruled that the Texas law prohibiting Negroes from voting in Democratic primary elections was unconstitutional—which was a blow to the Texas Klan. But now in the fall there was much talk that Governor Al Smith of New York, who had campaigned unsuccessfully in 1924 for the Democratic presidential nomination, would try again. The KKK imperial wizard Hiram Wesley Evans vowed that the Klan would fight in every way possible to defeat Smith.

"They'll form an Anti-Al Smith Democrats of Texas group," Harry prophesied at a Sunday dinner at the farm, shared with Maura and Jeff. "They'll fight to persuade Democrats to vote Republican for president but Democrat for local, county, and state tickets."

"They'll stir up such Roman-Catholic hatred," Maura said with contempt, "that Smith won't stand a chance."

"I don't know about Texas voting Republican." Jeff was doubtful. "The state's always gone Democratic."

"I doubt," Harry said bluntly, "that we'll ever see a

Catholic, Jewish, or Negro president in our lifetime. No matter how often Al Smith says he won't let his church get in the way of the Constitution of the United States, he won't be believed by a lot of voters."

By the beginning of the new year Harry was planning a grand European tour for Katie and himself and the children. Warm, devoted Carmen was already fighting against her fears of traveling for four days and nights on an ocean liner. Harry decreed that they spend three days in New York City before boarding the *Olympic* for the trip to Southampton. They would stay at the Plaza, as on their wedding night—but this time Harry reserved a two-bedroom suite for family and nursemaid.

They celebrated Joanne's first birthday aboard a crack eastbound Pullman—with a birthday cake supplied by the dining-car chef.

In New York Katie and Harry settled Carmen and the children in their Plaza suite overlooking Central Park—all three fascinated by the bustling view below, particularly the parade of horse-drawn carriages favored by tourists. Now they set off for a nostalgia visit to the Lower East Side. A quick perusal of the telephone directory had told them that Harry's cousins were still without a phone.

As Harry helped her into a taxi for the drive downtown—neither thought once of taking the subway—Katie tried to gear herself to face the world they had left behind four years ago. *They were different people now.* They had left here with so little money for the trip west that they'd slept in a tent at the side of the road rather than pay for a tourist camp or tourist home. Now they had a Plaza suite overlooking the park.

Everything had happened too fast, she thought, while panic tightened a knot in her throat. Harry was obsessed by money. The need to acquire more and more money. And all the while they were building up this maze of installment payments.

Harry was right, of course. It was a way of life today.

"Pay as you ride," the carmakers urged. "Enjoy while you pay," advertisers seduced eager customers. But installment buying made everything cost so much more. How could that be good for the country?

"I don't see many changes around town." Harry's voice broke into her introspection. "Some new buildings here and there."

"Harry, we've been away only four years," Katie laughed.

Then the taxi was moving downtown in the narrow, unattractive streets of the Lower East Side. Noisy, cluttered with people and pushcarts. Everybody in a rush, appearing short-tempered and suspicious. Katie felt a sudden urge to be back in her beautiful house in Highland Park. *How had Harry and she endured living here?*

The taxi pulled up at the curb before the tenement where the Hirsch family lived. Katie hurried out and waited—feeling a stranger here—while Harry paid the driver. So much had happened to them so fast, she thought. Standing again on Rivington Street, she was starkly conscious of the difference in their lives now. It was inconceivable that such a little while ago she had shared a cell of a room with Celia Kornfeld—in a flat that could fit into the master bedroom of the house in Highland Park.

"Okay, let's go." Harry reached for her hand. For him it was a kind of triumphal homecoming, she realized.

Their only contact with Harry's cousins had been the set of silverware Harry sent as a Chanukah present a couple of years ago, a thank-you letter from his surprised cousin, and an exchange of postcards—theirs from the Grand Hotel at Mackinac Island, Izzy's from Grossinger's in the Catskills.

From the aromas of rendered chicken fat filtering from the Hirsch flat, Katie and Harry knew his cousin Sophie was home. For a few moments the air crackled with the barrage of questions that ricocheted between them.

The flat had changed somewhat from what Katie remembered. Sophie pointed with pride to the new "living room suite"—"we paid fifteen dollars down and twelve dollars a month." She brought out her new vacuum cleaner. "Izzy bought it for me. He pays four dollars a month. After this he's buying me a sewing machine.

"Come, sit down. I'll make tea. Just this morning I made hamantaschen. I remember, Harry"—Sophie wiggled a finger in triumph—"you always loved hamantaschen."

Sophie was plainly impressed to learn that they were on their way to Europe. Katie had been aware of Sophie's shy glances of admiration at her chic Neiman-Marcus designer dress.

"Katie, I always knew Harry would be special. From the very beginning I knew it."

Sophie was disappointed that they would not stay for supper, but Harry changed disappointment to pleasure by insisting that the following evening he and Katie would take the whole family to Ratner's on Delancey Street.

"Sophie, you cook enough. For one night, somebody else will cook," Harry decreed.

On their third and final day in the city—because Harry wished it—Katie accompanied her enthusiastic young husband on a visit to the cavernous New York Stock Exchange. From the visitors' gallery she watched with hordes of others as gray-uniformed guides pointed out big-name traders on the more than one-quarter-acre floor below, where nine hundred brokers—each a Stock Exchange member—crowded around the stockade-shaped trading counters. Over a thousand manned telephones in operation. Five hundred page boys, 280 tube attendants and quotation clerks—which Harry had been in the early stages of his brief career—a stream of bond clerks and specialists' clerks milled about the room.

"I've never seen anything more exciting," Harry whispered in satisfaction. "A bull market going top speed.

Prices have never been so high, or the volume so huge. Every day new millionaires are born!"

That same evening Katie, Harry, the children, and Carmen boarded the huge, four-funneled black *Olympic*—nearly nine hundred feet long and eleven decks high—and were directed to their luxury first-class quarters. Carmen was impressed that they had their own private promenade space.

"Carmen, watch the children every minute," Katie exhorted nervously, secretly vowing to spend much of her time with them. "They both move so quickly." From her first shaky steps Joanne had progressed to a run.

"I wish to hell they had a brokerage firm aboardship," Harry grumbled when Katie and he were dressing in their stateroom for dinner.

"Harry, how on earth could you expect that?" she scolded. "You can survive for five days without talking to your broker."

"They'll have it within a year or two," Harry predicted. "Look, the technical problems will be worked out. Radio transmission makes it possible. Secret codes. The Stock Exchange will insist on that. Think of it, Katie. A businessman will be able to cross the ocean without losing a day of market transactions!"

At their assigned table Katie and Harry discovered they had been seated with middle-aged couples, all of whom seemed to be involved with the stock market, along with a charming fortyish Frenchman who spoke impeccable English and his attractive young British "secretary." As usual, the men talked shop, the women discussed clothes and current movie stars. But as always, Katie managed to eavesdrop on the masculine conversation.

While she appeared to be only vaguely knowledgeable about the market, in truth Katie understood far more than even Harry realized she did. Her inborn caution kept her ever wary of the manipulations in the stock market. How could people—even Harry—trust themselves to buy "on margin"—just one step away from disaster? An unexpected drop in prices sent them scurrying to cover themselves—and if they couldn't, they lost what they had invested. To Katie, the gambler at the casino was on a par with those on the stock market who bought "on margin."

After dinner Katie and Harry were invited to join Pierre Simon and his secretary—Daphne Winthrop—in his suite for champagne. Pierre—at home in major cities around the world and conversant in six languages—was candidly fascinated by the stories about Texas money that circulated around the world.

"I'm not in oil," Harry explained with an air of apology. "Though, of course, that's the main scene in Texas these days. We've seen some real gushers coming in right in our area in the past few months," he added with pride.

"What's your field?" asked Pierre, his eyes narrowed in speculation.

"Basically I'm in the stock market. I've done well," Harry said with an apologetic smile. As though, Katie thought, he felt he should be a business tycoon—as Pierre Simon appeared to be. "I started out writing quotations on the board. Then I began to play the bucket shops. That led up to the big show."

"Harry has a phenomenal memory plus an analytical mind that anticipates price fluctuations," Katie told Pierre, almost defensively—quoting what others said about the secret of Harry's success on the stock market.

"In a small way I'm dabbling in grain," Harry said. They owned a small, inactive farm, Katie silently rebuked him. "Corn at present, but I'm thinking of moving into wheat. I'm convinced that grain is even more important to civilization than oil. The world needs grain to survive."

"I'm a grain merchant." Pierre was delighted. "We've been established in Paris for two generations. Simon and Simon Grain Company. We're not as big as Louis Dreyfus or Bunge, but we do well," he said with pride. "I've been visiting your country with an eye to expansion there. What your wife just said about your ability to anticipate price fluctuations will serve you well in the grain field. It's the ability to read the future—whether it's how good the crop will be or whether the weather will permit the grain to be moved out before the ice freezes over, as can happen in your Great Lakes states—that makes the difference between failure and tremendous success. Contrary to what people think, a grain merchant can build up a strong organization without enormous capital. You're not growing the grain—the farmer does that for you. What you need is a sharp mind, the right contacts, and credit. At any rate"—he reached into his jacket pocket and pulled forth a business card—"hang on to my card. One of these days we might just do some business together."

Katie listened as absorbedly as Harry while Pierre Simon talked with enthusiasm about the grain business—while Daphne made unsuccessful efforts to conceal her boredom. A business, Katie conceded, she could regard with respect. Mama had planned to open her own shop, she remembered nostalgically. With a business you were dealing with more than pieces of paper and stock quotations.

All the way across the Atlantic Harry and Pierre explored the grain business, both in Europe and America. Katie listened. Names that she knew from grocery-store shelves—Pillsbury, General Mills, Kellogg—surfaced as major players in the grain market, along with unfamiliar names.

At the moment Pierre was fascinated by the quiet maneuvering of Continental Grain, founded in France early in the decade by two brothers, Jules and René Fribourg.

"For almost a century before the war the Fribourg family had been prosperous in the grain business in Antwerp, at one point even investing in flour mills. Jules and René ran a brokerage firm—Fribourg Frères—in

Antwerp, but had broader ambitions. During the war they fled to London, made a lot of money speculating on Australian wheat shipments. These were great times for all of us in the field—the Allies bought everything we could deliver. The profit margins were high—and our expenses were small. Jules and René opened up Continental in 1921, and they've been soaring ever since. My sources tell me they're moving into the States now—they've just leased a grain elevator in St. Louis."

Pierre talked with infinite respect about the major grain families—the Andrés, the Hirsches, the Cargills, the Dreyfuses. Names not known to the general public but ones that commanded awesome respect among the grain world. Only now—as Pierre expressed his pride that three major grain dynasties were Jewish—did Katie and Harry realize that Pierre, too, was Jewish.

Harry seemed mesmerized by the stories Pierre wove. In some way, Katie guessed—though how this could come about she couldn't conceive—Harry meant to become involved in the grain business. She felt cheered. This was a business, not a fantasy world. Harry was brilliant—everybody said that. Harry would accomplish whatever he set out to do.

Katie fell in love with London. The people, the sights—and the Claridge Hotel, where Harry had through devious means been able to acquire choice reservations.

"Queen Victoria stayed here," he told Katie complacently while Carmen tried to put Leo and Joanne down for naps in the bedroom that would be the nursery for the next two weeks. "Royalty from all over Europe has stayed here."

"That accounts for the footmen in knee breeches," she guessed, but she was highly respectful of the elegance and privacy that the Claridge provided its often-illustrious guests.

While Carmen took Leo and Joanne to see the comic antics of the pelicans in St. James Park and to watch the kite-flying in Hyde Park, Katie and Harry visited Westminster Abbey, the Tower of London, and all the favorite tourist haunts. They shopped for Maura and Jeff and their children at Harrods, and rode on the Underground. Together with Carmen and the children they saw the Changing of the Guard at Buckingham Palace and—for the sake of the children and Carmen—made a second trip to the Tower of London.

Two evenings were spent with Pierre Simon and Daphne, dashing about London in his rented Rolls-Royce. They dined in quaint French restaurants in SoHo, while Harry mourned about the paucity of fine restaurants in Dallas. Afterward they made brief stops at private parties—one at the exquisite all-white ballroom of Mrs. Somerset Maugham, where guests included Lady Mendl, actor Adolphe Menjou, and the beautiful American-born Lady Cunard.

Later they engaged in what Pierre referred to as the favorite British evening sport, the pub crawl. In London—unlike in the States—drinking was illegal only between certain hours, but every district had different closing hours. The game was to continue pub crawling as late as possible.

A habitué of the London pubs, Pierre took them to the most favored. They saw Sophie Tucker—adored in London—at the Kit Cat. They danced at Ciro's, at the Hambone, at Elsa Lanchester's the Cave of Harmony in Seven Dials. They saw the Midnight Follies at the Hotel Metropole.

"Nothing like this in Dallas," Harry said complacently when he and Katie were back in their suite and preparing for bed.

"It's like the New York we didn't know," Katie said reminiscently. "Except from the outside looking in."

"We've come a long way, Katie." He reached for her in sudden arousal. "But this is just the beginning."

"Lock the door," whispered Katie, conscious of the nearness of Carmen and the children.

"Carmen would sleep through a tornado," Harry chuckled. "And the kids wouldn't understand if they walked in on us." But he went to lock their bedroom door.

Katie was terrified when Harry decided on impulse that they would travel to Paris by plane. Since 1919 there had been daily flights between London and Paris. Imperial Airways in London offered a thirty-to-forty-minute cruise every afternoon, with tea served in flight.

"Katie, we can fly to Paris in less than three hours!" he chortled, and Katie gritted her teeth and pretended this was an exciting adventure. Carmen prayed every moment they were aloft.

In Paris—spilling over with tourists this summer of '28—in a suite overlooking the Place Vendôme, though Katie would have preferred one that faced the quiet back garden, Harry was smug about the favorable rate of exchange in Paris. A meal—table d'hôte, *vin compris*—at a sidewalk café cost the equivalent of fifteen cents in American money.

Katie was enthralled on their second day in Paris to recognize Coco Chanel strolling from the Ritz, and the following afternoon to discover that the rather handsome young man at a table opposite theirs at the Ritz was F. Scott Fitzgerald. They sipped Pernod at a café on the Champs Élysées, explored Montmartre, as in London visited all the places beloved by American tourists. Harry took endless snapshots of Leo and Joanne—in the Luxembourg Gardens, at the Arc de Triomphe, in the shadows of the Eiffel Tower.

At Cherbourg they boarded the *Île de France* for the return trip. For hours each day Harry talked about the possibilities in the grain market, mulling over all that he had learned from Pierre Simon. Katie mirrored his enthusiasm. This meant, she realized, that Harry would transfer money from the stock market into land. He talked about building up a land empire, to be rented out to farmers who would raise wheat.

"Katie, it's a natural," he said zealously while they sat at a table of the ship's Parisian sidewalk cafe. Leo and tiny Joanne were in the children's playroom, which provided a real carousel with colorful ponies and gay music. "The world can't exist without wheat. I'll control all the wheat grown by our farmers. In five years I'll be an important grain merchant. In ten years I'll go international." He smiled tenderly. "You'll like that, won't you?" He knew how she distrusted the stock market—despite all that his manipulations bought for them.

"Oh, Harry, yes!"

"Next year," he decreed, "we'll go to Europe in October when the tourists have all gone. It'll be great for the kids." His eyes brightened with pride. "At their ages we never got further from home than Coney Island."

Back in Dallas Harry began to diversify his investments, though the stock market continued to be his major source of income. He drove around Texas in search of property that he could buy cheaply. Land suitable for growing wheat. Despite the prosperity throughout Texas the farmers continued to suffer.

He took Katie with him on occasion to view his latest acquisition. He knew her love for land matched his own. They would stand arm in arm and gaze with undisguised joy at the seemingly endless fields that were now their own. But Katie worried that his bank loans were soaring. Harry was convinced his stock-market earnings could comfortably handle these. His knack for judging price fluctuations remained phenomenal.

Leo and Joanne were a continuing source of joy. Both were happy, affectionate children, and Katie was ever touched by the closeness between the two of them. Joanne always rushed to Leo's side in any childish battles with other youngsters. Katie wished that they could see more of Maura and Jeff and their two children, but the planting season—followed by harvest-time—occupied the Warrens from sunup to sundown. They were fighting for survival—like most Texas farmers. Jeff's novel continued to move from one publisher to another without any indication of a sale.

The first of October the Newhouses, together with the ever-faithful Carmen, set forth for Europe again. Now Katie insisted they take the children with them to the fine art museums in London and Paris. She was delighted that Leo—two years older than Joanne—was enchanted by many of the paintings they saw in the museums. Later, she told Harry, Joanne, too, would appreciate them.

In the last week of October they boarded the *Île de France* for the voyage home. Harry was pleased that the ship had been equipped since August with its own brokerage office, an exciting innovation for trans-Atlantic travelers. Just a few feet away from "the longest bar afloat," the Compagnie de St. Phalle had set up a Wall Street-style customers' room.

Harry was faintly troubled by what was happening at the Bourse—the French equivalent of Wall Street—during their stay in Paris. The French press was attacking Wall Street for the sudden drop in the price of stocks. Still, he told himself, there was no real cause for alarm. He knew that some passengers—heavily involved with the stock market—were bombarding their brokers with wireless messages about the state of the market. But the general feeling was that the market would rally. Passengers—many of them American millionaires—were planning strategy for beating the market even while aboardship.

On Monday evening—with the *Île de France* approaching midocean—Harry sat up late in their luxurious apartment and planned his operations for the following day. Because of the time difference it would be tomorrow afternoon before the ship's brokerage office opened for trading. He anticipated a lively afternoon of buying and selling.

"Harry, come to bed," Katie called from their bedroom. "This is supposed to be your vacation."

"In a few minutes, Katie. I just want to go over these figures once more."

Minutes after the brokerage office opened—with company clerks chalking stock quotations radioed from the Bourse and Wall Street on the office blackboard—Harry felt a sudden sense of imminent doom. Figures were being erased and revised. Ever plunging. *What the hell was happening?*

The brokerage office was crowded to capacity. Others stood in the corridor, fighting to see the blackboard. The noise level rose ominously. With his magnificent memory for figures Harry computed the "margin call" needed to bail him out in the face of the unbelievable collapse of prices. *He couldn't meet the call.*

"Sell!" called one voice after another. "Sell at the market!" An air of hysteria permeated the room.

It was almost impossible for the brokers to write orders fast enough to satisfy the stricken passengers.

"God, the bottom's dropping out!" screamed a diamond-encrusted matron. "I'm ruined!"

Ashen-faced, Harry pushed his way through the crowd into the equally jammed corridor. Subconsciously aware that others reflected his own shock. He fought his way through the mobs in the area adjacent to the brokerage office to the grand saloon where he knew Katie would be waiting for him.

Pale but poised, she sat in the near-empty saloon—normally crowded with festive passengers at this hour of the day. Here and there a zombielike man or woman sat slumped in disbelief. Katie's eyes told him she understood the disaster that hung over every investor.

"Katie . . ." His voice was hoarse with the effort to speak. "The market's gone crazy. I've never seen anything like this. There's no way I can meet my margin calls. We're broke. We've lost everything. . . ."

Part Two

Chapter Eleven

THE ATMOSPHERE aboard the *Île de France* was that of a funeral barge. Hundreds of passengers—men and women—walked about in a deathlike silence, too numb to deal with their financial debacle. But the luxurious liner continued its daily routine as though the world as known for the past decade had not just collapsed. Elaborate meals were served as usual in the seven-hundred seat gray marble dining room, but few diners appeared. In the evening bands played for dancing, but few danced.

Harry cursed himself endlessly for bringing his family to ruin.

"I should have listened to you, Katie," he railed as he paced in their shipboard apartment. "You always worried about the stock market. Look what I've done to you and the children."

"Harry, we'll be all right." How many times had she said this in the last twenty-four hours? But it was necessary for her to seem unafraid of the future. For Harry, she must do this.

"In three months at the most the bank will take over the house and the cars." His face was white and drawn, his eyes anguished. "Every shop in town will be dunning us. I won't be able to meet the bank loans on the land I've bought. Katie, we'll have nothing. We'll be on the street."

"We'll be on the farm." Thank God, Harry had put the farm in her name. That couldn't be touched. "We'll sell my pearls and my mink coat. The situation will change." She refused to succumb to panic.

"Back to the farm again?" Harry paused in his pacing to stare at her. "Back to where we began?"

"You're twenty-four years old, Harry. You can start all over again," she said urgently. "We're both young—we can handle this."

At Katie's insistence Harry agreed that they would forgo the planned layover in New York. It was she who arranged to exchange their pair of expensive drawing rooms aboard the westbound Pullman for three modest berths. And she promised Carmen—devastated at the prospect of leaving the Newhouse family—that she would help her find another job immediately.

"You're a treasure, Carmen," she comforted. "Any family will be happy to have you."

The *Dallas Morning News* reported that the business in the country was fundamentally sound, that only "amateur speculators" had been hurt. The city appeared determined to remain optimistic about the state of the economy—though newspapers across the country labeled the situation disastrous. In the past year many new firms had come into Dallas. Its building industry was booming. Those untouched by the Crash felt secure—or pretended to feel secure.

With staggering swiftness, it seemed to Katie, their lives were turned upside down. The banks descended to take over the house, the furniture, the Cadillac, and the recently bought Stutz Torpedo. They moved back to the farm. Katie was grateful that—out of sentiment—she had insisted on keeping the old Ford that had brought them to Texas. Now—one by one—the farms Harry had bought, with minuscule down payments and extravagant dreams, were reclaimed by the banks. And with them went Harry's dreams of being a grain merchant.

Despite the air of optimism that continued in Texas,

many were hurting. Unemployment was increasing. Each day Harry drove into Dallas. The beat-up Ford was their lifeline to the city. He searched for a job in the brokerage firms; and when none was available, he tried for sales jobs, work at gas stations, construction jobs. He found nothing. He had no marketable skills—in an already tight market. Even experienced carpenters, bricklayers, and electricians were taking cuts in wages.

"Damn, I should have gone to law school," he told Katie as they sat in the kitchen on a blustery February evening after Katie had put Leo and Joanne to bed. "A man needs a profession to succeed in this modern world. I tell you, Katie, Leo will go to law school. I know the prospects look rotten, but somehow we'll come out of this. Leo will be an attorney—he won't ever face what we're facing. And Joanne will be a schoolteacher."

"We'll put in a crop of corn," Katie said warily. "If we're careful, we'll have enough money left to handle that."

"Jeff says we're lucky we don't have mortgages." It pained Katie to see him so frustrated, so humiliated. "He forgets about the taxes that'll be coming up. He knows how the banks are tightening up on loans."

"Maura told me to put in a good-sized vegetable garden come spring. We'll have food on the table and some we'll can for later."

"Why didn't I see the crash coming?" Harry slammed a fist on the table. "I should have seen it. I didn't want to."

"We'll manage, Harry. We've had some great years. We'll survive a bad year." Didn't the Dallas newspapers refer to this as a mild recession?

She had tried—futilely—to find a job at one of the women's wear shops and department stores in town, though she knew Harry's pride would be hurt if he was faced with taking care of the children while she went into the city to work. But sales in the stores were dropping. There were no jobs.

When the bank rejected their request for a loan in the spring, Katie and Harry went from pawnshop to pawnshop until they found one that would make the highest offer for her pearls. A few days later they returned with her fur coat. These funds enabled them to put in a crop of corn.

Again, they were working from sunup to sunset. Katie and Maura set up a schedule where each would watch the four children on alternate days so that the other might work in the fields. As always, they worried about the price of corn when the harvest season arrived. Prices on everything seemed to be plunging. And Jeff had abandoned his bootlegging after a scare last month. "*Jeff wouldn't look good in stripes,*" Maura had said flippantly when they told Katie and Harry about Jeff's close scrape with federal agents.

Late in the year there was a spectacular oil boom in East Texas. Harry berated himself for not investing in oil fields. When the harvest was in, he tried to find work in the oil fields. With other desperate men he lined up to wait overnight in the blustery cold to file an application for work. But experienced men were fighting for jobs.

Katie and Harry struggled to pay their taxes, relieved that they could handle this—though meat rarely appeared on their dinner table and there were days when they burned corn to keep the house warm rather than touch their small cash reserve to buy coal. Harry acquired a cow by helping a neighbor short on cash and needing labor to repair his roof. Leo and Joanne, Georgie and Willa, had milk every day.

Dallas took pride in the report that the city had less unemployment than any other community in Texas or Oklahoma, but Maura derided this.

"Try telling that to people who're starving."

"There are people here in Dallas who aren't hurting at all," Harry said with frustration. "They still go to plays and symphonies and fancy dinner parties. All we can afford is to play dominoes with Jeff and Maura. But the rich Texans," he said with contempt, "refuse to look beyond their safe small circles. They don't want to know about all the millions of people who've lost their jobs. About the companies who've gone out of business."

"But the governor and that State Committee on Drought Relief are fighting for government help for the farmers," Katie reminded him. "We're all for that."

"Nothing will happen," Jeff predicted contemptuously. "The government rushes to help foreign governments and rich American industries. They hardly know the small farmers exist. We're not asking for preferential treatment," he said in exasperation. "Just equality with big business."

Through a plan devised by the Northwest apple-growers in 1931, the jobless were standing on city street corners trying to sell apples. The Bureau of the Census considered apple-sellers as employed. In Dallas—as in other towns and cities across the country—soup kitchens and breadlines were in operation. On farms families lived on what they could grow. Meat and eggs and butter disappeared from the tables of the unemployed.

Cotton dropped to five cents a pound. In June 1931 Dallas declared a "Cotton Week," pleading with local women to buy cotton products.

"It's a finger in the dike," Harry scoffed. "When will Texans learn not to put so much land into cotton?"

The corn crop, too, brought lower prices than ever. But farmers' mortgages and taxes were based on higher 1920s prices. Many banks suffered from speculation on the stock market, and were moving to foreclose on farm loans when in earlier days they would have extended more time. Farm-machinery companies were taking legal action against local farmers.

Katie and Harry watched with pain when they saw sheriffs post dispossess notices. They hurt for farmers when auctioneers arrived to sell off a farm that had been in a family for generations. In some of the richest farmland in the world the Red Cross was now setting up food centers to give food to starving farm families.

A few days before Christmas Katie and Harry went to the Warrens' home for supper—each family contributing to what was on the table. Maura was proud to serve tomatoes that she had just grown in the small greenhouse Jeff had built for her.

"Maura, these are great," Harry said with relish. "You'd think we were eating in some fancy restaurant."

"Who's eating in fancy restaurants these days?" Jeff's smile was sardonic. "I hear the Junior League has just enlarged its soup kitchen."

"Plenty of people in Dallas are still filthy rich." Harry's eyes glittered with frustration and rage. "They still go for dinner at the Adolphus or the country club. And when they eat at home, they eat well. The rich sit down at the kind of tables you'd see on Park Avenue in New York."

"Maura, are these the tomatoes you grew in the greenhouse Jeff set up for you?" All at once Katie's quick mind was absorbing what Harry had just said, tying it in with Maura's greenhouse efforts.

"You know Jeff's passion for tomatoes," Maura said. "I figured, if we have to live on rice, pasta, and corn, he'd notice it less if we had real, honest-to-God tomatoes on the table."

"Jeff, would you show Harry and me how to set up a greenhouse?" Katie asked, excitement charging through her.

"Sure." Jeff gazed curiously from Katie to Harry. "You want to go through what Maura does for a few tomatoes?"

"We could raise other stuff besides tomatoes, couldn't we?" The anticipation in Harry's voice told Katie he was following her thoughts.

"Of course. Any kind of summer vegetable. But I wouldn't try corn—that might bring up space problems." Jeff was amused but puzzled.

"Harry, couldn't we develop a business raising summer vegetables all year round? Like you just said, there are plenty of rich people still in Dallas—and they'd pay anything to have tomatoes like this in winter months—or fresh peas and carrots and beans."

"We could work up a circuit of the few high-priced restaurants, the country club." Harry radiated fresh confidence. "And, of course, families who set great tables. My old customers," he pounced. "The ones we sold when we were bootlegging, Jeff! It's a natural."

"I think you're off your rocker," Jeff said flatly.

"Look, there are people in Dallas with money to burn." Harry envisioned an untapped market in a city less hurt than most by the terrible Depression. "Women still go to Neiman-Marcus and spend as much for a dress or a coat as a family on relief gets for a year. Dallas still has its fancy affairs at the country club and at the big hotels and in their mansions. Let's get some of that money for ourselves."

"It's one thing to fuss over a few tomatoes because Jeff loves them, but it's a whole different ball game to try to raise enough to sell," Maura exhorted.

"To Maura it's a labor of love," Jeff interjected.

"To sell greenhouse produce will be a labor of love for me," Katie countered. "A love for the money it'll bring in."

"I never know what's going to come up when I put in my tomatoes," Maura said. "Sometimes there're tomatoes, sometimes nothing."

"We'll learn what we need to know to keep them coming," Katie said with conviction. "These are the slow months in farm country. What have we got to lose?"

"Money," Jeff said. "Better worry about how we'll manage to put in corn in the spring." He gazed from Harry to Katie with a flicker of exasperation. "Katie, you've usually got your feet on the ground. Tell Harry he can't afford a big greenhouse. That means a lot of lumber and—"

"We've got all that lumber sitting in the barn since Amelia's day," Harry remembered. "She bought it cheap from some farmer down the road who was selling out. She'd meant to put up new fencing and another tool-shed, but the cash was never around for the labor. Help us put up the greenhouse, Jeff," he urged. "We'll cut you in on the profits. Unless, of course, you get called for a job. . . ."

"Pipe dreams," Maura drawled. "What kind of job is going to pop up for any of us now? Jeff, help them with the greenhouse."

The following day—with the four children watching the construction as a fresh diversion—Harry and Jeff set to work on the framework for the greenhouse. Reluctant to spend money on gas but determined to learn what she could about greenhouse produce, Katie drove into Dallas with Maura to visit the public library, to ask endless questions at the produce stores. They must know every possible way to make this new venture a success, she told herself. Not just a few tomatoes for the table. A new business.

Lingering over supper—while the children played on the blanket laid on the floor before the stove—the four adults explored the prospects of Katie and Harry's new venture.

"Look, to produce in volume enough to be commercial will be hard," Jeff cautioned for the dozenth time. "It'll keep you on your toes sixteen hours a day. You heard Maura—even the little she's raised for our table kept her running."

"Tell us what to do," Katie said stubbornly. "We'll do it."

Jeff explained that not only must they create the proper temperature for their plants, they would have to create the best possible soil conditions.

"You can't go out and buy all the junk the salesman will try to push on you. Everything has to be natural. The soil has to be the best. You have to create the perfect

146

home for those tomatoes and cukes and string beans and whatever you set your mind to raise," Jeff ordered.

"You tell us what to do," Harry said. "You and Maura. We'll learn how to do on a big scale what Maura did small. I tell you, there's money in this."

The following morning Katie and Harry left Leo and Joanne with Maura and drove into Dallas. With high expectations they visited the agricultural stores, checked on prices for what they would need. Katie tried to conceal her nervousness at the cash outlays that would be required.

Their first impasse arose when they learned the cost of the glass necessary for the greenhouse—far more than they had anticipated.

"Damn!" Harry's hands tightened on the wheel of the car as they headed away from the city toward the farm. "Prices are so low for everything else. Why does glass cost so much?"

"We'll raise it somehow," Katie said defiantly.

"How?" Harry challenged with an attempt at humor. "Have you got another string of pearls tucked away that I don't know about? Somebody's coming out to buy oil rights for the farm?"

"We'll find the money," Katie insisted. "And I don't mean to print it," she added shakily.

When they stopped off at the Warrens' to pick up Leo and Joanne, Katie admitted they hadn't bought the glass that had been their objective today.

"Cut down on the size of the greenhouse for now," Maura—ever practical—suggested.

"We need that size to make sure we'll have produce to deliver," Harry pointed out. "If only half of what we plant comes up, we can still fill orders."

"Maura, remember when you sold that Chippendale bed to some antique dealer in the city?" asked Katie, searching her mind for possible assets.

"Yeah, that paid our taxes," Maura recalled.

"We've got some old beat-up chairs out in the

barn—you know how Amelia used to say her mother never threw anything out. Do you suppose they might be antiques?" All at once Katie was optimistic.

"Let's clean them up and take them into town," Maura said. "They may not be Chippendale, but you might pick up some cash for them. Folks buy the strangest things."

"I almost burned those for wood when we ran out of coal last month," Harry mused. "Now maybe they'll buy us glass."

Two days later Katie and Maura drove into Dallas with the pair of fiddleback chairs Katie had found in the barn. Though Katie worried about the dents and bruises on the legs and that the upper side of the rungs were worn almost flat, the antique dealer offered what Katie considered an astounding price. But she caught the barely perceptible shake of Maura's head. The dealer was not offering enough, Maura was telegraphing.

"I don't know...." Katie pretended disinterest. "Maybe I ought to just hang on to them for a while."

Katie and the dealer haggled for a few minutes until Katie capitulated. She was awed by the money he handed over for the two chairs. Later Maura explained that his eyes had told her these were genuine antiques.

"He's probably got a customer just dying for a pair of chairs like these," Maura said exuberantly. "Let's treat ourselves to some window-shopping at Neiman-Marcus before we go home. It's kind of nice to see that some people have money to spend on clothes."

"Harry and I are going to make this work," Katie told her. "You'll see."

Jeff became their adviser. He showed them how to keep the greenhouse warm in bitterly cold spells.

"You use coal or coke because you can store them up in offseason—and with them you don't worry about power cuts. You remember the boiler has to be cleaned of ashes every day," he exhorted. "You've got to watch ventilation and shading. You make sure you don't overcrowd your plants."

He worked with Harry to pipe water into the greenhouse so they could avoid the backbreaking trips with buckets. He explained how some vegetables needed to be protected from direct sunlight and how to arrange this.

"We're getting the benefit of four generations of farmers," Harry told Jeff. "Plus you're a guy with imagination."

"I'm a guy who loves the land," Jeff said. "It's in the blood."

By early spring Katie and Harry were preparing to take their first shipment to eager Dallas customers. As Harry had predicted, she remembered, they hadn't blinked an eye at the price he asked. Finally, she thought with a surge of gratitude, there was a glint of light at the end of Harry's tunnel of despair.

Chapter Twelve

WITH KATIE spending long hours each day in the greenhouse, Harry began to prepare the fields for the spring planting. Once a week he went into Dallas to conduct business for the new venture. The other days he worked in the fields. But it was soon obvious—as he had suspected—that he couldn't work alone. He talked to Katie about their letting the field go fallow this season.

"Like Jeff," he reminded her over a supper that included their superb tomatoes and green beans, "you're always saying how farmers overwork their land. Here's a chance to give it a rest."

"Harry, no!" Katie was shocked at the prospect of no corn harvest.

"We break our butts to put in a crop, and when we

harvest it, what do we see? We're lucky to pay our taxes and put aside a few dollars to put in the next crop."

"With a corn crop I know there's food on the table," she said bluntly. "If we don't have money for coal, we can burn the corn."

"Haven't you any faith in what we're doing with the greenhouse?" he challenged.

"I have faith," she conceded. It wasn't just the money she welcomed. It was Harry's fresh confidence in their future. Maybe the business wouldn't become the big industry he envisioned, but it brought hope—and Harry needed this desperately. "But the corn crop's insurance." She forced a smile. "The world is going crazy, but with the farm we have a roof over our heads and food to eat. That helps me sleep nights."

"You know, Katie," he said wryly, "I'd be happy if I never ate another ear of corn, another dish of succotash, corn bread, chowder, pudding, fritters. I don't even like popcorn anymore."

"Don't say that in front of Leo and Joanne," she said quickly.

"I won't." His smile was gentle. "But I'm going to have to hire a hand. Katie, I can't put in a crop alone," he said before she could protest. "You're wet-nursing those greenhouse plants eighteen hours a day. Anyhow, we can afford it, the way the money's coming in." He tried not to show his pleasure in this, Katie understood, because the sums were unimpressive in comparison to what he had earned in the good days of the stock market. But *she* was impressed. Maura and Jeff were impressed.

Katie and Harry were doing well with their produce route—even when they had to compete during the summer with local produce. Katie's relief at their own improved financial state was edged with guilt because of the devastation they saw on all sides. Wages of day laborers in Dallas were reduced from thirty cents an hour to eighteen cents an hour—and this was to be paid in groceries. Over eighteen thousand men and women in

Dallas were out of work and looking to the Public Welfare Department for survival.

In Washington, D.C., seventeen thousand World War veterans—many accompanied by their wives and children—camped in record-breaking heat near the Capitol, vowing to stay until Congress voted for immediate cashing of soldiers' bonus certificates. Across the country entire families tried to live on two-dollar-a-week welfare payments. The lucky ones. In vast areas of the country there were no relief agencies. President Hoover considered federal aid a disservice to the country.

Banks were failing across the country. Huge lines of desperate depositors lined up before bank doors in hopes of withdrawing their life's savings before the bank ran out of funds. Even the great banks in New York and Chicago and Detroit were failing. State governors were declaring bank moratoriums to avoid the panic of a rush on the banks.

"No problem for us," Harry kidded with bitter humor. "What farmer has money in the bank?"

With over 13 million people out of work a million hit the road, hoping for something better just beyond. Katie lay sleepless on the nights when the local papers wrote about the starving children, millions of whom dropped out of school to wander with their parents in search of the always elusive jobs. She cried for the women and children digging in garbage cans for food. Why couldn't Harry understand that they were *lucky*? Harry was still obsessed by his failure to push his way up into what he called "real money."

"How can you be satisfied to live this way, after what we've had?" he reproached Katie. "Leo goes to a crummy rural school. I meant for him to go to a fine private school like Terrell School for Boys. How the hell will he ever make it into Harvard and Harvard Law from a shitty rural school?"

"Leo's seven years old. We don't have to worry now about Harvard Law." She fought against exasperation.

"We can't afford a new car or to fix up the house decently. When I buy a new pair of shoes, it's a four-dollar pair from Thom McAn."

"But the business is growing. In another year we can buy a new car." Not the fancy Packard he kept looking at down in the city that cost over two thousand dollars—but a good used late-model Ford.

"I let you down, Katie," he said with the anguish that was like a knife in her heart. "I let the kids down."

"You're not responsible for the Depression." How many times had she said that in the last two years? "And it can't go on forever. Everybody says Hoover won't be elected again. Franklin Roosevelt will be president by next March—things will be different with a Democrat in office," she repeated. Everybody said that any Democrat would win in November.

Ever since she and Harry first heard Franklin Roosevelt in a radio speech back in April—when he chastised the Hoover administration for helping the big banks and the corporations and doing nothing to help the farmers—she'd felt a surge of hope for the country.

A few days before the opening of Leo's school Harry returned from his Dallas route with two large cartons in tow.

"What'd you buy?" Katie asked, faintly uneasy. Harry rarely succumbed to his old habit of impulse buying, but Katie worried that this might return as their finances improved.

"An encyclopedia," he announced with relish. He dropped the two cartons on the floor and began to rip one open. "Secondhand, so it was cheap. If Leo needs to know something for school, he'll have it here at home." He pulled out a volume of *The World Book*. "It's a good investment for the kids," he said defensively, and paused. "For us, too." Harry had never overcome his self-consciousness at ending his education with high school graduation.

"We'll all read them," she told Harry tenderly.

"Where're the kids? Let me show them the books."

"They're sleeping over tonight with Georgie and Willa," Katie told him.

He grinned. "Aha, we're alone tonight."

"That's right," she drawled.

"We'll have music with supper. Dinner," he corrected himself insouciantly. "We might even dance."

"It's been a long time," she said softly.

"Have you forgotten your French?" he challenged, grinning. "Let's talk only French at supper twice a week," he decreed. "Let Leo and Joanne pick it up, too. But not tonight . . ."

"Candlelight dinners twice a week," she proposed. This was the old Harry. She hadn't seen him in a long time. "With a white tablecloth instead of the oilcloth. And red roses from the garden on the table. We'll pretend we're in Paris again."

"Remember our suite at the Ritz? There's one thing that's never changed," he said with pride. "No matter where we make love—the farm, London, Paris, the house in Dallas—it's always the same. Sensational."

"Are you making a play for me, Harry?" she teased.

"Damn it, I'm sure trying."

"Try harder." Her face was radiant. "Dinner can wait."

In 1928 Texas had broken from its Democratic tradition to vote Republican. It was clear that the state would not repeat that this year. Not when latest statistics put unemployment figures at 15 million. Not when farmers were fighting mortgage foreclosures with shotguns and nooses. When Hoover insisted there would be no federal "interference" in economic or social areas, that high tariffs and a balanced budget took precedence over welfare programs.

As the campaign progressed, the Republicans became frantic. They indulged in scurrilous name-calling. The secretary of agriculture called Roosevelt "a common garden variety of liar." The secretary of the navy warned that "if Roosevelt's elected, the homes and lives of a hundred million Americans might be in danger." President Hoover warned that "the fundamental issue that will fix the national direction for one hundred years to come is whether we shall go in fidelity to American traditions or whether we shall turn to innovations," and he harangued against "false gods arrayed in the rainbow colors of promises."

Campaigning in Texas, Governor Roosevelt promised that an important part of his program for the nation would be "to restore purchasing power to the farming half of this country. Without this the wheels of the railroads and of the factories will not turn." And hope took root in many listeners.

On election eve the Newhouses and the Warrens gathered together to listen to election news on the radio. Katie had prepared a festive dinner for the four grownups. The children had eaten earlier and been put to bed for the night, delighted by the party atmosphere. The adults were determined to sit up until one candidate or the other had conceded the election.

"A lot of voters don't give a shit about either candidate," Harry said bluntly. "Or either party."

"Did you read what Will Rogers said?" Jeff's smile was wry. "He said, 'The way most people feel, they would like to vote against all of them if it was possible.' "

"I like FDR," Maura said. "He looks like a man who could pull us out of this craziness."

"You don't pick a president by the way he looks," Jeff scolded.

"I know what Maura means," Katie said after a moment. "He kind of exudes hope—and that's contagious. We need to feel hope."

The four sat stubbornly before the radio, listening to election reports. By early evening indications were that FDR would win. He was carrying one state after another. But not until 12:17 A.M. Eastern time did President Hoover concede the election. FDR had carried forty-two of the forty-eight states.

Like many others, Katie and Harry grumbled that the new president wouldn't take office until March 4. Still, she considered, for Harry and her, life was improving. Shortly after the election he hired Jeff to help him build a second greenhouse because he had a waiting list of customers. He brushed aside Jeff's embarrassment at being paid.

"Hell, Jeff, it's a job. The way things are today I don't expect you to work for nothing—not now when we're making a living of sorts." It frustrated Katie to hear Harry downgrade their income.

Jeff's novel was still circulating among the New York publishers without any sign of success.

"We left New York to come to the farm so Jeff could write," Maura said somberly to Katie while the men worked outside on the greenhouse and the children sprawled on the kitchen floor to play dominoes and munch on chunks of bread fresh from the oven. "So he writes a few months out of each year. I think we'd know more how to handle the book if we were in New York and talking to people in the business. The last publisher sat on it for five months—and then it came back with one of those form letters."

"But he's had some near-sales," Katie consoled. "Two editors think he has a lot of talent."

"Near means nothing," Maura said dryly. "It's a sale or it's a rejection. But I keep telling Jeff—we're not starving, we're not on the road like a million others with no place to live and not much hope."

"After Inauguration Day we'll see things happening," Katie predicted.

On Inauguration Day—the morning when every bank in the country had to close its doors—the two couples, along with Leo and Joanne and Georgie and Willa, gathered at the Warrens' house to hear FDR's inaugural address. It seemed to Katie that his words were burned into her brain: "Let me assert my firm belief that the only thing we have to fear is fear itself."

Katie gazed at her husband and wished he could understand that they were among the lucky Americans. They were surviving the unbelievable devastation that was assaulting the country. At a time when millions went hungry, they were eating. At a time when countless families were without homes, drifting from city to city, they had a roof over their heads. They didn't have to apply for relief or WPA jobs.

The new president called for a special session of Congress; that reflected his inaugural speech—"This nation asks for action, and action now." Four days after he took office the banks reopened. Such was the hope Roosevelt had implanted in the people that deposits exceeded withdrawals. In the next hundred days he launched his "New Deal" program. He wanted Congress to pass new laws to help the unemployed, the farmers, to halt home foreclosures, to repeal Prohibition. Farmers waited anxiously for changes.

In April the country went off the gold standard, which was supposed to make it easier for farmers to meet their obligations. Then in June the federal government set up the Home Owners' Act to refinance home mortgages, which would save millions of farmers and urban dwellers from foreclosure. In the early part of the year it had been estimated that there were one thousand home foreclosures each day. But nevertheless, the first summer of FDR's New Deal was traumatic for farm owners. The unemployed in the cities couldn't afford even the low prices that farmers were forced to offer. Many were working for starvation wages.

This summer the farmers began to strike in an effort to starve the cities into recognizing their desperate straits. Trucks bringing produce into urban areas were stopped by farmers with shotguns and pitchforks. The National Guard was brought out, and violence erupted. In some states martial law was declared. Local businessmen—fearing financial ruin—organized vigilante groups.

Katie and Harry were furious when Secretary of Agriculture Henry Wallace announced that the Agricultural Assistance Administration—with summer fields about to provide bumper crops that would only lower farm prices even more—was setting up regulations to destroy crops and pay farmers from AAA funds to cover their losses.

"How the hell can we destroy crops with thousands of people out there starving to death?" Harry exploded.

"It's sacrilegious. . . ." Katie was pale with disbelief.

But the AAA laid down the rules, and fields were burned or crops ploughed under.

Katie felt especially protective toward her greenhouse these days. She enjoyed the feel of rich black Texas earth beneath her fingers. It was the land that gave them life, she thought with infinite respect. And later in the year she was grateful when restricted planting replaced the destruction of crops.

Harry was straining to build their gourmet produce into a high-volume business. By sheer power of his personality he persuaded Jeff—who felt Katie's reverence for the land—to help him build yet another greenhouse, which Jeff and Maura would manage. Maura admitted to being upset that Jeff would not be writing in the between-harvests period, but she knew how important the extra money was to them.

Katie was proud of their growing business, though Harry glumly warned that they were reaching the saturation point.

"We're doing fine." Her eyes defied him to deny it.

"We can't go beyond this," he pointed out in frustration. "Katie, there's no real future for us here."

"Harry, we're living comfortably. All right, you're not driving a new Packard, and I don't buy my dresses at Neiman-Marcus. But we are living better than any farming family in this county. We're saving money." Hidden away in secret corners of the house because they were not yet ready to trust the banks. Back on March 12 the president—in the first of his "fireside chats"—had told a wide radio audience that the banks were safe now under the new law. Katie insisted they wait a year before trusting the banks again.

"I've got a lid on my life. I'm in prison," Harry railed. "I can't rise out of this vacuum. Damn it, Katie, a man can't live without hope of something better."

"We're going through a bad period. It's like that all over the world." His anguish was always so close to the surface. What could she do to lessen it? Endlessly she asked herself this. "But once this Depression is over—and with Roosevelt in the White House it will be—we'll be on the move again," she encouraged him. Harry must believe this. "But this is not the time. Not yet, Harry."

Chapter Thirteen

KATIE FOUGHT constantly to deal with Harry's ever-present frustrations at not being able to push their produce business—now called Newhouse Gourmet Foods—into a major venture.

"Harry, we're doing fine, considering the times," she exhorted as they sat in the kitchen in the early afternoon and settled up the business records for the first two weeks of March 1934. "And if Dallas gets selected for the Texas Centennial Fair, we know we're in for some upgrade in the economy."

"What makes you think Dallas will be chosen?" he challenged. "Both Houston and Austin far outweigh Dallas historically. I doubt we have a chance." Still, Katie saw a glint of hope in his eyes. "If we did get the Centennial, it could put Dallas on the map. Most people outside of Texas have this vision of Dallas as an overgrown country town, populated by newly rich oil millionaires, loud-mouthed politicians, and sharecroppers."

"That's not true, Harry," she reproached. "People outside of Texas are beginning to talk well about it. It's a special place. People here are Dallas boosters. Look how Industrial Dallas, Inc., has been fighting to promote the city. And with Thornton on the new permanent Texas Centennial Commission . . ." The commission was in the process of being set up. "Well, we've got a great chance of seeing Dallas as the home of the Centennial. Do you realize how many people that will bring into town? How much extra business?"

"I'd better get moving." Harry began to gather together the papers scattered about the table. "I like to be at the school before the kids are out of their classes." This school year Harry had arranged for Leo and Joanne to attend another school a half hour's drive away. It was a larger, better-equipped school and Harry was becoming a fanatic about the children's education. Neither the heavy driving chores nor the expense of the new school—since they lived out of that school district—concerned him.

"I'll drive down for them," Katie offered. "You promised to help Jeff with the repairs on the new greenhouse," she reminded him. The last dust storm had caused some serious damage.

"Sure you don't mind?" Harry asked, but she knew he was glad to be relieved at intervals of the school shuttling.

"I'll pick up Maura to keep me company," she said. Maura was always glad for a break from the farm routine.

"Jeff's mad as a hornet at me," Maura confided as she joined Katie on the front seat of the Ford. "He got to the mail before I did."

"The book came back again?" Katie asked compassionately.

Maura nodded. "Jeff's pissed that I wasted postage on it. But the editor did say he thought it was very good. Just 'not for our list at this time.' Nobody wants to read about the troubles of a farm family," she said bitterly. "They want to go to the movies and see Ginger Rogers dance with Fred Astaire, or listen to Jack Benny or Fred Allen or Charlie McCarthy."

"How's Jeff doing with the new book?"

"When does he have time to write?" Maura challenged. "Not that I'm complaining about the work." Her smile was wry. "If we weren't working for you and Harry, we'd have lost the farm to taxes this year. You know what the drought did to our crops."

"I worry about the dust storms." Katie was somber. On top of all their other troubles, how were farmers going to cope with these? "Did you listen to the radio last night? About that storm up in Meade County, Kansas? It pulled up the wheat right from its roots."

Maura nodded. Even down here they were feeling the effects of that dust storm. A cloud of powdery earth cut down on visibility, kept housewives on a frenzied path of cleaning. "We don't have to read about it. We walk outside and we know what's happening."

"It's grim." Katie shuddered expressively. "Still, not as bad as the storm last November. That one sent soil from Texas all the way out to Lake Superior. Why are these storms happening?" Katie was recurrently baffled.

"Why do they usually happen in the spring?" Maura shook her head. "Some questions go forever unanswered."

"I heard Mr. Crane say that some dust storms are good for the farms," Katie recalled. "That it mixes the soil and helps keep it fertile."

"That idea is not something new in this part of the country," Maura pointed out. "You've heard Jeff carrying on about how we've got to learn to strip-crop if we're to cut down on wind or dust erosion." Katie knew that strip-cropping meant planting soil-holding crops such as wheat alternatively with cane, sorghum, or small grains—which help to stabilize the fields. "Not that we can stop wind erosion that way alone. But enough of farm problems," she ordered. "How do the kids like the new school?"

"They're getting used to it after all these months," Katie admitted. "They miss Georgie and Willa. But Harry's happy—he's sure he's giving Leo and Joanne a better education." She paused. "At least, he's happy about the kids' education."

"Harry won't be happy," Maura said bluntly, "until he's a rich man again."

"I wish I could make him understand we don't have to be millionaires to be happy. We're fixing up the house. We're buying a new car next month—not a Packard"—she smiled—"but brand new. We're putting money away every week. The kids are our riches—why can't Harry see that?"

"Katie, you sound so damn Pollyanna-ish," Maura chided good-humoredly, but her eyes were tender. "I know what you mean, though."

"I could be happy right now—except that so many others are hurting—if Harry would just stop this obsession to be the richest man in Texas."

"And in Texas," Maura laughed, "that's a big order."

"You and Jeff are happy," Katie said after a pause. "It kind of shines from you."

"We laugh a lot. We make a big fuss over the kids, and it's good. But there's always that shadow over us. Jeff's so good—and he can't get anywhere with his writing. I keep telling him his time will come—but will it?" Pain crept into Maura's voice. "Sometimes I think talent is a curse—not the blessing it's supposed to be. Because if you can't get it off the ground, you spend the rest of your life asking yourself, What did I do wrong? Or you're bitter and angry at the world because it didn't recognize what you were trying to give it."

"I think maybe we're meant to be happy just in small

bursts," Katie said softly. "We have to clutch at those moments and cherish them."

"God, we're being heavy," Maura clucked. "You're twenty-seven and I'm thirty-two, and we sound as though we're sixty and bemoaning our lost years. Katie," she said reflectively, "do you ever wish you and Harry had never come to Texas?"

"No," Katie said with conviction. "This is where I want to spend my life. What about you?" All at once she was curious.

"Sometimes I get restless," Maura confessed. "That's when I laugh the loudest and bake a lot. I work out most of my frustrations in the oven. Maybe if we had a lot of money—a house in Dallas and a busy social life—I wouldn't be restless. But mainly," she said, groping for words, "I think I'm restless because I see Jeff breaking his back—and his heart—and getting nowhere. Everything in life is timing. And this isn't Jeff's time to make it as a writer."

"What about you, Maura?" Katie asked gently. "Do you ever think about what might have happened if you'd stayed in New York and tried to make it as an actress?"

"Sure, every once in a while it sneaks into my mind. When I read something in *Theatre Arts Monthly* about some new young actress wowing them on Broadway. But I can live with that. What kills me is that Jeff can't get published, when he has so much to give." Maura glanced at her watch. "You'd better step on the gas, baby—or the kids will be out of class and wondering where the hell we are."

Katie knew the moment she saw Leo emerge from the schoolhouse that he was upset. He was so sweet and sensitive. So vulnerable, she thought, with a passionate wish that she could wash away all the hurts that lay ahead of him in life.

"Ma!" Joanne burst through the door with her usual exuberance, ran toward the car. A seven-year-old replica of her mother with a zest for living that Katie relished. "Hey, Leo, Mom's here!"

"Hi, kids." Katie kissed each from inside the car while she reached to open the sometimes-recalcitrant back door for them. "Maura's brought an oatmeal cookie for each of you." The original "Aunt Maura" and "Uncle Jeff" had given way to first names, because this was what the children heard all the time.

"Thanks." Joanne leaned forward eagerly as Maura extended this treat. Katie monitored the amount of sweets the children ate.

Leo was silent on the drive home. Joanne—who adored everything on four legs—was plying Maura with questions about a neighbor's litter of mongrel pups. But Leo huddled silently in a corner of the backseat. In hurt Leo retreated into himself. Joanne—like Harry—exploded.

Not until Katie dropped Maura off at her house did she question Leo.

"Leo, you're not happy about something," she chided gently. "You want to tell me about it?" Always Leo's champion, Joanne was suddenly alert.

"I got a seventy-two on my arithmetic test," he whispered in anguish. "Daddy's gonna be mad."

"You got a hundred on your English test," Katie said, trying to sound matter-of-fact. *Why must Harry push Leo this way?* He wasn't nine years old yet. Next month he'd be nine. "And you passed the arithmetic test," she pointed out.

"Daddy'll yell," he said in anguish. "He'll say I didn't study."

"I'll talk to him," Katie promised. The only times she and Harry fought were over the kids. So Leo had a kind of panic at dealing with numbers—that wasn't a cardinal sin. Despite this, his teachers always said he was very bright.

When they arrived at the house, Katie sent Leo and Joanne to the barn to bring in a few chunks of wood.

"We'll have dinner tonight in the living room, before the fireplace," she said, meaning to make this a small adventure. The "parlor" had become the "living room" when they'd bought the house in Dallas. "You'll like that, won't you?"

"Yeah." Joanne's small, lovely face glowed in anticipation. "Remember that poem Leo wrote about the fireplace the last time we had a fire going?"

"It was a beautiful poem." She smiled at her troubled son, hoping to wheedle a smile from him. She brushed from her mind Harry's biting reaction to the poem. *"That comes from hanging around Jeff. Let him do better in his arithmetic."* "I'm going to frame your poem and hang it by my bed."

"Come on, Jo. Let's go get the wood." But for an instant Katie thought she saw a glow of pleasure in Leo's eyes.

In the house Katie found Harry at the kitchen table. He was working over a sales letter to possible new customers.

"Where are the kids?" He glanced up with lifted eyebrows.

"I sent them out to bring in some wood for the fireplace. Harry, I don't want you to yell at Leo when he shows you his arithmetic test." This was a family ritual. "He's upset that he didn't do better. Don't make it worse."

"I helped him for almost two hours the night before the test." Harry's voice soared in exasperation. "He knows this stuff. Why doesn't he think?" He paused. "How bad was it?"

"He passed," she said. "Don't yell at him."

"You're making a baby out of him. How do you expect him to grow up to be a man when you're always pampering him?"

"He's a little boy, Harry. Let him be." She met his eyes in stubborn defiance.

"All right, spoil him rotten," Harry retreated. "But I'm

thinking of his future. He's not going to be a failure like his old man."

"For God's sake, Harry, will you stop this 'I'm a failure' routine!" Katie's voice was shrill despite her earlier promise to herself to remain calm. "We're doing all right. We have everything we need."

"If you're willing to settle for small change. You never used to be like that, Katie." His eyes were disconcerting in their scrutiny. "You were as ambitious as I was."

"Everything in its own time, Harry. Like you said, we get the Centennial here in Dallas, business will be booming." She smiled cajolingly. Sometimes she was furious with Harry, yet she loved him so much. "I promised the kids dinner in the living room, before the fireplace."

"If business expands, we'll add a dining room," Harry said. "It's time to stop living like we were on home relief." He squinted in reflection. "Or maybe instead of a dining room, we ought to look around for some cheap land. To hold for later, when we're out of the Depression. We can pick up acreage for almost nothing these days."

"If you buy it outright," Katie stipulated. She couldn't go through losing land again. "No bank loans. No options."

"It's a deal." His smile was rueful. He knew her fears of losing everything again. "As soon as we expand, we'll buy some land. Acreage that's right for wheat. I tell you, Katie, wheat's going to be the road up for us again." Ever since they'd met Pierre Simon, Harry had been mentally building himself a grain empire. "Unless—" he grimaced in irritation—"unless all this government control over agriculture screws it up."

"What would you like for dinner?" She strived for lightness. Let her avoid an ugly encounter between Harry and Leo over that low grade in arithmetic. "I know," she laughed, "no corn on the table in any shape."

"I brought hamburger home from the market this morning," he reminded her. "Leo and Jo think hamburgers are the greatest. We'll have a picnic on the floor before the fireplace. They always get sleepy before the fireplace. They'll go to bed early." His eyes held hers. "And so will we. . . ."

Harry was proud that after all these years their love-making never lost its power. In bed Harry and she were sixteen and eighteen again.

A cup of coffee at his elbow, Harry sat at the kitchen table and perused the current edition of the *Literary Digest*. Katie had gone out to the bedroom to make sure the children had brushed their teeth and washed their hands and faces before they went to bed. He could hear the faint sound of voices down the hall. Joanne was wheedling Katie to let her come out and "listen to the radio for just ten more minutes," and Leo was stalling on putting aside his book for the night.

In a burst of impatience Harry closed the magazine and put it aside. What the devil was the matter with Leo, coming home with such rotten grades in arithmetic? What would happen when he got into high school and had to face algebra and geometry? How would he get into a top college without good math grades?

He left the table and walked to the kitchen door that led outside. He opened the door and walked out into the night. The air was crisp but hinting at the approach of spring. The sky splashed with stars. Right now everything was so calm and beautiful, he thought—but they were approaching the dust-storm season again. In the spill of moonlight he could see the earth through the straggly grass. Hard from the lack of rain. Of course, there had been a lot of snow up in the panhandle this month—that ought to ease worries about another summer drought.

"Harry?" Katie appeared in the doorway.

"The kids in for the night?"

"They'll probably be out cold in five minutes. Joanne

was begging to go out to listen to the radio again—but her eyes were already closing."

"Maybe instead of a dining room, we ought to think about adding on a bedroom. At his age, Leo ought to have his own room instead of sharing with his sister."

"We can do that soon," Katie said carefully. "If we keep it small." She hesitated. "We're going along with the AAA on cutting back on planting, aren't we?" Harry knew Katie was ambivalent about this, at a time when hunger had spread around the world.

"You bet we are. It's a load off my mind not to have to worry about keeping the business going and putting in a full crop of corn. We won't have to be paying for help—and the federal subsidy checks will come in handy."

"I have half an apple pie in the refrigerator. Shall I warm it in the oven, and we'll have it before we go to bed?"

"You like having a refrigerator again?" he joshed.

"It was expensive but nice," Katie conceded. "I'll go put up the pie."

What had happened to the old Katie? he asked himself, with a wistful sense of loss. Her dreams in the old days had been as big as his. Why had she allowed herself to be frightened into settling for so little in life?

All through spring and summer Dallas groups fought to convince the Texas Centennial Commission that Dallas was the logical choice for the Exposition. It was situated in the state's greatest density of population, most accessible not only to residents of Texas but to out-of-state visitors. And Dallas, its supporters proclaimed, was Texas at its most progressive. There was high jubilation in the city in September when the commission chose Dallas over Houston and San Antonio. Now it was up to the state legislature and the federal government to make the necessary appropriations.

Katie was happy that the Exposition was to be in Dallas. She knew that Harry would be caught up in the excitement, the possibilities the Exposition would bring into the city. It would be the greatest event in Dallas's brief history.

Harry was jubilant when the state legislature put through an appropriation bill the following April. In less than fourteen months the Exposition—expected to bring in millions of visitors—would be opened. It seemed impossible, Katie thought, considering the scope of the State Fair as planned—actually a World's Fair. But Texans enjoyed this kind of challenge. And in this way Harry was 100 percent Texan.

While Harry continued to be obsessed by land—as was Katie, she understood that he cared little about working the land. It was ownership that enthralled him. Land was his private empire, and he yearned to own half of Texas. Slowly now he began to acquire small, cheap tracts of land. Bought outright, as he proudly pointed out to Katie.

With seven thousand men working three shifts at Dallas's Fair Park to construct the Centennial exhibit buildings, Harry launched a box-lunch program in addition to their normal business, with Katie supervising the needed employees while Harry himself arranged for daily deliveries. New restaurants were being set up to cope with the incoming hordes, though the doors would not open until June 6. And Harry was expanding their gourmet-produce business daily.

There was an advance sale of 2 million Centennial Fair tickets. The city of Dallas prepared for a steady overnight invasion of 150,000 people. The Dallas Hotel Association offered 5,917 rooms in a price range of $1 to $8 for singles and a $1.25 to $10 for doubles. Another 858 rooms were available from hotels not members of the association. Southern Methodist University turned over its dormitory facilities—except for a few rooms occupied by summer-school students. There were 27 tourist camps with 659 cottages, plus private homes offering rooms. At the corner of South Haskell and Fitzhugh Street was the Texas Tent City, which offered units consisting of wood-framed walls and floors and tent tops.

By the end of May excitement was running high. Downtown nightclubs and restaurants were offering big-name bands, movie stars. Freddy Martin's orchestra would open the Peacock Terrace summer season in the Baker Hotel. George Raft would be guest of honor at the grand opening of the French Casino. Chez Maurice, "a terrace restaurant" atop the Santa Fe Building, would open on June 4.

On Saturday morning, June 6, every factory whistle and train whistle blew at full throttle at 8:00 A.M. to signal the official opening of the Texas Centennial Exposition, the first air-conditioned World's Fair in history. For the past two days people had been pouring into the city by train and the new airline flights. Along with Dallasites and those from the nearby area, they lined the streets to wait for the parade.

At 10:30 A.M.—with sixteen Army Air Corps planes flying above, the Centennial parade began to move along Main Street en route to the fairgrounds three miles east. The Newhouses and the Warrens had arrived early to assure that their four children would have front-row views.

"When are we going to the fair?" demanded Joanne, avidly watching the procession.

"In a couple of weeks," her father told her. "When they've got all the kinks out."

"Will they have pink cotton candy?" Willa asked.

"For sure," Maura said solemnly, and turned to Katie. "Remember the pink cotton candy at Coney Island?"

"Remember Nathan's hot dogs?" Jeff asked with a rhapsodic sigh.

The parade was led by eight motorcycle policemen, who were followed by six men on horseback carrying the six flags that represented the state's four-hundred-year history. The grand marshal rode in the first car. Behind him came twenty-five Texas Rangers on horseback, followed by the United States Marine Band playing "The Eyes of Texas." The governor and the Dallas County sheriff led an entourage of high-level dignitaries.

"That's Secretary of Commerce Daniel Roper," Harry remarked, impressed that a Cabinet member was here.

Now came representatives of the many units of the country's armed forces. Twelve hundred national guardsmen policed the line of march while the three-mile-long parade moved slowly ahead.

"How many people do you think are here?" asked Katie, viewing the exuberant crowd.

"At least quarter of a million," Jeff guessed. "This is the finest occasion in the history of Dallas. There's been nothing like this in all of Texas since Sam Houston beat the pants off the Mexicans at San Jacinto a hundred years ago."

From the first day it was clear the Texas Centennial Exposition would be a success. It might not make money, Harry conceded, but the publicity for Dallas was invaluable. Six days after the opening President Roosevelt and his wife arrived in Dallas to be greeted by half a million people. After the presidential parade the president and Mrs. Roosevelt toured the Exposition by car, leaving at the Cotton Bowl, where the president delivered a national radio address.

"This great Centennial Exposition is not for Texas alone—it is for the people of all the other forty-seven states as well," Roosevelt declared.

With their income growing, Harry decided to add two rooms to the farmhouse—both a dining room and another bedroom.

"We can't keep stalling on giving Leo his own room. Maybe then he'll grow up a little. He's still 'Mama's baby boy.' "

Joanne, of course, was delighted that Leo was being moved out. Now Willa could come visit for "overnights."

Harry ordered a subscription to the *National Geographic* for the children and two sports magazines for Leo in the futile hope that he would become interested in baseball. For himself he bought a subscription to *The Wall Street Journal*. In what little free time he could contrive, he devoured farm journals, business magazines—anything that could enlarge his knowledge of wheat and the corporations that controlled this market. Grain, he kept telling Katie, was even more important to the world than oil. Somehow, in that mysterious world of grain merchants there would be a place for him—if he could find the key to open the right door.

Night after night—when Katie slept from the tiredness of a long, work-strewn day—Harry lay gazing into the darkness of their bedroom. He would never be at peace with himself until he could restore to Katie and the children the life they'd known before that awful day in October 1929.

Late in the summer Harry learned—through a bank clerk to whom he tunneled bags of gourmet produce at intervals in return for information about upcoming farm auctions—that a huge tract of land some miles to the north would shortly be up for sale. His interest soared when he realized this was prime land for raising wheat.

The next morning he drove up for a personal inspection. It was far too large a tract for him even to consider bidding on it. He stood there visualizing a fine wheat harvest grown by tenant farmers—and prices were going up for farm products. Not merely because of the AAA program, he acknowledged, but because the black dust blizzards had destroyed the crops of many Midwest farms.

He knew that the shortage of wheat in some states would send the market price to record heights. The market was something he understood, he thought with grim pride. He wasn't a man who wanted to dig in the earth—but he yearned to control a chunk of the wheat market. He remembered Pierre Simon saying—as clearly as though it were only yesterday—that his talent to anticipate price fluctuations would serve him well in the grain business. *"It's the ability to read the future that makes the difference between failure and tremendous success."*

Telling himself he was acting out of curiosity, Harry went to call on his banker.

"Any chance of that tract being broken up into smaller chunks?" he asked.

"No way," the banker said expansively. "But, Harry, it's going cheap. You know how tight money is around here."

"It's too big a bite for me," Harry said. "I came by on the off-chance that it would be divided up."

"You're healthy these days," the banker told him. "Your business is going great guns. You've got your farm subsidy from the AAA. If you want a loan, we'll carry you."

"Let me think about it." Harry's heart was pounding. "When's the auction?"

"Monday morning, eight A.M. sharp."

Harry waited until Leo and Joanne had gone off to bed to talk to Katie about bidding on the tract of wheatland. She swung around from washing dinner dishes to stare at him in disbelief.

"How can we think about buying something that large? Harry, we don't have that kind of money."

"I was discussing it with Bill Randall at the bank." He tried to sound matter-of-fact. "He said, considering the way our business is going, the bank would give us a loan. . . ."

"On the business plus the farm!" Katie's eyes blazed. Harry flinched. Katie was right. Randall meant for him to put up the farm, too, as security for the loan. "With one bad season we'd lose both! Harry, how can you stand there and talk to me about putting us in that position again?"

"We're in good shape," he insisted. "The bank will give

us a long-term loan. The monthly payments will be small enough for us to handle. And that land is—"

"We can't gamble, Harry. Once was enough. Do you want to see us on the road with Leo and Joanne? Living in cardboard shacks or what's left of the car? One more migrant family that's lost its farm and is looking for its next meal. I won't let you subject the children to that, Harry."

Katie didn't come out and say it, but Harry understood. The farm was in her name. He couldn't make a deal at the bank without her.

"Forget it." His voice was terse. "It just seemed a way out of this goddamn vacuum we're in."

"You'll need more than wheatland to set yourself up as a grain merchant," she said bluntly. "You'll need heavy financing."

"I told you, Katie. Forget it." He pushed back his chair and rose to his feet. "It feels like a furnace here in the house. I'm going to sit outside for a while."

On Monday morning at 8:00 A.M. Harry stood among those at the auction. Only a few prospective bidders had showed up. Harry told himself this was crazy, to put himself through this torment. Why the hell had he come?

As he expected, bids were astoundingly low. Sick with helplessness, he stood by while the land was sold for a fraction of its value. Why couldn't Katie see the possibilities for them in that tract? They could have handled a bank loan spread out over ten to fifteen years.

At regular intervals in the next few weeks he thought wistfully about that spread. Then, on a hot October morning—after a sweaty drive into Dallas to make a delivery—he sat on the porch with a glass of lemonade and the day's *Morning News*. Hoping to find some relief from the heat. He opened the newspaper, read the lead story, and felt suddenly dizzy with shock.

NEW GUSHER NORTH OF DALLAS.

"Son of a bitch!" His hands shook as he read the newspaper report. The tract of land he'd wanted to buy had gone to an oil developer. *Not wheat but oil could have made them rich.*

In rage Harry rose to his feet, the newspaper brushed aside. In a surge of frustration he smashed the lemonade glass to the floor.

"Harry?" Katie appeared anxiously at the screen door. "Are you all right?"

"No, I'm not all right," he snapped at her, his eyes furiously accusing. "You know that tract of land you wouldn't let me buy? The one the bank offered to finance for us?"

"What about it?" Katie was wary.

"The new owners just struck oil! You've got so damn narrow in your thinking that you've cost us millions! We could have been rich! Leo and Joanne could have been set for life. How did you become so scared and petty? What happened to the Katie I married thirteen years ago?"

He swung away from her, strode down the steps and to the car. He wanted to put distance between himself and his wife. *Because of Katie's stupidity they'd lost millions of dollars.*

Chapter Fourteen

IN THE WEEKS ahead Katie tried to forget Harry's ugly accusations. She told herself he'd been terribly tired and upset, that he hadn't meant to lash out at her that way. She worried that she had failed him—and at the same time was failing Leo because she could not bring father and son together. She knew that Harry was hurt that Leo seemed to turn more to Jeff than to himself. He was baffled and angry.

With the arrival of the new year Harry decided it was time the family joined a synagogue. In fifteen months, he pointed out to Katie with candid anticipation, they would celebrate Leo's bar mitzvah.

"Leo has to study with the rabbi," he reminded her. "He has to learn Hebrew."

Katie was not surprised when Harry arranged for the family to join Temple Emanu-El, where the Marcuses were members. And at the synagogue for Friday evening services she recognized some of their cherished customers.

"Why not?" Harry chuckled when she remarked about this. "Jews who can afford it love to eat well."

She hoped that Leo's approaching bar mitzvah would bring father and son closer together, though she was disturbed in the coming months as Harry plotted an extravagant party to celebrate the bar mitzvah. True, she conceded, conditions in the country appeared to be improving. Some pundits were predicting that by early 1938 conditions would be normal.

But in August 1937 the economy suddenly collapsed again. Everything that had been gained was lost. By January over 2 million people had been thrown out of work.

"Harry, you've got to cut back on Leo's party," Katie protested while he proceeded with his lavish plans.

"We can afford it," he said stubbornly. "We'll cut corners other ways. How many times will Leo celebrate his bar mitzvah?"

In a corner of her mind Katie heard Harry saying to Izzy at their wedding, when Izzy was shocked to learn they were spending the night at the Plaza, *"How many times do I get married?"*

"It's obscene to spend so much money on a party when children are digging into garbage cans for food!" She trembled with indignation. "When people are fighting over rotten vegetables in the streets! Cities like Chicago closing down their relief stations!"

"Roosevelt is working to change things." Harry refused to be dissuaded. "He's sending new relief bills to Congress. The economy will pick up—you'll see."

Like many Americans, Katie and Harry were disturbed by the rising voices of William Dudley Pelley's Silver Shirts—drawing thousands into their promotion of Fascism and anti-Semitism, of the return of Father Coughlin and his Christian Front—a Jew-baiting Fascist group with a rifle-training camp in New Jersey, and of Fritz Kuhn's German-American Bund—which mimicked the Nazi thinking.

As Harry predicted, new government money was thrust into the economy. Roosevelt asked Congress to appropriate $300 million for defense. American industry began to receive heavy orders from England and France for planes, guns, tanks. All at once Europe was demanding American food imports—to stockpile against an imminent outbreak of war. By the day of Leo's bar mitzvah unmistakable signs were visible that prosperity *was* "just around the corner."

Katie knew that gentle, reserved Leo was not comfortable at being the center of the extravagant party that followed the always-impressive ceremony at the synagogue. Harry was ecstatic. According to Jewish law, his son had become a man.

"This is a landmark in your life that you'll always remember, Leo," he said emotionally. "Along with the day you graduate from Harvard and from Harvard Law School."

But Leo was silent, staring at the floor in distress. Katie saw Joanne's small face tense in reproach. She was becoming openly rebellious about their father's insistence on planning their lives.

As Harry moved away to accept congratulations from a guest, Katie heard Joanne's grim whisper to Leo:

"Don't listen to him. You don't *have* to go to Harvard. You don't *have* to go to law school."

Harry was constantly upset over Leo's mediocre or low grades in math and science. It meant nothing to his father that Leo excelled in other subjects.

"How will he get into an Ivy League college without top grades in math and science?" Harry ranted regularly to Katie. "Why can't he concentrate? He's not stupid. He doesn't want to learn."

"Let him be, Harry," Katie pleaded tiredly when Harry brought up the subject yet again as they settled in bed that night. "You're making a nervous wreck out of him."

"I'm thinking of his future. Leo won't be a failure like his father."

"Go to sleep, Harry. It's been a tiring day."

Katie turned away from him and closed her eyes. Didn't Harry understand? Leo was still a child. Maybe at thirteen Harry had wanted to be a lawyer. Leo had no such desire. In time Leo would know what he wanted to do with his life. Harry would have to accept that.

Now, in 1939—with the economy improving—more Americans were concerned about what was happening outside the country. The Depression at home had done much to avert American eyes from the rise of dictatorships in Germany, Italy, from the Japanese aggression.

In the last year German troops had seized Austria and had taken the Sudetenland from Czechoslovakia. In March of this year Hitler's troops seized the remainder of Czechoslovakia, then took Memel from Lithuania. In April Italy grabbed off Albania. Now Hitler was complaining about the "frightful treatment of the German-speaking people of Poland." Tensions escalated around the world.

While she worried about the international situation—and was painfully conscious that the economy at home was improving because of this, Katie was pleased at the soaring success of the business. Harry continued to grumble that it would never extend beyond a local enterprise.

"You still think in terms of nickels and dimes," he upbraided Katie for her optimism. "In this world you have to think big."

But Katie knew Harry was as proud as she that their bank account was swelling—even while he derided himself as a failure in business. They'd bought a few small tracts of land—outright—but now Harry focused on saving for the children's education. Another two years, Harry rejoiced, and Leo would be heading for college.

"What his father couldn't do, Leo will do," Harry vowed. "My son will be a college graduate. He'll become a lawyer."

On a sweltering late May afternoon Leo walked despondently from the school building to wait for his customary pickup. His shirt clung damply to his back. Perspiration stained his unruly dark hair. The last week of school was always unbearably hot. He thought longingly of the air-conditioned movie houses and restaurants so welcome in Dallas. And more and more—since the Centennial fair, folks were air-conditioning their houses.

He prayed that today it would be his mother who would drive up in the parking area. He longed to delay a confrontation with his father as long as possible. *Let Dad forget that they were to get their math finals back today.*

Dad exploded when he came home with a "C." What would he do when he saw an "F"? He knew a lot of the answers, Leo told himself defensively. He just froze when test time came around. *Later*—after he'd handed in his test paper—he remembered all the right answers.

Some of his anguish retreated—temporarily—when he saw his mother at the wheel of the new Chevy. As usual, Joanne had been picked up first. Next year Joanne would be in high school, too. She couldn't wait to be in the same school with him again.

"Hi, darling." His mother smiled at him with that special warmth that had sustained him through many bad moments. "There's a Thermos of lemonade in the back."

"Great. I'm dying of thirst." With an effort at high spirits he joined Joanne on the rear seat.

"What did you get on your math final?" Joanne asked as he reached for the Thermos.

"Sssh." He glared at Joanne. Mom hadn't heard, he realized with relief. She was talking to somebody who had just pulled up beside the Chevy.

"Well?" Joanne prodded in a whisper.

"I flunked," he whispered back agitatedly. "I don't want to talk about it." He pretended to be involved in drinking his lemonade.

"Want a piece of gum?" Joanne offered in instant sympathy.

"No," he rejected her offer. He wondered if Mom had forgot about the math final, or was she just waiting for him to tell her? Dad wouldn't wait. The minute he came into the house, Dad would ask. He'd start yelling right away. A "C" was bad. An "F" was awful.

"If this heat wave doesn't break, we'll have a picnic by the pond on Saturday," his mother said, keeping her eyes on the strip of road ahead. "Maura and Jeff and the kids will come with us."

Mom knew he was supposed to get the math final today, he decided, his distress soaring. He could tell by the tone of her voice. He hated it when Mom and Dad started to fight over him. Mom always taking his side, Dad insisting she was making a baby out of him. But it wasn't like he was going to have to take the whole year over, he thought defensively. He'd just have to take math in summer school. *But Dad would be so ashamed of him for flunking.*

By the time they arrived at the house, he felt sick with

apprehension. Still, he couldn't bring himself to tell his mother about the failing grade. The test paper lay hidden away in his notebook.

"Mom, it's so hot," Joanne wheedled. "Could we have some ice cream now?"

"If you do, you can't have it with dinner," her mother warned.

"Let's have it now," Joanne said ebulliently, hurrying out of the car. "Leo wants it now, too."

"No," he rejected. If he ate anything now, he'd just throw up. "I'd rather have it after dinner." He tried to sound logical because his mother was gazing at him in that funny way that said she was worrying about him.

"Okay." Joanne shrugged. "I'll have mine now. You can have yours after dinner."

At the front door Joanne made a dash down the hall for the kitchen.

"There's mail for you, Leo. There on the hall table," his mother said. Another odd look on her face.

"Thanks." Puzzled, he reached for the large manila envelope without bothering to glance at the return address. It must be another sports magazine Dad had subscribed to for him. Always hoping he'd become interested in baseball or football. It didn't mean he was a sissy because he wasn't nuts about sports.

Not until he was in his room did he look at the envelope. He read the return address and broke into a cold sweat. For a moment he was sure he was going to be sick. The manila envelope was from Harvard. Numbly he ripped it at one end and pulled out the college catalog. He stared at the cover, his throat so tight he felt as though a rope were squeezing out his breath. Then, in a surge of revulsion, he dropped the catalog on his neatly made-up bed.

Now he understood. Dad had sent away for it in his name. He wouldn't be a high school junior until next year, but already Dad saw him registering for Harvard. *With his grades in math and science?* He'd never make it.

He didn't want to go to Harvard, he told himself in shaky defiance. He didn't want to go to a college far away from home. Why couldn't he go to school right here in Dallas? No matter what Dad said, he wasn't going to law school after college. He'd hate being a lawyer.

What did he want to be? The truth leapt traitorously into his mind. Up till now he'd never admitted it, even to himself. He wanted to be a writer. Like Jeff. But Dad would kill him if he said that.

He recalled a conversation between his parents a few nights ago, when Mom talked about Jeff starting a new novel. Mom had sounded pleased. But Dad said with such contempt, "*How can Jeff pretend to be a writer? What's he ever sold?*"

The only time Dad had ever been proud of him was at his bar mitzvah last year. *The only time.* It wasn't his fault that he didn't get an "A" on every test. He could get into lots of colleges, Mom said, even with his grades. Why did it have to be Harvard?

But in a couple of hours Dad would be back from making his deliveries in the city. He'd ask to see the math test. Mom would be disappointed that he'd failed, but she'd remember it was the first time he'd ever flunked a test. Dad would carry on as if he'd disgraced the whole family.

He sat on the edge of his bed, fighting against a bout of nausea. His eyes galvanized to the Harvard brochure. Math wasn't going to be any easier next year. It would be worse. He'd have to take geometry. He'd never pass. *He'd never get out of high school.*

Suddenly a strange calm settled over him. He knew what he had to do. He had to take the only escape open to him. He'd never have to worry again about failing a test. He wouldn't have to listen to Dad yelling because he couldn't make it into Harvard. He wouldn't have to fight about not going to law school.

He rose from the bed and walked to his closet, his mind dealing with practical details now. There was that jump rope Dad had given him last month—trying to make him work out like prize fighters did. And Dad had put up that basketball hoop in his room last summer. The fixture was strong, because Dad always said things should be put up to last. He'd put the loop around that fixture, climb up on a chair, put his head through the loop, and then jump off.

After that he wouldn't have to be afraid of anybody.

Chapter Fifteen

IN THE KITCHEN Katie lifted the lid from the pot roast, aromas of herbs and spices rising pleasingly from the Dutch oven. But her mind was not on dinner preparations. Once again she worried about the conflicts between her husband and her son. From the moment she saw Leo waiting in the schoolyard, she knew he was upset. She hadn't pushed him about the math test. In his own time he would tell her. But she knew that the moment Harry walked into the house, he would ask about the math final. And instinct told her that Leo had received a low grade—or worse, a failing one. He'd never failed up till now.

What had possessed Leo to write away to Harvard for that college bulletin? Was he having some last-minute change of heart about trying for admission? It wouldn't happen. Even Harry must realize that. Not just the grades. It seemed to be common knowledge that Harvard—like other Ivy League colleges—had quotas for Jewish students.

Katie crossed to the table to set four places. With the sun going down, the heat was less intense, though the air was still oppressive. Finishing up, she heard a car pull into the driveway. Harry was home.

All at once the churchlike quiet of the late afternoon was pierced by shattering screams.

"Joanne!" Immobile with terror for an instant, Katie raced from the kitchen now. "Joanne!" The screams agonized, coming one on top of another. *From Leo's room.*

"Katie?" Harry was charging through the door now.

"Joanne!" Propelled by the suspicion of some unthinkable horror, Katie hurried to the door of Leo's room. "Oh my God!"

Even before she fell to her knees beside Leo—the rope about his neck, the basketball hoop and fixture brought down by the weight of his falling body—she knew he was dead.

"Joanne, darling . . ." She scrambled to her feet to pull her daughter into her arms, trying to avert her gaze from the prostrate body on the floor. "Darling, don't look at him. Please, don't look at him."

"What did he do?" Harry's voice was at the edge of hysteria. "Katie, what happened?"

"It's your fault." All at once Joanne was no longer screaming. She swung accusingly to her father. "You made him do this! He couldn't tell you he'd failed his math final. You did it! You did it!" Now Joanne sobbed uncontrollably, her small frame shaking as her mother held her.

"I shouldn't have given him the brochure from Harvard," Katie chastised herself. *This was unreal. A nightmare. In a little while she'd wake up and know it was a nightmare.* "I should have thrown it away." Leo was gone. Her son was gone. He'd never talk to her again. He'd never smile at her again in that sweet little way that said he loved her.

"It came already?" Harry was frozen in shock. Trying to cope with reality.

"*You* sent for it?" Katie stared at him in disbelief. "And

it had to come today of all days! Harry, how could you do that to him?"

"I wanted only the best for him." Harry's voice was leaden, his face drained of color.

"You killed him!" Joanne shrieked. "I hate you! I hate you!"

"Darling, I want you to lie down in your room." Katie half-carried Joanne from Leo's room and down the hall to her own. "Please, darling, lie down for a while. Then we'll talk." She stood there beside the bed while Joanne sobbed heartbreakingly into her pillow.

Knowing she must remain in control, Katie made her way to the telephone. Maura would help her do what must be done. In accordance with Jewish law, Leo must be buried as soon as possible. While Katie talked in agonizing whispers with Maura, she heard Harry at last emerge from Leo's room and move slowly down the hall and out of the house.

Only when she was off the phone with Maura and had gone back to sit beside the body of her son did Katie see the note Leo had left. Too stunned to cry, she reached with a trembling hand for the sheet of paper on the bed. *"Dear Mom and Dad, I can't ever be what you want me to be"*. Not *her*, Katie thought in anguish. She'd made no demands of Leo. *Harry* did. *"I'm sorry. I love you. Leo."*

She sat on the floor, one of Leo's hands in hers, until Maura and Jeff arrived. Now she was caught up in their shock and sympathy.

"You're not to blame yourself, Katie," Maura reiterated, finally drawing Katie away from Leo's room while Jeff made the necessary phone calls. Harry had gone off into the fields to deal with his grief. "You're not to blame for what happened."

For Katie the next twenty-four hours passed in painful confusion and disbelief. Joanne was under sedation. Through the night Harry sat alone on the porch, while Maura sat with Katie over endless cups of tea. Why did women always seek comfort in tea? Katie asked herself.

At last the family and a few friends gathered for the funeral service and then the burial, in a hastily bought plot in a nearby cemetery because Katie rejected Harry's wish to see Leo buried in a field behind the house. Even as she stood at the gravesite, holding her sobbing daughter in her arms, Katie was trying to cope with the days ahead. There was no way she could stay on at the house with Joanne. It would be too agonizing for both of them. Where could she go with Joanne?

Already there was a wall between Harry and herself. A wall that Joanne had erected with her accusations. Katie made no effort to examine her own feelings about this. She could deal only with the knowledge that Leo—her precious son—was dead. How was she to survive this? Yet for Joanne's sake she knew she must.

Not until the evening—when the family was at last alone in the living room of the farmhouse—did Joanne speak again to her father.

"You killed Leo," she said with a calm that disturbed Katie more than her hysteria. Her eyes too old for her years. "You made him do it. Why don't you go away now and leave us alone?"

"Joanne, don't talk that way to me," Harry blustered. Seemingly relieved, though, that she had abandoned her unrelenting silence toward him. "Leo was my child. I loved him, the way I love you."

"I don't want your love!" Joanne lashed back. "It's selfish and mean! It killed Leo!" Again her voice edged toward hysteria.

"Katie, talk to her," Harry pleaded. "Make her understand I didn't do this."

"We'll talk later," Katie said, her gaze focused on Joanne. How many times had she pleaded with Harry not to badger Leo the way he did? The contents of Leo's brief letter were etched on her brain. They had failed him. They had failed their son.

"You don't blame me. Do you, Katie?" Uncertainty crept into his voice.

"No more tonight," Katie said exhaustedly. "This has been the most awful day of our lives. . . ." What could compare to losing a child?

"I don't want to have to see you anymore," Joanne told him. "Go away and leave us alone." She turned to her mother. "Divorce him! He's a murderer! He killed Leo!"

"Joanne, I want you to go to your room and try to sleep," she said unsteadily. She knew Joanne would never forgive Harry for Leo's death. She had to tread carefully—or she'd lose her daughter, too. "I'll turn on the fan for you."

"I don't want the fan!" Joanne's voice rose to a high, thin wail. "I want Leo. I want my brother."

"You blame me, too," Harry accused Katie.

"No," she denied, while doubts taunted her.

"Don't lie to me, Katie. I know you too well." He paused, seemed to struggle for breath. "We're not a family anymore. You and Joanne don't want me in your lives."

"Harry, don't say that!" Terror welled in her. Yet deep within she sensed that this was the way it had to be. She couldn't think of Harry and herself now. She must think of Joanne. Whatever Joanne needed to survive, she must have.

"You've already decided." Harry read the message in her eyes. "You and Joanne will go one way, and I'll go another. I'm leaving this house tonight. . . ." For an instant he wavered. Katie understood; he wanted her to insist he remain. But the words refused to come.

"Then I'll never have to see you again." Joanne's eyes were overbright. "That's what I want."

"Tomorrow morning I'll see our lawyer," Harry told Katie. Waiting, she thought, for her to refute this. After a moment of loaded silence he continued. "He'll arrange for the divorce. I'll sign whatever papers are necessary before I leave the city." *This wasn't happening. It was unreal.* "I'll take a thousand dollars from the savings account. I'll need that to get me back to New York and into a new life. Everything else is yours. You can run the business without me."

"I'll try. . . ." Katie was in shock, yet she knew this was the only way to save Joanne. She knew she must choose between her husband and her daughter.

Harry walked slowly from the living room into the bedroom Katie and he had shared for sixteen years. Katie lowered herself into a chair, her strength ebbing away. Joanne stood beside her with eyes fastened to the doorway. Waiting, Katie thought in agony, to see her father leave the house.

Katie heard Harry's footsteps in the hall. He appeared in the doorway, carrying one large valise.

"I'll make all the arrangements with the lawyer tomorrow morning," he told her. Ashen, dispirited. "I'll leave the car at the airport tomorrow night—I'll take the 'sleeper' to New York. You can pick up the car there the following morning."

Katie watched as he turned away. She flinched at the sound of the front door opening, then closing. She closed her eyes in pain as she heard the car start up and move down the driveway. How was she to survive without Harry in her life?

But for Joanne she must survive. Somehow, she must make up to Joanne for the horror of these last thirty hours.

Part Three

Chapter Sixteen

KATIE STIRRED fretfully beneath the sheet, reluctant to come awake. She had slept little in the course of the night, succumbing at last from a blend of physical exhaustion and enervating heat. She'd had such a terrible dream, she thought; and suddenly reality slapped her across the face. She had not been caught in a nightmare. The horror was real.

She lay still, conscious of being alone in the bed she had shared so long with Harry. But Harry was on a plane bound for New York. Last night Jeff and Maura had driven out to the airport—after Harry's plane took off—so Jeff could bring back the car for her. Harry was gone. Leo—her precious son—was dead. And Joanne was desperately hurt.

Again last night Katie had slipped a sedative into the chocolate milk she had forced Joanne to drink. The doctor was convinced that within a few weeks Joanne would begin to emerge from the frightening apathy that had replaced her grief.

"Katie, she's a child," he said compassionately. "She's had a terrible time. She's faced what no child should have to face, but kids bounce back."

It would be a long time before Joanne came out of that closed little world she'd built around herself, Katie warned herself. But her every action, her every thought, must work toward helping Joanne. She mustn't think about Harry now. Only about Joanne.

They couldn't stay in this house. It was a torture chamber of memories. In a need for action she left the bed and went to the closet, pulled out the pair of valises that remained from their trip to Europe almost ten years ago. In her nightgown she began to pack.

Later in the morning she explained to Joanne they were driving into town. They would stay for a few days at a hotel. No reaction from Joanne. It was as though Joanne hadn't heard her.

"We'll stay there just until we can find a nice little house," she said, disturbed by Joanne's continuing apathy.

They would take one day at a time, Katie told herself. She mustn't push Joanne. When they settled in the car, she drove away without a backward glance at the house. She didn't dare look back.

Joanne stared out the car window in silence during the long drive into town. Seeing nothing, Katie guessed. At intervals Katie forced herself to make some casual comment. Joanne's silence was more frightening than her hysterical grief. When they were settled in their hotel room, she instructed Joanne to unpack her valise.

"I'll be right back, darling. I have to talk to the man at the desk about how long we're staying," she fabricated.

In a lobby phone booth she called Joanne's school to report on the situation, knowing Joanne could not return for the final three days of classes.

The principal was warmly sympathetic. She'd read the tiny item in the Dallas papers about Leo's death.

"Joanne's a fine student. She's taken all her finals. There's no need for her to come back for these last three days."

Later that afternoon Katie reluctantly left Joanne alone at the hotel to meet with the attorney who would handle her divorce. She'd had a brief phone conversation with him yesterday. Harry had taken care of all the necessary paper work, he'd explained. Now there were papers she must sign. But how could a few pieces of paper, some words in a courtroom, dissolve what Harry and she had shared?

After talking with the lawyer, Katie phoned Maura. They arranged for the four of them to meet for dinner early in the evening. Both women realized the urgency of keeping the business moving without interruption.

"I'm sorry to drag you and Jeff into town," Katie apologized, "but I can't take Joanne to the house. Not even to your house, Maura." She fought against tears. "Too many memories."

"Katie, it's no problem. Jeff and I will drive in."

"Thank God for you and Jeff," Katie said softly. How could she have managed in these past days without them?

She stalled as long as possible in telling Joanne that they were to meet Maura and Jeff for dinner.

"You go," Joanne said. "I'm not hungry." She crossed to one of the two windows and gazed down into the street. Her poor, forlorn baby, Katie thought in fresh pain.

"Darling, you have to come with me," Katie tried.

"Why?" Joanne reproached her, without turning from the window. "I told you I'm not hungry."

"But Maura and Jeff will be disappointed if you aren't with me," Katie told her. "They're driving all the way into town to be with us. Not Willa and George," she added. "Just you and me and Maura and Jeff. We won't stay long. I have to ask them some questions about finding a house in town." The hotel room was like a cage. "One with a garden." Joanne adored flowers.

"All right," Joanne said after a moment. "I'll go."

"Change into your pink dress and brush your hair," Katie said. "We'll wait for them in the lobby."

In the next few days she'd have to make inquiries about a private school for Joanne. It would be unthinkable for her to go to Leo's high school. And all at once she felt a touch of panic. How was she going to manage these extra expenses? A house in Dallas plus a private school. Somehow she would manage, she vowed defiantly. For her daughter she would manage.

Katie avoided taking her small group to dinner at the Adolphus dining room. That would be full of ghosts—memories of special dinners there with Harry through the years. Instead, she chose a new restaurant in town. Praying that in some small fashion this would divert Joanne from her anguish.

When they had finished their main course and had ordered dessert, Maura contrived to take Katie off to the ladies' room for a few moments. Katie understood she was chafing for a private talk.

"Jeff, tell Joanne about the new litter of puppies," Maura persuaded him. "They're adorable."

"We can't keep Willa out of the barn," he chuckled. "She's practically living in there with them."

Katie was grateful that the ladies' room was empty except for themselves.

"Katie, how could Harry walk out that way?" Maura demanded. "I couldn't believe it when you told me."

"He wouldn't have walked if I'd tried to hold him." Katie forced herself to be honest. "Maura, he didn't want to go." Her voice broke despite her efforts to be in control.

"Then why?" Maura spread her hands in a gesture of mystification.

"He had to go—for Joanne's sake. I have to choose between my husband and my child. I know there are many women who would disagree with me," she acknowledged. "Who'd say, 'A wife clings to her husband. Children grow up and live their own lives—but your husband will still be there.' Maura, I can't feel that way. Harry and I gave life to Joanne. I'll feel forever responsible for her. I have to do what I believe is right for my child."

"We love you, Katie." Tears filled Maura's eyes. "We

love Joanne. We'll always be here for you. But it seems so wrong for you and Harry to be apart. You've been through so much together. You and Harry share a kind of love that's beautiful."

"I'll always love Harry." *He was part of her.* "But Joanne has to come first. Harry and I will manage to survive—but she's so vulnerable."

Katie insisted on Joanne's accompanying her on the search for a house in town. In truth, she was fearful of leaving her alone. Then—miraculously, it seemed—at the end of the second day of looking at houses, Katie found a charming one at an acceptable rental. It was full of sunlight and with a lovely small garden—and close to the school where she hoped to register Joanne.

The large bedroom with rosebushes climbing up to its three windows would be Joanne's, she plotted. One of the two small bedrooms would be adequate as her office. She was always conscious that she must be able to carry on the business if she and Joanne were to survive. She clung to the knowledge that Harry was convinced she could.

She signed a lease on the house, tried to cajole Joanne into helping to choose furniture. Nothing from the farmhouse would come into their new home. Nothing that would remind Joanne of the past.

Katie contrived to bring Willa into the furniture-buying project, hoping Willa's presence would help to draw Joanne out of the suffocating apathy that engulfed her now. She cautioned Willa never to bring Leo's name into their conversations.

And this year Joanne's birthday—her twelfth—passed without incident.

Katie plotted with Maura to have Willa spend many of the school-vacation days with Joanne. She dreaded the long, hot summer in town, but the movies were air-conditioned, and she counted on Willa to coax Joanne into long sessions at the movie houses. With the two girls occupied she would be free to handle business.

This was a terrifying new existence, Katie admitted. Desolate without Leo and Harry. But she forced herself to be realistic. She must not allow herself to succumb to her own grief, though she knew there would not be a moment in the days and weeks and months ahead when she would not cry within for Leo. Not miss Harry.

At thirty-two she was alone, with a fragile twelve-year-old daughter to raise.

Chapter Seventeen

HARRY LEFT the cheap furnished room he'd rented for himself on West Fifty-seventh Street near Ninth Avenue and climbed down the three flights of dreary stairs to the sultry outdoors. Each midmorning he made this same trek to the cafeteria at Fifty-seventh and Eighth, where he sat over coffee and eggs and tried to face yet another day.

For the past five weeks each day seemed to fade into the next. He felt ravaged by constant insomnia. Night after night he awoke in a cold sweat, hearing Joanne's ugly accusations, seeing those same accusations in Katie's eyes. Visualizing Leo's body lying there on the floor, his neck at that terrible angle—the basketball hoop lying incongruously beside him.

Often he left his room at two or three in the morning to walk over to the all-night cafeteria that was becoming his refuge from reality. To sit there over cups of coffee and to talk politics with other nocturnal wanderers.

God, how New York had changed in fifteen years, he thought as he headed across West Fifty-seventh Street this morning. He felt like a stranger. He'd taken a subway down to the Lower East Side his second evening in town, but he couldn't bring himself to go to the house where he'd lived with his cousins. How had they survived the bad years? After the stock crash he'd lost contact with them.

At this hour there were always plenty of empty tables in the huge cafeteria. Scattered groups of people—mostly men—sat here and there. Occasionally a solitary patron like himself. He went to the counter, ordered his eggs, exchanged impersonal conversation with the counterman while he was being served. He slid the plate onto his tray, moved down the line to order coffee. Beside him a pair of elderly men—pushing away the empty hours of their obvious retirement—were arguing about the German troops in Czechoslovakia.

The world was in such a mess, Harry thought tiredly. Here at home the economy was looking up, but only because of all the war orders coming into American factories. Everybody said war was unthinkable, but how was it to be avoided?

Sitting at his table, he considered enlisting in the army. If this country got into the war, the army wouldn't be fussy about his age. Hell, at thirty-four he was strong as a bull. He was too cowardly to kill himself—but why did he keep hanging on when he'd lost everything in his life that counted?

Joanne and Katie blamed him for Leo's suicide. They hated him. *But everything he did was meant for Leo's good. He wanted the best of everything for his children.*

He didn't leave Katie destitute. She could manage the business without him. She and Joanne would be all right. But what was he going to do with the rest of his life? He ate his breakfast without tasting, sipped at coffee that held no flavor for him. Where did he go from here?

A woman holding a small child by the hand walked into the cafeteria, glanced about as though in search of someone. He saw her eyes light, and then the little girl broke loose to run forward.

"Daddy! Daddy!"

He winced as the father lifted the little girl off her feet and into the air. How many times had he done that with Joanne? There was little chance that Joanne and Katie would ever accept him in their lives again, he thought—but all at once numbness seemed to give way to something new in him. An inchoate hope that in some way he *could* share in their lives, though at a distance.

Could he pull his life together enough to provide for the two most precious in the world to him? Not just the everyday things because Katie would manage that through the business—but the special things that real money could buy.

Would there ever be a time when Joanne and Katie would welcome him into their lives again? The divorce—when it came through—would be just a piece of paper. In his eyes Katie would be forever his wife. Katie and he had shared so much together. Without her, life was nothing. Would she understand one day that he had meant only to help Leo, to give his son all the opportunities that had been denied him? Hope invaded his despondency. Could he earn himself a place in Katie and Joanne's lives again?

What could he do to prove his worth to them? Katie was always anxious for security. *Money* brought them security. How could he get back on track again? He searched his mind for a route, frustrated that no instant answer penetrated his mind.

His eyes fell on a copy of the morning *New York Times* that lay on the chair beside him. Not the whole newspaper, he noted. The business section. He reached for the newspaper, scanned the front page, was about to turn to the inside when a small item at the bottom captured his attention. His heart began to pound. Pierre Simon was in New York on business.

Of course, it was eleven years since they'd spent time together, first on the *Olympic*—en route to England—and then in London. Would Simon remember

Harry Newhouse? Could he latch onto Pierre Simon to put himself back on track?

He recalled that many grain merchants had gone under because of the stock-market crash, but he had bet that Pierre—always astute and with top-notch connections—would survive. Obviously he had.

Harry made his way with purposeful strides to the phone booths at the rear of the cafeteria. In a phone book he found the number of Pierre Simon's New York office and called.

"I'm sorry, Mr. Simon is in a meeting," a British-accented feminine voice explained. "May he return your call?"

"I'll be on the outside most of the day," Harry improvised. "Will you please tell him that Harry Newhouse called. I'll try him later in the day."

On the chance that he might be seeing Pierre that afternoon, Harry returned to his room, took one of his well-tailored suits—though hardly Savile Row—from the makeshift closet. He'd run down and have it pressed, he told himself. He couldn't show up for a meeting with Pierre Simon looking as though he was on his uppers.

As the hours dragged past, he vacillated between heady optimism and taunting contempt for this effort. Pierre Simon had been fascinated by his memory for figures, by his skills in evaluating stocks—but he'd been a twenty-three-year-old boy wonder in those days. Would Simon even remember him?

At last he was able to reach Simon on the phone. *He remembered Harry Newhouse.*

"Can you be here in about forty minutes?" Simon asked briskly after a brief exchange.

"No sweat," Harry told him. "See you in forty minutes."

Though a subway would possibly get him downtown faster, Harry splurged on a cab. When the cab approached the Wall Street area, Harry was assaulted by memories. He and Katie and the children had stayed in New York for three days before heading for Europe on that first trip, and he had brought Katie down here to visit the New York Stock Exchange. She'd been as fascinated as he when they sat in the visitors' gallery and watched the action on the floor below.

Emerging from the cab, he checked his watch. He was a few minutes early. Walk around the block—don't let Pierre Simon know how anxious he was for this meeting. Play it lowkey, he exhorted himself. That was Pierre's style.

At just past 4:00 P.M. he was sitting in Pierre Simon's office in the Wall Street district. The two men were sizing up each other with pleasure. The years had barely touched Pierre, Harry thought. Then, at Pierre's prodding, he reported with candor on his personal situation, his tone faintly strained but matter-of-fact.

"I'm sorry as hell about your son," Pierre said gently. "And about your marriage. But you're a young man, Harry. The mind's still sharp. You'll come back."

"I gather you sat out the Depression without any real problems," Harry said with respect.

"We had some bad times," Pierre told him. "We had to carry a million bushels of wheat that we'd brought at pre-Crash prices. We lost on every bushel we sold. But the troubles in your dust bowl saved us. American wheat dried up—and we recovered." His eyes were somber for a moment. "My father died in '33. I wish he could have lived to see the firm pull out of trouble. It's still Simon and Simon," he said, "even though my father is gone." He paused, his eyes narrowed in a quizzical inspection of Harry. "How would you like to work for me? Out of the Paris office."

"I'd like it very much," Harry told him. Struggling to conceal his excitement. "But my French is weak."

Pierre chuckled.

"It's not your French that I'm hiring. I remember you, Harry. You've got a phenomenal memory—and a sharp, analytical mind. In the grain business that's very useful. I'm sailing for Cherbourg in five days. Can you be available to go with me?"

"No problem."

For a few moments—five evenings later—Harry was unnerved when he boarded the *Île de France* with Pierre. His mind shot back to the return trip from Cherbourg with Katie and the children in October '29—when they learned about the stock market crash aboardship. But that was almost eleven years ago, he rebuked himself. *Concentrate on today.*

With astonishing swiftness Harry found himself living in high style. In Paris he was set up in a small but elegant apartment not far from the French Bourse—the Paris equivalent of the New York Stock Exchange—and close to Pierre's townhouse. Pierre sent him to his own tailor for custom-made suits and to his shoemaker for custom-made shoes, all charged to the company account.

Conscious of the need to communicate with business associates, Harry spent every free moment concentrating on learning to be fluent in French. He joined Pierre in entertaining clients at Maxim's or the Ambassadeurs. The two men took business associates to hear Negro singers at Bricktop's and to enjoy the antics of Kiki at the Boeuf sur le Toit. But for hours each day Pierre and Harry studied the figures reported at the Bourse.

Late in August Harry learned that he was to leave in twenty-four hours for Romania to try to consummate a deal on wheat. Pierre's secretary was arranging accommodations to Bucharest via the Orient Express.

"You'll have no language difficulties," Pierre assured him. "The people with whom you'll deal are sure to speak either English or French—or both. Just buy all you can—as cheap as you can." He hesitated. "There has been some trouble for Jews in Romania. The Iron Guard has been acting up, with Nazi backing. But you're an

American. You'll have no problems." Harry realized that Pierre was gravely concerned about affairs in Nazi Germany.

With his usual thoroughness—and a zest for this new venture—Harry familiarized himself with every aspect of the business transaction to be handled. Arriving in Bucharest, he checked into the hotel where a suite had been reserved for him. He made his contacts, bought with a shrewdness that he knew would please Pierre—and then discovered that a trade treaty signed with Germany in March put all of Romania's export products at the command of Germany.

Pierre had said nothing of this. He must have known about it, Harry thought in momentary annoyance. And then he understood. Pierre wanted him to handle this as though there were no complications. To come to it with no reservations in his mind. Pierre trusted him to think fast, work out a solution.

"Of course, we are as anxious to ship as you are to receive the grain," the spokesman for the trio of Romanians assured him. "But you must understand that we must first clear the order with the German government."

"But it's my understanding that Germany wants no part of wheat," Harry said with a contrived air of indulgence, drawing on his phenomenal memory for a way out. He'd read recently that the Nazis—worried about Germany's need to import wheat—had declared that Germans must consume only rye. "Nazi propaganda," he pursued, "blames wheat bread for 'weakening the fighting will' of the German armies in World War One. Rye has become the national grain."

The faces of the three Romanians brightened. Though he had driven a tough bargain, Harry sensed they were eager for the transaction to go through.

"What you say is true," the spokesman conceded. "The German government should not be concerned since we are shipping wheat."

"But first we must check," one of the other two said

uncomfortably after a visual exchange with his associate. "The German government is—"

"Of course, if the wheat is moved to the port overnight," Harry interrupted, "who is to know? And I have a ship standing by. . . ."

The obvious spokesman smiled knowingly.

"With a fair amount of lei in the right hands, we should be able to handle this problem. But it will cost," he warned.

Harry haggled with him briefly, made the deal more attractive—though still satisfactory to Simon & Simon. The three Romanians exchanged smiles. The spokesman extended a hand to Harry.

"We will proceed as planned. The wheat will arrive in Marseilles on schedule."

Pierre was delighted with the way Harry had handled the business in Bucharest.

"Tomorrow morning I'm going to the château for the weekend," Pierre said, in high spirits. Harry had learned since his arrival in Paris with Pierre that his new employer had a wife—and two daughters in their early twenties—who lived on a huge country estate on the outskirts of Paris. Pierre made it clear that Yvette Simon was a wife in name only. "You take Friday off, too, and drive up with me."

Up till now Harry had spent his weekends holed up in his apartment, working on laborious computations for the business, polishing his French—and fighting against devastating loneliness.

"Sounds great," Harry said with an anticipatory smile. He understood that being invited into Pierre's country house was a signal of total acceptance.

Early Friday morning Harry joined Pierre on the rear seat of his chauffeured Rolls-Royce for the drive to the château. Harry was not surprised when Pierre initiated a discussion of a current business deal. The time rushed past as they explored the subject.

"We'll soon be at the château," Pierre interrupted the

business conversation an hour out of Paris. "My grandfather—who had done well as a banker—bought the place when my father was a small boy. At one time it was the country estate of French royalty," he said with candid pride.

They drove along a tree-lined winding road now, both men silent. Harry was caught up in pleasant anticipation. The chauffeur slowed down to turn into a private avenue lined by towering elms. At last the imposing French baroque château appeared. It was huge, Harry thought. He could envision French royalty living here in past centuries.

The chauffeur pulled to a stop before the entrance. Already a manservant was hurrying forward to take charge of their luggage. The air was fragrant, the atmosphere relaxed. Another world from Paris, Harry mused, understanding Pierre's desire for weekend escapes into this serenity.

A maid was already opening the massive front door as they approached. Pierre instructed her to have breakfast brought to them in the library, and he prodded Harry down the elegant hall lined with what were surely old masters.

"You'll meet Yvette and the girls at dinner," Pierre said dryly, and Harry understood that he and his family lived separate lives.

Over breakfast—served on individual tables in the library—the two men discussed the nonagression pact signed between the German and Russian governments, news of which had circulated just a week ago.

"The whole world assumes Germany and Russia are deadly enemies." Pierre shook his head in disbelief. "Now suddenly they're signing treaties."

"That assures Hitler he won't have to fight on two fronts," Harry pointed out grimly.

"Monsieur Simon . . ." A manservant hovered in the doorway, pale and clearly disturbed.

"Yes, Jean?" Pierre gazed up in concern.

"Perhaps you would like to listen to the wireless," he suggested. "Word just came through that the Germans are marching into Poland."

"Turn it on!" Pierre swung about to Harry. "It's happening, Harry! What we've all been dreading for months."

While Jean hovered close by, Harry and Pierre listened to the account of how German troops had marched across the Polish border at dawn. France and Britian had ordered Hitler to withdraw the troops at once, warning that if he didn't, they would declare war.

"It's a matter of days," Pierre predicted. "War in Europe."

"We've had war in Europe for years," Harry said. "What else but an act of war was Hitler's taking over Austria and then the Sudentenland, and in March Czechoslovakia?"

"I'm too old to be called up," Pierre said, "and you're an American. But we'll be losing some of our 'bright young men.' " His face was somber. "I spent three years with the French infantry in the Great War. I'm glad I'm past the fighting age."

It was clear this was not to be the relaxing weekend Pierre had promised. The two men spent much of the next three days listening to the news. Friday evening and again on Saturday they joined Yvette and her daughters at the dinner table. The three women were annoyed at all the talk of war.

"I don't want to hear another word," Yvette said arrogantly when Pierre reported that German planes were at that very moment bombing Warsaw.

Pierre's wife and daughters tolerated him, Harry thought compassionately—and remembered with pain the love he had shared with Katie and the children. A love that had driven Leo to his death—because he feared he couldn't please his father, Harry tormented himself.

On Sunday both France and Britain declared war on Germany. Over an early Sunday dinner—scheduled to allow Pierre and Harry to return to Paris that same evening—Yvette reared at Pierre's vituperous description of Hitler.

"Pierre, you are prejudiced," she said with distaste. "I suppose it is natural, since you are Jewish." She turned to Harry. "I am of the Catholic faith. My daughters follow my faith."

"That won't make you safe if the Germans invade France," Pierre said grimly.

"The French Army will not allow that," the younger of Pierre's daughters scoffed in amusement. "France is not Poland."

An hour later Harry and Pierre were settled in the Rolls and headed back for Paris. Both men sat in silence for the first mile. Both caught up in the drama of the weekend.

"We won't have to worry about the shipment from Romania," Harry tried for a touch of humor. "The Nazis have other things on their minds right now."

But Pierre was not to be derailed from his somber mood.

"Every able-bodied Frenchman under thirty-five will be leaving to join a regiment," he predicted. "Heating fuel is going to vanish. And worst of all, we are not prepared for war. Paris will fall if the Germans decide to invade."

"Are you considering sending your family out of the area?" Harry asked. The prospect of Paris being invaded seemed unreal.

"They wouldn't go. What I suggest to Yvette means nothing to her. Yvette and I have not shared a bed in fifteen years," Pierre said after a faint pause. "She was a lump of lead, putting up with a husband. That's why there's been a series of other women in my life." Harry remembered the beautiful English secretary with Pierre eleven years ago. "She married me for money. I pay the bills. All that expensive Louis Quinze and Louis Seize furniture she adores. Her collection of gold snuffboxes and antique porcelain. And of course," he drawled, "I pay for the fabulous clothes the three of them buy from Chanel and Molyneux and Mainbocher. But not one of those three women," he said with a sardonic smile, "has ever forgiven me for being a Jew."

The first day of school was hot and humid even by Dallas standards. Katie rolled down the car window before she reached for the ignition. She strived for a casual smile as she turned to Joanne, huddled against the door on the other side of the car.

"It'll be easy for me to drive you to school every morning," she told Joanne. Actually the posh private school Joanne was to attend was only five blocks from their new house.

Joanne offered no comment. Katie's throat constricted with tension. Poor baby. She dreaded starting school today. Facing a classroom of strangers. But this was a girls' school—no boys to remind her of Leo.

"That's such a pretty dress," Katie tried again. She'd never spent so much on clothes—not since that golden period before the stock crash, when Harry was doing so well—as she had on Joanne's school wardrobe. It meant no new clothes for *her* for the next year. No domestic help. "Neiman's is a wonderful store, isn't it?"

Katie pushed down an urge to pull up at the side of the road and draw Joanne into her arms. She knew her daughter—her precious baby—would only recoil from any physical contact. But going to school every day—after the painful emptiness of the summer weeks—would draw Joanne out of her pain, she promised herself. The doctor kept saying it was a matter of time.

Each night she went to bed fearful that this would be another night when Joanne suffered a nightmare. She'd awake to the sound of Joanne's screams, hurry into the bedroom across the hall to awaken her. She would hold her precious child in her arms for just a few moments before Joanne—shivering, her nightgown damp with perspiration—would thrust her away and pretend she'd dreamed somebody had broken into the house and was going after her with a knife. She knew that Joanne blamed her, too, for Leo's death. *She was Leo's mother. She should have protected him.*

Katie drove in silence until they arrived at the long, exquisitely landscaped circular driveway that led to Miss Walters's Academy for Girls. The school was housed in a white Greek Revival mansion. Katie winced as she remembered the annual tuition required for attendance. But this was important for Joanne.

Katie joined the procession heading for the school entrance. An air of gaiety pervaded as students emerged from cars, here and there from a chauffeured limousine. Pampered young girls from wealthy homes. But Joanne was dressed beautifully, Katie comforted herself—she could hold her own with any of them.

"You have your house key?" she asked Joanne, feeling again a spurt of guilt because business would keep her away until after five.

"I have it." Joanne stared into space.

"I'll see you around five, darling." Katie struggled to sound matter-of-fact. "You look lovely."

Without a word Joanne opened the car door and walked toward the entrance. Katie followed the parade of departing cars, ordering herself not to look back. Joanne would be fine.

Joanne walked toward the school entrance in grim silence. She didn't know anybody here, she remembered—panic closing in about her. All she knew was Miss Walters—not even her own teacher. She clung to the knowledge that she had been given a guided tour of the school, that she knew the number of her classroom.

It was going to be awful here. She'd hate it.

The first day of school seemed endless. All the other girls knew each other, she tormented herself. They smiled and laughed a lot—and stared at her because she was "the new girl." But they were friendly, she conceded after a while—though she made little response to their overtures.

From almost the first day she was conscious of Betty Forbes's presence in her class. Betty was unlike anyone she'd ever known. She exuded merriment, as though daring anyone to challenge her high spirits. Joanne saw the glint of rebellion in her eyes.

It didn't bother Betty when Miss Lawrence scolded her for lack of attention. Nothing seemed to bother her. Somebody had whispered that Betty was expelled last year—nobody was sure why—and her parents had only got her back in school by giving an endowment for the library.

At the end of the second week of school Betty invited Joanne to go with her that afternoon to see the new Tyrone Power movie.

"We have a family year-round pass," Betty explained. "My father's their landlord. I'll just say you're my cousin visiting from out of town."

"Sure." Joanne's face lighted up.

"Come to my house first," Betty said. "We'll have cookies and chocolate milk, and then the chauffeur will drive us over."

While Joanne and Betty sat in the Forbes's breakfast room and gorged on homemade cookies and chocolate milk, Betty talked about her parents. She'd come right out and said she *hated* her father and mother, Joanne thought with awe.

"My mother's always running off to Santa Barbara or Palm Beach or New York. Before the trouble started in Europe, she was in Paris twice a year. All my father ever thinks about," Betty said contemptuously, "are his oil wells and his ranch. Of course, that means I can get away with an awful lot. . . ."

"My mother's like that." Joanne's color was high. Her words tumbling over one another. "Even at night—when I'm in the living room doing my homework or listening to the radio—she sits there on the sofa with papers all around her and figures out business stuff."

Betty and she were real friends, Joanne told herself in triumph. *She was going to learn to be just like Betty.*

Katie watched anxiously over Joanne. She had tried to persuade her to see a psychiatrist who had been highly recommended. She'd sought out a female psychiatrist, suspecting Joanne would be more receptive to a woman. But when she'd tried to talk to Joanne about it—oh so tentatively—Joanne had locked herself in her room and wouldn't come out until the next morning.

For a few minutes she had been in panic. Then she heard the small Emerson radio she'd bought for Joanne's room blaring out the evening's episode of *Amos 'n' Andy* and drew a sigh of relief.

The holidays were especially difficult. At Thanksgiving she invited Maura and Jeff and the children to come over. She stressed to Joanne that Maura was working so hard for the business that she would be too exhausted to make a big dinner. But she was upset by Joanne's coldness to the Warrens.

Joanne wasn't cold, she analyzed finally while they sat at the dinner table and talked about the turmoil in Europe. Joanne was polite but impersonal. Maura and Jeff and the children might have been strangers.

Moments after they left the dinner table, Joanne received a phone call from Betty.

"That was my friend Betty," she explained self-consciously. "She's coming over with her chauffeur to pick me up. We're going to the movies."

Katie understood the two girls had arranged this earlier. She managed a tight little smile of acquiescence—when she wanted to go over and shake Joanne for such blatant rudeness. For all her life—until she started that fancy private school—Joanne had considered Willa her best friend.

"My heart hurts for those British kids." Maura ignored Joanne. "Either sent away from their families or sleeping in bomb shelters every night."

"This whole mess will be worse before it gets better," Jeff warned.

Usually the Warrens came to them for Chanukah, and they went to the Warrens' for Christmas. Not this year, Katie resolved. Probably, she thought cynically, Joanne would ignore Chanukah and spend most of the Christmas school vacation in Betty's company. But they were at that age, Katie tried to comfort herself. Approaching their teens and all wrapped up in themselves.

It wouldn't always be this way. Joanne would come out of this in time. The way the doctor kept telling her.

Chapter Eighteen

HARRY SPENT New Year's Eve alone in his apartment. The spacious living room was dark except for the muted illumination provided by the gray-edged logs in the fireplace grate. The only sounds in the room were an occasional pop from the slow-burning wood. Earlier—in a need for silence—he'd turned off the radio with its depressing news of the war.

He had been invited to several affairs, including a party given by Pierre at his townhouse, but he had known that this last day of the year would be a special torment to him. It was the first New Year's Eve in seventeen years that he had not spent with Katie.

In the months since he had come to Paris he had

written—and torn up—half a dozen letters to her. Each time hope gave way to despair. Katie didn't want him in her life. He was a pariah to his wife and daughter.

At close to midnight he walked to a window, pushed aside the drapes, and looked out upon the almost-blacked-out city. Never had he experienced such loneliness. He was a man in exile. What a rotten way to welcome a new year, he mocked himself.

After the initial excitement brought on by the declaration of war—plus the establishment of air-raid shelters and the distribution of gas masks—Parisians had shrugged their shoulders and settled down to a life that was almost normal. French formality had weakened. The city was colorful with the splash of military uniforms. British, French, and Polish young men converged on Paris on their first leaves or on weekend passes.

He and Pierre had heard a marvelous new singer at the Élysées Bar. They saw Maurice Chevalier at the Casino de Paris. The theaters were beginning to reopen, but nightclubs closed at 11:00 P.M. sharp.

Still, Harry realized, there were many Parisians who grumbled that this was a phony war. Of course, they'd been shocked by the six-week campaign that devastated Poland. That and the fighting in Finland seemed to be part of another world. The raids by German U-boats against Allied convoys on the Atlantic seemed remote to them. Even Frenchmen in uniform complained about sitting still behind their Maginot Line, while the Germans dug in behind their Siegfried Line. The French went through each day, he thought, with the conviction that the Maginot Line fortifications prevented any invasion of the country.

Now Harry turned away from the window to inspect the French ormolu clock above the marble mantel. The hands moving inexorably into the new year. A year that Leo would never see.

He was not an evil man, Harry thought with fresh anguish. No father could love a son more than he'd loved

Leo. He'd wanted only the best for his children. And in wishing for that, he'd lost everything that held meaning for him.

Thank God, he told himself as the hands of the clock met at the top, the war would never reach America. Katie and Joanne were safe.

In the early months of 1940 Harry welcomed the business trips that kept him on the move, allowed less time for painful introspection. The war created problems; but once these were solved, the profits were high. The company had never been more prosperous.

He and Pierre dined with friends at the Ritz on occasion, but more popular with Pierre's circle were the small dinner parties at private houses. They attended the theater and afterward went to someone's home for scrambled eggs and champagne—champagne being more available than coffee. Harry was ever amazed at socializing with such celebrities as Lady Mendl, who had been the famous decorator Elsie de Wolfe, and with Coco Chanel and Sacha Guitry and Jean Cocteau. The guests at a memorable dinner included the Duke and Duchess of Windsor, who had returned to Paris after an early flight at the declaration of war.

Inevitably at these affairs Harry visualized Katie's excitement if she had been here with him. He remembered their Sunday trips from the Lower East Side to the regal lobbies of the uptown hotels, when he and Katie pretended to be part of the scene. Katie could hold her own with anybody, he thought with nostalgic pride. She had a special aura of gentility and elegance. He had never envisioned a life without her.

Almost overnight, it seemed to Harry, Paris lost its drab winter grayness. The sky was a radiant blue. Varicolored hyacinths pushed through the earth into glorious bloom in all the public gardens. The chestnut trees were ablaze with yellow blossoms.

It appeared to Harry that every Frenchman not in uniform was fishing along the *quais* of the Seine, where the book markets were thriving now. Suburbanites thronged the garden shops for seeds and fertilizer. Soldiers on leave sought out the pet stores along the Seine to buy mascots for their units.

Harry and Pierre—escorting a pair of attractive French models—attended the gala starring Maurice Chevalier and Gracie Fields at the Opera, a benefit for soldiers' recreation centers. Harry knew both girls were sleeping with Pierre—and he could have his choice of either. But Harry remained celibate.

The never-drastic regulations about food rationing appeared to be easing up. Officially Mondays, Tuesdays, and Wednesdays were meatless days. But on Mondays restaurants were allowed to serve beef, veal, and mutton in the form of stews or croquettes. On Tuesdays sweetbreads and liver were not regarded as meat, and on Wednesdays pork was not considered meat. At all times poultry, game, and baby lamb could be served.

Paris in the spring would have been intoxicating for him except that he was haunted by his personal anguish. On a beautiful afternoon in early April—en route to the Ritz Bar to meet a client—Harry watched a pair of pretty early teenagers half-skipping along the street in some private delight. One with lush dark hair cascading down her back reminded him of Joanne. His mouth went dry as he remembered Joanne's lovely exuberance, her *joie de vivre* that he had destroyed. But she was so young, he sought to comfort himself. She would be the old Joanne one day soon.

She would be thirteen in June! His daughter almost an adolescent. But he wouldn't be there to watch the changes, to see her budding into womanhood. Katie had been only sixteen when they were married. Mother and daughter were so physically alike it was astonishing.

All at once he was assaulted by a need to reach out to

Joanne. To make her understand that she never left his thoughts. Pierre was sending one of his "bright young men" to the United States next week, he recalled. Despite the dangers from the U-boats, Pierre's representative would travel from England to neutral Portugal to catch Pan Am's *Yankee Clipper* for the twenty-six-and-a-half-hour flight to New York. He would carry with him a birthday present for Joanne, Harry resolved.

He would buy a wildly expensive Paris frock for Joanne's thirteenth birthday and have it mailed from New York City to assure its arrival. Joanne had adored pretty dresses since kindergarten. He hesitated an instant. Instinct warned him that Katie would not be able to bear staying on at the farm. She would continue the business, but she would have moved with Joanne into another house. They had been mentally attuned too long for him not to realize this. Send Joanne's birthday present care of Maura, he decided. Maura and Jeff would never leave their farm.

Changing his destination—so he would be a little late for cocktails, that was accepted in Paris—he headed in the direction of a small, smart shop admired by Simon & Simon secretaries. They admittedly could not afford to buy there, but he'd often heard them chattering with wistful delight about a dress displayed in the window. He'd know what size to buy, he thought in a surge of high spirits. Joanne was surely as tall as her mother now. Slim like Katie.

Fifteen minutes later Harry emerged from the dress shop, whistling, pleased with his choice, envisioning Joanne's eyes when she opened the box and saw the dress inside. Perhaps it was a little grown-up for thirteen, Harry conceded, but Joanne would love it.

He tried to push aside the wistful hope that Katie would accept this as a peace offering and write to him. He knew the odds were against this. Yet hope lent a bounce to his steps as he turned into the Ritz to meet his client. The man would assume, of course, that the elegant box held a gift for his mistress. But there had been no woman in his bed since he'd left Katie.

Maura heard the car pull up in front of the house. That would be Jeff, returning from the city. He'd be hot and thirsty, she guessed, and reached into the icebox for the pitcher of ice tea.

"Hey, Maura!" Jeff yelled as he strode into the house. "What the hell is this?"

Maura put down the pitcher and walked to the doorway.

"What the hell is what?"

"I found this parcel on the front porch. We must have been back in the greenhouses when the postman arrived."

"I didn't order anything from Sears Roebuck," Maura began, while Jeff walked into the kitchen and dropped a handful of letters on the table, simultaneously holding up the parcel with an air of triumph.

"It's not for you. It's addressed to Joanne."

Maura stared at him in bewilderment.

"Why would something for Joanne come here?"

"Because it's from Harry. He's in Paris!"

"He sent her a birthday present," Maura guessed, reaching for the box. "Her birthday is in June."

"What's Harry doing in Paris? Doesn't he realize there's a war on? Sooner or later Hitler's going to invade France."

"Leave it to Harry not to care. Did you pick up the seedlings?"

"Oh, sure."

Jeff was as excited as if they'd struck oil, Maura thought, inspecting the box with awe.

"Get them out to the greenhouse before they burn up in this heat," she scolded. "Oh, have some ice tea first."

"Where are you going?" Jeff asked in astonishment as

she reached into a drawer for her purse and clutched the box under one arm.

"Into the city to give this to Joanne. Jeff, this is the first word they've had from Harry since he left!" Maura was enraptured by the possibilities this offered.

"Joanne's in school, and Katie will be out on her route. You may have to hang around for an hour or two."

"I have a key to the house," she reminded him. "I'll leave the box on the hall table and come back home. Jeff, I can't just let the box sit here until Katie comes out tomorrow morning!"

In a becoming summer print that was her latest acquisition from Neiman's—and shockingly expensive, even to her—Joanne lingered with Betty on the rear seat of the Forbes's chauffeured Cadillac, parked now before the Newhouse residence.

"Ask your mother if you can sleep over on Saturday night," Betty coaxed. "My mother's going to a house party in Waco. My father has some business convention down in Houston. He'll be away, too. We can sneak into his bedroom and dig out the doctor books he hides in his closet. Wow, they tell everything about you-know-what."

"She won't let me if she knows both your mother and father are out of town," Joanne said rebelliously. It wasn't enough that the Forbes had a live-in housekeeper plus Zeke and the maid.

"Don't tell your mother," Betty giggled. "Say I'm having a slumber party. Then she won't ask questions."

"Miss Betty, your mama is gonna want the car in a few minutes," Zeke called good-humoredly from behind the wheel. "You better lemme take you home."

"I'll call you later, Jo. Just tell your mother you're coming to my house for a slumber party."

Joanne remembered her mother wouldn't be home until close to dinnertime tonight. It was the second time this week. But *she* didn't care. It make her feel important to run around on business appointments.

Joanne unlocked the door and walked inside. The foyer smelled of lemon oil, she thought, frowning in distaste. That meant Millie—who came in for four hours twice a week now—had been here cleaning.

She gazed in curiosity at the box on the hall console table. She put down her school books and picked it up. Had Mom bought something for her? Not something mail order! She never wore anything from the catalogs anymore.

She glanced at the label. It was addressed to her. Then her gaze moved upward to the return address, and suddenly her heart was pounding. She felt a wave of nausea that immobilized her for a moment.

Did he think he could come back to them? She wouldn't let him. She'd run away if he tried. Mom wouldn't let him come back, would she? In a need to express her rage, she reached for the carton and tried to rip it open. She shrieked in frustration, then ran to the kitchen for a knife to undo the careful wrapping. But before she lifted out the contents, she slashed the return address—again and again until it was illegible. *She never wanted to see him again. Not ever.*

She pulled the exquisite printed silk dress from the protective layers of tissue and attacked it with the knife, determined to reduce it to shreds. *He killed Leo. He was a murderer.*

Holding the torn remains of the dress in her hands—the knife thrown aside—she stood swaying in anguish, reliving that awful moment when she walked into Leo's room and saw him lying there with the rope about his neck.

"Leo, why did you do it?" she sobbed. "You shouldn't have left me!"

Her voice soared into hysterical weeping as she collapsed on the floor . . . still clutching at what was meant to be a thirteenth-birthday gift.

Guilty that she was so late in coming home—normally she was in the house by six, and it was a few minutes past seven—Katie let herself into the house. She had phoned three times to tell Joanne she would be late, but Joanne hadn't answered. Probably she had gone to the library to look up something for a school paper.

"Joanne?" she called from the foyer. Noting the school books that lay on the foyer table. Surprised that no sounds came from the living-room radio. Like 30 million other Americans, Joanne was addicted to *Amos 'n' Andy*. "Joanne?"

Puzzled, Katie walked down the hall to Joanne's bedroom. Millie had made the bed up and picked up after Joanne. *Where was she?* Alarm began to tug at her. She hurried from the bedroom and out toward the kitchen.

She'd meant to tell Joanne to take the tuna-noodle casserole out of the refrigerator and put it in the oven so there wouldn't be a long wait for dinner. They'd have that, she thought in a corner of her mind, with steamed vegetables and fruit salad.

"Joanne . . ." She paused at the kitchen doorway and stared at the small, huddled sleeping figure on the floor. Galvanized in shock. *What were those rags she was holding?*

Katie dropped to her knees beside Joanne. What new nightmare had come to taunt them? Her eyes fell on the discarded, ripped carton. The knife on the floor. Something had come in the mail that upset Joanne terribly.

"Joanne," she tried again. She had to know what happened. "Baby, please—"

"I don't want to talk to you. I don't want to talk to anybody," Joanne whimpered.

"Darling, what happened?"

"Don't let him come back to us!" *Him? Harry?* "I'll run away if you do. You'll never see me again."

"Darling, you mustn't lie on the floor that way." She

struggled to sound calm, though inside she was falling apart. Harry had sent a present, and Joanne had been thrust back into those awful days, Katie interpreted. "I want you to go into your bedroom and lie down. Come on now, darling." She fought to lift Joanne bodily from the floor. "Everything's going to be all right. In a little while I'll bring you a tray in bed."

Joanne allowed her mother to help her to her bedroom. Katie subdued her initial impulse to cradle Joanne in her arms and rock her as though she were a baby again. Instinct told her that part of Joanne's rage reached out to herself.

At her mother's persuasion Joanne changed from school clothes to pajamas, then sought refuge in the bed. Katie stood still for a few moments, gazing down with love and apprehension at her tormented child. Joanne lay with her knees drawn up to her blossoming young breasts, her face buried in the pillow. Trying to hide, Katie thought, from a memory too painful to bear.

She left Joanne's bedroom and hurried out to the kitchen. Her hands trembling, she reached for the wrappings. She crossed to the telephone to call Maura. In moments of crisis she always went to Maura.

She listened with a pounding in her head while Maura explained about how the package had arrived at the Warren house.

"It was addressed to Joanne. From Harry. I shouldn't have left it in the hall that way. I should have put it in your bedroom," she reproached herself, "so you could have handled it best. Katie, I'm so sorry."

"Maura, do you remember the address?"

"Only that it was Paris." *Paris? The French were fighting a war! What was Harry doing there?* "I was too excited to think straight. Here was your first word from Harry in all these months. . . ."

"It's just as well that you don't remember. I might have written to him—and that would have been wrong."

"Katie, I think Joanne needs some professional help,"

Maura said apologetically. "I know how hard you try to make things right for her, but—"

"I've tried to talk to her about that." She'd shared everything with Maura except this. "Joanne wants no part of it. I said, 'Darling, just talk to this doctor'—but she refuses. You know how kids feel about psychiatrists. And I've gone and asked for advice. Two different doctors. They've told me the things I already know. But they said that unless Joanne will cooperate, they can't do anything."

"Katie, I feel awful about this. If I hadn't left the box there, this wouldn't have happened."

"She had to know, Maura." All at once Katie felt drained of strength. "Her father made an effort. She rejected it. I won't do anything to upset her. Together we'll work through this."

"Of course you will," Maura comforted.

"But, oh God, I dread her birthday." For weeks now she'd debated about giving a fabulous party for Joanne. Thirteen was so important. And she'd been so sure—until today—that Joanne had come to accept Leo's death. Now it was as though it had happened yesterday. "How do I know what's right for her, Maura? How do I protect her from more hurt?"

Chapter Nineteen

IN THIS spring of 1940 most Parisians took the war for granted, reconciled to its existence into the unforeseeable future. It was still "the phony war," though the lack of fuel to heat houses plus the defection of servants to the war effort had persuaded many of the wealthy to close up their homes and move into such refuges as the

Ritz. Pierre had shut off much of his townhouse and made do with one elderly manservant. Harry had the services of a woman who came in to clean twice a week.

At daybreak on Friday, May 10, Harry was awakened from deep, troubled slumber by the sound of air-raid sirens. There had been no daylight *alerte* since the first weeks of the war. He threw aside the bed covering and—conscious of the sharp chill—hurried to a bedroom window. From other windows on the square he spied anxious faces, all eyes gazing up into the gray morning sky.

The antiaircraft guns were roaring. Tracer shells were being fired to brighten the sky. The drone of plane motors was ominous. Were they German bombers or French pursuit planes looking for Germans? No way that a bomber could be brought down over the city, he thought grimly. It would cause too much devastation.

But in a matter of minutes faces began to disappear from the windows as residents retreated from the uncomfortable early-morning cold to seek another hour or two of sleep. Harry lingered, caught up in the drama of the moment. Below he saw a milkman urging his two horses onward as though nothing had occurred to disturb the morning calm.

He withdrew from the window, went to a closet for his robe, and walked out to the kitchen to put up coffee. He knew sleep was over for the night. When he finally dressed and left the apartment to head for the office, he discovered that hordes of residents were impatient to buy the morning newspapers. The police had been called to herd purchasers into queues that extended for almost a block.

Now he learned that Hitler's forces were simultaneously invading neutral Luxembourg, Belgium, and the Netherlands. The French confidence about the status of the war had suffered a staggering blow.

Some wealthy socialites left for Biarritz. Pierre held agitated phone conversations with his wife and daughters, Harry knew, but the three women refused to leave the country estate. They refused to believe that German planes were capable of dropping bombs in every corner of the country. They were convinced their area was too lightly populated to warrant attack.

"What the hell's the matter with them?" Pierre railed in frustration as the two men sat in Pierre's office long after the staff had left for the day. "Do they think they're immune to the whole German Army?"

"Pierre, have you thought about yourself?" Harry asked tentatively. "If the Germans take Paris, you'll be in an especially hot spot. Every Jew here must be aware of that. Except myself," he mused. "I'm an American citizen."

"I don't know why you stay," Pierre said, his eyes reflecting his gratitude. "Your passport will get you out of the country. The *Yankee Clipper* is still flying out of Lisbon."

"I'll stay for now." Harry clung to a meager hope that some word would arrive from Texas. That Katie would want to bridge this terrible gap between them. He'd stay in Paris until the last moment. Like Pierre, he suspected that the city would eventually fall to the Germans.

"But we should make plans," Harry said.

"If the Germans approach Paris, we'll run," Pierre said grimly. "I live with the hope of a miracle."

On the morning of May 17, Harry sat at his desk and tried to consider how the company could continue its operations in the face of the escalating war. He looked up with a start when the door swung open and Pierre strode into the room.

"The Germans are heading for Paris. We have to get out fast."

"How do you know?" Harry had not expected anything so swift.

"A friend at the embassy just alerted me. He told me, also, that I'm on the Nazi hostage list. A rich Jew," he mocked himself. "A prize. I'm leaving the staff in charge of the company. Meet me in exactly two hours"—he checked with his watch—"at my house. Don't bring more than one large bag. It's wise to travel lightly." He hesitated. "Perhaps it would be all right for you to stay. The United States isn't in this war. But I don't trust the Nazis."

"I don't trust them either," Harry said. "We'll get out of this together."

In little more than an hour Harry was ringing Pierre's doorbell. Pierre himself responded. His manservant, he explained, had packed up and moved out.

"As I said before, it's bad enough to be a Frenchman at a time like this. It's far worse to be a Frenchman and a Jew." His smile was wry. "We'll take the Rolls and head for the border. But first I have some important packing to do."

Harry joined Pierre in the library, where Pierre proceeded to remove two paintings from their frames. Both old masters, Harry recalled with respect.

"This is my stake for the future," he told Harry. "I bought them to hang in the drawing room of the château. Yvette disliked them. They'll bring a good price in the States."

Pierre told Harry that he had managed to see his lawyer and transfer the deed to both the country estate and the townhouse to Yvette's name.

"Yvette will bring a bunch of nuns into each place," Pierre surmised. "The Germans won't confiscate the property." He paused. "At least, not for a while."

By the time Harry and Pierre were driving south, the roads were clogged with those seeking escape. Only two valises plus a hamper of food accompanied them.

"Biarritz and Bordeaux will both be madhouses," Pierre predicted. "We'll miss that by going directly to the border at San Sebastian. We'll have to cross Spain and make our way to Lisbon."

"The only airport with flights to America." Their sole

route out of Europe, Harry realized. The luxury ocean liners had been refitted, painted gray, and consigned to military duty.

Their progress to the border was agonizingly slow, and overnight accommodations were difficult to obtain. They were without gas coupons, but Harry managed to bargain for gas when the Rolls's tank was almost empty.

"Thank God we left when we did," Pierre said tiredly when they finally approached the border. Both had acquired visas for Spain and Portugal. "Another few days and these roads will be almost impassable. Not a bed available. We'd have to sleep in the car."

Once inside Spain, Pierre decided to sell the Rolls. He urged Harry to haggle with the dealers. The price offered for the immaculate Rolls was shockingly low, but Pierre accepted when Harry conditioned acceptance on their being provided seats on the train for Lisbon—already hard to come by.

They were forced to linger in Lisbon almost a week, sleeping in a rundown hotel twenty miles out of town. Finally the morning arrived when they boarded the *Yankee Clipper* and left Lisbon behind. Just under twenty-seven hours later the plane landed at La Guardia Airport in New York.

"How does it feel to be home again?" Pierre asked Harry as they walked through the busy airport.

"Unreal," Harry said after a moment.

"At fifty-one I'm starting out all over again." All at once Pierre appeared a decade older than his fifty-one years. "But, by God, Harry, we'll make it up the ladder again. More than ever before," he said with a touch of his more familiar insouciance, "the world will need wheat. We'll find it, and we'll sell it."

Katie completed the week's billing, switched off the fan that sat at a corner of her desk, and headed for the kitchen for a quick lunch. The late May heat wave was in its third day. The scent of roses behind the house was intensified by the recordbreaking temperature.

Thank God, Katie thought, that Joanne had come out of that awful time brought on by the arrival of Harry's gift last month. She'd been terrified that Joanne would retreat again into that frightening withdrawal. Betty had helped, Katie acknowledged, just by being Joanne's friend.

In the kitchen Katie poured herself a tall glass of iced tea, made a hasty sandwich from last night's chicken, and with glass and sandwich plate, went into the living room. She deposited her dishes on the coffee table, crossed to switch on the radio.

The news continued to be ominous for the Allies. Nazi troops had marched through Belgium, Holland, and Luxembourg. Their destination—the world knew—was Paris. *What was Harry doing in France?*

"Fearing the worst," a news commentator was reporting, "several million refugees have taken to the roads." *Was Harry on the run?* "In the course of the savage Nazi advance thousands of civilians—women and children among them—have been killed or wounded. . . ."

Her throat tight with anguish, Katie darted to switch off the radio. *Enough.* An instant later the phone rang. Not the business line—what she and Joanne called the residence phone.

"Hello?"

"Mrs. Newhouse?" The voice was faintly familiar.

"Yes."

"This is Sandra Mitchell. Joanne's teacher."

"Oh yes, Miss Mitchell." Katie tensed. Bracing herself for unpleasantness. She'd spoken with Miss Mitchell last month—at her request. Joanne's grades were going downhill. Not failing—as Joanne had pointed out in defiance. Not yet. Katie hadn't dared more than a gentle reproach, remembering Leo—fearful of Joanne's reaction. "Is there a problem?" She'd tried to make Joanne cut back on her radio listening, to persuade her to spend more time on studying.

"She's failed math this term," Miss Mitchell reported. "She's exceptionally bright—there's no reason for her to have failed." Frustration blended with exasperation in the teacher's voice. "I know that Joanne is capable of top grades."

"I'm so sorry. We've had some d-difficulties this year," Katie stammered. Did this mean Joanne would not be accepted for next term?

"She'll have to attend summer school," Miss Mitchell said. "And if she passes math during the summer, she'll be admitted again, but on probation."

"I understand this isn't your fault," Katie said conscientiously. Why hadn't she taken a firmer stand? Always so afraid of pushing Joanne onto dangerous ground. *She should have removed both radios from the house.* "I'll have a serious talk with Joanne. Of course she'll attend the summer session." Would she? Katie asked herself in apprehension.

Katie tried to focus on work, but this was difficult. Her eyes constantly sought out the clock. She was impatient to confront Joanne—and simultaneously dreaded it. Most afternoons Joanne and Betty were together after school. She might not be home until almost six.

Katie froze at the sound of a car pulling up before the house. That would be the Forbes's car—bringing Joanne home. She listened now, hearing the light sounds of young girls' voices. She left her office and strode down the hall toward the entrance foyer.

"Hi." Joanne tugged at the neckline of her peasant blouse. "Wow, it's hot. It's so nice at Betty's house, with the air-conditioning."

"The Forbeses can afford air-conditioning," Katie pointed out. Joanne was forever needling her because their house—like the houses of other people of their means—lacked this amenity so loved by wealthy Texans. "Joanne, Miss Mitchell called me today. . . ." She paused, took a deep breath.

"She couldn't wait to tell you. I flunked math!" Joanne's eyes were contemptuous. "She hates me."

"She's concerned about you. She knows you're capable of passing grades." Katie chose her words carefully. "She said you'll have to go to summer school to make it up."

"Betty flunked, too. Her mother's going to arrange with the school for private tutoring." Triumph radiated from Joanne. "I'm invited to spend the summer at the ranch with Betty so we can be tutored together out there—she'd hate it alone. Mrs. Forbes will call you about it as soon as she's worked it out with the school. She wants to take us out to the ranch the minute school closes."

"Do you want to spend the summer at the Forbeses' ranch?" Katie asked after a moment, masking her dismay. Joanne would be away for her thirteenth birthday.

"Sure. It'll be terrific." Joanne's eyes dared her to reject this.

"We'll talk about it after I've discussed it with Mrs. Forbes," Katie hedged. "Go wash up for dinner."

Trembling—dizzy at sudden comprehension—Katie walked toward the kitchen. Joanne had deliberately flunked math—knowing she'd be terribly upset.

Two days later Della Forbes called to invite Joanne to spend the summer at the ranch with Betty.

"I can't wait for the end of school so we can take off for the ranch," Mrs. Forbes said enthusiastically. "Dallas is uncivilized once the hot weather descends. I'm sure Joanne will love it—and Betty and she can have their tutoring together."

"It's very kind of you to invite Joanne." Katie felt self-conscious about accepting the Forbeses' hospitality. But then, it was the Texas way.

"Good, it's all settled," Mrs. Forbes said with an air of relief. "Can't you just die with these kids? But they're teenagers—what else can we expect?" Betty was thirteen two months ago. Joanne would be thirteen next month. Katie didn't want to think about Joanne's birthday. It would be traumatic for both of them—coming right after the first anniversary of Leo's death.

That evening Katie told Joanne that Betty's mother had called, and it was arranged that she would spend the summer at the ranch.

"Okay." Joanne shrugged nonchalantly and returned to turning the pages of *Life*.

Katie settled down to read the farm journal Jeff had given her this morning. The only sound in the house was that of the pair of oscillating electric fans that offered meager relief from the heat.

The phone rang. Joanne tossed aside the magazine and leaped to her feet.

"I'll get it. It's probably for me."

Katie tried to focus on the farm journal. She was attacked by mental visions of summer alone in the house without Joanne. She would worry a lot, she admitted—but she mustn't allow Joanne to know that. She would phone the ranch once a week—that shouldn't bother Joanne.

The final days of school rushed past. Joanne clamored for new clothes that must be shopped for in a hurry.

"You don't have to go with me," Joanne said with deceptive sweetness. "Just let me charge at Neiman's—like Betty does."

"I'll go with you," Katie insisted.

"All the kids at school charge at Neiman's!" Joanne flared.

"Not my kid," Katie said flatly. "We don't own an oil well."

"You're mean!" Joanne screeched.

"If you want to go to Neiman's this afternoon, then I'll have to switch an appointment with a customer. Make up your mind, Joanne."

Katie and Joanne went shopping for clothes. For a

heartbreaking little while Joanne was her old joyous self. But Katie knew she must draw the line on spending. The light disappeared from Joanne's eyes. She was silent as they waited for the selected items to be wrapped. On the drive home she clung to her side of the car, offering monosyllabic responses to Katie's efforts at conversation.

"I'm not hungry," she told Katie when they arrived at the house. "I'll have a glass of milk and go to my room to pack." They were leaving in the morning.

Katie knew not to press her. Later Joanne would wander out to the kitchen and check out the refrigerator. She would make herself a sandwich, take it back to her room, and listen to the radio behind the closed door. Couldn't Joanne understand that she didn't have the Forbeses' kind of money? Had it been a mistake to send her to a private school?

Later in the evening Katie went out to water the flowers. The heat was devastating to them. She found a kind of relief standing out there hosing down the garden.

She dreaded tomorrow morning—when the Forbeses' car would draw up before the house and Joanne would hurry out to greet Betty and her mother while Zeke would stash Joanne's luggage in the trunk of the car. She debated about giving Joanne her birthday present—a beautiful watch she'd long planned for a thirteenth birthday present. No, send it out "special delivery" just before Joanne's birthday. Or maybe, she thought wistfully, Joanne would ask her to come out to the ranch for her birthday. It was just a two-hour drive from Dallas. Yet instinct told her this wouldn't occur.

The morning was cloyingly hot. Katie showered and dressed early to give Joanne the freedom of the bathroom. Now she went out to the kitchen to prepare breakfast. Joanne's last breakfast here at home until the summer was over, she thought with a surge of loneliness.

She'd make banana fritters, she decided. Joanne loved them.

With the fritters removed from the pan and covered with a lid to keep them hot, she left the kitchen to go to Joanne's bedroom. The door was closed, as always.

"Joanne, breakfast is ready," she called. "Banana fritters."

A moment later Joanne opened the door.

"I'm not hungry. It's so hot in the house. We'll have an early lunch out at the ranch."

"All right." Katie forced a smile. Joanne was all excited about being away for the summer.

She returned to the kitchen and made a pretense of having breakfast. Joanne didn't emerge from her room until the car pulled up before the house. Betty darted up the walk to the front door, Zeke at her heels to carry Joanne's luggage to the car.

The two girls exchanged light conversation. Joanne submitted to a kiss from her mother, and then they were off. Katie stood at the door and watched the car drive away. Her view blurred by tears. She would not see her precious baby for weeks. Not unless Joanne called and invited her to come out. . . .

Katie ran a hand across her eyes. *Stop being a sentimental idiot.* She had no time for that. She had a morning appointment with a smart new restaurant opening in town. Her dress already clung between her shoulder blades. *Change into something fresh.*

She hurried back into the house, chose a cool cotton that wouldn't look wilted right away. She went into the bathroom for the bottle of Blue Grass cologne that Maura had given her on her birthday and which she used only a special occasions. A prospective new account was a special occasion, she told herself with an effort at humor.

Walking into the bathroom, she was startled by the pungent scent. Joanne had dipped into her Blue Grass, she thought tenderly. She reached for the bottle and froze in disbelief. Her eyes swung to the toilet bowl. Joanne had dumped the entire bottle of Blue Grass into the bowl. Furious at her, Katie interpreted, because she had refused to spend more money at Neiman's yesterday.

What did she have to do to win her daughter back?

Chapter Twenty

HARRY AND PIERRE took up residence in a modest hotel in the West Seventies and began to explore their options. As Pierre had feared, the New York office of Simon & Simon was closed, the small staff gone because the office had run out of operating capital. It had been impossible for Pierre to forward funds.

After several weeks of negotiations with art dealers—while Harry dug into the grain-market scene in America—Pierre made a deal for the pair of old masters he had managed to smuggle out of France. This would be his stake in starting up fresh operations.

"We're moving into decent quarters," Pierre decreed when the check for the paintings had cleared. "I can't operate from this kind of setting."

"Right," Harry agreed. If Pierre was to follow up on his American contacts, they would have to do some high-style entertaining.

Pierre and Harry moved into a suite at the Waldorf. Pierre called up prestigious contacts to announce his adventurous escape from France and his arrival in the United States.

"We're not sure just where we'll settle yet," Harry heard him say repeatedly in response to inquiries from the other end of the phone lines. "I brought Harry New-house along with me. He's very knowledgeable about the American wheat market—and we know this is a time when profits are going to climb up into the sky."

Harry understood that it was important for Pierre to set up that he had high-powered American contacts. The wealthy men Pierre contacted—none of them specifically in the grain business—might not know Harry New-house, but the fact that Pierre considered him an asset on his staff was enough to guarantee his acceptance.

"We don't need an enormous amount of financing," Pierre pointed out over breakfast in their suite on their seventeenth morning in New York. Harry was anxious now about their expenses and lack of success in finding a backer. "In the grain business a man's biggest assets are his connections and his experience."

"That was true up until a few years ago," Harry contradicted. He saw Pierre wince. Up till now they'd ignored this truth. "The situation has changed with the Depression. We need large capitalization to play in the American market." Maybe he'd made a serious mistake in believing Pierre could propel them back into the international wheat market. And there was all that talk about drafting American men—all this might be a big laugh on him. In three months he could be in the army.

"We'll raise the capital," Pierre said after a moment. Harry noted that he'd said "we." "We're having dinner Friday evening with Arnold Sinclair. He's a tough character, but sharp. He represents a lot of money—and I gather he's looking for some action. We'll have dinner downstairs, then bring him up to the suite for more talk. Work up some impressive statistics about the future of the grain business and the profits. This is important, Harry."

Harry and Pierre had a leisurely dinner with Arnold Sinclair downstairs in the Palm Garden. Harry managed to conceal his dislike for the pretentious, pudgy, ruddy-faced man whose expensive suit seemed a little tight, his pinkie ring coarse and ostentatious, his tie too flashy for the role he played in life. Harry forced himself to remember that Arnold had a genius for raising capital, contacts to guarantee excellent distribution, and European and South American connections.

In Pierre's suite the three men worked out a possible partnership. Harry understood they must contrive to survive until Sinclair brought in the necessary capitalization. Arnold Sinclair was greedy, Harry thought with amusement—he'd make sure the money came in. Sinclair knew that every indication pointed to a tremendous wartime and postwar market for wheat. But Sinclair needed him and Pierre to build a powerful organization. All his money, all his contacts, were nothing without the skills to run the business.

"This country will have to feed the world, you know," Harry said with studied casualness as Sinclair prepared to leave. "We're talking about a longtime, highly profitable venture."

"You're sure that Minneapolis is where we should locate?" Sinclair pressed for the third time.

"That'll be the core of the firm," Pierre insisted. "Harry and I will carry on operations up there. You'll handle the New York operation. Of course, we're counting on your shipping contacts. Nothing is more important than getting grain to market."

"I've got that tied up." Sinclair's smile was smug as he exchanged handshakes with the other two. "They need us as much as we need them."

For Katie the summer was a constant torment. The house seemed painfully empty without Joanne. Every Sunday night she phoned the Forbeses' ranch and talked with Joanne—careful to call after the girls' favorite radio programs were over.

After the first three weeks Joanne began to call at

midweek intervals. She was homesick, Katie thought tenderly. Brief calls when she chattered about inconsequential happenings—but Katie cherished them. But when Katie suggested that she and Betty might like to come into the city for a day or two, Joanne rejected this.

"We're having a terrific time," she insisted. "We lie around the swimming pool all day, and sometimes Mrs. Andrews—the housekeeper—drives us into the village to see a movie or have a shake." But her voice told Katie she needed to touch base with her mother. Katie clung to this knowledge.

"How's Mrs. Forbes?" Katie asked. Mrs. Andrews drove them to the village, she noted.

"Oh, she's out in Bar Harbor," Joanne bubbled. "But she'll be back in another two weeks. Mrs. Andrews is great."

"Is there anything you need?" Katie asked. *Mrs. Forbes was in Bar Harbor.* She'd said she'd be at the ranch all summer.

"No," Joanne said. "Unless you want to send me another bathing suit. A two-piece," she emphasized. "I'm tired of looking at the ones I have."

"I'll run over to Neiman's tomorrow," Katie promised.

She'd hoped Joanne might wish to come into the city a day or two—or ask her to drive out to the ranch—even if just for the day. But clearly that wasn't to be.

Though he disliked Arnold Sinclair, Harry admired the speed with which he handled the negotiations for the new company. By autumn capitalization had been set up, offices had been secured in downtown Minneapolis, and Harry and Pierre—for the moment sharing a comfortable hotel suite—were searching for apartments.

Harry was frustrated that he owned no shares in the company, though his contract called for the new firm—Simon & Sinclair Grain, Inc.—to hold stock in escrow for him to purchase within a ten-year period at a stated price. Still, his salary was impressive, he reminded himself, and his responsibilities ego-coddling.

Today—their second Saturday in Minneapolis—Harry and Pierre were on the track of apartments available for rental in prestigious neighborhoods. They were traveling about town in the company car—a Cadillac, at Pierre's insistence—that would be at their mutual disposal until a second car was acquired for Harry.

"We should consider this place," Harry told Pierre as they drove away from an attractive, meticulously landscaped building. Two choice apartments were available.

"Nobody's grabbing them at those rentals." Pierre shrugged. "Next week we'll call and make arrangements to sign leases. For now they'll do. Until we can afford one of those estates around Lake of the Isles or on River Road—or something further out on Lake Minnetonka," he said with an insouciant smile. "What do you think of this town, Harry?"

"It's where we want to be for the business," Harry said. The state's wheat crop was huge. Its transportation facilities were admirably suited for moving grain to its ultimate destination. Grain elevators dominated the skyline. "And I think it'll be an interesting place to live. It's not Paris," he joshed, knowing how Pierre missed his posh apartment there and the château. "But the university gives it class." The University of Minnesota was the third largest in the United States.

"Let's drive out on the River Road," Pierre said. "It's beautiful this time of year."

Harry had been amazed to discover that in Minneapolis Mark Twain's "mighty Mississippi" became a small stream, moving in and out of the Twin Cities of Minneapolis and St. Paul. Now, as they turned onto the River Road and saw both steep banks ablaze with autumn colors, reflected in the waters of the river, Harry thought of Katie. She would be ecstatic at the sight of this painting by nature, in magnificent yellow, orange, scarlet, and—here and there—purple.

Both he and Pierre made a showy pretense of living for the moment, but Harry knew how Pierre worried about his family in France—just as he worried about Katie and Joanne in Dallas. This deprivation of family was a special tie between them.

He'd have the office subscribe to the Dallas newspapers, he told himself on impulse. After all, the company was interested in every area that grew wheat. In some small way he'd feel closer to Katie and Joanne if he knew what was happening in Dallas. As though he were sharing their lives. Instinct told him Katie would remain there. She could run the business without him. And to Katie that kind of security was precious.

"The winters out here are rough," Pierre interrupted his introspection.

"We'll be too busy to notice," Harry laughed.

The months seemed to race past. Harry spent fourteen-hour days—along with Pierre—in building Simon & Sinclair. He was grateful to be so involved. He was subconsciously aware of the rigors of the Minnesota winter, though the houses were built to cope with this. Fortresslike dwellings with powerful furnaces protected residents from temperatures that dropped well below zero.

Harry was astonished by the brilliance of the January sun, which—even in below-zero weather—flooded his apartment, taunting the icicles. He was aware of myriad children skating on the frozen-over lakes and remembered ice-skating as a child on New York's Central Park Lake. A pleasure never enjoyed by Leo or Joanne.

Always he worried about Katie and Joanne. He knew they were not in financial want. Katie was a sharp businesswoman—no doubts in his mind she was carrying on the business successfully. But how were they faring emotionally? *Were they all right?*

At intervals he thought about sending monthly checks to Katie. Instinct warned him they'd receive the same rebuff as his gift to Joanne from Paris. *Katie and Joanne wanted no part of him. Not even the intrusion of checks.*

On this spring morning Katie sat in the kitchen with Maura over coffee while Jeff loaded the car with the day's deliveries for Newhouse customers. She was exhausted from last night's battle with Joanne.

"Joanne's all upset because she was rejected by that summer camp that she'd hoped to attend with Betty."

"You mean they didn't want their girl campers contaminated by a Jewish camper?" Maura interrupted. "Their brochure didn't read, 'Dietary rules strictly enforced'?"—the code that said Jews were acceptable. "It's like me trying to buy a house at some fancy beach resort. Irish Catholics are not accepted. Of course, we can't afford to buy a beach house, so that's no problem."

"As I was trying to tell you," Katie scolded good-humoredly, "she and Betty are off on another track now. There're two openings for a school tour to San Francisco and down the West Coast to Acapulco. Joanne couldn't be rejected, since she's a student at the school."

"That sounds like big bucks. Are you letting her go?"

"I've been stalling," Katie admitted. "I'll have to let her go. Last summer she was at the Forbeses' ranch with Betty—but Betty says she'll go on the tour this year."

"You're spoiling her rotten," Maura warned yet again. "You don't own an oil well."

"I may have to take out a personal loan to pay for the tour." Katie sighed. "I'll go to the bank this afternoon. My credit's good—I know I can get a loan. Then I'll stop off at the school tomorrow to make arrangements for the tour."

She needed to expand the business, she reproached herself. Increase her income. She remembered how

Harry had complained about feeling in a vacuum—that the business was going nowhere. But didn't most people reach a certain level and stay there the rest of their lives? In the same jobs, same houses, same circle of friends.

Jeff appeared in the doorway.

"The car's loaded. The sun's getting hot as hell. You ought to get moving, Katie."

"I dread another summer." Maura grimaced. "Here it is early April, and we had the fan on at dinner last night."

"I'll talk to you later." Katie drained her coffee cup and rose to her feet. "Can't keep our customers waiting."

Halfway into town Katie decided to stop off for gas. She always patronized the independent station that had opened up on the road about three years ago. She liked Bill and Angie Meadows, the older couple who ran the filling station. They'd come out to Texas a dozen years ago from northern New York to avoid the harsh winters—never suspecting the "blue blizzards" that infested Dallas.

She swung off the road and drove to the pumps. Bill was letting the filling station go to pot, she thought. He really should have the place painted, spruced up a bit.

"Hi." She leaned out the window as Angie approached and reached for the hose. "Where's Bill this morning?" It was strange to see Angie manning the pumps.

"You haven't stopped by for a few days," Angie said softly. "I guess you haven't heard. Bill had a heart attack three nights ago."

"Oh, Angie, I'm so sorry." Katie was cold with shock. "How is he?"

"He's still in the hospital, but he's doing all right. He'll be coming home tomorrow. But he won't be working for a while—and you know how hard it is to find help today. Everybody's running to the defense plants. I'm anxious to sell the station and take Bill down to Florida. Living's cheaper down there—and the doctor says these winters are bad for him."

"It would be easier for him down there," Katie said sympathetically. "A lot of retired people are going down to Florida these days."

"If you hear of anybody interested in buying, you send them over to us, Katie. We'd appreciate that."

"I'll mention it around," Katie promised.

They talked a few minutes about local affairs, then Katie drove away from the station and down the road. But an odd excitement charged through her. She remembered Amelia and the farm—how out of nowhere they had bought a farm. Filling stations could be good business if they were handled right. Bill was too tired—he hadn't been well enough to keep the station attractive to customers. Was she crazy to be thinking this way?

In sudden determination—feeling herself at a turning point in life—she turned into a driveway, backed out, and swung in the direction of the station again.

She wasn't thinking like Katie now, she told herself. She was thinking like Harry. If Harry were here, he'd see the potential of that filling station. It was in a good location. The nearest competitor was four miles down.

Did she dare borrow on the farm? Her heart pounded at the prospect. Guiltily she remembered how she'd refused to allow Harry to do this—and they'd lost out on what turned out to be rich oil land. All right, do what Harry would do if he was here. Buy the filling station from Bill and Angie. Dress it up with a fresh coat of paint. Pay good wages—she'd find workers if she offered that. Maybe she wouldn't make a cent the first year, but she'd figure out a way to make it profitable. People in these parts couldn't live without their cars. A gas station was essential.

Angie glanced up with surprise when Katie drove in again. Quietly Katie told her she was interested in buying. They talked business terms for a few minutes, and Katie agreed to come to the house the following evening to work out the details. Angie looked so relieved, Katie thought. She and her husband would be able to move to Florida as soon as the legal papers were drawn up and signed.

Was she taking on too much? Katie asked herself as she drove away again. But she had to make a move upward. She was playing the game the way Harry would play it. She had to gamble now. Even if Jeff was right and the car manufacturers were cutting back, people would hang on to their old cars, make every possible repair. Cars were part of their way of life—and the need would only increase.

Chapter Twenty-one

JOANNE FOLLOWED Betty into the girls' locker room—deserted during class time. Both had asked to be excused from gym today because of "cramps." Both were sure that the gym teacher was doubtful that this was true.

"Miss Blackmon couldn't ask us to prove it," Betty giggled. "I told you we'd get away with it."

"We can't stay in here for more than five or ten minutes," Joanne warned. "We'll have to go back to the gym and sit on the sidelines."

"After we have our smoke," Betty drawled, reaching into her locker.

"You have cigarettes?" Joanne was simultaneously intrigued and alarmed.

"A whole package of Lucky Strikes." Betty was opening up the pack with a triumphant smile.

"I've never smoked." Joanne was uneasy. "I'll bet you haven't either."

"I have, too. At home. My mother and father leave cigarettes all over the place. Take one and light up," Betty ordered.

Amid self-conscious giggling the two girls managed to light their cigarettes, puffed awkwardly.

"You have to learn how to inhale," Betty began—and suddenly the locker-room door was open and Miss Blackmon hovered there in outrage.

"Not only did you lie to me about your gym excuse," she seethed, "but you have the audacity to come in here to smoke!"

"My mother smokes," Betty said defiantly. "She doesn't care if I do."

"The school cares. We'll discuss this right now with Miss Walters."

"What about your gym class?" Betty countered while Joanne's eyes pleaded for discretion.

"Never mind my gym class." Miss Blackmon was grim. "Come with me."

Were they going to be expelled? Joanne asked herself in alarm. Mom would be livid. Betty's mother would be livid. She was always threatening to send Betty off to boarding school. *I don't want Betty to go to boarding school.*

At Miss Walters's office they were ordered to sit in a small room off to one side. Joanne and Betty gathered Miss Walters was trying to reach their mothers.

"My mother will yell at me, but she won't do anything," Betty whispered. "But boy, will she be mad that she has to come down to the school!"

She could handle Mom, Joanne tried to console herself. She'd just say that Bette Davis looked so gorgeous when she puffed away at cigarettes—and they were pretending they were Bette Davis. She wasn't afraid of Mom. But she was scared to death Mrs. Forbes would send Betty off to boarding school. That would be awful.

The two girls sat—growingly restless—for over an hour before their mothers arrived, within minutes of each other.

"Let's try to hear what they're saying," Betty whispered at the sound of their voices.

The exchange between the two mothers and Miss Walters was brief. Joanne and Betty were to be suspended for a week. Any repetition and they would be expelled.

"I don't need to tell you that we consider such behavior a dreadful example for the other students," Miss Walters concluded. "Now if you'll please excuse, I have a meeting to attend. The girls are there in the adjoining room."

The door swung open. Mrs. Forbes gestured menacingly to them.

"You both know you have to be punished." Mrs. Forbes exchanged a meaningful glance with Katie. "Betty, you're to stay in your room for the week of your suspension—except for meals. And this is my final warning. One more nutty act like this, and you're off to boarding school!"

"You'll stay in your room," Katie echoed Mrs. Forbes. "No radio playing. No phone calls." She knew the moment she walked out of the house Joanne would be on the phone with Betty—her bedroom radio blaring in the background.

"That goes for you, too, Betty," Mrs. Forbes added. Now she turned to Katie. "What did we ever do to deserve this from our kids?"

As Katie had anticipated, she was able to take out the necessary business loan to buy the Meadowses' gas station. There was money, too, for Joanne to go on the summer tour. Six weeks after Katie made an offer, she sat down with Bill and Angie and their respective lawyers and went through the mechanics of taking over the station. Afterward she met Maura and Jeff for an early dinner at one of Dallas's fine new restaurants to celebrate her new ownership.

"You bit off a lot, lady," Jeff said warily after they'd ordered dinner.

"You think I'm crazy," Katie guessed.

"George wants to know if he can have a summer job with you," Maura said.

"As soon as I reopen the station," Katie promised. "I was going to ask him if he'd like a summer job."

"Summer and after school, later," Maura told her. "He's already thinking ahead to college, and he knows he'll have to help."

"I can't believe he'll be a senior next year." Leo would have been a senior, Katie remembered with fresh pain.

"When we went to school back in New York, there were eight years of elementary instead of the seven George and Willa have here," Maura mused. "That puts them in college so young."

"What are you doing about hiring—outside of George?" Jeff asked curiously. "You've got a lot of hours to fill—and seven days a week."

"We'll be closed on Sundays." She'd explored the current business situation in detail, reading newspapers from all over the country. "That's already being talked about in a lot areas." She chuckled. "So I'll be an innovator in this area."

"People are going to cuss a lot if gas stations close on Sundays," Jeff said. "This country isn't at war—they don't feel any patriotic urge to keep their cars in the garages on Sundays to save gas."

"I don't expect this first year to be easy," Katie said slowly. "I'll be happy just to break even. But next year I want to open a second station. And then another. This is a business I can see myself handling," she said zealously. "With labor problems what they are, the big oil companies won't be expanding their stations. They won't find that many ambitious would-be owners wanting to invest a thousand dollars to lease a station. Not with wages jumping upward the way they are."

"What makes you think you can carry this off?" Maura challenged, but the glint in her eyes told Katie she expected an optimistic response.

"I've sat down and figured out all the angles." The way Harry had taught her, she thought to herself. "I know exactly how much profit I have to make to stay out of the red. I've studied every report I could get my hands on. I need four-to-four-and-a-half cents a gallon profit. I have to remember not to get involved in price wars. And I have to keep a steady staff that's trained to be polite and efficient."

"Where do you expect to get them?" Jeff asked seriously. "In the summer, sure—with school vacations and all. Maybe some after-school help. But otherwise . . . ?"

"I'm hiring women," Katie said and watched for the anticipated gasp of astonishment from Jeff. "Married women who want to earn money."

"Why not?" Maura said with a defiant glance at Jeff. "Women can handle a gas pump."

"What man's going to want to ask a woman to put air in his tires?" Jeff was skeptical.

"Times are changing, buster," Maura told him. "Thousands of American women are working in defense plants. In England they're overhauling planes, serving in the military. I'm not talking about little Dallas debutantes," she mocked. "And don't forget, old boy, these two women were out there in the fields working right beside you and Harry. So why can't a man ask us to put air in his tires?"

"I'm going to make a go of this gas station," Katie vowed. "And once it's on its feet," she repeated, "I'll buy a second and get that rolling. All at once I have this insane sense of confidence," she laughed. "Or is it just that I know I *have* to be a financial success?" All at once she was somber. "I *must* do this—for Joanne."

But would money ever make up for what she and Harry had allowed to happen to Joanne's fragile young life?

Business throughout the country was booming. Wheat was in great demand in Britain. The major problem in the grain market was transportation. Harry wrestled with this daily—despite Sinclair's important connections. Merchant ships with intrepid crews had to struggle through enemy mines and torpedo attacks.

Both Harry and Pierre were impatient as governmental restrictions steadily increased.

"Damn!" Harry railed repeatedly. "We're not grain merchants anymore. We're a public utility."

"But when peace arrives," Pierre pointed out, "the demand for wheat will be mind-boggling. Farms in France, Italy, and Germany are being wiped out. Harry, great times are coming for the grain merchants."

At rash intervals Harry considered enlisting. He was sure it was a matter of months before the United States was drawn into the war. He knew, also, that there were anguished moments when Pierre felt he should be with the Free French organizing in England under General de Gaulle. But both Harry and Pierre realized they were involved in an industry providing urgent wartime services.

In September President Roosevelt ordered attack "at sight" upon any German or Italian ship encountered in U.S. defensive waters by American ships or planes. By now a number of American vessels had been sunk or fired upon by German submarines. On October 17 the U.S. destroyer *Kearny* was torpedoed by a German submarine off the coast of Iceland. Two weeks later the U.S. destroyer *Reuben James* was sunk by a German submarine, with one thousand lives lost. Yet even with these losses the United States did not consider itself at war.

"Every morning I wake up and ask myself," Pierre said to Harry, " 'Is this the day the president will announce we're at war with Germany and Italy?' *What are we waiting for?*"

Katie sat with Maura and Jeff in their living room, where a blazing fire helped alleviate the December cold.

They sat in stunned silence, listening to the reports of the disaster at Pearl Harbor. Then Jeff leaned forward to switch off the radio.

"We'll listen again later. They're just repeating the same stuff over and over now."

"I'll bring us more coffee." Maura rose to her feet, her face taut with anxiety.

"Maura, Jeff won't be drafted," Katie said gently. "Not a married man with two children."

"One of whom will be seventeen in April," Maura reminded. "This war won't be over fast. George will be drafted."

"Stop being dramatic," Jeff ordered with a calm Katie suspected he didn't feel. "George doesn't even have to register for the draft until April 1945. By then this war will be over."

"Why didn't the world stop those maniacs before now?" Maura blazed. "Why did we sit back and let this happen?"

"Maura, go get the coffee." Jeff leaned back in his chair with an air of exhaustion. "It's going to be a long day."

"Five years ago Harry was already worrying that we'd be dragged into another world war," Katie remembered. She gazed into the orange-red flames in the fireplace grate. "I hope he got out of France. . . ."

"Harry's sharp. He got out," Jeff comforted. "And neither of us will be called up. At least, not unless the situation gets wild. The kids will go first—and that's kind of tragic, because they've had so little time."

Leo had less time, Katie thought. But how many mothers would feel her pain before these maniacs were stopped? She'd been a little girl during World War I, but even now she remembered the shrieks of grief when a mother in the flat above theirs received a telegram from the War Department, reporting the death of her son. She remembered Armistice Day, November 11, 1918, when they were awakened by the screech of sirens of factory whistles blowing all over the city, and the ringing of myriad church bells. She had never imagined that there would be another such war in her lifetime.

"How's business at the station, Katie?" Jeff interrupted her introspection.

"I've met some resistance because of our shorter hours," she admitted. Still, it was easier to keep help without the late evening and Sunday shifts. "But now with the chains cutting back, too—no Sunday openings and closing at eight o'clock—I'm right in line. I've made our rest rooms more comfortable and attractive. I'm playing up the angle that we use 'gas girls' to free men for defense work. And now," she said somberly, "that will hit customers right between the eyes."

"What about Jeff's worries that men wouldn't want to ask the girls to put air in their tires?" Maura asked.

"Are you kidding? It's a running gag at the station. 'Hey, honey,'" Katie mimicked, "'you think you can handle putting some air in that rear left tire?' And that's one of the reasons I have them wearing slacks." There was a touch of laughter in her voice for the moment. She glanced at her watch now. "I'd better head home. Joanne said she might be back in time for dinner."

"Is she still thick as thieves with Betty Forbes?" Maura asked.

"They're like Siamese twins." Betty was Joanne's only close friend, Katie thought with recurrent unease. She wished wistfully that Joanne and Willa had remained close. She looked ahead with anxiety to the day when Betty blossomed into a Dallas debutante and Junior League member. Joanne could not follow her into that world. "But you know how kids are at their age."

"I can't stand some of their darling little habits." Maura shook her head in incomprehension. "Why is it so fascinating to them to walk with mismatched shoes and socks? And what's this craziness about some new singer named Frank Sinatra?"

When Jeff left the two women to make a routine check of the greenhouses, Maura confided to Katie that he was working on another novel.

"I pestered him," Maura said with satisfaction. "He's been fooling around with a plot for months—and I know he's dying to put it down on paper. It'll take time because he only works about an hour a day plus some extra time on Sundays. But he's happy with it. He's always happy when he's on a book."

"This one will sell," Katie predicted. "I still don't understand why the others haven't found a publisher."

Maura reiterated her usual lament: "You have to be at the right place at the right time with the right material. I'm praying this will be it for Jeff." She squinted in thought. "You know, it's funny how we can sit here and talk about our lives as though we haven't just been plunged into a war. How can we plan ahead when maniacs have taken control of the world?"

Americans suffered disconcerting shocks in the months after Pearl Harbor. U.S. forces encountered crushing defeats in the Pacific Islands. The Japanese occupied Manila, driving General MacArthur and his troops to Bataan. And in mid-March Bataan fell to the Japanese after a heroic defense.

General Wainwright with around thirty-five-hundred soldiers and nurses retreated to Corregidor while American and Philippine prisoners taken at Bataan began a "Death March"—eighty-five miles in six days, peppered with atrocities—that cost the lives of fifty-two-hundred Americans and even more Filipinos.

At home in April rents were stabilized. There was talk of sugar rationing. In the East there were plans afoot to ration gasoline. And with the chains closing a number of company-owned filling stations because of the labor shortage, Katie decided to look around for a second station to buy. The first was showing a profit already.

She was playing Harry's game, she told herself. It was as though he were hanging over her, directing every move. In wartime the economy had to be excellent—and everyone agreed that this country would not become a battleground. It was time to expand. After the war, she was convinced, cars would be in tremendous demand. And she meant to be there to sell them gas.

Late in May she attended George's high school graduation with Maura, Jeff, and Willa. Walking into the auditorium—buzzing with the animated conversations of parents, relatives, and friends of graduating seniors—she tried to brush aside the depression that had invaded her since morning. A ghost would be on the stage tonight. Leo's ghost. Tonight Leo, too, should be graduating.

She had made no effort to persuade Joanne to attend the exercises. Especially tonight Joanne would be remembering Leo. But for Maura's sake, Katie told herself, *she* had to be here. Maura was so happy that George had graduated with good grades and would be starting college in the fall. The University of Texas, down in Austin.

On occasions such as this Katie was sharply conscious of Harry's absence from her life. *Was he all right? Had he been caught in France when the Germans invaded?* So many nights she battled insomnia. Harry a barrier between her and sleep.

If he was back here in this country, he wouldn't do something rash like enlisting, would he? He was thirty-seven years old and a father. He was safe from the draft.

"The girls' bouquets are pink roses," Willa leaned forward to tell her. "Don't you love pink roses?"

Now the music teacher sat down at the piano. It was time for the processional. The girls down the right aisle, the boys down the left. Katie fought against tears. Leo should be walking down the aisle with those boys. Harry should be sitting here beside her and bursting with pride that their son was graduating and would soon be a col-

lege student. But Leo was dead—and Harry was forever
gone from her life.

Chapter Twenty-two

JOANNE AND BETTY lingered over breakfast in the air-
conditioned family dining room of the Forbeses' ranch
and debated about how to spend their first full day here.
Zeke had driven them out last night, and they were to
remain here for the ten days before they were to leave
for this summer's tour. Early this morning Betty's
mother had left for a flight to Santa Barbara, where she
was to attend a wedding.

"I'm so mad that I didn't pack the new shorts I bought
at Neiman's yesterday. They're really snazzy," Betty uttered a wistful sigh.

"You'll take them on the tour," Joanne consoled. It
hadn't taken a lot of carrying on this time to persuade
Mom to let her go on another tour. Mom was glad to
have her out of her hair for six weeks.

"I know what!" Betty's smile was electric. "We'll drive
down to the city and pick them up."

"Zeke's driving your mother to the airport—and you
said he'd be staying at the Dallas house. And Mrs. Andrews is in bed with an awful cold," Joanne reminded
her.

"I can drive." Betty's eyes glowed with a blend of triumph and defiance. "Daddy lets me drive all around the
ranch."

"You don't need a license to drive on private property." Joanne parroted what Betty had told her on those
occasions when they'd taken a car from the garage and
driven about the ranch.

"So who's to know I don't have a license?" Betty shrugged. "Daddy says I'm a real good driver. I dare you! Drive with me into the city. We'll pick up the shorts, pop into Neiman's to look around, then drive back."

"Betty, it's kind of scary," Joanne hedged, but the prospect was enticing.

"We'll take my mother's Cadillac convertible," Betty decided exuberantly. "We'll leave a note for Mrs. Andrews, in case she gets up. Well?" she prodded. "Are you with me?"

"Sure." Joanne's face lighted up. It was a crazy adventure. Something to brag about to the girls on the tour.

Betty scribbled a note for Mrs. Andrews.

"She'll screech, but it'll be too late," Betty said while they went out to the kitchen to give the note to the maid—who read no English and spoke little.

"We'll be back this afternoon, Conchita," Betty told the good-natured Mexican maid. "If Mrs. Andrews wakes up and asks about us, give her my note. If she doesn't ask, just hold it till we're back."

"*Si, si.*" Conchita smiled broadly.

Fifteen minutes later—the convertible top down, a light summer breeze relieving the morning heat—the two girls were away from the ranch and headed toward Dallas.

"Betty, you're going fast. . . ." Joanne was uneasy for a moment as her eyes rested on the speedometer.

"Don't you like it?"

"Sure!" She loved seeing everything go by so fast. She wouldn't care if Betty went even faster. But suppose a cop stopped them for speeding? Betty didn't have a driver's license. She was too young to drive.

"Nobody's on the road right now," Betty soothed. "We won't see much traffic until we're closer to the city."

Joanne laughed as Betty stepped harder on the accelerator. This was terrific! It was as if they were laughing at the whole world.

"Oh, Betty, you're terrible!" she squealed in delight.

Then delight switched to alarm as they heard the sound of a police siren.

"Oh shit." Exchanging a swift glance of fear with Joanne, Betty pulled off at the side of the road.

Katie listened in shock to the voice at the other end of the phone. Betty and Joanne had been picked up in a white Cadillac convertible that was going eighteen miles past the speed limit. Betty had no driver's license, no car registration. She claimed the car was her mother's.

"We couldn't reach Mrs. Forbes or Mr. Forbes," the police officer reported. "We don't even know if the girl is the Forbes's daughter. The other young lady said you were her mother. You could identify them."

"Where are they?" Katie's voice was uneven. "Of course I can identify them."

Katie left immediately for the police station. What the devil were Joanne and Betty up to now? She shivered at the image of their speeding along the highway. Where did Betty learn to drive? *They might have been killed.*

Katie walked into the police station and immediately spied the two girls, huddled pale and frightened on a bench.

"Mom!" Joanne darted toward her, hugged her tightly. "Oh Mom, I love you!"

Katie spoke with the officer on duty. She assured them Betty was the only child of the oil-rich Mr. and Mrs. Forbes. She agreed that it was certainly necessary that the girls be punished—but added that an appearance in juvenile court would be a waste of taxpayers' money.

"I promise you, they'll never do anything like this again. And I know how grateful the Forbeses will be if this can be written off as a childish prank. Betty's allowed to drive on their private property. She let herself be carried away—"

"Driving eighteen miles past the speed limit," the officer pointed out grimly. "Without a license."

"I'll have Mr. Forbes come out and personally thank you," Katie promised with an ingratiating smile. "The Forbeses will be so grateful."

"If they were my kids, I'd make sure they couldn't sit down for a week." He gazed at the two girls as though they were an exotic exhibit. "All right, you're free to go."

"I'll arrange for someone from the ranch to pick up the car," Katie told the officer. "Thank you so much."

Katie didn't trust herself to speak while she drove back to the ranch.

"Mom, we're sorry," Joanne said desperately when they turned in at the ranch entrance.

"Don't you know you could have been killed?" Katie's knuckles were whitening from her grip on the wheel. "It's a miracle the police officer released you."

"We're sorry," Betty echoed Joanne. "It just sounded like fun—and I *can* drive."

"Not off the ranch," Katie pointed out. In her mind she saw the relief on Joanne's face when she walked into the police station. "*Oh, Mom, I love you.*" Katie clung to the memory of Joanne's spontaneous greeting.

"We'll just stay around the pool every day. We won't even drive on the ranch," Betty promised.

"I'm not sure I should leave Joanne here. . . ." Mrs. Andrews couldn't watch them every minute. They shouldn't need to be watched every minute.

"Mom, please," Joanne cajoled. "I'll call home every day. Please let me stay."

Sitting alone in the living room with her after-dinner coffee, Katie still questioned her judgment in allowing Joanne to remain at the ranch. But it was awfully hot in town, and Joanne was sensitive to the heat. Anyhow, they'd had a real scare, being hauled into the police station that way.

The sound of the phone ringing was a raucous intrusion in the quiet of the house. With her usual compulsive swiftness Katie reached for the receiver.

"Hello."

"Katie, I've just heard about a gas station that's up for sale," Maura told her. "It's in the area you said you liked."

"Fill me in," Katie urged.

Maura did, and Katie immediately pursued this lead. She was able to negotiate a favorable sale. On the morning she saw Joanne off on her tour, Katie went to a meeting with the station owners, their lawyer, her lawyer, and a bank representative. By lunchtime she was the owner of her second gas station. Already she was contemplating a third.

Joanne might be a replica of her physically—as Harry used to enjoy pointing out—but in so many ways, Katie thought, she was very much Harry's child. She had Harry's charm—when she chose to use it—and on occasion Harry's explosive temper. Harry's obsession for the lifestyle of the Texas rich. And *she* was determined to provide Joanne with the luxuries that brought her pleasure, helped her forget that awful day three years ago.

Early in the fall Katie was approached by a man who was eager to buy out Newhouse Gourmet Foods. Not the farm and the house, he emphasized. Just the greenhouses, their records, their customers. She was polite in her refusal to consider selling, though the prospect of having all of her time to devote to building a chain of filling stations was enticing. Out of loyalty to Jeff and Maura—who were earning their living from the company—she couldn't sell out.

"Think about it for a month," the man persuaded. "I'll contact you again."

Katie was furious when Maura mentioned the following morning that the prospective buyer—Craig Winters—had talked with her and Jeff about the operation of Newhouse Gourmet Foods. They'd thought he was writing an article for a farm journal about their methods.

"He was after information about how we handle our greenhouses. How we keep our production so high. He came to me with an offer to buy the company."

"Was it a good offer?" Maura's voice crackled with excitement.

"I wouldn't sell," Katie chided. "We're in business together."

"You'd be happy out of it," Maura guessed. "All you talk about these days is how to promote your filling stations. And if you're thinking about Jeff and me, we'd just as soon see you sell. We'd move back into regular farming. Jeff has this weird conscience, you know. He's always feeling guilty because we're putting so much effort into feeding a few people with loads of money when there's such a need for food in Europe."

"You and Jeff want to go back to regular farming?" Katie was astonished.

"Katie, this is a boom time for farmers. We're becoming the breadbasket of the world. And new farm machinery is coming onto the market. High-yielding seeds are being developed. But we figured you needed us for the company."

"I'll sell." Katie felt a surge of confidence in tomorrow. "I'll haggle a bit," she admitted. Harry had taught her that. "But Craig Winters can buy out Newhouse Gourmet Foods. He's even talking about freezing vegetables and selling them across the country."

"Let him do whatever he wants," Maura crooned. "Just take the money and run."

"Joanne will be sixteen next June," Katie said softly. "You know what I'll give her for her sixteenth birthday?" Katie's smile was brilliant. "Her own convertible. That's what Betty's parents have promised her. Maura, she'll be so thrilled."

"Katie there are no cars coming off the assembly lines," Maura cautioned.

"For a price I'll find one," Katie said with conviction. "Joanne will love it."

But in a corner of her mind Katie wondered if she would ever erase her towering guilt at having failed her children. Joanne blamed her for Leo's death, almost as much as she blamed her father.

Chapter Twenty-three

EARLY IN the new year Harry sat in Pierre's ornately furnished oversized office and made a pretense of listening to Arnold Sinclair's complaints about the progress of Simon & Sinclair. He and Pierre were both aware that this was Arnold's way of pushing himself into a key position in the Minneapolis office—where the real action existed.

Didn't the bastard understand that right now the grain trade was controlled by the Department of Agriculture and the War Food Administration? They did what they could, and that was damn good. At regular intervals he was attacked by guilt at not being in uniform. Hell, he was still a young man. But what he was doing was essential to the war effort, he reminded himself.

"What's this nonsense about our buying prefab storage bins, Harry?" Arnie demanded arrogantly. "Look at these figures—the cost is preposterous."

"It'll be more preposterous to lose our wheat because we can't lease elevator space, Arnie. The wheat surplus is colossal—and that's great *if* we work out a way to store it till we can ship. These lumber people have come up with prefabs that can save our hides. The farmers are storing in their barns, even their houses. Some are renting empty stores." He paused, willing himself not to lose his temper with Arnie. "I'm working up a study on milling. We should make a real effort to expand into flour mills. The army is buying flour like crazy."

For over an hour they argued over the course to follow, Harry ever conscious that Arnie was leading up to saying he wanted to be part of the Minneapolis picture. He didn't like Arnie Sinclair. He loathed Arnie's way of reminding him that he wasn't a partner in Simon & Sinclair. That, in truth, the syndicate Arnie represented was in control. But he knew Pierre expected him to ignore his personal distaste, because they needed the financing Arnie brought into the business.

"I've discussed the situation with the board," Arnie wound up with a smug smile. "We've agreed that I should come into the Minneapolis office sometime after the first of the year."

"There're a tough couple of years ahead of us," Harry acknowledged. "We can use all the help we can get up here." *The fucking bastard. It was going to be hell with him underfoot.*

"It'll be great to have you aboard." Pierre contrived to sound sincere. "Now, shall we go out for lunch? There's a new restaurant that Harry and I—"

"Why not the Minneapolis Club?" Arnie interrupted with a devious smile.

"I think you'll enjoy this restaurant." Pierre was polite but firm. Harry understood—like Pierre—that Arnie had pointedly suggested the Minneapolis Club. The son of a bitch knew Jews were not welcome there. It made Arnie feel so smug to point out that he was accepted where they were not.

The three men left Pierre's office and walked down the hall to the reception area. Harry noticed the smirk Arnie shot in the direction of the new receptionist. She was a tall, attractive blonde of about nineteen. What was her name? Eileen something or other. Eileen Stanton, he remembered.

"If any calls come for me, tell them I'll be back in two hours," Arnie said importantly. His gaze fastened to her high, small breasts, the nipples outlined by her black sweater.

"Yes, Mr. Sinclair," she said sweetly, while her eyes glided past him to rest on Harry in sultry invitation.

She was ready to jump into bed with him, Harry surmised self-consciously. Hell, she was just a little older than Joanne! Yet he felt a familiar stirring low within him. He might be exhausted from long hours at the office, he thought with a touch of humor—but that young bitch could make him forget that. If he'd let her.

Arnie managed to criticize the near-perfect restaurant where they lunched. He was pissed, Harry guessed, because Eileen had made a subtle pitch for *him*. But he was not about to mess around with a girl in the office. Also, instinct warned him not to increase Arnie's hostility toward him.

He was living high, he analyzed, because that was expected of him here in Minneapolis. It was part of the image. But damn, he existed from paycheck to paycheck. Nothing went into savings. He continued to be haunted by a need for wealth—not for himself but to make life easier for Katie and Joanne. To give them the luxuries Katie and he had enjoyed before the Crash.

After a long three-martini lunch the three men returned to the Simon & Sinclair offices, each to go his separate way. As usual, Harry remained long after the last of the staff had left for the day. Pierre had joined Arnie for a final drink before seeing him off on his flight for New York.

Leather briefcase in one hand, Harry walked out into the near-zero temperature of the night and turned up the collar of his tweed topcoat, bought at Burberry's Paris shop three years ago. He glanced up at the sky, a murky gray with an undertone of burgundy that hinted at imminent snow. Conscious of hunger, he debated about where to go for dinner, decided on a small, undistinguished restaurant two blocks north.

Harry held the door wide for an amorous young couple, then entered the steamy warmth with a sigh of gratitude. He was tired of the bastardly cold nights. He was tired of the meager winter socializing, in such contrast to the years in Paris. Pierre spent the weekends at a ski lodge with the most recent of his mistresses—of which there was a never a shortage.

The restaurant was colorful with holiday decorations. An exuberant departing diner paused to scrawl "Merry Christmas" on the steamed-over window. Harry settled himself at a small table at the rear and tried to evince some interest in the menu. He knew not to expect anything beyond routine food. Generous in portions but bland and unappealing. Still, he was not in the mood for solitary dining in one of the places he normally favored.

"What'll it be?" a pretty, dark-haired waitress somewhere in her early thirties asked with a bright smile. She looked tired, Harry thought sympathetically. Slinging hash was not an easy way to make a living.

"The roast-beef dinner," he told her. "And I'd like coffee right away."

"Sure thing." She took the menu and hurried off. She was small and curvaceous, he noticed, his eyes following her to the kitchen. Like Katie.

When the waitress brought his coffee, he reached into his briefcase for one of the two Dallas dailies delivered to him through the mail. Somehow, reading the Dallas newspapers made him feel closer to Katie and Joanne. He skimmed the front page, mostly concerned with the war news. Now he turned the paper back to glance over the inside articles. All at once his throat tightened in excitement. Katie's name jumped at him from the page.

She had sold Newhouse Gourmet Foods to some guy named Winters. And what was this shit about her buying a third filling station? *When had she bought the first two?* What set her off on that track?

He sat motionless, the coffee forgotten. His mind in high gear, struggling to assimilate this new information. Gas Girls, Inc.—that was a sharp angle. At least, as long as the war continued.

Even before she sold the business, she'd bought two filling stations. How had she managed that? And now a third. She was thinking like him. Building a chain, he told himself.

Hell, Katie didn't need him—she was doing fine on her own. It was a tormenting realization. He was forever cut out of her life.

"Be careful now," the waitress cautioned as she set a plate down before him. "It's awful hot."

"I'll be careful." He managed a casual smile. "What about you?"

"Am I awful hot, or did I get burned?" she said saucily. Her eyes met his with candid interest.

"Both," he drawled. What the hell? His wife didn't want him. His ex-wife, he taunted himself. *God, it had been so damn long.*

"There's one way to find out." She reached for the salad and the bread-and-butter plate and deposited them on the table, managing an inviting view down the front of her uniform. She hesitated. "My husband and I split up eleven months ago. A girl gets lonely."

"What time do you get off?" All at once he couldn't wait to get into bed with her.

"It's slow tonight. I can leave in forty minutes." He sensed her own arousal. "My name's Dolores, but everybody calls me Dolly."

"I'm Harry," he told her. No last names. "You live near here?" He didn't want to take her to his place. That could get sticky.

"Finish your dinner. Then I'll call us a cab. We'll be there in ten minutes." She understood why he didn't want to take her home with him—but she accepted it. Lots of girls were giving it away to soldiers. So he wasn't in uniform. Anyhow, she wanted it as bad as he.

He thrust the Dallas newspaper back into his briefcase and ordered himself to focus on dinner and what would follow. What kind of a crazy dream had he been living in? Staying away from women because he was still in love with his wife. This had nothing to do with love. And after this maybe he'd get a decent night's sleep for a change.

Harry dawdled over the soggy apple pie while Dolly disappeared into the kitchen. He swigged down the last of his coffee as she went to the telephone and made a call. For a taxi, he assumed. He understood they were to exit separately. She didn't want the counterman or the other waitress—now doubling as cashier—to realize they had something going.

They had something going for tonight, he emphasized to himself. He'd never see her again. But for a few hours they'd both have something they needed very badly.

By early spring—with her plans for further expansion of Gas Girls, Incorporated, already taking shape—Katie began to plan for Joanne's "sweet sixteen" party. Each year she dreaded that brief span of time between late May and early June. Each year she grieved again for Leo—as though it had been only a few days since she heard Joanne's screams and walked into Leo's room to find her precious son gone forever. And each year Joanne's birthday was haunted by that memory.

She would involve Joanne in all the planning, Katie promised herself. A "sweet sixteen" party was so important in Joanne's circle. This year Joanne would be caught up in coming birthday celebrations. *This year would be different.*

She worried about Harry. Had he been trapped in Paris when the Nazis invaded the city? Had he come home, enlisted, and was he somewhere overseas? Fighting guilt—knowing Joanne would be upset if she discovered this action—Katie wrote to the Hirsch family in New York. This didn't mean she'd make up with Harry, she comforted herself—just that she had to know that he was all right. *Joanne would not find out that she had written.*

Her letter to the Hirsches in New York was returned. They'd moved away without leaving a forwarding address. She was simultaneously disappointed and relieved. It would have been difficult, she admitted to herself, to establish contact with Harry without Joanne's knowing. But it would have been so reassuring to know that he was not in danger—not fighting in Europe or the Pacific.

Though her schedule was frenetic, she decided to become a volunteer at a Red Cross canteen. She ought to do something toward the war effort, she told herself. After her first night she resigned in rage—the canteen served only officers.

Maura kept pushing her to socialize. Despite the shortage of men in wartime Texas, she was pursued at regular intervals. She brushed aside all overtures.

"Maura, I have no time in my life for that," she protested when they met for lunch on a beautiful April Saturday. Maura had come into the city to help Katie with the preliminary arrangements for Joanne's birthday party. "Besides, you know the attitude of men toward a divorced woman. She's supposed to be delighted to hop into any empty bed."

"It wouldn't hurt you to have an affair," Maura said bluntly. "You're not the type to sleep alone."

"I am now." Katie forced a smile. "I have Joanne, and I have my business. That's all I need."

"Are you still trying to track down a convertible for her birthday?" Maura asked. Cars were not coming off the assembly lines with factories focusing on military needs.

"I have a lead on a late-model Cadillac. They're asking a fortune; but if it's as good as it's supposed to be, I'll buy it for Joanne."

"And you're driving a seven-year-old Chevy," Maura jibed. But Katie knew she understood.

"I'll drop a hint three weeks early," Katie said. Before the anniversary of Leo's death.

"Oh, Katie . . ." Maura sighed. "You're spoiling her to death."

"I'm trying to decide where to have the party." Joanne would like to have it at the country club; but, of course, they weren't members. "Maybe at the Adolphus."

All at once Katie was tense. Last night she'd talked to Joanne about how many were to be invited to her "sweet sixteen" party. Joanne had suggested—in that deviously charming manner she'd inherited from Harry—that it would be better not to invite Willa. *"She'd feel so uncomfortable with my friends."*

"That's one problem I don't have," Maura laughed. "Willa will have a backyard barbecue and a hayride afterward. And we'll be lucky if George gets the day off and can come home for his birthday later in the month."

Katie understood how upset Maura was about the draft registration age being dropped to eighteen, though George had pushed off going to agricultural college to take a job in the defense industry in Forth Worth. As long as he was in a defense job, it appeared, he wouldn't be drafted.

"Katie . . ." Maura hesitated. "I don't want you to think about inviting Willa to Joanne's party. The girls have grown so far apart. Let's don't try to push them on each other."

"Maura, I love Willa." Katie's face betrayed her anguish. Maura understood that Joanne wouldn't want Willa at her party.

"I know you do, darling. And she loves you. But Willa and Joanne live different lives now. They're not comfortable together."

"It shouldn't be that way. . . ." They'd been so close as little girls.

"Katie, a lot of things 'shouldn't be that way.' But we have to go on with our lives. You'll come out for Willa's party?"

"I wouldn't miss it," Katie said.

This was so wrong. Maura was right—she spoiled Joanne rotten. But how could she do otherwise after what Joanne had gone through?

Chapter Twenty-four

BY EARLY May Harry knew the Minneapolis office was too small for both Arnie and himself. It wasn't only the business conflicts—most of the time, with Pierre approving of his strategy, he had his way. There was this uncomfortable personal hostility between them.

Right now Arnie was pissed because he couldn't get anywhere with Eileen. She came right out and told him she didn't go out with married men. He'd be more pissed if he knew the two of them had something going.

With Arnie down in New York for a few days, Harry was able to breathe more freely, but he knew it was time to put distance between them. Over a late dinner with Pierre he brought up the subject.

"Arnie can't stand the way Eileen gives you those long, lingering looks," Pierre chuckled. His eyes were speculative. "You got something going with her?"

"She's a kid, Pierre," Harry hedged. "Three years older than my daughter."

"That one was born old," Pierre laughed. "And she's sharp."

"I've been studying up on the situation in Argentina," Harry told him. "We can buy grain from the farmers down there so cheap it'll make your head spin. Maybe right now we've got a wheat surplus in the country; but once this war is over and the shipping lanes are open, we'll have the wildest market you've ever seen. And instinct tells me this wheat surplus won't continue. Europe's wheat fields are shot to hell. The same thing is happening in Asia. I want to see Simon & Sinclair sitting there with enormous supplies when this war is over—and, Pierre, it can't go on for more than another year or two."

"You're saying you want to set up in Argentina," Pierre said thoughtfully.

"I won't need a big setup down there," Harry pushed. "A good team of agents to go out there and buy the wheat—each one personally trained by me. Thank God I'm fluent in Spanish after all those years in Dallas. Terminal space will be cheaper than here. We may have to sit a while, but we stand to make a fortune."

"It'll take some real pressure to make Arnie agree," Pierre warned.

"I'll work up the figures that'll whet his appetite," Harry promised. "And drop a hint that I'm seeing Eileen on the side." He chuckled softly. "He'll be glad to get me out of town." But mainly Arnie's shrewd mind would see the profits for Simon & Sinclair.

Harry fretted over the delay in selling Arnie and the board on establishing the company in Argentina in the midst of a war. He knew, though, that the board would accept whatever decision Arnie made. Arnie had a colossal ego problem when it came to his success with women, but he was brilliant when it came to juggling money.

It amused Harry to have discovered Eileen's ambitions to marry rich—though rich alone was insufficient. She yearned for a husband who commanded attention from others. He saw the way her eyes lighted when he took her to dinner and people in the restaurant stared. Probably they were staring because he was out with a beautiful girl half his age, he thought with wry humor—but Eileen thought he had some special magnetism. But he made it clear he wasn't in search of a wife. Merely an attractive woman to satisfy his sexual needs.

Finally—well into May—Arnie capitulated. Simon & Sinclair—tricky though it would be to operate in Argentina when the world was at war—would have South

American representation. Harry would be in charge. Immediately he went about making arrangements to settle in Buenos Aires—ignoring Eileen's reproachful stares because he was leaving the country—and her.

"You'll live well," Pierre congratulated him. "American dollars go far in Buenos Aires. Stay at the Alvear Palace—it's very French—until you find a townhouse to rent. Then hire two or three servants to run things for you. When that's settled, establish an office downtown."

On the afternoon when word came through that the red tape had been cut to facilitate his traveling to Buenos Aires, Harry received the latest copies of the *Dallas Morning News*. As always, he skimmed through the pages. He stopped short and began to read an item on the society page. A report on Joanne's sixteenth birthday party. Katie was climbing up socially, he thought with respect as he read with bittersweet slowness a colorful description of Joanne's "sweet sixteen" birthday party. "Joanne Newhouse, daughter of Mrs. Kate Freeman—"

She had taken back her maiden name, he thought in pain. Yet at the same time he was conscious that she had not remarried. Obviously she was doing well—a lavish birthday party at the Adolphus must have cost her a small fortune.

He sat at his desk and stared into space, his mind hurtling back through the years. All his dreams had revolved around his family. Katie and the kids. He'd wanted only the very best for them. *He'd made a fucking mess of all their lives.*

"Harry?" He'd been too wrapped up in the past to be aware that Eileen had come into the office. Now she closed the door behind her.

"What?" He hadn't meant to sound irritated, but she had jolted him. "What is it, Eileen?"

"It's such a gorgeous day. Why don't we pick up some cold cuts and drive out to the lake for a picnic dinner? Then we can have something tall and wet at your place." Eileen always said rum and Coke made her passionate.

"I have to make a couple of calls before I leave. Meet me downstairs in the lobby in twenty minutes." Though Arnie suspected he was seeing Eileen outside the office, there was no need to rub it in, he thought. Arnie was obsessed by Eileen—there was no other word to describe it. But didn't he understand she wasn't ready to settle for being his bed-mate? She still held out hopes—waning though they might be—that she'd become Mrs. Harry Newhouse.

Harry sat in the car while Eileen—with the twenty-dollar bill he'd provided—shopped in the delicatessen for cold cuts and sodas. Tonight he fought against depression. He remembered other picnics—when he and Katie had been in their teens and Central Park had been their special picnic rendezvous. They'd come so far through the years—yet he was left with so little.

Then Eileen was emerging from the delicatessen with a convivial smile.

"The bastard tried to overcharge me, but I wouldn't let him," she laughed, handing over bills and change to Harry. "He thought, Oh, a dumb blonde, she won't know the difference."

"You're not dumb," he said. Pierre was right—Eileen was shrewd. Sophisticated beyond her years. "Why don't we go to your place and picnic there?" he said in sudden arousal. "I'm in the mood to make love."

"I'm always in the mood," she drawled, dropping a hand on his thigh. "You're going to miss me like hell when you're down there in Argentina," she taunted.

At her tiny apartment—which she had tried to make attractive despite its limitations—they stashed the food in the refrigerator and went into the bedroom. While he stripped and settled himself on the bed, Eileen disappeared into the bathroom. Moments later she emerged in the sheer black negligee she kept for such occasions. Nothing beneath it except sleek, sexy, nineteen-year-old body.

"Wow," he murmured in appreciation, knowing this was expected. "You look like a blond Rita Hayworth in that getup."

"And you're Clark Gable," she teased, sliding out of the black negligee—which looked as though it had been borrowed from a Hollywood wardrobe department—and allowing it to drop to the floor.

"Then treat me like Gable," he ordered. He was thirty-eight years old, he thought in amusement—and women still chased after him.

"When are you leaving?" she asked, joining him on the bed. Her hands moved adroitly about him, her secretive little smile a potent invitation.

"In two or three weeks." *Where the hell did she learn so much at her age?*

"You'll miss me," she warned.

"Maybe not," he said, his eyes clashing with hers. All at once she was immobile, eyes flashing at the implication. "Maybe you'll be in Buenos Aires with me." All at once he recoiled from starting life anew in a strange city. A strange country. Alone.

"I won't go down there as your secretary," she said after a moment. "There's no future in that."

"Go down as my wife," he said. *Why not?* "We can get married at City Hall before we leave. Unless," he mocked, "you want to get your mother's permission." He knew her father had died when she was a toddler, in a drunken brawl. Her mother and she saw each other at Christmas. Her two brothers—older than Eileen by several years—had long ago gone off on their own. "Well?" he challenged.

"I'm almost twenty. I don't need anybody's permission." He could feel her exhilaration, though she was playing casual. "You mean it, Harry?" All at once she seemed young and vulnerable.

"I mean it," he told her.

"Oh wow, will Arnie be pissed!" she laughed.

"Hand in your resignation tomorrow," he ordered. "But don't tell anybody why. Say your mother's dying and you have to go home."

"I'm glad I took Spanish in high school." She dropped a hand between his thighs. "We're going to have a great old time in Buenos Aires. I hear Americans live like royalty down there."

"We'll talk about that later. I've got other things on my mind right now."

"Harry," she murmured moments later, "I don't want to get pregnant. Even if we are going to get married. I never want to get pregnant."

"You won't, sugar," he promised. "No more of that crap for me."

He leaned across for his wallet. Eileen knew he always kept a condom there. But why did she have to talk about getting pregnant? All at once he was remembering Katie pregnant—each time he'd been so scared for her. So proud when Leo was born, and then Joanne.

It was time to forget those years. *Look ahead.* That was the road to survival.

Within twenty-four hours after he asked Eileen to marry him, Harry was besieged by doubts. Yet the prospect of coming home to an empty house in yet another strange city was unnerving. It was the right move, he told himself. He wasn't meant to live alone.

Then—almost wishing for a reprieve—he phoned the attorney in Dallas who had handled the divorce.

"I've been out of touch," he explained when at last his call was put through. "I wanted to make sure everything had gone through as anticipated."

"You're divorced, Mr. Newhouse. You signed all the necessary papers before you left Dallas. We had no forwarding address to advise you when the decree came through."

"I've been on the move," Harry explained. "New York, Paris, Minneapolis. Now I'm leaving for Buenos Aires." He hesitated a moment. "Let me give you my new address."

He wanted desperately to ask about Katie. He couldn't bring himself to do this. If Katie had cared to contact him, she would have written him in Paris, he tormented himself for the thousandth time.

Not one word had come from her—or Joanne—when he'd sent that dress. Praying for a reconciliation. He'd been in Paris for a month after Joanne had received it. Despite the war situation they had still been receiving mail in Paris. Katie and Joanne had not cared to respond to his overture.

Harry and Eileen were married in Pierre's grand new house on Lake Minnetonka, by the judge who had sold him that house. Harry struggled not to remember his marriage to Katie in the flat on Rivington Street. In marrying Eileen he was admitting to himself—truly for the first time—that Katie was forever out of his life.

Despite his expectations to be aboard a ship bound for Buenos Aires within a few days, it was the end of August before he and Eileen were able to acquire passage to South America. When they arrived in Buenos Aires, which sits on the banks of the mud-washed Rio de la Plata, they took up temporary residence at the Alvear Palace Hotel in the smart residential district.

"The Plaza in the downtown area is for the rich tourists," Pierre had told them. "You'll like the Alvear Palace—it's very French. In fact, Buenos Aires is often called the 'Paris of South America.' "

They arrived near the end of the winter in Argentina, but the season was still in full swing. Rich Buenos Aireans remained in residence in their fine townhouses. The opera season was at its height. The ladies went to tea every afternoon at five or six—at Harrods' Buenos Aires branch department store or at Desty's on the Calle Florida or at the Confitería Ideal. Limousines with liveried chauffeurs carried them to the elegant shops on the Calle Florida and the Calle Santa Fe.

Though Eileen reveled in the grandeur of their hotel suite—"Harry, I feel like Marie Antoinette, sleeping in a bed in an alcove!"—she loathed the constant rain and the raw cold that was in such contrast to the balmy weather they'd left behind. She quickly forgot this when Harry took her shopping in one of the posh fur stores and bought her a mink coat. This gesture was not entirely to please his bride. He meant to show that Harry Newhouse and the firm of Simon & Sinclair represented wealth.

Harry was fascinated by Buenos Aires. It was unlike any place he'd ever known. Here nobody seemed aware that the rest of the world was involved in a war, though Argentina itself had just undergone a military takeover, led by Colonel Juan Perón. The United States recognized the new government with the understanding that it would be on the side of the Allies. But there were those in the English and American colonies, he quickly learned, who suspected the Argentines of favoring the Axis.

It wasn't just that Argentina was a neutral country—presumably—he thought. It was as though it were isolated from the rest of the world. Hardly anyone strolling along the Avenida de Mayo bothered to glance at the news board in front of *La Prensa*. The rich here seemed to live in an almost feudal society.

Harry and Eileen dined in the attractive grill of the Alvear Palace—where she was eloquent in her approval of the chartreuse curtained room with its gleaming wood paneling and crystal chandeliers—or at the Plaza with its white-turbaned East Indians tending to exotic curried dishes. While he focused on setting up an office and finding a house for them, Eileen shopped. The American dollar went very far here.

Harry was pleased to observe that Eileen's taste was

excellent. It was important that his wife be a credit to him. He knew they were a couple who attracted admiring eyes, and that was part of the image he meant to project.

By the end of ten days he had an office on the Avenida de Mayo, the semblance of a staff, and was arranging a lease on a fully furnished house on Avenida Alvear, overlooking Palermo Park.

"You're renting a house without my seeing it?" Eileen scolded, but he knew she was pleased.

"You'll see it soon enough," he told her while they dressed for a night at the opera. On Tuesdays and Fridays the opera—presented at the magnificent Teatro Colón—was a white-tie gala. "Oh, tomorrow night we're having cocktails at the Jockey Club."

"Harry," Eileen asked, inspecting her reflection in the mirror with an air of triumph, "how long will we live in Buenos Aires?"

"Who knows?" His smile was philosophical. "As long as it's good for the company." And for his bank account. "Get your coat. We don't want to be late for the opera."

Harry—who considered himself too sophisticated to be awed by any structure—was awed by the belle époque grandeur of the huge Teatro Colón. Someone had said it was the most beautiful opera house in the world, he recalled. Gazing at its gold brocade walls, its seven tiers of boxes adorned with red velvet, its parade of chandeliers, the block-long stage, he believed this.

Then, traitorously, his mind shot back through the years to those occasions when he and Katie—so young and full of dreams—had wandered through the elegant lobbies of Manhattan's fine hotels and promised themselves that one day they would be part of that scene. Not merely observers. For a little while, he thought bitterly, they'd had it all. And then came the descent into hell.

Once he and Eileen moved into the house and the business was launched, Harry found their lives assuming a pattern. They were surrounded by every luxury. Their servants performed impeccably. Eileen complained that

273

all the women thought about and talked about was clothes, but she enjoyed being part of this world. Everybody in Buenos Aires seemed to be satisfied with their lives, Harry decided. Even the office workers and salespeople and tradespeople—who ate filet mignon twice a day and commuted twice a day to their nearby suburban homes to have lunch and a siesta.

Argentineans were smug at not being bothered with the rationing that plagued most of the world. Only gas and tires were rationed—and for a price these could be had. Cars were no longer coming in, and coal was expensive and hard to acquire. But dried corncobs—available at seven dollars a ton—were being used as fuel in railway stations and power stations. And Harry remembered burning corncobs in Texas when he and Katie couldn't afford coal.

In the months ahead Harry discovered that Buenos Aireans considered most Americans gauche and without culture. The aristocratic families rarely socialized with any foreigners. And foreigners tended to form their own colonies. The English socialized with other English, entertaining one another at their homes and at the Hurlingham Club. The Americans entertained their fellow exiles and lamented about the absence of new golf balls, five-and-dime stores, and canned baby food. The Americans Women's Club had become a canteen for American sailors.

Harry sensed that the Porteños—natives of Buenos Aires—were growing suspicious of United States policies and, particularly, of the U.S. press. Bored with shopping after a while, Eileen had become an avid moviegoer. She reported that the American war newsreels that preceded each American film were cut to eliminate anti-Nazi sentiment.

"How do you know that?" Harry challenged, but he was not surprised. The feeling among the Americans was that Argentina was secretly pro-Nazi.

"I listen to people," Eileen told him. Harry recognized her ability to soak up Spanish. "They look at me and think, Oh, a dumb, rich blonde, and they talk. They don't like Americans, Harry."

"So they don't like us." Harry shrugged this away. "I'm setting up a terrific wheat pipeline here." He was working his tail off, driving around to hundreds of small farmers; but he was training agents to do the follow-up. "I pay just a fraction more than the other buyers—and they're mine."

He was handling the transportation problem. The syndicate backing up Simon & Sinclair owned ships. Buying low and selling high, the company was reaping enormous profits.

At the end of each day—no matter how exhausted he was—Harry devoured the American newspapers sent to him. He read the Dallas newspapers with an obsessive need to learn whatever he could about Katie and Joanne's daily lives. With an odd pride he read about Katie's expanding chain of stations, now situated across Texas. He cut from the Dallas newspapers the article about how Gas Girls, Inc., was handling the rationing problem.

Smart, he approved, the way Katie had issued membership cards to regular customers. Unlike other stations—which gave out a minimum amount to all comers or sold till the tanks were empty—Gas Girls, Inc., apportioned its supplies among club members. Their loyalty for this consideration earned the chain a big following. Now Katie was embarking on an expansion program to include all the southwestern states.

Gradually—while the war turned in favor of the Allies, with American troops forging ahead in the Pacific and in Europe—Harry and Eileen collected a circle of friends. They were mostly from the café society crowd—considered slightly déclassé by the Argentine aristocrats. Still, Harry thought with satisfaction, their social circle included several renowned European refugees and a pair of Argentine playboys. At regular intervals they were invited to cocktail parties at the posh Jockey Club.

In the midst of a world war they were living well. And Harry fought off recurrent bouts of guilt that he was not personally involved in fighting the war. This was not the image of himself he had nurtured in earlier years. Did every boy approaching manhood envision himself as changing the world?

Chapter Twenty-five

IN A dressing room at Neiman-Marcus Joanne—her beloved loafers discarded because they clashed with the sophistication of the dress she was trying on—inspected her reflection in the mirror. She was triumphant at being on the expensive second floor of the posh department store rather than the less expensive Younger Set Shop on the third floor, where she usually shopped. But she had permission to charge at Neiman-Marcus, she thought defiantly. Mother never said on what floor she was to shop.

"It's sensational, Jo," Betty gushed. "You look about twenty."

She had seen the dress—a designer original—in this issue of *Vogue*. She knew she'd die if she didn't get it.

"I'll take it," she told the cordial saleswoman, who knew both Joanne and her mother as regular customers. "Please charge it to my mother's account."

"It's so expensive," Betty said with awe when the two girls were alone, though her own wardrobe bill was impressive. "My mother would scream. She won't let me buy a designer dress until I'm in college." The two girls would enter their senior year of high school in four weeks.

"My mother will look pained when the bill comes in." Joanne shrugged this off. She'd learned how to handle her mother better than Betty handled hers. Betty's parents were oil-rich, but she could go just so far before they'd threaten to ground her or cut off her charge privileges. "I'll tell her it can be my high school graduation present."

"Hurry and get back into your clothes," Betty ordered. "I'm dying for a hamburger and a Coke."

Joanne dressed quickly, brushed her pageboy into its customary sleekness, and went with Betty into the elegant enclave of the designer selling floor. Nobody in their classes owned a designer dress, she thought with satisfaction. And not another store in town could sell the designer dresses that were shown at Neiman-Marcus.

"How are you doing on the deal about college?" Betty asked when they were back in Joanne's convertible and headed for a favorite teenage hangout.

"Mother's having a mild fit," Joanne admitted, "but don't worry—I'm handling it. I told her if I couldn't go to college with you in New York, then I wouldn't go at all. She just hates the thought of me going to a junior college—but I told her I might switch to a Texas college for my junior and senior years."

"You're really going on for a degree?" Betty radiated disbelief. "I can't believe it, Jo. . . ."

"I don't want to just float around when I'm out of school," she said self-consciously. She knew the college where they expected to go was really a fancy finishing school. Everybody said it was gauche to get married early these days, but that's what all the debutantes did. "I think women should have careers."

She didn't want to think about what would happen after college. Betty—her "best friend"—would come out and join the Junior League and go to parties all the time. But Joanne Newhouse wouldn't be invited to join the

Junior League. Even girls from really rich Jewish families were not invited to join the Junior League or the Shakespeare Club. People were always talking about how successful Mother was—but she wasn't, really. Not like the Sangers or the Marcuses.

She'd be famous someday and make them all sorry they were so mean to her, Joanne vowed. Maybe she'd be a movie star or go to New York and be a star on Broadway. One thing for sure, she thought defiantly. She'd get far away from Dallas—and from her mother.

Katie followed the progress of the war with soaring hopes for an early peace. On August 25, 1944, Paris was liberated. Early in September the U.S. First Army pushed its way into Germany. On October 20, Americans landed at Leyte, in the Philippines—fulfilling MacArthur's vow to return.

On November 7 Roosevelt was reelected for an unprecedented fourth term. Like many Americans, Katie now felt that the end of the war was near—that the country needed FDR to see them through this last hurdle to peace. But the following April FDR died in Warm Springs, Georgia, and much of the world mourned for him. How sad, she thought a few weeks later when the news of V-E Day ricocheted around the world, that he had not lived to see this.

By spring of '45 it was necessary for Katie to make arrangements for Joanne's college enrollment. Reluctantly she agreed to allow Joanne to go to the posh junior college in New York where Betty would go.

"It'll be a wonderful experience for the girls," Betty's mother told Katie. "They'll have the theater, concerts, opera. All those marvelous shops. It'll give them a touch of polish."

Della Forbes had no knowledge of that other New York, Katie thought wryly, where she and Harry had grown up. Joanne would never know it. She could give her daughter so much, she thought bitterly—but it meant so little to Joanne. For all her air of effervescent gaiety Joanne was still seeking to forget the brother she had lost. The wall Joanne had erected between them remained in place.

At their request Joanne and Betty shared a splashy high school graduation party. Katie felt uncomfortable about this extravagance, because—though the war was over in Europe—American soldiers were still dying in the South Pacific.

Now Joanne and Betty went to spend a month at the Forbes ranch. Early in August the girls returned to Dallas and focused on buying their college wardrobes. They haunted Neiman's, devoted hours to studying the pages of *Mademoiselle* and *Glamour*—new magazines dedicated to feminine fashions. They alternated between their beloved blue jeans and sloppy shirttails and a yearning for sophisticated designer dresses that made them feel awesomely grown up. To Joanne, Katie thought wistfully, V-J Day and the end of the war were just newspaper headlines.

Then, all at once, the date of their departure for New York arrived. Their mothers went to see them off at the Dallas airport.

"Betty, always remember you're a lady," her mother emphasized when she saw her daughter gazing flirtatiously at a young marine waiting for his flight to be announced.

Katie tried to match the girls' high spirits as they waited to board their plane. New York was so far away. And she knew with painful clarity that for Joanne this was the grand escape. She was escaping the past. She was escaping her mother's tenuous hold on her.

Then, in a rush of conviviality and anticipation, Joanne and Betty kissed her and Della Forbes good-bye and left them to board their plane. Long after the plane lifted off from the runway—with Della dashing off to some committee meeting—Katie stood gazing into the sky with tear-blurred eyes. *Let Joanne be all right off at school. On her own.*

It was going to be so awful to go into that empty house tonight. As long as Joanne had been there, she had hoped—she had prayed—to scale the wall that separated them. She'd thought she'd discovered a chink in that wall the day she went down to the police station to extricate them from their last scrape. But that had been a momentary hope. Joanne had retreated behind that wall again. Still, Katie consoled herself, there had been no further such escapades—and for that she should be grateful.

Enough of this, she rebuked herself now. Maura would be waiting at the restaurant to have lunch with her before she returned to the office. Bless Maura for suggesting lunch. For knowing the devastating loss she would feel today.

Maura was at their table, sipping a glass of white wine, when she arrived.

"I'm sorry to be so late," Katie apologized. "The plane took off ten minutes past schedule—and I just stood staring into the sky for a while. I can't believe my baby's off to school. All the way off in New York." Not the New York she had known, she thought—the one she and Harry had yearned to know.

"Joanne will be fine," Maura said with calculated conviction. "Wait till she discovers Saks and Bergdorf's and Lord and Taylor."

"I wish Willa and Jeff were not so stubborn about letting me help with Willa's college." Willa was taking a year off to work and save for college. She'd been in Katie's office since high school graduation. "It isn't really that much. It's not like that school of Joanne's."

"You know Willa and Jeff—too proud to accept a cent they haven't earned. George starts school next week," Maura reminded her. "And paying most of it from his savings. I'm so glad he'll be close enough to come home some weekends."

"Joanne won't be home till Christmas," Katie said

wistfully. "I was hoping for Thanksgiving, but both Joanne and Betty say it's too far for such a short school holiday."

"It's time to start living a life of your own," Maura said gently. "You're thirty-eight and look about twenty-eight. You don't have to spend the rest of your life alone."

"I'm buying a new house," Katie quickly changed the subject. "At least, I'm going to start looking for one. In Highland Park." This was the most expensive Dallas suburb. "I decided last night. I'll have a decorator do Joanne's room. . . ." Maybe with a beautiful new house Joanne would want to stay home next summer.

"You didn't hear a word I said," Maura scolded.

"I heard," Katie admitted. "But Harry's the only man I'll ever love."

Would there be a chance for them, with Joanne grown up and into a life of her own? A time when she and Harry could be together again?

Chapter Twenty-six

LATE IN October Katie was shown a house that she knew would delight Joanne. This feeling only deepened as the broker escorted her through each of the nine rooms.

"It's one of the loveliest houses in Dallas," the broker said with pride, and mentioned the asking price.

"One of the most expensive, also," Katie surmised with a reproachful smile.

"But you know how Dallas property is going up in value," the broker gushed. "It's a marvelous investment."

Always conservative in spending, Katie was unnerved by the price the broker quoted. Still, she reasoned, the business was succeeding beyond her most extravagant expectations. And the woman was right—Dallas property was a solid investment.

For two days they haggled over the selling price. This was a game she had learned well from Harry. At last, she accepted the terms and prepared to go to contract. By the time Joanne came home for the Christmas school break, she thought in exhilaration, this beautiful house would be theirs.

The thinking in Dallas in these first months after World War II ended was divided. Some Dallasites were convinced the war-created prosperity would erode now, that the city would experience unemployment. And in truth, during the first weeks of peace many workers were laid off. But Dallas citizens were determined to keep prosperity alive.

Bond issues were voted to create public improvements: the library, a new City Hall, Love Fields, a fine downtown auditorium, new streets, and a better water supply. There were those who were predicting that by 1955 metropolitan Dallas would have grown into a city of close to a million people. That the whole skyline would be changed. And Katie was predicting that, within ten years, Gas Girls, Inc., would be nationwide.

Now Katie launched a fresh venture. She negotiated with a New York investment firm to set up a second corporation—actually a subsidiary of Gas Girls. Her chain would now have access to its own oil refinery. By early November she scheduled a meeting in New York for her new associates. The trip to New York was largely motivated by her eagerness to see Joanne. She was plagued by Joanne's absence and the lack of any real communication other than telephoned requests for money and brief letters.

"I could handle this through letters and phone calls," she admitted to Maura and Jeff as they waited with her at the airport for her early-morning flight to be announced. "But I can't resist a chance to see Joanne."

"The last time you were in New York was 1929,"

Maura reminisced. "When you and Harry were en route to Europe. You were living high in those days. We were all so intrigued by Harry's success."

"Harry was the financial wizard, and I was going to be a famous writer," Jeff said with wry humor.

"You ought to be writing now," Maura scolded. "And I don't mean those occasional farm-journal articles you sell for peanuts."

"Maura, a time comes when you read the signals. I spent years of my life writing novels, and I earned nothing but enough rejection slips to paper an outhouse. I like farming—I put in a crop and something comes up. I'm fascinated by all the new developments in farming. If we learn to take care of the earth properly, then it will feed the world. That's more important to me than writing novels."

"That's my flight being announced," Katie said with a lilt in her voice. Tonight she would be in New York. Tomorrow afternoon she would see Joanne.

Aboard the plane Katie remembered the flight from London to Paris the summer of '29. She'd been terrified, though she had never admitted this to Harry. Now she flew regularly between cities where her stations were located because this was part of the business scene.

What had taken Harry to Paris? she asked herself recurrently through the years. Instinct told her it was in some way related to Pierre Simon. He'd never made another overture toward reconciliation after he'd sent the birthday present for Joanne from Paris. He couldn't know that she never saw the return address on the box. He assumed she and Joanne wanted no part of him.

Would she have written him if she'd known his address? Katie asked herself. She'd been terrified of upsetting Joanne even further. *She couldn't have written.* She would have lost Joanne completely. But there should have been some way to reach out across the miles to Harry without Joanne knowing, she reproached herself in retrospect.

On the trip into Manhattan Katie was enthralled by the night-illuminated view from the taxi. Maura had warned that the city would be hardly recognizable after all these years. That must be the Empire State Building, rising 102 stories into the sky, Katie thought with excitement. The tallest building in the world.

She remembered how she and Harry had said good-bye to the city twenty-two years ago on the pedestrian walk of the Brooklyn Bridge. She remembered the myriad lights that had suddenly appeared as sunset gave way to dusk. All these years later she could hear Harry's voice—*"Good-bye, New York. When we stand here again, we'll be rich."*

Briefly, they'd been rich—until the stock crash. Now *she* was rich. In dollars and cents she was rich. But she'd always known—though this seemed to elude Harry—that richness was in family and the love that was part of that. Now she had lost one child, and she'd lost her husband—and the second child was not truly hers. Joanne had held a wall in place between them since that awful day when Leo died.

With nostalgia she had instructed her secretary to reserve a suite for her at the Plaza. But once settled in her suite—with a view of the park—she was assaulted by bittersweet memories. Harry and she had spent their wedding night here—in the smallest, least expensive room in the hotel. Even that room had been a wild extravagance. But they had come to it with such hopes and dreams for the future.

Despite the hour she left the hotel for a brief walk in the cold crisp night. She would have liked to phone Joanne, but they had arranged to meet at the hotel after classes were over. Joanne might be annoyed if she called this late. The girls were probably studying.

If it had been Maura, and Willa were at school here, Maura would have called from the airport. But she still weighed every word she uttered to Joanne, Katie recognized in a moment of rare candor. Always fearful of upsetting her, of triggering terrible memories.

Katie slept little that night. The Plaza was a torture chamber of memories. It had been a mistake to come here, she rebuked herself. By 7:00 A.M. she had showered and was dressing. At this hour the day was gray and cold. She would wear the gray wool Mainbocher she'd bought at Neiman-Marcus, she decided. She meant to look smart, expensive but understated. With it she'd wear pearl earrings and her triple strand of pearls. Her tailored gray cashmere coat. Contrary to fashion's dictates, she refused to wear furs.

Think about business, she exhorted herself. Supposedly that was why she was here, though most of the details of her anticipated second corporation were in place. From Harry, she thought involuntarily, she had learned the fine points of running a business. Today's conference was a triumph for her.

She debated about having breakfast at the hotel, then—in a surge of restlessness—decided to walk first. At nine-thirty she arrived for her business conference. As ever, she was conscious of the astonishment of her male business associates that a woman was successful in operating a chain of gas stations. She enjoyed their respect, their eagerness to cooperate in this new venture.

By the time the conference was over, the day had brightened. Sunlight washed the city. Empty hours loomed ahead before she was to meet Joanne. She could shop, go to a museum, she considered—but she was in the mood for neither. Nor was she ready to go to lunch. On impulse she decided to go to a beauty salon for a facial. That was a relaxing way to push away an hour. Maybe a facial would relieve some of her tenseness. Then she'd have lunch. The beauty salon at B. Altman, she decided, then lunch at the Charleston Gardens. And after that she'd shop for some small gift for Joanne.

At the beauty salon she discovered that despite the

lack of an appointment she could have a facial within half an hour because of a cancellation. She debated about going out into the store to shop, then discarded the thought. She'd settle down with a magazine and wait.

She flipped through the supply of magazines, chose a recent edition of *Town & Country*. Hardly absorbing what she saw—the magazine lying across her lap—until a familiar face jumped at her from the pages. Her heart pounding, she gripped the magazine and brought it closer to her eyes. It was just someone with a startling resemblance to Harry, she told herself.

She read the caption beneath the photograph of the man who so resembled Harry. A man with a tall young blonde. "Mr. and Mrs. Harry Newhouse at an American embassy party." *Harry had remarried.*

Trembling, light-headed from shock, she inspected the photograph closely. That tall, smartly dressed blonde was Harry's wife. She looked so young. Half his age. *Not much older than Joanne.* Why had she nurtured the absurd belief that this would never happen? The divorce had meant nothing to her. It was a piece of paper needed to convince Joanne that her father was forever out of their lives. In her heart had lingered the dream that one day this nightmare would be over, and she and Harry could be together again.

Why did she feel betrayed? Harry wasn't her husband any longer. She had driven him out of her life. Why did she keep playing this ridiculous game? *There would be no tomorrow for Harry and her.*

Katie managed to survive the day. She had her facial, went upstairs for lunch at the Charleston Gardens—eating without tasting, bought a cashmere sweater for Joanne. She met Joanne as planned, but the joyously anticipated brief reunion was shadowed by the memory of what she had seen in the current issue of *Town & Country.*

286

At La Guardia—waiting for her return flight—Katie found herself inexorably drawn to a newsstand. Her hands trembling she reached for a copy of *Town & Country*, dug into her purse for a bill to pay for the magazine. Her heart pounded as she steeled herself to gaze again upon the photograph of Harry and his new wife. It would haunt her forever, she thought in anguish.

Again—back in Dallas—Katie was plagued by insomnia. Only Maura knew about Harry's remarriage. She'd asked Maura not to mention it even to Jeff. She brushed aside Maura's repeated pleas to start circulating socially. *"Katie, you're thirty-eight years old. Too young to put yourself in mothballs."*

She tried to focus on business, on the knowledge that Joanne would soon be home for the college's "winter break." In mid-December—with Dallas preparing for a festive Christmas season—Maura reminded her of an imminent benefit dinner for the symphony.

"Maura, I forgot." Katie was contrite. She had bought three tickets when she'd been solicited—for herself, Maura, and Jeff. But she was in no mood for such socializing, she thought in distaste. "Why don't you ask Willa to go in my place?"

"You're coming," Maura insisted. "You're running yourself ragged with business. You're getting so thin a good Texas breeze could knock you down. It'll be a fun evening. And I'll have a chance to wear my one dinner dress."

On the afternoon of the dinner Katie was disconcerted to discover that Maura had made a beauty-salon appointment for her.

"You've got half an hour to get over there," Maura told her calmly. "You need a trim, a shampoo, and a set for tonight. You can't spend the rest of your life avoiding beauty salons." Maura was compassionate about the painful memories the trip to the hairdresser would evoke, but she determined that Katie break this fear.

"The appointment is with Pam?"

"Of course. Doesn't Pam always do your hair? She couldn't understand why you haven't been in since before your trip to New York. I just said you'd been working your butt off. And that's true, too."

"All right, I'll go. But you're a bossy woman, Maura." Katie tried for a touch of humor.

Later—home from the hairdresser's and admittedly feeling more cheerful—Katie told herself she was glad she had shopped extravagantly at Neiman's yesterday for a new dinner dress—forest-green velvet cut with the new fullness embraced by the couturiers now that the war was over. The green emphasized the auburn glints in her honey-colored hair, the green in her blue-green eyes.

Maura and Jeff were lavish with their compliments when they arrived to pick her up.

"Katie, you'll never look like the efficient businesswoman you are," Maura clucked, "but in that dress you look like a movie star."

"Good thing we decided to leave our jalopy here and drive over in your car," Jeff said humorously. "That dress demands fancy wheels."

"Can you imagine what it took to get Jeff into a dinner jacket?" Maura whispered as they rushed through the night cold to the car. "If I hadn't found it on sale and brought it home, he'd never have one. And Dallas is a city that loves to dress up."

Approaching their table, Jeff was delighted to discover a longtime acquaintance was seated there. The two women watched while Jeff and Sherwin Kirk exchanged greetings.

"Maura, you remember Sherwin," Jeff said pleasurably. "He teaches at Southern Methodist."

"I remember," Maura said with warmth. "We met at a campus play several years ago."

Now Jeff introduced Katie to the tall, slender, meticulously groomed college professor. She was immediately conscious of his admiration as they exchanged small talk.

MORE PASSION AND ADVENTURE AWAIT... YOUR TRIP TO A BIG ADVENTUROUS WORLD BEGINS WHEN YOU ACCEPT YOUR FIRST 4 NOVELS ABSOLUTELY *FREE*
(AN $18.00 VALUE)

Accept your Free gift and start to experience more of the passion and adventure you like in a historical romance novel. Each Zebra novel is filled with proud men, spirited women and tempestuous love that you'll remember long after you turn the last page.

Zebra Historical Romances are the finest novels of their kind. They are written by authors who really know how to weave tales of romance and adventure in the historical settings you love. You'll feel like you've actually gone back in time with the thrilling stories that each Zebra novel offers.

GET YOUR FREE GIFT WITH THE START OF YOUR HOME SUBSCRIPTION

Our readers tell us that these books sell out very fast in book stores and often they miss the newest titles. So Zebra has made arrangements for you to receive the four newest novels published each month.

You'll be guaranteed that you'll never miss a title, and home delivery is so convenient. And to show you just how easy it is to get Zebra Historical Romances, we'll send you your first 4 books absolutely FREE! Our gift to you just for trying our home subscription service.

BIG SAVINGS AND FREE HOME DELIVERY

Each month, you'll receive the four newest titles as soon as they are published. You'll probably receive them even before the bookstores do. What's more, you may preview these exciting novels free for 10 days. If you like them as much as we think you will, just pay the low preferred subscriber's price of just $3.75 each. *You'll save $3.00 each month off the publisher's price.* AND, your savings are even greater because there are never any shipping, handling or other hidden charges—FREE Home Delivery. Of course you can return any shipment within 10 days for full credit, no questions asked. There is no minimum number of books you must buy.

4 FREE BOOKS

TO GET YOUR 4 FREE BOOKS WORTH $18.00 — MAIL IN THE FREE BOOK CERTIFICATE T O D A Y

Fill in the Free Book Certificate below, and we'll send your FREE BOOKS to you as soon as we receive it.

If the certificate is missing below, write to: Zebra Home Subscription Service, Inc., P.O. Box 5214, 120 Brighton Road, Clifton, New Jersey 07015-5214.

FREE BOOK CERTIFICATE

4 FREE BOOKS

ZEBRA HOME SUBSCRIPTION SERVICE, INC.

YES! Please start my subscription to Zebra Historical Romances and send me my first 4 books absolutely FREE. I understand that each month I may preview four new Zebra Historical Romances free for 10 days. If I'm not satisfied with them, I may return the four books within 10 days and owe nothing. Otherwise, I will pay the low preferred subscriber's price of just $3.75 each; a total of $15.00, *a savings off the publisher's price of $3.00.* I may return any shipment and I may cancel this subscription at any time. There is no obligation to buy any shipment and there are no shipping, handling or other hidden charges. Regardless of what I decide, the four free books are mine to keep.

NAME

ADDRESS _____ APT

CITY _____ STATE _____ ZIP

TELEPHONE
(   )

SIGNATURE _____ (if under 18, parent or guardian must sign)

Terms, offer and prices subject to change without notice. Subscription subject to acceptance by Zebra Books. Zebra Books reserves the right to reject any order or cancel any subscription.

God, what a new dress and a visit to a hairdresser could do, she joshed to herself.

"I remember when I used to spend summers with my grandparents on their farm—just a piece down the road from the Warrens' place. Jeff—though he was several years younger than I—used to come over and coax me to go swimming with him." Sherwin smiled reminiscently. "Then we started to talk books one day, and I was amazed how much he'd read for a kid his age."

"There wasn't much else to do on the farm at night," Jeff reminded him. "Thank God, we had electricity."

All through dinner Katie was conscious of Sherwin Kirk's covert—almost shy—glances in her direction. He must be about fifty, she guessed. Trim and distinguished, with a quiet charm.

"He's been divorced for years," Maura whispered at a moment when the two men were earnestly involved in dissecting a new novel.

"Maura, shut up," Katie scolded. But it was difficult to ignore Sherwin's interest in her. A pleasing balm for the rejection she had been feeling.

After the dinner—where Katie discovered that Sherwin shared her love for Strauss waltzes—the four of them lingered for further conversation.

"This has been so pleasant," Sherwin said with obvious enjoyment. "Why don't the three of you come over to my apartment one evening next week for dinner? I'm not a gourmet chef," he conceded, "but I can promise you a decent meal. And Strauss waltzes."

"We'd love it," Maura accepted for herself and Jeff, and turned to Katie. "Right, Katie?"

"It sounds like fun," Katie agreed. She was reluctant now to return to her empty house. A house full of ghosts, she thought in revulsion. Oh yes, another evening with friends held vast appeal.

"Then let's set a night," Sherwin picked up, smiling approval.

*   *   *

Katie was astonished by the importance the prospect of a small dinner party at Sherwin Kirk's apartment assumed. It was absurd to be counting the days, she derided herself. But everywhere she looked in her house, she saw Harry's face in the shadows. She had been able to handle her life until she discovered that he had remarried. Now she fought futilely to wash that knowledge from her mind.

She was conscious of a rush of anticipation when she went with Maura and Jeff to Sherwin's apartment on the appointed evening. The apartment was small but comfortably attractive. Jeff immediately headed for the bookcases to scan titles. Sherwin and Maura disappeared into the kitchen, going for glasses to serve the wine Katie had brought. A fire had been started in the fireplace grate. "What can I do to help?" she asked when Sherwin and Maura reappeared with wine-filled stemware.

"Just sit there and look beautiful," Sherwin ordered. His eyes told her of his pleasure at her presence.

Sherwin had prepared cream of asparagus soup, filet of sole poached in white wine, baked potatoes, and a tossed salad.

"Nothing fancy," he said with a deprecating smile. "And dessert's from the bakery."

The table talk was sprightly, eclectic. They discussed books, music, Sherwin's pre-war travels about Europe. For a moment fresh pain invaded Katie. She remembered her own trip to London and Paris—with Harry and the children. The trip that began with such joy and ended with despair. Then conversation turned to talk of the late war, and for a while the mood was somber.

"I was too old to fight in this war," Sherwin mused, "and married during World War One. Married men were mostly exempt." Unexpectedly he chuckled. "I was having a war of my own at home."

"What about dinner at our house one evening next week?" Maura asked. "I know it's a haul, but I promise you Black Forest cake like you've never tasted. You, Sherwin. Katie knows."

"The best in this world," Katie agreed. "But Joanne's coming home for the school holidays. I won't be free until she goes back to school."

"All right, the night after you see Joanne off," Maura decreed. "And no need for you two to drive out separately. . . ."

"I'll pick up Katie," Sherwin said with a warm smile. "I still can't believe you have a college-age daughter, Katie. I envy you three for being blessed with children. My wife and I had none. Just as well," he said with wry humor. "She would have made a horrible mother."

Katie was joyous at having Joanne home for the "winter break," though she sensed immediately that Joanne was restless here.

"Mother, Dallas is just an overgrown small town," Joanne complained over dinner at one of the city's charming new restaurants. "I don't know how you ever gave up New York to live here. I adore the shops and the theaters and the terrific restaurants in New York." She tolerated school because it was her means of remaining there, Katie understood all at once. "It's exciting just to walk around New York streets. What's Dallas got—except for Neiman's?"

"Don't sell Dallas short," Katie warned. Uneasy that Joanne might—in the future—reject her hometown. "It's really on its way up." She rattled off a stream of statistics. None of which—she noted with misgivings—seemed to impress her daughter.

Still, Katie tried to comfort herself, for all Joanne's putting down of Dallas, she was impressed by the new house—which would be ready for occupancy by the time she came home in the spring. She, too, looked forward to the move—as though another move would put more distance between herself and the painful past.

"I told Betty you'd hired an interior decorator to do the house," said Joanne, clearly pleased. "She was so surprised."

By the end of Joanne's fifth day home, Katie was worried by her admitted boredom.

"There's nothing to do here," Joanne complained when they sat down to dinner. "And the girls I know from school are so snooty. Betty's being invited just everywhere, but they act as though I wasn't even in town." Her eyes were accusing. Blaming *her*, Katie thought in frustration. Because they weren't Old Texas society.

"Joanne, you've been out three nights since you came home." Katie strived for lightness. "That makes you a very popular young lady."

"Betty goes out every night," Joanne sulked. "I wish it was time to go back to school."

Katie sent Joanne on a shopping spree at Neiman-Marcus to compensate for her missing out on some of the socializing. She strived to provide diversion on those evenings when Joanne was not involved in the holiday festivities. She tried—knowing it would be futile—to bring Joanne and Willa together.

Then it was time for Joanne and Betty to fly back to New York. Katie and Betty's mother saw them off.

"Isn't it just exhausting to have the girls home?" Della Forbes effervesced. "I adore Betty, but at this age they are too much."

As Maura had determinedly arranged, Katie and Sherwin drove out to the farm together for dinner the night after Joanne returned to school. Sitting down in the Warrens' recently enlarged dining room, Katie was grateful that Maura had chosen tonight. She always felt so alone those first nights when Joanne went away from home.

It had been a lovely evening, Katie thought when Jeff went to retrieve her coat and Sherwin's. Maura was right—she needed some socializing besides the occasional benefits, the campus plays they saw three or four times a year.

Before she and Sherwin left, Katie arranged a dinner party for the four of them at her house ten days later. This was just a group of friends sharing a pleasant evening, she told herself self-consciously. Not a man-woman thing.

As they drove to Katie's house, Sherwin talked about the academic world. She was content to sit back and listen. He admitted to certain frustrations.

"There're the same petty jealousies and hostilities you find in business. But on the whole I manage to enjoy a comfortable life. Still, there are moments best shared with a congenial companion. Like seeing a play or attending a concert. I'm not being very adept at this, am I?" he said with a rueful smile. "What I'm trying to say is that I have a pair of tickets for the symphony next week, and I'd enjoy it ever so much more if you were there with me."

"I'd like that very much," she said after a moment's mental debate. Sherwin wasn't avid to make a pass at her. He was lonely. She understood that loneliness.

In the weeks ahead she found herself spending a couple of nights each week with Sherwin. Always the same nights because these fit in with his schedule. Certain nights were devoted to academic situations. Sundays he spent with his mother.

He was the youngest of three sons. The other two lived in Oregon and rarely saw their mother or Sherwin. He didn't condemn them, Katie noted, but his displeasure shone from his eyes. Sherwin was a man who would never shirk his responsibilities, Katie guessed. So on specified nights they went to the theater, the symphony, the ballet. On occasion they haunted his favorite bookstore.

"Katie, you mean to say Sherwin has never made a pass?" Maura demanded impatiently over an office lunch. "God, do you suppose he's a fairy?"

"Maura, no," Katie admonished. "We don't have a romantic relationship. We're just two very congenial friends."

"He's scared to rush you," Maura decided. "I guess he got badly burned in his first marriage."

"Maura, stop it," Katie ordered. "Neither of us is thinking about marriage. That would spoil it." But there were moments when he seemed about to take her in his arms—and she knew she wouldn't reject him.

A week before Joanne was due home for the spring holidays, Katie moved into the magnificent new house. And she explained to Sherwin that she would be tied up until Joanne left.

"The whole time?" he asked wistfully.

"It won't be long," she reminded with a smile. It was *good* to feel she would be missed.

Joanne arrived and was full of praise for the new house. She bubbled with high spirits, Katie thought gratefully. But almost immediately she understood. Joanne was out to charm her into approving a school-sponsored cruise that would begin after a three-day tour of Chicago and travel to Mackinac Island; Goderich, Ontario; Escanaba, and Sturgeon Bay.

Mackinac Island, Katie thought, enveloped in nostalgia. Harry and she had gone there with Leo when he was a baby.

"It's just for three weeks—but it'll be so exciting," Joanne wheedled. "I'll have to sign up fast—there's room for only ten girls. And two teachers. Betty's going, of course."

Those were the magic words. Joanne knew—and she knew—there could be no refusing. She understood, too, that Joanne meant to spend as little time as possible in Dallas.

Chapter Twenty-seven

WITH JOANNE back at school Katie and Sherwin resumed seeing each other. She was tenderly amused by the way he compartmentalized his life. She fitted comfortably into two evenings each week. Tuesdays and Saturdays.

There were moments when she read about some new cultural event in the city, and her instinct was to reach out to the phone to call and discuss it with Sherwin. It was ridiculous to feel she'd be intruding, she scolded herself. Yet he never called her—and she accepted this as part of their relationship.

Late in May Sherwin suggested extending their Saturday diversion of that week to include an afternoon's drive to one of the lakes.

"Let's make it a full day, starting with a picnic lunch," he said exuberantly. "Before the damnable heat settles in over the city."

"I'll pack us a lunch," Katie offered. Oh yes, a day by the lake would be most welcome!

On Saturday Katie waited almost forty minutes past the scheduled time before Sherwin arrived. Ten minutes earlier—worried because Sherwin was always punctual—she'd phoned his apartment. He wasn't there. She sighed with relief when she saw his Chevy drive up before the house. She reached for the picnic hamper and hurried out to greet him.

"Katie, I'm so sorry," he apologized. "Every Saturday morning I grocery shop for Mother. She always insists she can do it herself, but I can't see letting that happen.

She's pushing eighty and fragile—I don't want her lugging bundles. I don't even like her driving these days."

"You're a good son," Katie told him sympathetically.

"There were several things I had trouble finding—I thought I'd never get out. I tried to phone, but the one phone in the place was out of order."

"Sherwin, stop worrying," she soothed. "I understand."

"You're wonderful," he said softly.

Later—as they relaxed on the lush grass beside the lake, at a spot ignored by all but themselves—Sherwin reached to pull her into his arms. His eyes questioning. She lifted her mouth to his in acquiescence.

"I've wanted to do that for such a long time," he said when their mouths parted. "I was afraid of driving you away."

"You won't." What a gentle, unassuming man he was. She felt cherished, protected, in his arms. For a little while she could forget about Harry and that tall young blonde he'd married.

Katie felt guilty at banishing Sherwin from her life for the brief time Joanne was home from school before leaving on the cruise. But he understood that the hours she was away from the office belonged to Joanne now.

In a joyous flurry of excitement Joanne and Betty flew to Chicago. Katie resumed seeing Sherwin. She knew he was waiting for a sign from her that she was ready to go beyond increasingly warm kisses. It touched her that he was so solicitous. She knew that she must make the first move.

The Saturday after Joanne left for her tour, Katie told Sherwin she had rented a beach house at La Jolla for the following weekend. For years, she knew, there were well-placed Dallasites who made La Jolla their summer destination. For land-locked Dallasites the Pacific shore was enticing.

"We can fly out Friday afternoon and return sometime Sunday," she said casually.

"For a whole weekend?" His eyes lighted with pleasurable anticipation. Then the glow disappeared. He seemed all at once ambivalent. "All the way to La Jolla?"

Katie was bewildered.

"You don't like to fly?"

"I love flying," he said defensively. "I always fly when I go out to lecture or attend a seminar."

"It's my treat," she rushed to explain, self-conscious at this display of her affluence. "I've made tentative arrangements for a charter flight both ways. And there'll be a car for our use out there. Sherwin," she coaxed, "you're always picking up the tab. Let me do this."

Sherwin squinted in thought.

"I'll have to arrange for someone to do Mother's grocery shopping on Saturday morning. There's a woman who's done it in the past when I had to be away on university business. And if we're back Sunday afternoon, then I can be with Mother for dinner. It'll work," he said with relief. "Oh, Katie, I can't wait!"

The beach house Katie had rented was a small masterpiece, designed in the style of Frank Lloyd Wright—long, low, with a multitude of windows facing the gentle Pacific. They arrived from the airport in the evening, in the car provided by the owner, and explored the house with delight.

Now they emerged from the house to walk along the beach, having dug sweaters from their luggage because the night air was refreshingly cool. The moon dropped a swathe of shimmering silver over the night-dark Pacific. The sky offering a dazzling display of stars.

"Katie, this was a wonderful thought."

Sherwin reached to draw her close in the beautiful solitude of the deserted beach. Tonight his mouth, his hands, were passionate. No holding back tonight, Katie thought in glorious anticipation. It might not be what she had known with Harry, but it would be good.

"Let's go inside," she whispered.

While moonlight filtered into the master bedroom, Sherwin swayed with Katie beside the bed. They both needed this, she thought in joyous defiance. For only a moment she worried that the long years of sleeping alone might cause difficulties. But Sherwin was not rushing, she realized gratefully. He wasn't some overheated young man with one destination in mind.

She stood immobile while he swept away the sheer nightie she wore—knowing its tenure would be brief. He stripped to skin, his body still lean and firm, testifying to his years of swimming and playing tennis. Then he lifted her from her feet, placed her on the bed, and lay beside her.

"I don't deserve such splendor," he whispered, his hands closing in about her breasts. "I feel like Cortez when he stood and gazed with such wonder at the blue Pacific."

"Sherwin," Katie scolded with a hint of laughter, "the Pacific is out there. I'm here." No more waiting, she thought with silent impatience, and reached a hand to him.

"The wonder you stir in me, Katie," he said with accelerating passion, "is the wonder Keats attributed to Cortez on that peak in Darien."

"Spoken like an English lit professor," she teased. Her voice uneven. Then her hands tightened about his shoulders. "Oh, Sherwin!"

From habit Katie awoke early the following morning, left Sherwin asleep to trail into the bathroom. She hesitated. If she showered, would the noise wake him? Why not? She told herself in tender amusement. They could sleep back in Dallas.

Before driving to the house last evening, they'd shopped for groceries. Showered and dressed, she went out to the kitchen—with windows that provided a magnificent view of the Pacific. She put up coffee, brought eggs and Canadian bacon from the refrigerator, popped rolls into the oven. She hadn't felt this *joie de vivre* in such a long time. She'd feared she might never feel it again.

The day raced past. While Katie prepared dinner in the kitchen, Sherwin laid a fire in the grate. Then she heard him talking in the bedroom. He was phoning his mother, she understood. He was always solicitous about her health.

"Mother, there's no need for you to phone me tomorrow. I'll be home in time for dinner." Katie tensed as his words reached her in the stillness of the house. "No, I can't give you a number for tonight—I'll be a guest of another professor—I don't know who it'll be." He'd told his mother this weekend out of town was university business, she interpreted. "I'll be there in time for dinner," he reiterated with the gentle tones he might have used to a young child.

Joanne returned from the cruise, to remain in Dallas for just a week. She would spend a month with Betty on the Forbes ranch.

"You know how I hate Dallas in the summer," she reminded her mother. "Thank goodness Mrs. Forbes invited me to come out there."

With Joanne out of their lives again, Sherwin talked about taking Katie to meet his mother. She gathered his mother understood he was seeing her regularly. But that wasn't interfering with his mother's life. He never missed his Saturday shopping chores or Sunday dinners with her, except that one weekend when they were out in La Jolla. And she gathered he talked to his mother every day that he didn't see her.

"You'll like Mother," he told her with quiet satisfaction, "but I warned her I'm robbing the cradle."

"Sherwin, there are not that many years between us," she laughed.

Was his mother upset that he appeared serious about a woman? Neither of them ever mentioned marriage. They'd both been badly hurt. Both, she told herself, content to let things remain the way they were between them.

Then, on a hot August afternoon—when his mother, he said, was suffering badly from the heat yet refusing to have her house air-conditioned—Sherwin broke his usual routine of seeing Katie twice a week to call between classes to ask if he might come over to the house on Friday evening. She smiled tenderly as she listened. He knew the housekeeper, Melinda, was off on Fridays. They would be alone.

"Come for dinner," she invited. She rarely cooked these days, but it would be pleasant to cook for Sherwin. When he came on Saturdays, Melinda cooked and served dinner, then went out for the evening—as customary on Saturdays. "We'll eat on the patio." Enclosed and air-conditioned.

"Great," he approved.

At 7:00 P.M. sharp on Friday Sherwin arrived at the house. Dinner was on the range, ready to be served at any moment. A bottle of wine was chilling in the refrigerator. The lilting strains of "Tales from the Vienna Woods" filtered through the house.

"Oh God, it's wonderfully cool here," he said, and reached to kiss her.

"Isn't your air conditioner working?" she asked as they crossed from the foyer into the huge, airy living room.

"Mine's fine," he reassured her, sitting on the summer-slipcovered sofa and drawing her down beside him. "But I was at Mother's for the past two hours. She had another of her anxiety attacks." Twice in the past month Sherwin had been forced to miss an evening with her because his mother had suffered an anxiety attack. "It's hot as hell there. I offered to pay for the air conditioners, but she won't hear of it. When she was a girl, nobody had air conditioning. She thinks to have it now is a sign of weakness."

"You're probably starving," she guessed, some of her high spirits evaporating. Sherwin's mother always seemed to be intruding on their time alone. "I'll put dinner on the table."

"I'd just as soon we wait a while." He smiled sheepishly. "You know Mother—she kept stuffing me with food when her attack was over."

"Like the stereotyped Jewish mother?" she teased.

All at once Sherwin seemed ill at ease.

"Katie, when I take you over to see her, there's no point in mentioning you're Jewish."

"Why not?" Katie stiffened in defiance.

"Well, she might be a little upset if she thought I was seriously interested in someone out of my faith." He sighed, stared at the floor for a moment. "Katie, why do we have to go on like this? Just being together twice a week. Why can't we be married?" He reached for her hand. "Life could be so comfortable for us. We could be together without playing games. I'd get rid of my apartment. We could break through a wall between two of your guest rooms to make a little apartment for Mother. God, you have enough space." *Sherwin would expect his mother to live with them?* Every argument would be settled by an anxiety attack, she thought with a flash of clairvoyance. "There's even enough space for a nursery," he added archly.

Katie froze. Physically she was able to have more children—but how could she ever allow this to happen? *She had failed as a mother. She couldn't go through that again.* But she understood Sherwin. He was past fifty and afraid life was passing him by. He wanted children, a comfortable home, a wife to share the responsibility of looking after his mother.

"Sherwin, I don't think I want to marry again," she said unsteadily.

"Why not?" He was affronted by this rejection. *He had expected her to be grateful.*

"I've lived alone a long t-time," she stammered. "I have Joanne to consider. I—"

"Joanne's a grown woman—even if you do treat her like a child," he interrupted impatiently. "She'll marry and move out. Do you want to be left alone in this big house? We'll start a new family. You won't even have to give up your business. Mother will be in the house to supervise the nursemaid—"

"No, Sherwin." She was gentle yet firm. "I'll never marry again."

He stared at her in disbelief, then in anger.

"You've used me! You just wanted a stud. You're one of those damn independent women who think they need nothing on earth except themselves—and a man in their bed when they choose." He rose to his feet, his face flushed. "Don't call me the next time you want to fuck. We're through!"

Katie sat cold and trembling long after Sherwin left. Dinner simmering on the range and forgotten until the unmistakable aromas of food burning shot her into the kitchen. She shut off the gas, stared without seeing at the remains of dinner. She shuddered as she envisioned her life if she was Sherwin Kirk's wife.

Let her realize now and forever that she'd lost the one man whose wife she could ever be.

Chapter Twenty-eight

HARRY SAT in a burgundy leather lounge chair in the library of their magnificent rented house on Avenida Alvear and gazed without seeing into the winter sunlight of beautiful Palermo Park. A batch of American periodicals—which he'd meant to read—were on the table at his elbow. He was disturbed by the rumors circulating in Buenos Aires about Juan Perón—President Perón since June.

These last three years had been highly successful ones for him businesswise. He had learned quickly how to deal with the Argentinean wheat farmers. As anticipated, he had been able to buy cheap, and Simon & Sinclair sold high. But rumors about Perón's plans for Argentine wheat were ominous.

"Harry!" Eileen stood imperiously in the doorway. Wearing one of her dramatic Balenciaga evening gowns. "You should be dressed by now. We have to leave for Carlotta's party in half an hour." Carlotta Mendoza was a wealthy Buenos Aires widow who was a leader in the jet-set circle. She delighted in hosting lavish parties, where the guests sometimes included important political figures.

"I can be ready in fifteen minutes," Harry said with a shrug. He had no intention of being late for Carlotta's party. He hoped to collect inside information on Perón's plans for Argentine wheat before the night was over. "Keep your antennae up for the wheat situation," he reminded her. They'd discussed this at breakfast. Eileen had been upset at the prospect of their idyllic business being seriously downgraded.

"I'll collect for you," Eileen promised. Harry knew she was proud of her talent for acquiring gossip for him. Bored by the sameness of their daily lives—though she took off for frequent house parties at favored summer and ski resorts—Eileen relished sharing his business life, even in this unrecognized and unrewarded fashion. "Harry, we won't have to leave Buenos Aires, will we?" Her voice was strident with alarm.

While she complained about boredom, Eileen was reluctant to abandon their luxurious lifestyle. Here they lived as though he were a multimillionaire. Back in the

States, he thought dryly, his salary—large though it was—would not support them in their current fashion.

"We'll see what happens," he hedged. "But I don't like what I'm hearing. Perón is determined to industrialize the country. His close advisers are telling him that the best way to finance this would be with profits from grain exports. They're telling him to take over control of the grain trade."

"Can he do that?" Eileen stared at him in disbelief.

"This is not the United States," Harry shot back. "Perón will do whatever is best for his own interests. He realizes we're making tremendous profits. Oh sure, he'll talk a lot about taking over the trade for the good of the country—but he and his private clique will line their own wallets first."

"He'll have his hands full with other problems," Eileen said after a moment. Like himself, she was knowledgeable about Argentine politics. "It won't happen for a while."

"But we have to know which way he's leaning," Harry pointed out. "The company has to be ready to move in other directions."

"You said there's a real grain shortage back home," Eileen recalled.

"Right now," he conceded. "Of course, every year is different—depending upon that year's crop. For the next twelve months, at least, we're going to need every bushel of grain we can buy."

"Carlotta likes me," Eileen said with a devious smile. "I'll tell her I'm fascinated by the men who're important in Perón's administration. I'll ask her to give a dinner and invite some of Perón's top advisers."

"Do." Harry nodded in approval and rose to his feet. He hadn't expected Eileen to be a business asset—but she was proving highly useful.

Harry left the library and went up to his bedroom. He and Eileen had separate bedrooms with connecting bath and dressing rooms. He was frank in admitting he liked this arrangement. He had become an insomniac through the years, often reading far into the night. He was obsessed by American periodicals and newspapers, intent on ever increasing his knowledge about the grain trade. And instinct told him—though he refrained from saying as much to Eileen—that their months in Buenos Aires were numbered.

Changing into evening attire, Harry pondered for the dozenth time his suspicions that Eileen was having an affair with an Argentinean playboy ten years his junior. No, he rebuked himself, he was becoming a neurotic husband. Part of having just passed his forty-first birthday. Eileen flirted, sure. She liked to feel sought after by rich and handsome young men. But she wasn't sleeping around. She knew she had a good thing as Mrs. Harry Newhouse. She'd come a long way in a very short time.

Katie was distressed when Joanne wrote home from school early in her second year that she'd prefer to continue her education in New York City rather than in Texas. She talked vaguely about a "major in English lit" at New York University. "If I get accepted, of course," she wrote.

"What's she going to do with that?" Katie demanded of Maura and Jeff over Thanksgiving dinner in her exquisitely furnished new house. Joanne had rejected coming home for the holiday—as she had last Thanksgiving. She and Betty were houseguests of a classmate whose family lived in Westchester County.

"If she takes some education courses, she can teach," Maura suggested.

"Do you see Joanne teaching?" Katie challenged. *What did she see Joanne doing?* Marrying well, she tried to comfort herself. Becoming a beautiful young society matron.

"She could go into publishing," Jeff said slowly. "That's the destination of a lot of English majors."

"I'm going to insist she go on with her schooling here

in Texas," Katie resolved. This time she'd have to be firm. "I don't want her floating around in New York alone." After graduation in June Betty would come home and prepare to "come out." She would make her debut, join the Junior League, and become part of that esoteric world. Joanne would have to pursue her life without Betty.

"Katie, you never stand your ground with Jo," Maura interrupted her introspection. "Maybe this time you should."

"I'll insist." Katie battled with apprehension. It would be better to have a confrontation with Joanne now than to have her remain in New York for another two years. Without Betty, she thought with a flicker of panic. Knowing her belief that Betty would make sure she and Joanne didn't become involved with the wrong people was illogical. Betty had long been drilled by her parents to mix only with her "own kind"—but they were adrift alone in a strange city so unlike Dallas.

Fearful but determined, Katie was adamant about Joanne's taking her junior and senior years at a Texas college. Joanne was outraged at not being able to manipulate her as in the past. She uttered dire threats—*"I'll just stay here in New York and be a cocktail waitress or maybe a model."* Then—sullen and reproachful—she applied for admission to the University of Texas in Austin and was accepted.

In June Katie went to New York for Joanne's graduation. Sitting with Betty's parents in the flower-bedecked auditorium, she watched the ceremonies with eyes blurred by sentimental tears. So proud of her beautiful young daughter, completing two years of college. Imagining her own mother's pride if she could be here today. Remembering her aborted dreams to earn a college degree. And, inevitably, remembering Leo and his terror of being shipped off to college and failing to fulfill his father's dreams.

Katie and Joanne flew home together. Betty and her

parents were flying to Bar Harbor for three weeks. Katie realized that the division between Joanne and Betty was beginning—and she worried about the effect on Joanne. When Betty returned from Bar Harbor, she would be swept up in preparation for her role as an Idlewild debutante. The shopping, Betty told Joanne, would be endless. She'd need dresses for luncheons, for cocktail parties, for endless balls. Betty would have little time, Katie understood, for her longtime "best friend."

Betty would make her official entrance onto the Dallas social scene at the Idlewild Ball at the end of October—in a white gown, and her final bow—in a pastel gown—at the Terpsichorean Ball three months later. During those months she would attend two or three parties every day, six days a week.

"Mother says we'll probably go to Maine Chance for a week at the end of January to recuperate," Betty had confided. "The new Maine Chance, near Phoenix—not the old one in Maine."

To divert Joanne's thoughts from Betty, Katie talked—on the plane trip west—about her expansion plans for the business.

"I'm moving out into the Pacific Coast area," she said confidently. "All the key cities. Tacoma, Seattle, San Francisco, Los Angeles." But Joanne wasn't interested in Gas Girls, Inc., Katie realized.

Back in Dallas Katie waited anxiously to see how Joanne would occupy herself this summer. During past summers she had gone on trips with Betty, spent time with Betty on the family's ranch. She felt a surge of relief when—almost immediately upon her return—Joanne became involved with a pair of former classmates from her posh private high school. Girls like herself, who were from well-heeled families but lacked the credentials providing entrée into the Dallas social world of debuts, country-club memberships, and Junior League status.

She was pleased to see Joanne being pursued by eager-eyed young men who would be in demand as escorts for

Dallas debutantes but were happy—meanwhile—to date a Dallas coed with Joanne's obvious attractions. Not prospective husbands Katie acknowledged—these young men were often not of Joanne's faith—but a summer diversion. Katie told herself that Joanne would have an enjoyable summer.

Returning from an October field trip, Harry found a pile of American newspapers and magazines atop his desk. As always, he filtered through to dig out the Dallas newspapers for first perusal. On the society page of one Dallas newspaper he discovered an article about the planned college activities of a group of Dallas young people.

With his pulse racing, he read about Joanne's graduation from her expensive New York junior college. And then he recognized the name of the posh school. It was the college that Michelle Goncourt had attended all those years ago. Even today he could remember his pain the evening he discovered Michelle had left New York without a word to him.

Why had Katie allowed Joanne to go to school in New York? He thought about Michelle and felt a rush of anger that Katie had permitted Joanne—reared gently in Dallas—to go off into such freedom.

Joanne had celebrated her twentieth birthday in June, he thought. *She was going out with boys.* Young guys today were so brash, he worried. The war years had brought about a change in morals. Had Katie taught her not to hop into beds, the way so many young girls had done during the war years?

Joanne would work for a degree at the University of Texas, he read with pride. His daughter would be a college graduate. The first in the family. But why hadn't Katie sent her to Radcliffe or Barnard or Vassar? From what he read about her business ventures, Katie could afford the best colleges.

His thoughts turned, inevitably, to Leo. All through the month of May—every year—he was tormented by memories of his son. For everyone, he guessed, there was one month that was a time of painful recall. Like himself, Pierre hated the month of May. That was when the two of them fled from Paris, with Nazis at their heels.

Pierre's wife and daughters had refused to leave. They had survived the war—with all of Pierre's possessions transferred to their names. And the three women wanted no part of Pierre after the war. What they had from him they meant to keep.

"We were never a real family after the first few years," Pierre had confided. "But damn it, the girls are my *daughters*. How can they treat me like a total stranger?"

Now Harry turned to *The New York Times*, scanning for articles of special interest. Later he'd read every article. From the *Times* he moved to *The Washington Post*. He paused to read an article about Juan Perón, which labeled the Argentinean president a "sort of international black marketeer." The article confirmed the gossip he'd heard—that the Argentine government was paying Argentine farmers $1.25 a bushel for wheat and reselling it in Europe for $5 to $6 a bushel. Basically, Harry conceded, what grain merchants like Simon & Sinclair were doing.

In the next twenty-four hours Harry devoured his cache of American newspapers and magazines. At the moment wheat was in short supply in the United States. The European market was hungry for wheat. When would Perón move in to cut off foreign businesses from buying up Argentine wheat?

Their time was running out, Harry warned himself yet again. Perón would enact a law that would give him control of all Argentine wheat. What should be the next direction for Simon & Sinclair to take?

A couple of days later Harry focused on a report about the new food habits in Japan. Wheat bread had been almost unknown in Japan until General MacArthur arranged for wheat to be imported to Japan last year. The wheat was made into bread—and *the Japanese liked it*. Wheat bread was becoming wildly popular in Japan.

Of course, Harry conceded to himself, last year's wheat crop and this year's crop had not been good—but all indications from the Midwest were that the next crop would be heavy. Analysts were predicting a surplus. It would sell cheap—and could be exported to Japan at high prices.

In his usual thorough manner Harry began to research the situation of shipping wheat to Japan. He learned that for years the "white" wheat grown in the state of Washington had been exported to Japan. It produced the perfect flour for the noodles that were a mainstay of the Japanese diet, as well as the flour for cakes and biscuits.

But, Harry's research revealed, this low-protein wheat did not produce satisfactory bread flour. The Japanese were buying the more suitable high-protein wheat raised in western Canada—notably in Saskatchewan and Manitoba. And instinct told him this was a trend that would continue and escalate.

Wheat grain in the prairie belt—from Texas to North Dakota—was bread wheat, he pinpointed from past knowledge. But hell, it was far from the West Coast ports! How could they move that grain to the ports without raising its cost prohibitively?

Sooner or later, he reasoned, the government would move in to provide lower freight rates to sell off Midwest grain—but the government moved so damn slowly. The road to selling Midwest grain to Japan—most likely a huge crop in the coming season, he reiterated—was through a tie-in with a railroad line operating from the Midwest to the West Coast. Their shipping facilities—a tie-in with Simon & Sinclair—could move their operations from Buenos Aires to Japan.

Harry churned with anticipation. He knew just how

the company was to proceed. They'd buy in the Midwest, sell to Japan. They'd have a healthy replacement for the lost Argentine wheat.

Over dinner that evening he told Eileen he was flying to Minneapolis in a few days for a conference with Pierre and Arnie.

"Are you going to talk to them about closing down here?" Her voice was sharp, her eyes accusing.

"Perón is plotting a government monopoly on grain," he said. "What choice do we have but to move?"

"Wait until it's necessary," Eileen urged. "We might have another year here."

"I'll discuss it with Pierre and Arnie," he said evasively. "I have to tell them what's hanging over our heads."

"I'd hate living in Minneapolis again," she sulked.

"We won't be there long," he promised. Arnie wasn't becoming easier to deal with, Pierre had warned. *"He's a real bastard. He'll cut your throat or mine in a minute if he thinks it's to his advantage."*

Eileen frowned, a sliver of choice Argentine filet mignon impaled on a fork midway between plate and mouth.

"Where will we live?"

"Probably Seattle. I hear it's a great town." Anything except Dallas was exile, he thought subconsciously. "I'll have to go out there and set up port storage at Puget Sound."

"I'll hate Seattle," Eileen flared. "Where the hell is it, anyway? Off at the end of the country somewhere . . ." She grimaced in distaste.

"It's up in a corner of the state of Washington," he began, and she interrupted.

"Oh God, it'll be as cold as Minneapolis. Maybe colder."

"No," he soothed. "While actually it's further north than Quebec, it's warmed by the Japanese current—you'll never see zero weather in Seattle. And the summers are mild."

"I'll hate it," Eileen repeated. "Nobody we know ever goes to Seattle." She paused. "Is it near San Francisco?"

"Not really," he conceded. "It's almost a thousand miles north of San Francisco."

"Why can't we settle in New York?" She'd never seen New York except for their one day there before boarding a ship for Buenos Aires, but to Eileen New York was the most glamorous city in the world, after Paris and London. In New York, Harry interpreted, Eileen would see her jet-set friends at regular intervals. Seattle was not on their itinerary.

"Business calls for us to live in Seattle," he pointed out. Eileen understood business took precedence over personal preferences.

He'd done extensive research, as usual, even though he had not yet discussed this new venture with Pierre and Arnie in real depth. Seattle was the ideal location for them. It had terrific transportation facilities to the Orient, though he harbored some concern about the strength of the teamster union boss, Dave Beck—said to "run Seattle"—and possible expensive labor. Simon & Sinclair's railway connections guaranteed efficient transportation to the Seattle docks. And already he was receiving tentative interest from the Japanese grain buyers he had approached.

"I'm scheduled to fly to Paris with Carlotta in three weeks," Eileen reminded him. Geared for battle. She was ever conscious that their friends in Buenos Aires were veteran world travelers.

"You'll go, Eileen," he soothed. She'd spend a fortune at the couturiers, but he liked her to look smartly—expensively—turned out. It was part of his image as the supersuccessful grain merchant.

But his success was hollow, he thought with painful candor. He'd longed to lay a second success at Katie's feet—to make up for the debacle of '29. *But Katie didn't need him.* She'd become a wealthy woman on her own.

Like Ulysses, he was doomed to roam about the face of the earth. But after long years, Harry taunted himself, Ulysses returned home, was reunited with his wife, and lived in peace for many more years. Katie was no longer his wife—and she wanted no part of him.

Maybe—just maybe—he stipulated in sudden excitement—he could stop off in Dallas for twenty-four hours en route to Seattle. He should set up an agent in Dallas as soon as possible to buy for the company. But mainly he had an obsession to see Dallas again. To see for himself the house where Katie was living. He nurtured a wild longing to see her—and Joanne.

They wouldn't know he was there, he told himself. Joanne was away at college, Katie all involved in the business. But it would be a precious experience if he could see Katie—even at a distance. To see the house where she lived. To see the downtown building where she had her offices.

All at once he was consumed with impatience. He'd cable Pierre to say he'd be arriving in Minneapolis in a week. Before he returned to Buenos Aires to wind up company and personal affairs, he'd fly out to Dallas to set up an agent. Later he'd set up a network of agents. And he'd check out port storage in Seattle.

He'd be doing much traveling for the first six months, he judged. That was good—he needed that kind of activity. Eileen would be in a perpetual foul mood, he suspected. Furious that they were no longer able to keep up the old lifestyle—a mansion with five live-in servants. She'd have to settle for a housekeeper-cook and a part-time maid. The cost of living in Seattle was among the highest in the country.

Perhaps he'd bring Eileen into the office. She'd been hinting about that here in Buenos Aires. In Argentina that was unacceptable. In Seattle women in the business world were commonplace. It would make her feel important. She'd be less apt to bitch constantly.

In a way, Katie thought guiltily, it had been a relief when Joanne left for college. The tension between them had become horrendous those last weeks before the opening of school. Joanne was so resentful at not being allowed to return to New York. It had come down to a furious realization on Joanne's part—that there was a limit to her mother's forbearance. Despite her rash threats both knew she was too accustomed to her comfortable lifestyle to abandon this.

Katie was glad of a necessity to fly to Seattle—where she planned to open three new stations—shortly after Joanne left for school. The house seemed painfully empty without Joanne's presence—though, in truth, they'd been like the proverbial "ships that pass in the night," she thought with wistful candor. She'd rush in from the office and—most evenings—Joanne would be rushing off on some social engagement or other.

On the morning when she was to leave for Seattle, Maura drove her to the airport. For two months now Maura had been working in her Dallas office.

"I never thought I'd be thrilled to be working in an office," Maura confided as they headed for Love Airport. "But I was just vegetating there on the farm. Willa loves it. Can you imagine, my daughter going to agricultural college?"

"I saw it coming," Katie said gently. "I think it's wonderful."

"Maybe now I'll start taking off some of the lousy weight I've put on. I eat when I'm depressed." Katie knew Maura was depressed because Jeff had stopped writing. "I eat when I'm bored. And oh God, was I bored on the farm! I could handle it when the kids were growing up and Jeff was writing—but no more. I'm forty-five years old and staring at menopause. All of a sudden I see my life slipping away. I want something more exciting than defrosting the refrigerator and waxing the floors. Katie, thank God you coaxed me into an out-of-the-house job."

"Jeff isn't upset, is he?" Katie knew she'd asked Maura this several times in the past two months—and each time Maura's answer had been in the negative.

"It's taken him a little while to adjust," Maura admitted now. "He was used to me always being there to put his lunch on the table or bring him coffee out in the fields in the afternoon. I made more of a fuss over meals because I had so damn much time on my hands. But he respects the money I'm bringing into the house. He enjoys the extras it provides."

"That's good." Jeff was almost paranoid about accepting financial help, Katie remembered.

"But damn it, Katie, I wish he'd get back to writing something besides occasional farm articles. He's convinced himself that writing fiction is a waste of time."

"I liked that last article," Katie said. "The one that warned farmers against becoming caught up in all the new fertilizers—all the *chemicals*—coming into the market."

"You know Jeff." Maura smiled tenderly. "For all his youthful rebellion against being on the farm, he has such reverence for the land. Like his father and grandfather before him, he considers farmers the 'stewards of the land.' It upsets him to see so many farmers selling out to move into the city and work at dull jobs. As farmers they're their own men—answerable only to themselves."

"I've seen the For Sale signs on the McDougal farm a few miles down the road from you," Katie recalled. "It doesn't seem to be moving."

"They're getting desperate," Maura told her. "The house needs serious repairs—and they don't want to lay out the cash or take out a loan. They just want to unload it and move into town."

"They'll sell low." Katie felt a tug of excitement.

"Are you considering buying?" Maura was instantly alert.

"Maybe it sounds crazy—but, yes." Land was always a good investment when bought at a low price. "Would you ask them what their bottom price is, and call me tonight at the Olympic in Seattle? If it's a good price, I'll buy it." She felt exhilarated at the prospect. "I'll resell the house with a few acres and let the rest go fallow for a year." That was what Jeff always preached. *Give the earth time to repair itself.* "Later I'll rent it out."

"I never thought," Maura said whimsically, "when Jeff and I first met you and Harry that you'd one day own a chain of gas stations reaching halfway across the country. And buying up Texas land the way I buy up bobby pins."

"I've never gotten over my sense of awe at owning land."

Katie's mind darted back through the years to the day when she and Harry had taken over Amelia's farm. She had felt as though they had become rulers of a cherished empire. Harry, too, had felt that way. And she remembered—with fresh pain—the day Harry learned through a bank clerk about an auction of a huge tract north of their farm and how the bank had offered him a loan to buy it. But the loan would have meant a mortgage on their farm—and she had refused to allow this. Weeks later the land had produced an oil gusher. *How could she have known?* How could she have allowed him to gamble on their one chunk of security?

"I felt that way about the land when Jeff brought me out here and showed me the farm." Maura's voice was soft. "To me a quarter-acre plot had been a lot of land—and here we owned hundreds of acres."

"It's strange, Maura. Harry and I have been separated for eight years." Even now she couldn't bring herself to say "divorced." Not even though she'd discovered he'd remarried. "But Harry's still guiding my life. I'm thinking Harry's way. It's as though Harry still walks beside me."

Chapter Twenty-nine

HARRY WAS relieved when the conferences with Pierre and Arnie were over. As always, there was conflict between Arnie and himself. Arnie might be a genius at raising capital, Harry conceded to Pierre as they waited at the airport for the flight to Seattle, but he was totally lacking in vision.

"To hell, you got your point across," Pierre soothed. "Arnie knows you've pushed us in the right direction. It was a brilliant decision."

"What do you hear from your daughters?" Harry asked. Only in the last two years had Pierre resumed some sort of relationship with his two daughters, though they continued to hold on—with their mother—to the fortune he'd left behind.

"They're both very pregnant. I can't believe it. I'm going to be a grandfather. Twice!"

"It won't cramp your style," Harry joshed. Even now—in his late fifties—Pierre never lacked for attractive women in his life.

"I can't believe it, Harry," Pierre said softly. "I'm going to have grandchildren. I'd just about given up—both girls are in their thirties."

"That's my flight they're announcing." Harry rose to his feet. "Take care of yourself, Granddad."

Usually Harry used flying hours to study reports, read business journals. The news of Pierre's imminent grandfatherhood had thrust him into somber contemplation about Joanne and Katie. Family had always been so important to him. Even now he remembered his

317

pain—how old had he been then, fourteen?—his feeling of desolation, when his whole immediate family died in the flu epidemic of 1918. And his life had been devastated a second time when his daughter and his wife banished him from their lives. They had ceased to be a family.

Harry was caught up in an air of unreality when—at last—the DC-4 approached Love Field. He remembered with what anguish he had left Dallas—via a "sleeper" from Dallas to New York—a little more than eight years ago. Even from the air he saw signs of a changing city. New buildings on the skyline, much construction in progress. He'd yearned to be a part of Dallas's expansion—but that was not to be.

Tense and beleaguered by recall, Harry took a taxi from the airport to the Hotel Adolphus—where he and Katie had enjoyed festive dinners on special occasions. Gazing from his taxi window without seeing, dizzy with the effort to remember he was not here to try for a reconciliation with Katie. Hell, he had another wife now! And Katie had made it clear she didn't want—didn't need—him.

As the taxi approached the city, Harry pushed himself to focus on the passing scenery. With a start he stared at an immaculate, well-maintained gas station just ahead. His throat tightening with comprehension he read the sign: GAS GIRLS, INC. *One of Katie's stations.* One of many, his mind taunted.

Settled in his room, he questioned this choice of hotels. For him the Adolphus was inhabited by ghosts. He remembered the first time he had walked with Katie into the Adolphus dining room. Ashamed of her shabby coat, she had taken it off in the lobby and carried it over her arm. He'd silently promised himself that one day she would wear the most expensive furs.

Without bothering to unpack, he reached for the local telephone book on the night table, turned to the Highland Park section—where he knew she lived. His heart hammering—his hand not quite steady—he flipped through to the *N*'s—then remembered that Katie had assumed her maiden name. He flipped the pages back and ran one finger down the *F*'s.

Here it was. The house where she lived. Katie wouldn't be there now—she'd be at her office. He'd take a taxi over and just have a look, he told himself self-consciously. He needed to see where Katie lived—how well she lived.

A hand on the door, he paused, returned to the telephone. *He was so close to Katie.* Let him hear her voice. He wouldn't say a word, just listen for a moment, then hang up. Crazy, he admitted to himself—but he couldn't deny himself this.

He sat immobile, planning what to say that would get him through to Katie. *"I'm Izzy Hirsch from New York—I knew Miss Freeman years ago."* He'd hang up as soon as she answered. Katie would think Izzy got cold feet and aborted the call. Screwy, sure—but he'd plotted this trip to Dallas just to feel closer to Katie. He could have delayed interviewing prospective agents until after he'd checked out Seattle.

In a cold sweat he waited for the switchboard at Katie's firm to reply.

"Gas Girls, Inc.," a cordial yet businesslike voice replied.

"I'd like to speak to Miss Freeman, please. I'm—"

"Miss Freeman is out of town," the young, feminine voice told him. "Can somebody else help you?"

"Thank you, no." He hung up, sick with disappointment.

Katie was out of town, and Joanne was away at school. But he could see the house where they lived and the office where Katie carried on business. And then he'd forget this craziness and focus on what he needed to do for Simon & Sinclair. He had half a dozen appointments set up in town. Go through the interviews and get the hell out of Dallas.

Katie sat over a late room-service dinner in her posh suite at the elegant Hotel Olympic and listened to Irene Leslie, the office manager of her newly established Seattle headquarters. Irene had been with the company for four years, moving up rapidly. Most recently she had been office manager in their Kansas City office.

"If we're to keep our employees happy in this area," Irene told her, "we're going to have to up our wage scale. Wages are high in Seattle."

"Okay, we can handle that," Katie agreed. Prices at the pumps were higher here than in other locales. "And as I always stress, Irene, I want us to work toward a low turnover." This, too, she had learned from Harry.

They discussed the properties she had bought in the area for the three new stations in the Gas Girls chain, worked out opening dates and promotions. Thank God for ambitious, bright young women like Irene, Katie thought. The success of the company depended upon hiring the right people. No longer just women, she recalled with whimsical amusement, though she continued to hire only feminine attendants at the stations.

"I'll drive you to the airport in the morning," Irene said warmly when she was about to leave.

"I can take a taxi," Katie told her, though she was touched by Irene's solicitude.

"I'll be there," Irene insisted. "And hope for a clear day," she laughed. "So you can say good-bye to the mountains."

In the morning Irene arrived on schedule. As they drove away from the hotel, Katie realized how much she enjoyed these few days in Seattle. Not only because of the beauty of the city and its spectacular views—the Olympic range across Puget Sound, snow-crowned Mount Rainier in the opposite direction—but because away from Dallas she escaped the past. Each time she traveled on business she felt this heady sense of escape.

Though a newcomer to Seattle, Irene already harbored a sense of pride in being a Seattleite. This morning she was full of talk about the coming Centennial—in November 1951 but already the subject of much interest in the queen city of the Pacific Northwest.

"It'll be great for business," Irene said enthusiastically. "Can you imagine the cars that'll be pouring into Seattle?"

While Irene outlined the city's plans for the Centennial, Katie's mind hurtled back through the years to the Dallas Centennial. She remembered the excitement—the hopes that gripped the city, even in the midst of the Depression. Though Harry mourned their losses in the stock crash, they had survived. They weren't rich, but they were building a substantial business. Why must Harry always demand so much of life—and of himself? And of Leo? Except for that, they would still be a family.

"It's beginning to look as though cocktail bars will become legal in a year or so." Irene's voice brought her back to the present. "The rest of the state may vote dry, but analysts are saying Seattle's votes will be heavy enough to put it across."

Katie tried to evince interest in Irene's talk about Seattle, but the mention of the coming Centennial had set off a flood of anguished recall in her. At the airport she insisted that Irene drop her off and return to the city.

"There's no need to hold you up," she said firmly. "I know how busy you are."

"It's always such a pleasure to work with you, Katie." Irene radiated admiration. Because she was a woman who had made it in a man's world, Katie thought. "I think the locations you chose for the new stations are great."

They said swift good-byes, and Katie hurried into the airline terminal. She'd fought off an urge to fly first to Austin to spend a few hours with Joanne before returning to Dallas. Instinct warned her Joanne would be annoyed at an invasion of private turf. Would there ever be a time when she could act on impulse with her daughter? When Joanne would truly accept her again? Or had that disappeared forever when Leo died?

Katie walked with compulsive haste toward the boarding area. Her luggage checked through, briefcase in one hand—contents to be studied on the flight to Dallas. Her black wool suit—with Dior's new fitted jacket and full skirt—was becoming, emphasizing the feminine contours of her slender figure.

All at once she froze in place—her heart pounding as she stared at the profile of a man talking absorbedly with another at her left. *Was that Harry?*

"Excuse me!" The young woman holding a toddler in her arms apologized, but her eyes were reproachful when Katie swung around to face her. "I didn't expect you to stop short that way."

"I'm s-sorry," Katie stammered. "Is he all right?" she asked solicitously, because the small boy had begun to cry.

"He's okay," the woman said briskly, and reached to pick up the valise she had dropped.

"I'm sorry," Katie said again, but the young woman was already sweeping past her.

Now Katie turned to the man who so resembled Harry. But he was gone. It couldn't have been Harry, she told herself, her throat tightening in disappointment. Harry was in Buenos Aires.

Waiting to board her flight, she fought to brush aside the emotion-laden memory of that moment when she thought Harry stood no more than thirty feet away from her. What would it have mattered if it had been Harry? He was gone from her life—there would never be another time for them. He'd married some girl half his age. It was almost incestuous—as though he were trying to replace Joanne in his life.

She'd lost Harry and all but lost Joanne. Once Joanne was out of college, would she be content to come home? Inchoate fears lashed at Katie. What kind of life lay ahead for her precious child? Joanne lived on the surface, terrified to do more. Terrified of a second awful loss.

What about herself? Katie pondered while she waited in festering impatience to board her flight. She was forty years old—with a lot of empty years stretching out ahead of her. What was she to do with the rest of her life besides keep up the frenzied race to make more money? Money that was *not* buying Joanne happiness. Only a fragile facade always on the point of destruction.

Seeing that man who so resembled Harry made her realize how empty her life was. She must have something in her life besides this eternal watch over Joanne if she was to survive. She must find something that would provide personal satisfaction. For *her*, Katie.

Buy land, she thought. Buy land and learn to preserve it—as Jeff always talked about with such love and respect. She remembered that trip across the country with Harry twenty-four years ago, when she had been so awed by the endless stretches of land. Yes, she thought with exhilaration. She would buy land all over the Southwest. Not just the small tracts she had been buying at intervals these last four years. Large farms.

Now her mind was charging ahead. She felt a surge of pleasurable excitement. She would buy land and lease it to young farmers—much like herself and Harry in earlier days, she thought with wistful nostalgia. And these young farmers must first agree to farm as "stewards of the land."

It would be a commitment to the future, she told herself. Jeff was horrified by the rush to fill the earth with fertilizers—myriad chemicals that would in time, Jeff was convinced, destroy the earth. A time would come, he insisted—and she believed this—when farmers must learn the old respect for nature if the world was to survive.

It would give her pleasure to know that *she* was preserving what land she could afford to buy up. It would give her enormous satisfaction, something she'd experienced at rare intervals during these last years.

When she was settled in her window seat on the eastbound plane, Katie allowed her briefcase to remain unopened on the empty seat beside her. The sight of that man who so resembled Harry had been disturbing. How different all their lives would have been if he had not been so overly ambitious for Leo. They would still be a family.

So often she lay alone in the darkness of her bedroom and remembered making love with Harry. That had always been spectacular. The brief affair with Sherwin had been a pallid substitute.

She was not one of those women who tolerated her husband in bed—or worse, fabricated excuses to avoid sex. Harry had always been so proud that she enjoyed their lovemaking as much as he.

She was forty years old. It was frightening to look ahead to the rest of her lifetime. What was there in store that really mattered? Watching over Joanne, yes—*but what was there for her as a woman?*

Chapter Thirty

IN THE months ahead Harry buried himself in the arduous task of setting up a Pacific base for the company. He was fascinated by Seattle, which he regarded as an exciting blend of metropolis and wilderness. He'd laughed aloud when a native-born new employee boasted, "What other city in the country can boast of a territory for a suburb?"

Alaska was hardly what he would call a suburb, but he understood. The tie between Seattle and Alaska was strong. Seattle's history was linked with that of Alaska. It had played host to endless thousands of gold-seekers, en route to the frozen Yukon back in 1897.

Today the Alaskan trade amounted to over $150 million a year. The men's clothing stores in Seattle offered fur-lined parkas and beaded Eskimo mukluks for Alaska-bound customers beside the latest in double-breasted suits as favored by corporate executives. Seattle newspapers printed special editions to be sold on the Yukon River docks. Seattle radio stations provided special programs to Alaskan families scattered over the frozen tundra.

Harry bought a house—with a private boat dock and yards of picture windows, in the California tradition—in a prestigious residential area on Lake Washington. While Eileen concentrated on furnishing their new home, Harry roamed through the breadwheat belt, hiring and training agents for the company. Late in the spring he flew into Dallas for a meeting with the Dallas agent—conscious every moment that Katie was somewhere in the city. Yearning for a glimpse of her, the sound of her voice, he forced himself to focus on business.

On occasion—in his travels about the prairie belt that runs from Texas to North Dakota—he was unnerved by the sudden appearance of a Gas Girls station along the side of a highway. A constant taunt of Katie's independence. He'd worried about her in the early years, hoping she could run the business he'd left behind—an unnecessary anxiety.

There were men who would love one woman all their lives. As he loved Katie. Until he became aware of her fantastic success in business, he'd harbored a wistful hope that one day Katie might forgive him. Might find room in her life for him again. But that was a foolish dream. He'd known that before he married Eileen.

In Buenos Aires he had not been assaulted by constant reminders of Katie, though she was never completely out of his thoughts. In everyone's life, he thought, there are certain moments that remain forever. And most of those moments he had shared with Katie. He had shared the most painful few moments of his life with her—when Joanne ordered him out of their lives, and Katie said nothing to stop him.

On his return from Dallas Harry was met at the airport by Eileen, with the Mercedes. While she resented the lack of the large domestic staff they'd had in Buenos Aires, she was—thus far—pleased by the social life she was contriving for them.

"Thank God your flight was on time," she said after a perfunctory kiss. "You have to dress for a party at the French consulate."

"Tonight?" Harry grimaced in rejection. "I've been working like a dog for the past ten days."

"You won't have to work tonight," Eileen said coldly. "This party is important for business." Her eyes were triumphant. "I happen to know that the guests will include a very rich Japanese with a new flour mill operation near Tokyo. Somebody you don't know."

"You're sure of that?" Harry was immediately alert to business possibilities.

"He's stopping in Seattle on his way to Vancouver to buy wheat. You could pull off a terrific deal if you shave prices a fraction."

"How do you know this?" Harry challenged.

"Darling, I haven't been spending three days a week in the office without learning the facts. Figure a way to beat the Canadian prices, and you'll walk off with a deal."

"Okay, we go to the party at the French consulate," Harry agreed.

Katie had promised herself that she would be less of a recluse away from the office. She forced herself to socialize. She went out with a series of personable men without ever becoming emotionally involved, always

326

charming but aborting all efforts to form a close relationship.

"Maura, I can't play these games," she confided in a Neiman-Marcus dressing room while they tried on dinner dresses for a fund-raiser where she had taken a table for eight. Jeff would never know she was buying Maura's dress—she and Maura had devised a matching story about this. "I just back off every time a man makes a serious play."

"Katie, don't you miss making love?" Maura asked bluntly.

"I miss it," she agreed. "But after all those years with Harry—sixteen years, Maura—I can't accept somebody else. I have this awful mental block. . . ."

"You've got some weird puritan streak," Maura accused. "You haven't accepted the divorce—and so you'd be cheating on Harry if you slept with somebody else."

"Stop playing the amateur psychologist," Katie scolded. "Just tell me, does this dress do anything for me?"

Katie scheduled a two-day conference for her various station managers and high-level company executives. She selected Seattle as the site, to tie in with the opening there of her 150th gas station.

"Irene says May in Seattle is perfect," she told Maura. "The rainy season is over. The spring flowers are in full bloom. It'll be like a minivacation for me."

"You need a vacation," Maura said grimly. "A full-blown one. Why don't you take off two weeks and fly to Paris? Everybody's talking about the Air France Golden Comet service between New York and Paris. They have nonstop flights twice a week, and the food is supposed to be unbelievable. Pâté de foie gras, lobster salad, breast of chicken with truffles. Champagne and brandy and coffee. And Katie, they make the trip in just twelve hours!" Other airlines required sixteen to twenty hours for the trip.

"I'll settle for Seattle," Katie laughed. For her Paris was fraught with both lyrical and painful memories.

In Seattle Katie stayed again at the elegant Hotel Olympic. The two-day conference—together with the splashy opening of the new gas station—was a huge success. After the closing seminar this afternoon she and Irene had gone to dinner as guests of two local officials at the leaded-glass-domed dining room of the prestigious Arctic Club. The atmosphere had been convivial, the occasion a fitting climax to the two-day conference.

Now—settled in her suite at the Olympic—Katie talked on the phone with Maura.

"It's hot as hell down here," Maura reported. "Enjoy that gorgeous weather out there. Oh, Andrea scheduled an interview for you with a great magazine," Maura drawled.

"What kind of interview?" Katie tensed. Andrea Winston was the company's new public-relations woman. "And what magazine?"

Katie gasped in disbelief when Maura named a national magazine with a huge circulation.

"Why would they want to interview me?"

Maura laughed indulgently.

"Because you're recognized as one of the country's most successful businesswomen. And because your public-relations woman has a sharp eye for coverage. You're young, beautiful, and growing richer by the day. Katie, you've become sensational copy."

She'd soak in a warm tub, Katie told herself when she was off the phone. She needed to relax after the frenzied activities of the last forty-eight hours. But everything had gone so well, she thought with satisfaction. Andrea was terrific. They were picking up so much newspaper coverage here in Seattle—and now a national magazine would run a story on the company.

She fiddled for a few moments with the radio until she found a station offering classical recordings. With the accompaniment of Schubert's *Serenade* she undressed, went into the bathroom to run a tub. For a moment she dallied with the thought of calling Joanne at her dorm.

No, Joanne would probably be studying at this hour. Besides, school would be over in ten days—Joanne would be coming home.

Katie worried about how Joanne would occupy herself in Dallas for the summer. She'd kept busy last summer, Katie thought defensively—but already Joanne was complaining that last summer had been "just awful." There was talk about a few days at the Forbes ranch with Betty, yet Katie doubted this would happen. She'd promised Joanne a six-week European tour after graduation—sponsored by a well-established organization specializing in tours for young people. Joanne had talked vaguely about traveling Europe along with a classmate, but she had quashed that.

And what about after graduation? Katie asked herself while she stepped into the rose-scented bathwater. It disturbed her that Joanne refused to discuss the subject of a career. Money wasn't something they had to worry about, she conceded—but Joanne needed to do something with her life. She never knew what really went on in Joanne's mind, she thought with recurrent frustration.

The scented warmth of the bathroom was making her drowsy. Maybe she'd fall asleep tonight the minute she hit the pillow, she thought hopefully. She abandoned her original plan to soak for half an hour. Within ten minutes she was in her bed with the lights out. But drowsiness had abandoned her. *Don't let this be one of those nights when she was still staring at the ceiling at 3:00 A.M.*

She tried to clear her mind of concerns for Joanne—that was the sure route to insomnia. Minutes later she reproached herself for letting business intrude. With a sigh of impatience she reached to switch on the lamp on her night table. Read for a while.

She left the bed to settle herself in a lounge chair in the sitting room. Again tonight she'd brought up the Seattle newspapers. Read the papers for a while, she ordered herself.

She flipped through the selection on the table beside

her chair: the *Seattle Times*, and the *Star*, the *Post-Intelligencer*. With a paper resting across her lap, one hand trying to massage the tense area between her shoulder blades, she scanned the front page, then turned to the inside of the newspaper. Nothing was holding her attention beyond the first few lines.

The double-fold of the society page dealt with a major diplomatic affair of the previous evening and a fund-raising ball. There was a genuine diplomatic set here. That was because of the score of foreign consulates in Seattle, she mused, skimming one article. Then her gaze focused on a cluster of photographs taken at last night's fund-raiser.

All at once she was white and trembling. Her eyes clung to the print-blurred face that had to be Harry's. Now she tore her gaze away from the photograph to the caption beneath. Her heart pounded as she scanned the names until she found her quarry:

"Mr. and Mrs. Harry Newhouse, newcomers to Seattle. He is head of the Northwest division of Simon & Sinclair. Eileen Newhouse is active on several charity committees."

That had *been Harry she saw at the airport on her last trip to Seattle.* Simon & Sinclair? What kind of firm was that? *Grain*, she pinpointed. Simon was the name of that man they'd met aboard the *Olympic*, en route to London. They'd spent time with him in London. Pierre Simon. Harry had been fascinated by him.

She sat motionless. Caught up in emotional turmoil. The newspaper slid from her lap to the floor. *Harry was here in Seattle. She could pick up the phone and call him.* But she wouldn't, of course. He was married again. To that tall young blonde named Eileen. There was nothing for them to say to each other.

He must know by now that she had been in Seattle for the opening of her 150th gas station. Her photograph had appeared in all of the local newspapers. There would be more tomorrow. He'd know about Gas Girls, Inc., with headquarters in Dallas.

Why had he never tried to contact her in all these years? Had he been so bitter about their breakup? He'd tried once, she conceded—when he was in Paris. But why hadn't he tried again?

Oh, what was the matter with her? Harry walked out of their lives nine years ago. He'd been married again for probably five years. He never thought of her or Joanne. When was she going to stop behaving like a lovesick teenager?

Katie reached for the newspaper and picked it up again. She stared at the photograph of Eileen Newhouse. She looked like an arrogant young slut, Katie thought with instant dislike.

She closed her eyes and tried to thrust aside a mental image of Harry making love to his new wife. She must put Harry out of her mind—and heart—forever, she told herself. That part of her life was long closed.

Katie was astonished that Joanne was content to spend much of the summer at the Dallas house, playing hostess to a stream of college friends. The house was fully air-conditioned, and the swimming pool she had put in was the mecca for Joanne and her friends.

In addition to the constant demands of the business, Katie was caught up in local presidential campaign activities. Public-opinion polls revealed that only 36 percent of Americans thought Truman was doing a good job. His projected civil-rights program was creating anger throughout the South. There was talk among high-level Democrats that Truman must be dumped. Katie had enormous respect for him. Couldn't people understand what he'd accomplished? Every farmer, every laborer, every Jew, every black, ought to vote for him.

Katie was relieved when—on July 15, one day after

the States Rights Democrats nominated Governor Thurmond of South Carolina as their own candidate—the Democratic National convention reluctantly nominated Truman. His prospects appeared shaky. Every public opinion poll predicted he'd lose.

Katie tried—futilely—to enlist Joanne in the Truman campaign. Joanne made it clear she harbored no interest in the presidential election, though this would be the first election in which she would be old enough to vote. A dedicated group of women had fought so long and so hard to win the vote for their sex, Katie thought in frustration—dating back to 1639, when Margaret Brent appeared before the Maryland Assembly and asked for the right to vote—and yet today so many women wouldn't take the trouble to go to the polls.

Still, seeing Joanne off for the return trip to school, Katie imagined a new sense of responsibility in her daughter. She returned to the office from the airport to discuss this with Maura.

"I think Joanne is growing up. She was the perfect hostess this summer. She had a stream of friends from school in and out of the house. They all behaved so well."

"A bunch of spoiled, selfish young brats," Maura said bluntly. "You provided them with a free summer resort."

On election eve Katie invited Maura and Jeff for dinner and to watch on her new fourteen-inch television the first presidential election ever televised. Back in September Elmo Roper had written in his newspaper column that "Thomas E. Dewey is almost as good as elected." The November 1 issue of *Life* had carried a full-page photograph of Governor and Mrs. Dewey above the caption *The next president travels by ferry boat over the broad waters of San Francisco Bay.* Democrats were apprehensive about Truman's chances.

"The farm belt will put Truman back into the White House," Jeff predicted. "They don't trust Dewey."

As invariably happened, conversation at the dinner table turned to farming. Jeff was upset about the flood of new pesticides that were flooding the market since the end of the war.

"I distrust all these chemicals they're throwing at the farmers," he complained. "Sure, it's big business for the chemical industry, but how do we know this stuff is safe? I remember hearing my father talk about how farmers were bombarded—way back in 1910—by all these sure-fire cures for pests that kept killing off crops. It got so bad, he said, that the government had to come in and pass the Insecticide Act of 1910."

"Then it worked?" Katie asked. What was Jeff getting at?

"Hell, no," Jeff said contemptuously. "Within two years the salesmen were chasing after the farmers, counteracting recommendations made by the county agents—and the farmers were listening to them. By the 1920s the USDA's Bureau of Entomology was playing right along with commercial interests. But what's happening since the end of the war scares me."

"I read somewhere that if it weren't for DDT, we would have lost the war in the Pacific," Katie said. "That our soldiers would have died of malaria."

"How do we *know* what DDT does to our food? It has to seep right into the food chain, no matter how you look at it. What are all these chemicals—DDT and the rest—doing to us when they get into our bodies? We need to know a lot more about these things before I'm using them on our land." And Katie knew that included her own—because now Jeff was supervising the land she leased to tenant farmers.

"It's big business," Maura said cynically. "What chance do we have against that?"

"If enough people open up their eyes, we'll see some action," Jeff prophesied. "It may take a while until the problem grows big enough to burst out into the open—but it's coming."

"Why do people always have to be hurt—grow sick or die—before there's action?" Katie asked quietly.

"Let's worry tonight about the election," Maura said. "Let's pray Truman makes it. I don't want to see Dewey in the White House. That might be fine for the rich guys—but not for most of us."

By 10:30 P.M. it appeared that Truman's lead was unbeatable.

"Let's go home, Maura," Jeff said happily. "Truman's our president for the next four years."

The next day Katie and Maura laughed over the reports that Harry Truman—spending election eve at a Missouri hotel—had fallen asleep early in the evening to awaken around midnight to the voice of H. V. Kaltenborn on radio reporting that despite a lead in the vote counts the incumbent president was "still undoubtedly beaten." The president went back to sleep, to learn only this morning that he had, indeed, won the election.

When Joanne came home at Christmas, she reminded Katie that she'd been promised a European tour as a graduation present. Joanne and her roommate had checked out prospective tours. They'd come up with one they found exciting. They would spend two weeks in London, two weeks in Paris, and two weeks traveling around Switzerland.

"It'll be fascinating," Joanne said ecstatically. "We'll fly, of course. We'll sleep our way across the Atlantic!"

The cost was astronomical—geared for the offspring of Texas oil millionaires—but so were her earnings, Katie conceded. She approved the trip.

What about after the summer tour? Katie asked herself uneasily. Joanne refused to talk about a prospective job. No point in suggesting she come into the Gas Girls, Inc., offices. Joanne would ridicule this. But one day her daughter would inherit the business. She should know its inner workings.

Joanne would marry, and her husband would be interested in the company, Katie comforted herself. It had become a major firm. Not that she intended to retire in the foreseeable future, she thought with wry humor.

What would she do with herself if she didn't have the company? How much time could she spend driving around the Southwest and up into the prairie belt to scout for land to buy?

Katie chartered a small plane to fly her to Austin for Joanne's graduation in June and to fly them back home. She sat at the graduation exercises and watched, eyes blurred with tears of happiness that her daughter was receiving a college degree. The very first in the family. Tears of pain pricked her eyes as she remembered Leo—who had been so afraid of disappointing his parents that he took his life. And she thought about Harry and knew how proud he would be today to see his daughter fulfilling the dream denied her parents.

Katie put all business on hold for the three days Joanne was home before four of the girls met in Dallas for the flight to the new Idlewild Airport in New York, where they were scheduled to assemble for the flight to London.

"Drive up to the airport in the Mercedes," Joanne told her mother with a glint of triumph in her eyes. "The girls will be so impressed."

Katie managed a casual facade as she saw the girls off at the airport. But she struggled against fears for Joanne's future. She could never truly be a part of the debutante scene in Dallas—and in truth, Katie suspected, she'd be quickly bored if she were.

Joanne's roommate, Laurie—whose family was from Houston—already had a job at a publishing house in New York. The lowest rung, Joanne reported, but Laurie was thrilled. For a brief period Katie had been terrified that Joanne, too, would want to look for a job in New York.

Thank God, Katie thought, Joanne meant to live in Dallas. But what would she do with herself here?

Chapter Thirty-one

IN A BEDROOM of the suite at the Paris Ritz—which she shared with three other tour members—Joanne changed from the walking shoes she had worn for their fourth day of sightseeing to fashionable, high-heeled, blue-toned opera pumps. Sprawled in a chair by an open window—because early July in Paris could be brutally hot—Laurie watched with avid interest.

"Joanne, what'll I say if Miss Hyatt comes to our suite and asks where you are?" Laurie demanded. "Of course, it's crazy to have to be chaperoned at our age," she scoffed. "Texas parents are so old-fashioned."

"Miss Hyatt will stay in her own suite." Joanne shrugged this off with confidence. It was great that they were in the one suite that didn't have a chaperon sleeping in. "She was probably fast asleep by nine o'clock." She glanced at her watch. It was only twenty of ten. She had plenty of time before she had to meet Gordon Brooks at the Ritz Bar. "We just about walked her to death today. She hadn't planned on doing the Tuileries gardens, the Jeu de Paume, and the Louvre in one day.

"I can't believe we've been in Paris only four days and already you've met somebody from Dallas." Laurie giggled. "Of course, I knew about Gordie Brooks back home, but I never met him. He's two years older than us and always dashing off to boarding school or college and then to Paris to study art."

"I met him at a party at Betty Forbes's house three years ago. He didn't give me a second look then." He'd been sulking at spending time back home, she'd gathered from Betty. He'd come to the party under parental pressure.

"He's changed." Laurie giggled. "He couldn't take his eyes off you when we were roaming around the Louvre. He's gorgeous."

"He's smart, too," Joanne approved. "The way he approached Miss Hyatt and asked so politely if she was from Texas."

"After you told him so," Laurie reminded. "He's lost a lot of his Texas accent. . . ."

"We haven't," Joanne laughed. She smoothed her pale pink chiffon dress about her hips. She was pleased that skirts were shorter this year—she had good legs. "How do I look?"

"Sexy," Laurie told her. "Where are you going? After the Ritz Bar?"

"Gordie says they have great jazz on the Left Bank in the St. Germain-des-Près quarter—it's what Montmartre used to be."

"You don't like jazz. . . ."

"I do now," Joanne said smugly. "Gordie says the jazz clubs are in basements that are real eighteenth-century cellars. They're cool. And I'm not talking about the temperature."

Timing herself to arrive at the Ritz Bar minutes after their scheduled meeting, Joanne approached Gordie with a festive smile. What could Miss Hyatt do if she found out? Ship her back home? Not likely, considering what the tour company was making on this trip.

"We'll have one drink and then blast off," Gordie said. "We've got some *Nouvelle Orléans* jazz to hear."

She was drawn to Gordie more than to any boy she'd met so far, Joanne analyzed as the evening progressed. She could guess exactly what went on in the minds of most boys she knew. Gordie was different. He made her laugh a lot. And he wasn't forever trying to paw her.

"Tomorrow night we'll go to see Stéphane in *Le Silence*

de la Mer," he decreed when they were approaching the Ritz again at close to dawn. Taking for granted that he'd be seeing her as long as she was in Paris.

"What is *Le Silence de la Mer*, and who is Stéphane?" Joanne asked.

"A new movie and a coming-up new movie star," Gordie predicted. "Stéphane is Nicole Stéphane, who in private life is Nicole de Rothschild. Her father is Baron James de Rothschild."

"So?" Joanne drawled. "You're partial to titles?" Stéphane was Jewish, she noted. Did Gordie know *she* was Jewish? Would it matter?

"She went through the war as 'Stéphane.' " Gordie ignored the jibe. "She was imprisoned in Spain, escaped to England, and became a WAAF. After Liberation she joined a group that toured the concentration camps."

"I was too young for that." Joanne was faintly defensive. "But sometimes I wish there was a Foreign Legion for women."

"You're a runaway," he said softly. "Like me."

Every night for the next nine nights Joanne sneaked away from her assigned suite at the Ritz to meet Gordie. He was such fun, she told herself, yet she was puzzled that he never tried to make out. Not that she ever went all the way. She always pulled back at the final moment. But maybe with Gordie she wouldn't.

On their last evening together—in the seductive darkness of a cavelike *boîte*—he told her he'd be home for Christmas.

"I'll arrive three or four days before Christmas—leave three or four days after New Year's. Will you save that time for me?" His voice was flippant, yet his eyes were serious.

"I think I can arrange that," she said with a contrived air of amusement. Gordie was so *sophisticated*. Not like other Dallas boys she knew. "I'll make a note in my appointment book."

She realized by now how he disliked his family—his parents and two elder sisters. None of them appeared to approve of Gordie. What would they say if they knew he was seeing *her*? But that wouldn't stop Gordie, she thought with satisfaction.

Katie was happy to have Joanne home in Dallas, yet she worried that Joanne's life was so unstructured these days. While prominent Dallasites had enormous respect for Katie Freeman's growing fortune—and it was recognized that "new money" was winning places in Dallas society—she couldn't forget that the Dallas Junior League did not include Jews among their membership. Joanne was on the fringe of Dallas society—invited in some instances, ignored in others.

While Joanne was still in Europe, Katie learned from a disappointed mother—at a fund-raising luncheon at the Baker Hotel—that Betty Forbes had been invited to become an Idlewild debutante.

"Joanne and Betty used to be real good friends, didn't they?" the mother asked with the girlish sweetness of Dallas ladies from sixteen to ninety.

"Oh yes, they've always been close." Katie refused to recognize the snide implication that, having arrived at the debutante stage, the two girls were taking separate paths.

"I ran into Della Forbes this morning. She's already planning Betty's parties and all the shopping. The Forbeses will give the usual daytime party to introduce Betty to their own friends and a dinner dance at the Baker Hotel for the chosen debutantes." Envy sneaked into her voice. "They're bringing an orchestra all the way from New York."

Katie was not surprised when—early in the fall—Joanne was invited to join several charity committees. She recognized that these invitations were based on the assumptions that Joanne's mother would be enticed to make substantial contributions to their fund drives. Still, Joanne was pleased. Katie contributed.

Chanukah was celebrated as usual at home, with Katie taking time out to buy offbeat gifts for Joanne to commemorate the occasion. Long ago Joanne had refused to participate in temple festivities. Katie suspected this was because of the painful reminder of Leo's bar mitzvah, a year before he died.

Katie recognized the Christmas season as a time of "peace on earth." She welcomed the festive atmosphere that permeated the city. The Dallas social season became particularly frenetic during this period. To make Joanne less aware of not being included in certain festivities, she persuaded her daughter to give several small, informal dinner parties, which were duly reported on local society pages. It was tacitly understood that Katie would absent herself from the house on these occasions. Joanne was twenty-two—past the age when a chaperon was expected to be present. It was sufficient that the cook and a housemaid were present.

Now Katie became aware of the presence of Gordon Brooks in Joanne's life. Almost every night, it seemed, Joanne and he were together. She knew the Brooks family by sight. Cold and arrogant, she'd judged them. One of the oldest families in Dallas—though no family in the city went back more than four generations. One of the wealthiest families in Texas—and one of the most snobbish.

Gordie—unlike the others in his family—was charming, polite, eager to please. Yet in a way Katie was relieved that he was returning to Paris shortly after New Year's. It wasn't merely that he wasn't Jewish, she analyzed—and she admittedly hoped Joanne would marry within her faith. She sensed Gordon Brooks was a very troubled young man. That Joanne didn't need.

On New Year's Eve Joanne was hostess at an elaborate party at their Highland Park house. Katie saw the relief in Joanne's eyes when the invited guests began to pour into the huge entrance foyer while an orchestra played "Some Enchanted Evening." Poor baby, Katie thought with a rush of love, she was always afraid no one would come when she gave a party.

Under her breath—as Joanne greeted her guests with an insouciant smile that was so like her father's—Katie swore at the Idlewild Club. That group of ultraconservative prominent Dallas men who chose nineteen or twenty girls each year to be presented as the Idlewild debutantes. To Joanne this had been a personal rejection. No matter that dozens of other girls were similarly rejected.

For a moment she was brushed by rueful amusement as she remembered the Cotillion Idlewild, a club of professional colored men—taking their name from the Idlewild Club. The Cotillion Idlewild chose their own debutantes each year—basing their choices on the girls' intellectual achievements.

The following day Katie welcomed in 1950 with an early-afternoon dinner party for a small group of friends and business associates. The conversation was nostalgic in tone, settling at last around the events of the past year. Truman's inauguration in January, the formation of two Chinas—one Red China—Russia's development of an atomic bomb. The continued Red-baiting.

Inevitably Katie's mind wandered. Where was Harry today? He would have been furious this past year about the way careers were being destroyed by the people behind *Red Channels*. She remembered his hatred of the Ku Klux Klan in their early years in Dallas. Harry might have been doggedly ambitious—but part of him was always on the side of those oppressed.

"What does Joanne hear from her friend in publishing?" Maura asked when the other guests had taken their leave and Katie and she had settled themselves before a blazing fire in the library fireplace. Jeff had gone off to the kitchen to put up a pot of coffee for them.

"She says Laurie loves New York." Thank God, Katie

thought for the hundredth time, Joanne didn't want to go there to live. She'd abandoned her earlier affair with the city. "She's just been promoted from editorial assistant to assistant editor."

"Is she in a position to do something for Jeff?" Maura asked.

"I don't know." All at once excitement spiraled in Katie. She knew Maura never gave up hope that Jeff's novels would be published. "I've just assumed that she's too low on the totem pole—but she's in touch with the right people. Let me talk to her, Maura."

"Great. But don't say anything to Jeff. . . ."

Katie felt some doubts about Joanne's reaction. There had always been a kind of separation between her and Joanne's friends. It was as though Joanne meant to keep them in separate worlds. But that same evening she approached Joanne about making overtures to Laurie on Jeff's behalf.

"You mean, ask Laurie if she could have her boss read one of Jeff's books?" Joanne was familiar with his writing background.

"Yes."

"Sure." Joanne surprised Katie with this swift agreement. "I'll phone her in New York. Just tell me what to say."

Katie was touched by Joanne's eagerness to be helpful. At last, she thought sentimentally, her daughter was growing up. Maura smuggled a manuscript out of the house without Jeff's detection and shipped it off to Laurie.

"If nothing comes of it, then he won't be hurt. But if it does—oh, bless Joanne for coming through this way!" Maura was euphoric with anticipation.

Five weeks later Joanne called Katie to say a letter had just come in the mail. Laurie's boss wanted Jeff's address so she could contact him directly.

"They want to publish Jeff's book," Joanne said triumphantly.

"I'll have Jeff write immediately. Give me the name and address, Joanne."

"Coming right up . . ."

"Darling, I'm so happy for Jeff and Maura," Katie told her. "And so proud that you're responsible for making this happen."

Now she summoned Maura into her office and gave her the news. Maura was transfixed.

"Katie, I can't believe it. After all these years."

"Laurie warned Joanne they don't pay much for first novels—"

"Jeff and I wouldn't care if they pay twenty-five cents for it! Right now it's enough just to know Jeff's going to be published!"

"Take the rest of the day off," Katie ordered with tender laughter. "Drive home and tell Jeff."

"Good night, Mother." Joanne hurried past her as they met on the stairs. "Gordie's waiting outside in the car—"

"Is that coat warm enough?" Katie called after her. "The temperature's dropped ten degrees in the last two hours."

"It's fine." Joanne's voice drifted up to her as she sped across the foyer to the door. "See you. . . ."

She'd be asleep by the time Joanne arrived home. Tomorrow was a workday. She had to be up by seven. God knows what time Joanne would come home. At Joanne's age she couldn't ask questions.

Was Joanne getting serious about Gordie? Katie asked herself in sudden anxiety as she walked into her bedroom. The Brookses were wealthy, but Gordie was twenty-four and still playing the art-student role. Usually Joanne flitted from boy to boy. Instinct warned her this relationship was different.

She dropped into the lounge chair before the fireplace, where Melinda had laid and lighted a fire earlier. She hoped Gordie would drive carefully—the roads were icing up tonight. She always worried when Joanne drove in weather like this—she had such a passion for driving fast.

Gazing at the orange-red flames that enveloped the cluster of birch logs, Katie remembered the years when a fireplace had been a strictly utilitarian object—to keep their small farmhouse less painfully cold. She remembered the times—during the Depression—when they had burned corncobs for lack of cash. She was richer now than even Harry had ever envisioned in those days—but part of her had died with Leo.

"Will you drive me to the airport tomorrow morning?" Gordie asked Joanne while they headed for the country club.

"Sure," Joanne said. "But I wish you weren't going back already." Her voice was faintly reproachful.

"You know the problem, Jo." He took one hand from the wheel to squeeze hers. "I can take just so much of the family. To them, nothing I ever do is right. My mother is always whining because I wouldn't go to law school. My old man is always making noises about my coming into business with him—like his two son-in-laws. I'd die of boredom in the oil business. All this shit in Texas about how nothing is like bringing in a gusher. Once a week my father drives out to the oil fields. The rest of the time he sits there in his office and makes deals."

"Gordie, you can't stay forever in Paris," Joanne scolded.

"I've got money to live on. I told you—since I was twenty-one I get monthly checks from my grandmother's trust fund. They can't tell me what to do now. Anyhow, they're glad I'm away and out of their hair." In the spill of light as they waited in traffic, Joanne saw his hands tighten on the wheel. "I never really knew the old lady. She died when I was four. But she did me one big favor.

344

My sisters got trust funds, too—but for me, it's like a release from prison. And after my twenty-fifth birthday the monthly checks go way up."

"I'll miss you," Joanne said softly.

"Why don't you come with me to Paris, too?" he said. "I've got enough money to keep the two of us afloat."

"My mother would find a way to stop me. She's smart." Gordie was such a bohemian, but that wasn't for her. She'd die if she had to live in that creepy fifth-floor walk-up flat where Gordie lived.

"You said she doesn't give a damn about you," Gordie reminded her. "That the only thing that matters to her is the bloody business."

"Oh, she plays the heavy mother," Joanne said distastefully, "though all she cares about is how many new stations she can open up. That's been good for me, though," she said with smoldering defiance. "Because she lets me get away with a lot—it's easier than fighting with me." The only time Mother fought her was about going to NYU after junior college.

"My mother never wanted another child. She said she'd gone through enough having my sisters. But my father thought he had to have a son to carry on the family name," he mocked. "Only he didn't much like what he got. I hate football. I don't see anything exciting about working in the oil fields. He wanted me to start from the ground up—work in the fields like some dumb jerk who couldn't do anything else. *He* didn't do that. Oh, his father did," Gordie conceded. "My grandfather worked his butt off to make it big. Now my old man thinks he can use his money to haul me in. He's always threatening to disinherit me." Gordie shrugged. "He won't. He wants Gordon Brooks the Third to be a Texas wheel some day."

"What do you want to be, Gordie? Besides an artist, I mean." Gordie said he didn't have enough talent to be a real artist—painting was just something that kept him away from Dallas.

"I want to be happy," he said quietly. "To wake up every morning and feel I have a reason to stay alive. I wish I could really paint. I'd like to paint you, Jo. You're so beautiful."

"No, I'm not," Joanne rejected his praise. "I try hard to be, but I'm not."

"You and your mother are two of the most beautiful women I know. It's weird, how much you look alike."

"I don't look like my mother!" Joanne's voice was shrill. "I don't look like anybody in my family!" *Leo used to say they looked alike.*

"Are you going to write to me?" Gordie asked. "I'm going to miss you so much."

"If you promise to answer," Joanne stipulated. Why did he carry on like that when he never tried to make out with her? Just a soft kiss when he brought her home.

"I'll answer."

"When will you be home again?" It had been fun, being with Gordie so much these last ten days.

"I don't know. Maybe I'll fly into New York for a few days in June. You said you have a friend in publishing in New York. Maybe you could visit her there and we could meet."

"Maybe."

"Unless you'd rather come to Paris in April. You know, Paris in spring." He smiled whimsically.

"I could handle New York," she surmised. "My mother might not buy Paris again."

"Then let's work on New York," he said, a lilt in his voice. "I can't believe I walked right past you at Betty Forbes's party three or four years ago. You're so special, Jo."

She wasn't special, Joanne thought bitterly. Not in this town. For all Mother's money, they were still nobody. To be somebody, you belonged to the Junior League. Your mother belonged to the Shakespeare Club and your father to the Brook Hollow Golf Club and the Petroleum Club, and he was on the Dallas Citizens' Council. *To be somebody in Dallas you weren't Jewish.*

Three days after Joanne saw Gordie off at the Dallas airport, she learned from a former high school classmate that Betty Forbes was engaged to an attorney fresh out of law school.

"Didn't you know?" the classmate bubbled. "You two used to be thick as thieves. Of course, it hasn't been announced yet. My mother heard about it from the lady who does her hair. Betty's mother had been in earlier to have her hair done, and she was babbling to everybody."

"Betty's probably been trying to reach me, but I just haven't been at home except to sleep these last few days." *Betty was engaged and hadn't even called to tell her.* "Melinda's becoming so forgetful about giving messages."

Joanne went directly home from the committee meeting. She debated about phoning Betty, then decided to wait for Betty to call her. She hadn't even known Betty was going steady with Frank Bristow. They'd been best friends for so long—and Betty hadn't even told her about getting engaged.

Shortly before dinner, Joanne's bedroom phone rang. She rushed to pick up the receiver.

"Hello." Despite her determination to be casual, she felt a surge of resentment when Betty's voice greeted her.

"I've been meaning to call you all week," Betty babbled. "I have such exciting news. Jo, I'm engaged!"

"Betty, I don't believe it! You never even told me you were going steady! Who's the guy?" *Don't let Betty know she'd already heard.*

"We've kept it from everybody—even my family—until we knew Frank had passed his bar exams."

"Frank?" Jo managed to sound bewildered. "Betty, I'm dying to know. *Who* is Frank?"

"Frank Bristow," Betty said. "His father is Judge Bristow. Frank was starting Yale when we went into high school. We never ran into him back in those days. We're not formally announcing the engagement until after the Terpsichorean Ball. Let's have lunch one day soon. I'll call you as soon as I see some clear time ahead. Everything's becoming so hectic. We plan an early June wedding, and you know Mother—she's carrying on about not having enough time to arrange everything."

Joanne gave the first shower for Betty and attended two others. Two additional showers were strictly Junior League affairs. Joanne waited eagerly for Betty to invite her to be maid of honor—or at least a bridesmaid. But months went past without a word about the wedding party. Then shortly after Easter she learned through gossip that the maid of honor and the six bridesmaids had all been chosen. They were Idlewild debutantes of the past three years. *Betty was getting married, and she wasn't even a member of the bridal party.*

At a charity fashion show where she had been asked to be one of the models, Joanne heard the latest news about Betty's wedding plans.

"I hear the maid of honor will wear white organdy over lime-green taffeta with a bouffant skirt and a lime-green sash, and a picture hat," her informant effervesced with barely concealed envy. "The bridesmaids are wearing white organdy over lemon-colored taffeta with picture hats, and they'll carry yellow roses."

"Aren't they going to roast to death in taffeta—in June?" Joanne scoffed, fighting to hide her hurt. "I'll bet Betty won't be wearing taffeta."

"No." Her informant giggled. "Her dress is being made by Miss Effie, who made my sister's wedding dress last year. It'll be white embroidered Swiss organdy with a full skirt and a fitted bodice and a portrait neckline. I can't imagine why any girl as flat-chested as Betty wants a fitted bodice."

"What about her veil?" Joanne asked with an air of amusement. "Don't tell me Betty's walking down the aisle without a veil."

"Tulle fastened to a cap of lace and seed pearls. And

she'll carry white orchids, lilies of the valley, and stephanotis."

At a shower for another former classmate a few days later, Joanne ran into Betty. Everybody, Joanne thought with shaky amusement, was getting married this year.

"Jo, let's have lunch next week," Betty said. "At the country club. Tuesday? Yeah, Tuesday's clear—"

"I'm busy most of next week," Joanne lied. "Let's make it the week after."

"I'll have to check my schedule," Betty said vaguely. "I know I have a couple of fittings for my gown." All at once she was giggling. "Jo, you wouldn't believe it. Mother actually thought I could wear my grandmother's wedding gown. She wore it, too. But the damn thing's six inches too short for me, and my grandmother had a nineteen-inch waist. We're growing tall girls in Texas this generation."

Joanne tried to convey an air of high spirits as she waited for the invitation to Betty's wedding to arrive. *She didn't want to go.* Maybe she'd sprain her ankle or come down with the flu or something just that week, she fantasized.

She knew she was to be invited. Betty had said something about three thousand guests coming from all over the country—many of them Mr. Forbes's business associates. There'd be a reception after the afternoon ceremony, and then a wedding dinner for five hundred.

On an unseasonably warm late April evening Joanne sat down to dinner with her mother and spied the elegant envelope at her mother's place setting. Instinctively she knew this was the invitation to Betty's wedding.

"Joanne, would you please take care of this?" Her mother's smile was strained. "It's our invitation to Betty's wedding. I'm going to be out in Denver on business—I can't make it. Will you explain on the RSVP card?"

"I don't think I'll be able to go, either," Joanne said, her words tumbling over one another. "Laurie called me

349

last night from New York. She's taking off the first week in June as vacation time." A lie, but Laurie would cover for her. "She wants me to come out and stay with her. She's getting theater tickets to just everything! *South Pacific* and *Streetcar Named Desire* and *Kiss Me, Kate*. You know how I love Cole Porter music," she ended up breathlessly.

"Will you stay with Laurie?" her mother asked.

"Yes, of course. Laurie has this darling apartment right near Riverside Drive." She managed a smile as her eyes met her mother's. Feeling herself enveloped in her mother's compassion. *Mother thought it was awful that Betty hadn't asked her to be maid of honor.* Moments like this she loved her mother so much.

"Then you'll go to New York for the first week in June. Remind me to give you money for traveler's checks," Katie said gaily. "You used to adore shopping in Saks and Bergdorf's."

She'd write Gordie tonight, Joanne thought, bathed in relief. She wouldn't be here for Betty's wedding. She'd be with Gordie in New York. He'd meant it, hadn't he, when he'd said he'd come to New York to spend a week with her?

Chapter Thirty-two

JOANNE SPRAWLED on the studio couch that doubled as a sofa in Laurie's furnished Upper West Side brownstone apartment. Laurie was bringing mugs of coffee from her Pullman kitchen to the low table before the couch. How could Laurie be so excited about finding this creepy little apartment? Joanne wondered. Back home in Houston she lived in a gorgeous house.

"You mean Gordie is flying to New York just to see you?" Laurie asked in candid astonishment as she joined Joanne on the couch.

"Why not?" Joanne countered, a hint of defiance in her voice. Couldn't Laurie believe a man would be that attracted to her?

"Well, you know. . . ." All at once Laurie was self-conscious.

"Know what?" Joanne asked, reaching for a mug.

"Joanne, you know how folks gossip back home."

"About what?" she demanded impatiently.

"Last summer when I spent that week with you in Dallas, I heard some of the girls talking about him. About Gordie being—well, a pansy."

For an instant Joanne was shaken. Was that why he never tried to make out with her? But she felt a rush of protectiveness toward Gordie.

"Laurie, that's just crazy," Joanne reproached her with a bright, synthetic smile. "Why do folks always make up stories about somebody who's different from them? Gordie's so creative and exciting and—different."

"You're sure?" Laurie seemed dubious.

"I have proof positive," Joanne lied. "That's why Gordie's flying in from Paris. So we can be together. His parents don't even know he'll be here. I'm not supposed to tell anybody but you. He's coming just to see me."

"Oh God, that's romantic." Now Laurie glowed. "Is this serious, Jo?"

"We're just playing for fun now," Joanne hedged. "Anyhow, he told me he wired ahead to a ticket broker to buy tickets for several Broadway shows for us to see. And he wants to take me out to Southampton for a couple of days. He adores the beach, and he said it's just gorgeous out there."

"When will you see him?"

"He'll be here late tonight. He'll call me tomorrow morning. The three of us will have dinner. Somewhere wild," Joanne promised. "And then Gordie and I will head for whatever play he has tickets for tomorrow night."

"Maybe he'd rather have dinner with you alone," Laurie demurred, but she seemed wistful.

"We'll have dinner together," Joanne insisted. She knew Laurie's salary was tiny, hardly allowing for dinner at a cool place like Le Pavillon or "21." And Laurie had vowed she would live on her salary—with occasional checks from home for binges.

In the morning Joanne was drowsily aware of the activities in Laurie's minuscule bedroom and the antique bathroom. Then—leaving behind an aroma of freshly brewed coffee and Chanel No. 5—Laurie was hurrying out the apartment for the subway that would take her downtown to her job.

Joanne reached for her watch on the end table beside the studio couch where she had slept. It was barely eight-thirty—at home she never woke until nine-thirty or ten. She'd lie in bed and wait for Gordie to call. He said he'd be at the Plaza. He lived so cheaply in Paris, he said, that he could afford expensive sprees a couple of times a year. In April he'd spent a week in Morocco.

What she had attempted to put out of her mind last evening—when she and Laurie had sat around until midnight gossiping about everybody they knew back in Texas—now invaded her thoughts. *Was* Gordie a pansy? That would explain why he never tried anything with her. But he was still her dear, dear friend. Gordie was special. She felt warm and loved when she was with him. Never mind what folks said about him.

At noon Gordie called from the Plaza. He was in high spirits, full of plans for the week in New York. She met him for lunch at a new Italian restaurant a friend in Paris had recommended. After lunch they strolled about the city in the June sunlight.

"There's a movie I want to catch," Gordie recalled. "I saw it listed in today's *Times*. *The Bicycle Thief*. The uncensored version," he teased. "Think you can handle it?"

"I'll make a special effort," she laughed. "Where's it playing?" Gordie knew everything, she thought. It was so *nice* being with him.

"It's at the World on West Forty-ninth," he told her. "And I checked the time. We'll be out early enough to meet Laurie for dinner."

With Gordie, Joanne told herself with pleasure, she was even forgetting about Betty's wedding. They were going to see *Streetcar Named Desire* with Uta Hagen and Anthony Quinn, and *South Pacific* with Mary Martin—and *Kiss Me, Kate* with Alfred Drake and Patricia Morison. It was sweet of Gordie to remember she was mad about Cole Porter music.

Each day sped past in a haze of euphoria. Both Joanne and Gordie delighted to be in the city and away from all that was familiar. For their last two days in the city they were going out to Southampton. It sounded deliciously wicked to go to a beach house alone with a man, Joanne thought. Laurie was impressed. Joanne didn't ask Gordie where they would stay. He would take care of everything, she told herself.

The night before they were to leave—while they walked along the Hudson because the night had grown hot and humid—Gordie told Joanne to phone her mother when she was back at Laurie's apartment.

"Tell her you and Laurie are going to Southampton but that there's no phone out there. You'll call her when you get back—before you fly home."

"Where are we staying, Gordie?" Would they have to pretend they were married? Sometimes Gordie forgot that things back home were different from in Paris.

"This wonderful little old lady I know who spends most of each year in Paris owns a beach house out there. She rents it for a fortune in the summer—enough to live on all those months in Paris. But it'll be empty until June fifteenth, so she said I could have it until then. We'll rent a car," he plotted exuberantly, "and drive out in the morning."

"Gordie, that sounds fantastic!"

By ten the following morning they were en route to Southampton. Like Joanne, Gordie was addicted to speeding.

"Watch out for cops," Gordie ordered ebulliently. "Though if we get a ticket, who cares? I'll be back in Paris in a few days, and you'll be back in Dallas."

"It's going to be so dull," Joanne mourned. "At least, you'll be in Paris."

"I won't be there much longer," Gordie said, all at once serious. "I figure another ten months and that's it. Next April I start drawing big monthly checks from my grandmother's trust. I can live decently in this country then."

"Is that why you've stayed in Paris?"

"Sure. The dollar goes a hell of a lot further in Paris—plus it's been fun. Not much anymore," he admitted after a moment. "It's like living in exile now."

"You could live with your family," Joanne ventured.

"Not on your life," Gordie shot back. "You know how I feel about them. My mother's still trying to get me into law school—because her brother's two sons are both lawyers now. Mother's always wanted to show him how much better she could do—she wants to brag about her son the congressman. Or her son the senator. She figures with all the money in the family—on her side and Dad's side—they could buy an election for me. And Dad, of course, is still trying to get me out there in the oil fields."

"Why can't parents understand we have a right to make our own lives?" Joanne stared ahead, catapulted into the ugly past.

"They're always sure they know what's best," Gordie said with contempt. "My parents haven't done so hot. My mother's a closet alcoholic, and my old man's always chasing after some girl half his age."

"Nobody's telling *us* what to do." Joanne forced an air of triumph. "We live the way we want to live."

Wouldn't Mother just die if she knew about these two

days out at Southampton? Would anything happen between Gordie and her? Was Laurie right about him? It didn't matter. She liked being with Gordie. He made her laugh. He made her feel important.

Joanne was enthralled by the Southampton house. It was huge and rambling, sitting directly on the beach.

"Now is that a great view or isn't it?" Gordie demanded while they stood on the deck and gazed out at the gloriously blue, sunlit Atlantic.

"Gordie, I didn't bring a swimsuit!" Joanne was suddenly appalled by this admission.

"You can buy one in town—or we can wait till night and go in bare-assed. This early in the year there won't be a soul on the beach."

"Would we dare?" She adored his casual disregard of conventions.

"Sure. Now let's go into town and buy groceries. We'll have breakfasts and lunches on the deck, go out somewhere for dinners. After lunch let's drive over to Sag Harbor to sightsee. We'll have dinner there," he decreed. "Tomorrow we'll drive up to Montauk and have dinner at Gurney's, right on the ocean. My sweet old lady swears we'll love it."

With candid reluctance—holding hands—they left the deck and the splendor of the ocean to head back for the car.

"I'll take our luggage to our bedrooms later," he said nonchalantly. "We'll unpack after lunch."

Gordie said "our bedrooms," Joanne noted. They weren't going to sleep together. Oddly, she was relieved. She'd told herself she was ready for anything Gordie wanted, but she wasn't comfortable with "going all the way." Actually, she tried to rationalize her feelings, they hadn't known each other very long.

Joanne allowed Gordie to sweep her up into his own exuberant mood. They shopped for food, had lunch on the deck—feeling deliciously isolated from the world. After lunch—eaten on paper plates to avoid having to wash dishes—they drove over to the quaint small town of Sag Harbor.

"It's just like she told me it'd be," Gordie said with satisfaction as they roamed the streets of Sag Harbor. "God, some of these houses go back a hundred and fifty years," he said with awe. "Before anybody ever dreamed there'd be a town called Dallas."

They watched the fishing boats, walked endlessly—hand in hand, enveloped in an exquisite silence broken occasionally by the cawing of gulls. They drove until they found a small restaurant that faced the ocean, and over a superb seafood dinner—"you only eat seafood by the ocean," Gordie proclaimed—watched the sun slowly descend in a triumphant burst of color.

Later—on the deserted night-cloaked beach—they stripped to skin and waded into the dusky blue water. Each enthralled with the perfection of the other, but neither touching.

"Oh God, I wish I were good enough to paint you like this," Gordie whispered while they walked in brilliant moonlight to the pile of clothes they'd left on the sand. "A little talent is a curse, you know."

Back at the house—sprawled on a chaise on the deck—Joanne began to yawn. Gordie insisted they call it a night. At the entrance to her bedroom, he kissed her gently on the cheek.

"Sleep well," he murmured. "Thanks for a beautiful day."

Joanne expected to lie awake for hours. Instead, she fell asleep immediately. Gordie was right, she thought in her last waking moments. It had been a beautiful day.

Over dinner at Gurney's in Montauk, Gordie grew unexpectedly somber.

"The lobster was wonderful," Joanne said, striving to restore his earlier high spirits. "I wish I could pack a couple in ice and fly them back to Dallas with me."

"I wish *I* were flying back to Dallas with you," he said, disturbingly intense.

"You can," Joanne urged.

"Not until the big checks start coming in from my trust fund." But he exuded a painful loneliness.

"That's not far off," she consoled. "April, you said."

"Do you ever wake up in the morning afraid of the day ahead?" he asked. "Without knowing why . . ."

"Sometimes." All at once she was trembling. "I didn't think anybody else felt that way. . . ."

"You know what I wish." His hand reached across the table for hers. "I wish we could stay like this forever."

"Sitting in a restaurant by the ocean and eating lobster?" She strived for a flippant note.

"I hate the world out there. I hate being alone."

"I hate it, too," she confessed.

"Maybe together we could make a life for ourselves." He seemed wary, yet determined to pursue this. "I just want to be with you. Always. Not to make love," he said, and she felt his overwhelming anguish at revealing this. "We have a special kind of love that's above all that. I want to take care of you, watch over you, laugh with you. Does that sound crazy to you?"

"No," she said softly. Maybe—after a while—he'd love her that way, too. "I feel so warm and safe when I'm with you."

"Then you'll marry me?" he asked urgently. "Nobody has to know about"—he fumbled for words—"about our special kind of love. They'd never understand."

"I'll marry you, Gordie," she whispered. "Whenever you say." Gordie would be her dear, much-loved brother. She'd never be alone again.

"I'll come home at Christmas as usual," he plotted, radiating a joyousness that brought tears to her eyes. "That's when we'll tell our folks we're engaged. We'll get married in the spring."

"In June," she said, her smile dazzling. "I'll wear a white gown and a veil."

"It'll have to be a civil ceremony," he cautioned. "I'm

Protestant, and you're Jewish." He grinned. "I don't think the minister and the rabbi will share the marriage service."

"We'll be married by a judge. Somebody important," she laughed. Refusing—for the moment—to consider the battles with their families that were sure to come. "Our parents will insist on that. And afterward we'll have a huge reception and a dinner." As fancy as Betty's, she promised herself, giddy with exhilaration.

"And everybody will say, 'Joanne was the most beautiful bride Dallas has ever seen.' We'll go to Bermuda on our honeymoon," he decided. "It's not high season, but it'll be great without the tourists around."

"Gordie, we can handle this, can't we?" Her eyes pleaded for reassurance.

"We can handle it," he promised.

Chapter Thirty-three

DURING THE course of the summer and fall Katie was relieved and happy that Joanne seemed to have come to terms with life. She radiated a new serenity that Katie relished. Joanne was becoming a responsible young woman, she thought with tender pride.

Joanne worked tirelessly with one of Katie's cherished charities. She was home for dinner most evenings. And today she had made no effort to break away after the traditional early afternoon Thanksgiving dinner, with the Warren family—as usual—their guests.

Jeff and Maura were in a perpetual state of pleasure because his novel would be published in February. George and Willa were impatient for the publication date—both were so proud of their father. And Joanne,

Katie thought tenderly, had helped bring this about. She wished wistfully that Willa and Joanne were closer—but they lived different lives, she conceded. Willa and George were both so involved in agriculture.

"Katie, it's been a beautiful day," Jeff said. "Boy, were those sweet potatoes great! All gussied up with marshmallows and pineapple." Now he gazed through a window at the approaching dusk. "But we've got three dogs out there at the house who're waiting for their Thanksgiving dinner. We have to get moving."

"Isn't it terrible the way we let our dogs dictate our schedules?" Maura laughed. "It's a miracle Jeff didn't insist we bring them along with us."

"They don't like the city," Jeff chuckled. "Smart dogs."

After the Warrens left, Katie and Joanne cleared away the table. On Thanksgiving Katie made a point of dismissing the domestic staff once dinner had been served. She liked the feeling of being alone in the house with Joanne. Just family. But—as always on holidays—she thought about Harry. Every time she spoke on the phone with the Seattle office, she thought of Harry.

"Mother, I have something to tell you," Joanne began while they stacked the dishes in the sink, to soak until the domestic staff reappeared. "We said we'd wait till Christmas to tell our parents but—" Joanne paused. "Gordie and I want to announce our engagement on New Year's Day. We'll be married in June."

"Gordon Brooks?" Katie struggled to mask her dismay.

"We've been writing and talking on the phone, and I saw him when I was in New York visiting Laurie." Joanne was talking with a speed that told Katie she was nervous. She expected objections. "I know you're upset because he's not Jewish, but we won't let that stop us." Joanne's face was pink with color, her eyes defiant.

"You haven't seen very much of him, Joanne. . . ." She mustn't fight Joanne, Katie cautioned herself. That would be a disastrous move.

"He's coming home just before Christmas. To stay. We'll see lots of each other by June. Gordie's special." Her voice was hushed with a rare surge of emotion. "We'll be happy together."

"I gather he hasn't told his parents?"

"No. They'll carry on," Joanne predicted. "But we don't care. In June Gordie's money from his grandmother's trust fund jumps way up. We'll be able to live just fine. I don't know if we can afford a house in Highland Park, but—"

"The house will be my wedding present, darling," Katie told her. There was no way she could change Joanne's mind. To fight would be to lose her daughter altogether. "A house in Highland Park."

"Can Gordie and I choose the house?" Joanne asked tentatively.

"Of course you'll choose it, Joanne. It's where you and Gordie will live." It was her fault Joanne was marrying out of her faith, Katie chastised herself. She should have insisted on Joanne's being part of the temple crowd. They should have been more attentive to their faith. It wasn't enough just to observe the important holidays. "Have you set a date yet for the wedding?"

"Early in June," Joanne told her. "June weddings are so romantic."

"It'll have to be a civil ceremony," Katie warned.

"Gordie and I don't care about that." Joanne's smile was brilliant. Katie sensed her relief—she had been fearful of a scene. "But I'd like a big reception and dinner. Like Betty's."

"The best," Katie vowed, and reached to hug her daughter. Today, it seemed to her, Joanne reciprocated.

Sleep eluded Katie tonight. She wasn't worrying just that Joanne was marrying out of her faith, she analyzed. There was something so vulnerable about Gordie. And he had no profession, no job—only a trust fund that would probably provide for them well. What kind of lives would they lead? Could this marriage work? A failed marriage would be disastrous for Joanne.

She was bracing herself for an ugly battle between Gordie and his parents when they learned about the wedding plans. The son of an old Texas family marrying the daughter of a *nouveau riche* Jew. But if Gordie could make Joanne happy, then she would love him, too.

This should be one of the happiest days of her life. Her daughter was getting married. *Why did she feel this terrible sense of foreboding?*

The day was gray and bitterly cold, the wind shrill and venomous—but Joanne insisted on driving from the airport with the top of her new white Cadillac convertible down.

"Mother gave it to me as an engagement present," she told Gordie while he sat with his shoulders hunched in discomfort. *Didn't every girl in America want a white Cadillac convertible?*

"When did you tell her?"

"Oh, about a week ago." A little white lie, Joanne comforted herself. "And she's giving us a house in Highland Park. Gordie." At a traffic light she inspected him anxiously. "Aren't you pleased?"

"Sure." But his smile appeared forced. "I'm gearing myself to face my family."

"They can't stop us," Joanne reminded him softly. *Gordie wasn't changing his mind, was he?*

"Nobody will stop us," he said with a show of defiance. "I just hate the explosion when I tell them. I'm not asking," he emphasized. "I'm telling them."

"Call me after you've talked to them," Joanne urged. His parents didn't know exactly when he was coming home. He'd just said "a few days before Christmas."

"It'll have to be after dinner," Gordie reminded her. "When Dad's home, too."

"I'll be waiting by the telephone. Gordie, it's going to be good for both of us."

"Start planning the wedding." His smile was dazzling as he dropped an arm about her shoulders. "Make it something this town will remember!"

Gordie sat, tense, through dinner while his mother reported on the activities of various members of the family.

"Everybody's sure that within another five years Eric will be running for governor," his mother wound up with unspoken reproach. Why did she always have to throw dear old cousin Eric in his face?

"I have some news of my own," he said, discarding his original intention to wait until after dinner to tell them. "I'm engaged." He gazed from his mother to his father, bracing himself for what was about to come.

"To whom?" his mother demanded after a swift, silent exchange with his father.

"Some French girl?" His father was testy.

"No." Gordie smiled. "A Dallas girl." He paused before he dropped the bomb. "Joanne Newhouse." They had to know Joanne—her name hit the society pages often enough, even if she wasn't Junior League.

"The daughter of that woman who owns Gas Girls?" Mrs. Brooks was suddenly pale.

"Her mother is Miss Freeman," Gordie confirmed. "She uses her maiden name."

"They're Jews!" His father flushed in anger. "You're Protestant."

"Joanne and her mother are willing to overlook that," Gordie drawled. "We're announcing the engagement on New Year's Day. We'll be married in June."

"Gordie, you're not marrying that girl!" His mother's voice was shrill. "This is an old Texas family. We—"

"I'm marrying Joanne," Gordie broke in. "We don't need anybody's consent."

"She won't see a cent from this family," his father warned.

"She doesn't need it," Gordie laughed. "Her mother has as much money as we have."

"I don't want to talk about this." Mrs. Brooks rose from her chair. "Just remember, Gordie, that girl will never be welcome in this house. She and her mother are not received by the best families in Dallas. We have a tradition to uphold—"

"Tradition be damned! If you don't want to accept Jo as your daughter-in-law, the loss will be yours." He pushed back his chair. "If you like, I'll move to a hotel now."

"Oh, shut up," his father snapped. "This wedding isn't taking place yet. You'll come to your senses. You'll see how ridiculous this is. There are plenty of Dallas girls of your own kind who'd be delighted to marry into this family."

"I'm marrying Jo," Gordie said quietly. "In June. You'll be invited. Jo's asking her mother to give a small party on New Year's Day so we can announce our engagement."

"There's not enough time for her mother to arrange a party," Mrs. Brooks said with smug arrogance.

"You don't know Miss Freeman. She's the smartest woman I've ever met. She can arrange anything she likes."

"We'll be the laughingstock of Dallas," his mother raged. "After all we've done for you, how can you subject us to this?"

"You've been telling me since I got out of college that I should marry and settle down. Well," Gordie said with malicious humor, "I'm taking your advice."

Katie gave a small but spectacular dinner party on New Year's Day, to announce Joanne's engagement to Gordon Brooks III. Gordie's parents ignored the invitation.

"That was rude," Joanne railed when she was at last alone with her mother. "For Gordie's parents not even to acknowledge the invitation to the party."

"Being one of Dallas's oldest families doesn't insure good manners," Katie said gently. She was making a valiant effort to pretend delight at Joanne's engagement. "By the time of the wedding they may be more receptive."

"Gordie and I don't care." Joanne lifted her head in defiance, but Katie knew she was hurt.

"We'll have to start planning right away," Katie said tenderly. "I want this to be the most beautiful wedding Dallas has ever seen. For my beautiful daughter's sake."

It was decided that Joanne would wear a short dinner dress rather than a wedding gown, since the marriage ceremony would be performed by a judge.

"Something exquisite," Katie comforted her, because she knew Joanne was disappointed at being deprived of the traditional gown. "We'll talk to Mr. Stanley about a designer dress." Stanley Marcus of Neiman-Marcus was considered Dallas's ultimate voice in the fashion field.

"You'll be my only attendant," Joanne declared, and Katie's eyes filled with tears. She had never loved her daughter more than at this moment.

"What about Laurie, too?" Katie asked.

"Laurie can't take time off in June," Joanne explained. "She won't be here for the wedding. But she's coming home at Easter, and she's giving me a shower."

Katie concealed her astonishment that Laurie wouldn't attend the wedding. Yet she sensed that Joanne was not concerned. Had Laurie made disparaging remarks about Gordie back in New York? The young could be so careless.

Harry returned to Seattle from a Canadian business trip to find a pileup of Dallas newspapers at a corner of his desk. His private secretary had been trained to collect these during his absences from the city. On this first morning back at the office he gave the front pages of the most recent editions a quick survey, then put them aside for perusal at a more convenient time.

It was past seven—he'd just shipped his secretary home for the day and turned to the dinner tray sent up by a nearby restaurant—when he remembered he hadn't gone through the Dallas newspapers. He could go through them in his usual casual manner while he ate, he decided.

He scanned the front page for any important news. Dallas was growing beyond the expectations of even the most optimistic. The population soaring. Major office buildings changing the Dallas skyline. Business was booming.

Now he scanned the inner pages, determined to be thorough though it was the society section that was most precious to him. It was through this section that he saw his daughter growing into young womanhood. He had a secret scrapbook laden with newspaper photographs of Joanne and Katie.

All at once he leaned forward in excitement—almost overturning his dinner tray. Slowly he read—eager to extract every nuance in the article before him. Joanne was engaged to be married. *His little girl.* His throat tightening, he went back and reread the announcement. No mention of Joanne's father, he thought with pain.

He scrutinized the name of the prospective bridegroom. Gordon Brooks III. He squinted in recall. That was the Brooks oil family. Lots of money there—not that Joanne would need it. But why in hell did she have to marry a *goy*?

He'd be in New York next month. He'd go into Tiffany and buy Joanne a fabulous set of dinnerware. He'd have it shipped to their Dallas house—and just happen to forget to fill out the gift card. He'd pay by cash so there'd be no way to check on the sender. *Let something from him be there in his daughter's house.*

Joanne was to be married in June, he noted. He fantasized briefly about checking into a Dallas hotel—the hotel where the wedding reception or whatever would be held—and just catching a glimpse of Joanne and Katie. Realistic again, he dismissed this.

Would Katie think of him when she stood there and watched their daughter being married? Would she remember *their* wedding?

He felt a fresh surge of anguish as he remembered that hot Sunday afternoon in the Hirsches' living room. Katie so young, so beautiful, so earnest when they stood together beneath the *chuppa* and listened to the rabbi. He remembered their wedding night in the tiniest room at the Plaza Hotel—which had seemed so grand to them.

They'd acquired the kind of money they'd promised themselves they would one day own—but never, *never*, had he expected it to be in different worlds.

He started at the sound of the phone ringing. His private line. He frowned. That would be Eileen.

"Hello." Damn it, he'd told her he couldn't go to the symphony with her tonight. Not with all the work piled up during his absence.

"Harry, we're going on to an embassy party after the symphony," Eileen told him. "Will you join us?"

"I'm not dressed," he reminded. And in no mood for an embassy party tonight. "And too bushed. I'll finish up here, go home, and conk out."

Early in February Katie made up her mind to approach Gordie's parents about their attendance at the wedding—which, thus far, they ignored. She knew that both Joanne and Gordie were upset about this. After several attempts she was able to get through to Mrs. Brooks on the phone.

"I understand that you disapprove of Gordie's marrying my daughter," she began with politeness.

"We will never recognize it," Mrs. Brooks shot back, her voice ice-cold.

"I'm not happy about this marriage, either," Katie said coolly. "I would prefer that Joanne marry someone of her own faith. But since Joanne and Gordie don't need our consent, I've concluded it would be wiser to accept their decision. We're planning an elaborate reception and dinner after the civil ceremony. I'm sure it would be less embarrassing for you and your husband to appear at the wedding than to have people all over Dallas gossiping about a family feud. These things can become so ugly."

Katie waited for a moment of dead air to be broken.

"I don't like this. Not one bit," Mrs. Brooks said bitterly. "I'll have to talk to my husband." But Katie felt confident that Mr. and Mrs. Gordon Brooks, Jr., would attend their son's wedding. This was not to be a quiet affair they could casually overlook. The wedding would be reported in great detail on the society pages of the local newspapers. For the parents of the groom not to be present would carry a note of scandal. *That* Gordie's parents would wish to avoid.

The following months held a nightmarish unreality for Katie. She went through all the motions of the happy mother of the bride. She sent Joanne and Gordie on a tour with several real estate brokers until they found a house that pleased them. She hired a social secretary to handle many of the details of the wedding. She sat down with Joanne and Gordie and listened to their honeymoon plans.

"My checks from my grandmother's trust fund should pay for the honeymoon," Gordie said self-consciously.

"We'll stay just a week," Joanne said.

"Stay a month," said Katie, eager to see Joanne happy. "My gift. And when you return, the house will be ready for you."

The closing was to take place shortly. After that, Joanne planned to redecorate. They would order furniture—to be delivered while they were away and paid for by Katie. It was clear that Gordie's parents, his sisters and their husbands, plus assorted uncles and cousins, would attend the wedding reception. En masse, they conveyed the message that they would attend neither the ceremony nor the dinner.

"They're scared to death the family will be tainted by my Jewish blood," Joanne derided. "After all, Gordie's cousin Eric plans to run for governor in a few years."

Chapter Thirty-four

IN THE comfortably air-conditioned room assigned for the ceremony—fragrant with the scent of yellow roses—Katie watched with a chaotic medley of emotions while the judge read the marriage ceremony. Only a dozen guests had been invited to attend the ceremony itself. Six hundred would attend the reception, and three hundred of those the wedding dinner.

Normally Katie loathed such massive, showy affairs—but this was what Joanne wanted, and she was filled with pride that she could provide it. But her mind was assaulted at errant moments by a montage of poignantly sweet and painfully horrific memories as she listened to the judge say the words that would make Joanne Mrs. Gordon Brooks III.

How lovely Joanne looked in her ivory taffeta short dinner dress, Katie thought, dragging herself back into the present. The gown was wide-skirted, with deep-set neckline and bias sleeves. In her hair Joanne wore a chignon of yellow rosebuds. She had been afraid—until her delight with the dress pushed such thoughts aside—that the taffeta might be uncomfortably warm in the Dallas summer.

Thank God for air-conditioning, Katie thought. For Dallas, especially, air-conditioning made the summers bearable. She, too—at Joanne's insistence—wore taffeta. Smoky blue and cut in the princess line favored by Dior. Earlier Gordie had said with charming diffidence, "Nobody who didn't know you would believe you're Joanne's mother. You look like her sister."

Now Katie's mind focused on the expensive gift of dinnerware from Tiffany in New York that had arrived among the wedding presents. No card had been enclosed. When she'd spoken with the office of Tiffany, they'd been able to give her no information about the sender. Joanne had been briefly curious, then dismissed this as coming from one of Gordie's weird friends who maintained homes in Paris and New York.

Katie was convinced the exquisite porcelain dinnerware had come from Harry. She remembered that Saturday—endless years ago—when in an especially ebullient mood she and Harry had invaded the august premises of Tiffany to pretend to be shopping for a gift. And she had been so enthralled by the delicate porcelain on display.

Harry knew Joanne was being married today. He wanted to be part of his daughter's life, she thought. To know that a gift from him was there in her new house. As she often read Seattle newspapers—covertly hopeful of discovering some item about Harry, he read the Dallas newspapers. *Why hadn't he written to Joanne?* Yet even as she asked herself this, she understood he couldn't face another rejection.

Harry knew that Joanne would never forgive him. She would not have allowed his presence at her wedding. Standing here while the judge pronounced Gordie and Joanne husband and wife, Katie remembered the anguish—the grief in his eyes at their last encounter. His

369

desperate wish that, somehow, she would intervene to keep him in their lives.

Harry still loved his daughter. How could it be otherwise? But he had forgotten his daughter's mother. He had married that hard-faced young bitch who looked like a garment-center model. For some cheap line of dresses, she thought with rare vindictiveness.

The remainder of the day passed in a haze for Katie. She kept Maura and Jeff constantly at her side—her one real hold on reality through the glittering reception and sumptuous dinner. Gordie's family had stayed briefly at the reception. Katie was relieved when they left. She sensed that Joanne shared this feeling.

While the dinner guests lingered over coffee and petit fours, Joanne retired to a suite to change into her traveling dress. She and Gordie would be on a night flight to New York. From there they would fly to Bermuda for their month-long honeymoon.

It was close to midnight when Katie's recently acquired chauffeur left her before the house and drove the limousine into the garage. Tonight the house was deserted. Melinda was beginning a week's vacation. The rest of the domestic staff did not sleep in.

Katie unlocked the door and walked into the massive foyer, all at once conscious that she would henceforth live alone in this huge house. Joanne was off into another life. Harry had taken another wife. But she would survive, she thought defiantly. She would make a life of her own.

Despite the fact that—still revved up by the excitement of the wedding—she had slept little last night, Katie was at her desk by 8:00 A.M. She liked this hour alone in her office before the ever-escalating staff arrived for the business day. In the quiet—the switchboard not yet in operation for the day, no stream of employees demanding her attention on one matter or another—she was able to focus on the special problems of the moment and arrive at decisions.

Twenty minutes later Maura walked in, bearing mugs of coffee.

"How's the mother of the bride?" Maura teased.

"I think I'll survive," Katie said with tender laughter. "Joanne was so happy yesterday. There was an aura of almost breathless joy about her—that seemed to lift her above the rest of the mortal world."

"It's a day she'll remember always." Maura's eyes were aglow with sentiment. "For Jeff and me it was a city-hall wedding. I bought a new dress for the occasion. From Klein's basement."

"What are you doing here so early?" Katie asked in sudden curiosity.

"Talking about weddings . . ." Maura chuckled, but her eyes were somber. "Jeff and I had a wingding fight. I figured my smartest move was to put distance between us."

"What were you fighting about?" Maura could be explosive on occasion, but their battles were never serious, Katie remembered.

"His writing." Maura sighed. "That's usually what we fight about."

"He's not happy about the way the book is going," Katie guessed sympathetically.

"He got two really tremendous reviews. From prestigious reviewers. The others were so-so or bad. In this great, prosperous country nobody wants to read about the troubles of an earnest young farm couple. The publisher printed three thousand copies of Jeff's novel, sold most of them, but they're not reprinting. 'Lack of interest,' " Maura quoted. "Now I can't get him to finish the revisions he was doing on the second novel. His editor delicately warned him that it wasn't likely they'd buy the new one. 'You're turning out some of the best writing in the country, Jeff—but you're not commercial.' Zane Grey is commercial. Mickey Spillane is commercial. Jeff Warren isn't."

"Has he heard from his sisters?" Katie remembered that—in an effort to bring the family closer—Maura and the kids had suggested he dedicate the novel to his sisters. "I know he sent a copy of the book to them months ago."

"Didn't I tell you? Alice finally got around to writing. Usually there's a Christmas card each year, and that's it. He's seen them four times in the past twenty-nine years," Maura's face tightened in distaste. "Nobody can ever say that my family or Jeff's was close. But that Alice is a stupid bitch," she said viciously. "Jeff asked if she liked the book, and she wrote back—'I don't have much time to read what with taking care of the house and cooking and going to my bridge club every week.' It didn't mean a damn to her that Jeff had a book published—and dedicated it to her and her sister."

"Jeff has a wife and two children who love him dearly. He can survive a pair of unfeeling sisters."

"So now all he does is dream up articles for farm journals that pay next to nothing. I told him, 'Take time off and just concentrate on writing. Rent out our land to a tenant farmer. At the least, it'll pay our taxes. We can live on my salary. I can't bear his giving up now, just when he's finally had a book published. Wow, did he rear up at that!"

"I can imagine," Katie sympathized as Maura winced. "I remember Harry that first Christmas I went out to work. Why is it the average man can't stand seeing his wife earn money? Why do they consider it an insult to their manhood?"

"It's going to change," Maura predicted. "More and more women are going to work. Men are going to have to accept it. Damn, they ought to be grateful! We're taking some of the burden off of them. Anyhow, I won't talk about my job again for a while."

"Maura, is the supervising he's doing for me taking time he might put to writing?" Katie probed.

"Katie, he loves that. You're putting into practice on your land what he's been preaching for years. He's so proud of your rules for your tenant farmers—and damned determined that they keep to them. The dinner-table talk these nights!" Maura shook her head affectionately. "The three of them—Jeff, George, and Willa—so wrapped up in fighting for soil conservation they don't know what's put on the table before them."

"I know what they mean." Katie was somber. "I see it myself when I'm up there in a plane. Our farmland is overplowed, excessively pastured. Maura, you wouldn't believe the endless gullies made by water coming down from crop lands that are unprotected. Water that's robbing us of precious topsoil. Too many farmers are sure land will always be there for planting. You have to see it from a plane to realize how bad it is. And let's face it—our farmland has to feed much of the world."

"And now a few farmers like Jeff are beginning to worry about how we keep using more and more pesticides. *Chemicals.* Jeff's convinced they've got to get into the food chain and poison us. Every day, he says, the food on our table contains more and more of some poison."

"If you consider it logically," Katie said, "pesticides are running up big bills for farmers—who can't afford that. It's becoming big business. Everybody who owns farmland is besieged by the chemical-company salesmen."

"Oh, enough of this agricultural seminar," Maura laughed. "Let's get back to business. You have a nine A.M. appointment with Terrence Faith. He was scheduled to arrive in town on Saturday. I gather he has other job interviews here, but Ed Stoddard is sure this is the man to replace him."

"I wish Ed was staying on." Katie sighed. She loathed turnover in staff, and Ed had been with her almost since the beginning. But because of his wife's health they were moving to southern California. "I'm assuming Ed has checked out this Terrence Faith thoroughly."

"You know Ed," Maura scolded. "He double-checks a laundry list. Did you see the photograph of this guy?" she asked with a sly grin.

"Oh, photos that go out with job résumés are notoriously bad," Katie dismissed this.

"This one looks like a page from *Photoplay*. He's a mixture of Clark Gable and Laurence Olivier—only younger." Maura whistled eloquently. "Every Gas Girl in the chain will love your new marketing manager."

"He hasn't been hired yet," Katie reminded.

"You didn't read Ed's report," Maura guessed. "I put it there on your desk a week ago."

"Maura, you know what this last week has been like." But Katie was shuffling through folders in search of the report.

"He's thirty-two, a Harvard graduate, has been working for the past three years for Devlin Cosmetics in New York as their marketing director. They hated to lose him, according to Ed Stoddard's correspondence with the company. Like a lot of other people today, he wants to live and work in Dallas."

"If he's as good as Ed claims, I'll hire him," Katie said briskly. Terrence Faith was twenty years younger than Ed, but she wouldn't hold that against him.

"Don't dawdle," Maura advised. "He has other interviews here in town. He'll be grabbed up quick."

Exactly at 9:00 A.M. the receptionist buzzed to announce that Terrence Faith had arrived for his interview.

"Send him in, please," Katie said.

When Terrence Faith walked into the office with a diffident smile yet still managing to convey self-confidence, Katie sensed that here was a man who could handle Ed's job. There was a quality about him that reminded her of Harry in their early years together. An audacious optimism.

His almost military bearing gave him an appearance of greater height than Harry's—an innate grace that was unexpected in a man with rugged, almost sensual features.

She wasn't what he had expected, Katie sensed. He'd envisioned a hard-driving woman executive addicted to tailored suits and a no-nonsense coiffure. She wore a feminine printed silk dress and her hair in a short, fluffy arrangement that was immensely becoming.

Terrence Faith was shrewd, she realized quickly. And ambitious. That was good. Ed had suffered painful misgivings every time she'd announced opening yet another station. Ed was always sure she was moving too fast.

"I feel we can work together," she said after fifteen minutes of conversation that dealt mainly with his business background. She knew from his résumé that he had been born and raised in Lowell, Massachusetts, had worked for two years in Boston after college graduation, and had then moved to New York City. He had chosen to settle in Dallas because of all he'd read about its being a boom area with a comfortable lifestyle. "What's your reaction?"

"I like your approach to business." He was serious now. "I have a lot of fresh ideas about marketing that I sense you'd understand. Of course," he hesitated a moment, "I do have two other interviews."

"Let me give you a breakdown on what we can offer." She paused for an instant before settling on a salary, then escalated the original figure by 10 percent. She also mentioned fringe benefits and the amount of traveling that would be required—she sensed that with Terrence Faith on the team she could cut back on this aspect herself. "Now, go on to your other interviews. If I don't hear from you within the next week, I'll assume you've accepted another position."

All at once the atmosphere was electric. She had not meant to make this sound like a challenge, she thought with a touch of guilt.

"I won't go to the other interviews," he told her. His smile was brilliant. "I'll call and say I've accepted the position here. When do I start?"

Katie was pleased that Ed agreed to remain on the job for another four weeks to help Terry become familiar with every aspect of the job. She recognized and respected Terry's ambition, his need to prove his worth to Gas Girls, Inc. It was important to him, she understood, to make himself indispensable to the company.

It became a habit for him to drop by her office around 5:00 P.M.—when most of the staff was leaving for the day—and settle down for a conference that could end well past the dinner hour. Ed Stoddard attended some of these meetings, when she and Terry battled with a heat that was exhilarating. And Terry was at his desk even before she arrived each morning.

Katie gave a farewell dinner for Ed before his departure for southern California.

"The company is in good shape with Terry taking over for me," he told Katie at the end of the evening. "He has a sharp head on his shoulders. You two might battle some," he conceded, "but together you'll dig out every dollar of profit coming to you."

The following day Katie could think of nothing except that Joanne and Gordie would be arriving home from their honeymoon. She'd received three postcards from Joanne, casual and impersonal. She was anxious to see Joanne, to look into her eyes and feel that her daughter was happy in this marriage.

Today each hour seemed endless. Promptly at five she prepared to leave.

"Give Joanne my love," Maura said with a sympathetic smile. "I know how you've missed her."

"I can't wait to see her," Katie admitted. "The house is all set, the furniture delivered. I even arranged for the housekeeper to have dinner ready when they arrive.

Now the plane had better not be late!" She glanced up with a smile as Terry strolled into her office. "No work tonight," she apologized. Her face radiant. "I have to meet my daughter and her husband at the airport."

"You have a married daughter?" Terry gaped in amazement. "I don't believe it!"

"Maura was at the wedding," Katie laughed. "Tell him, Maura."

"I know how you feel," Maura told Terry. "Of course, she was a very young mother. . . ."

"I would think about seven." Terry was inspecting her with a disconcerting thoroughness.

"Tomorrow morning let's talk about a swing around the Southwest," Katie said. "I'd like to see you start working with the area managers."

Maura walked with Katie down the hall to the elevators while Terry returned to his office.

"Shall I drive you to the airport?" Maura asked. "Or is Juan waiting to drive you?"

"Juan will be downstairs," Katie assured her. "He's probably been waiting ten minutes. He's like me—he can't bear to be a minute late anywhere."

"You really startled Terry when you talked about Joanne." Maura chuckled. "People who don't know about Joanne usually think you're about twenty-eight. You're one of those rare women who'll still be sexy at seventy-five."

"Maura, I hope she's happy." Katie was suddenly serious. "I want that more than anything in this world. Without that, whatever I've accomplished means nothing."

Chapter Thirty-five

KATIE TOLD herself that Joanne and Gordie were happy in their marriage. They liked their lovely house. They were caught up in Dallas socializing. If they were hurt at being cut off from Gordie's family, they contrived to conceal this. It was Katie who was upset that the Brooks family ignored Joanne and Gordie's presence in the city.

During the first three months of their return to Dallas, Joanne and Gordie came to dinner every Friday evening—and Katie looked forward to these meetings. Joanne and Gordie always seemed delighted with each other, full of frothy conversation about their social lives. It was clear that they were content to live on the income from Gordie's trust fund, Katie thought—though at intervals Joanne borrowed from her until the arrival of the next check.

They were meticulous about repaying, Katie remembered with pride. Still, she wished that Gordie were pursuing a career. Maybe later, she told herself—when they started a family. She looked forward eagerly to this time. How wonderful it would be to hold Joanne's baby in her arms!

Joanne had never confided the exact amount of Gordie's income. Katie suspected it would not stretch to cover raising a child—not in the lifestyle they had embraced. Gordie was bright—he could fit into the company with little training if he chose. Yet instinct warned her not to make such a suggestion.

In November—admitting to taking out a loan against his income from the trust—Joanne and Gordie flew off to Acapulco for three weeks. They planned to return the

Sunday following Thanksgiving. Katie was unhappy that Joanne would not be home for the holiday. Maura suggested that this year they spend Thanksgiving together at the Warren house.

"Absolutely not. We'll have it at my house as always. Why should you have to spend hours fussing over dinner when you're holding down a full-time job? Anyhow, I think Melinda would be hurt if I told her she wasn't to prepare her usual Thanksgiving dinner." Katie paused in a moment of reflection. "Maybe I'll invite Terry. It's his first Thanksgiving in town, and he has no family here."

"And few friends," Maura guessed. "When would he have time to make friends the way you two work most evenings—and even some weekends?"

"Do you think I'm demanding too much of Terry?" Katie asked guiltily. Somehow, time seemed to run away when they were working together.

"He loves it," Maura said. "You'd think it was his own company—the way he's always so excited about the business."

"He comes up with some smart ideas. Not all of them. Sometimes he's a little quick to cut corners where somebody might get hurt. But that's because he's young. But he sees angles that are adding up to higher profits."

"He's superambitious." Maura paused, her eyes contemplative. "And I suspect he has a thing for the boss."

"Maura, don't be ridiculous." Katie felt color flooding her face. "He's a dozen years younger than me." But there were moments when their eyes met, and she sensed he wasn't seeing her only as his employer. "He's trying so hard to show me what an important asset he is to the company."

"Don't be surprised one of these days if he doesn't try to show you something else," Maura said bluntly.

"Maura, stop reading those confession magazines."

"Haven't read them since I was fifteen," Maura chuckled. "But you watch out. Terry'll make a play the instant he thinks he has a chance. He's smart. He's waiting for the right moment."

"That'll be never." If Leo had lived, he'd be twenty-six. Six years younger than Terry. Yet there were moments when she looked at Terry and felt an odd stirring. She'd told herself she had buried those feelings when Harry walked out of her life—but the body was often a truant.

"Ask him for Thanksgiving dinner. You're right—he is alone in town. Of course, there are half a dozen single girls in the office who'd love to have him over—and a couple who aren't single."

Katie was glad she had invited Terry for the usual midafternoon Thanksgiving dinner. He brought a charming warmth to the festive table. For a few minutes she thought he might be interested in Willa, who was clearly dazzled by him. She knew Maura was pleased. She remembered Maura's constant wail: *"Katie, when will that girl realize there are men in this world—and they're deliciously different from women?"*

Quickly Katie realized that Terry was making a determined effort to win approval from all of his dinner companions. Only Jeff seemed to hold him at a distance. Then—as though to break the spell Terry had cast over Willa—Jeff led the conversation into channels close to his heart.

"Did anybody read that article about oil pollution in our rivers and harbors?" he asked. "I think it was in *Newsweek*—or it may have been in the Audubon magazine."

Katie was surprised at the fervor with which Terry embraced this problem. Most people considered it trivial. Now even Jeff seemed to regard Terry with respect.

"We're wrecking the earth," Willa said passionately. "What has to happen to make people see that?"

After dinner Maura and Willa joined Katie in clearing

the table and stacking the dishes in the kitchen sink, to soak until the domestic staff was back on duty. The three men were watching football on television in the library, where Jeff had started a fire in the fireplace grate—not because the weather required this but because he knew Katie loved the splash of color this brought into the room, the crackling music of the logs.

The three women joined the men in the library. Katie was grateful for the presence of the others in the house. Without them she would be alone—and always on holidays her thoughts dwelt on Harry.

When the Warrens and Terry left, Katie was conscious of an overwhelming loneliness. Her big, beautiful house was a mockery, she taunted herself. A velvet prison for one. She wished with a burning intensity that Joanne had arranged to be home for Thanksgiving.

Terry was in high spirits as he drove toward his modest apartment in a nearby suburb. It was damnably hard to reach through to Katie, but at last she'd invited him into her house. That was the first big step in the relationship he meant to establish. Katie Freeman was the road to the kind of life he'd promised himself back in that New England milltown where he'd grown up—looked down on by the rich kids, who lived in fancy houses like Katie's and drove expensive cars, wore the best clothes. He didn't break his back to get through college to live in milltown, USA.

At a traffic light he checked his watch. Damn, he thought they'd be out of there well before now. Donna must be waiting at his door. But he wasn't giving her a key to the apartment, he warned himself. Let the hot little bitch from bookkeeping cool her heels. Anyhow, after today it might be smart to break off with her.

Katie was incredible. She didn't look a day over thirty. But then, with all her money why shouldn't she look great? Ever since he came into the company, he'd been breaking his balls to show her what a great asset he was. To make her understand he wasn't Ed Stoddard—*he* was indispensable. And every now and then—at calculated moments—he looked at her in a way that told her he saw her as something more than his boss. She might pretend she didn't get the message—but he'd got through to her.

He saw Donna's ancient Ford sitting at the curb before his apartment house as he approached. She'd be in a snit because he was late in getting home. Not that she knew where he'd been. He made a point of keeping his personal life private.

"You're late," Donna reproached him when he emerged from the elevator and walked to the door of his apartment. She sat on the floor, ignoring the damage to the felt skirt that was almost a uniform. She wore them to the office in gray and pink and turquoise and lavender, with a variety of appliqués glued in place. Today it was gray with a red poodle appliqué on one side. The red tube top emphasized her curvaceous breasts, outlined a nipple. He was sure she wore nothing beneath.

"I got hung up—you know how it is on holidays." He stretched a hand toward her, pulled her to her feet.

"I had to fight to get away from home." Her eyes scolded him, yet a hint of promise was there, too. "And then I come here, and I have to wait in the hall." She was still campaigning for a key. No dice. Especially not after today. He was taking no chances on losing ground with Katie.

"You won't have to wait much longer," he promised, reaching to unlock the door. "It's going to be great, baby."

With the door closed and locked behind them, he pulled Donna close—with the roughness she liked. Hell, she'd be one of those women who enjoyed having their men rough them up.

"Where were you that was so important?" she drawled,

nuzzling suggestively against him. "I thought you said you didn't know anybody in town."

"I had dinner with this family in Highland Park." That impressed her. "They know my sisters. My sisters would kill me if I turned down the invitation." He hadn't seen or spoken to his sisters since he got his degree from that two-bit college near Boston. They thought he gave himself airs. He was out of their blue-collar world. "I like what's under that thing you're wearing," he drawled, sliding a hand inside the sleazy tube to fondle a breast. "I was thinking about this all through dinner." He was thinking, *How long will it take me to get into Katie Freeman's bed?* It wouldn't all be work. He'd enjoy bringing a sharp and gorgeous woman to heel. Together, they could make Gas Girls the most important chain of service stations in the country.

"Terry, it'd make life easier for both of us if I had a key to your place," Donna murmured while he walked swiftly with her into the bedroom.

"Too dangerous," he rejected while they began to strip.

"Why?" she demanded, posing before him in nothing but black garter belt and stockings. Who taught her how sexy that was?

"Because if my wife ever found out I was playing house with somebody else, she'd call off our pending divorce and take me to the cleaners for money. She's a jealous bitch," he improvised while he neatly folded his slacks and dropped them across a chair.

"You never said you were married." So she harbored ideas about being Mrs. Terry Faith, he thought. When he married, it would be to a woman who was rich enough to supply all the best things in life. Like Katie.

"We're getting a divorce," he explained. "Back in New York. It won't be final for months yet."

"I don't think I ought to be doing this with a married man," she sulked while he shoved her across the bed. But already she was aroused, he thought with satisfaction.

"So we'll call it off," he agreed. "After today."

"You should have told me you were married," she said while he lifted himself above her and his hands began an erotic journey.

"Does that make you like this less?" he mocked, and dropped his mouth to one huge dark nipple, one hand between her thighs.

"You tell me when your divorce comes through," she ordered, her voice taut with excitement. "Until then this is the last time." Her hands tightened at his shoulders. "Terry, now! Now!" she cried out with encouragement as he moved within her.

Later, he contemplated the situation while he waited for Donna to emerge from the shower. It had been dumb to start off with somebody right in the office. Nothing—*nothing*—was to stand in the way of his rise at Gas Girls, Inc.—and a place in Katie Freeman's bed.

On New Year's Eve Katie was giving a party at her house for the Dallas staff of the company. The company had become her family. Joanne and Gordie had left two days earlier for Palm Beach. While Katie had searched her mind for a suitable Chanukah-Christmas gift for Joanne and Gordie, Joanne had ebulliently suggested two weeks at the Breakers in Palm Beach.

"Gordie's mother and sisters will be there," Joanne had said with a pretense of malicious humor. Katie knew Joanne longed to be accepted by her mother-in-law and sisters-in-law. That would bring about total social acceptance in Dallas society.

The office closed at noon, on the last day of 1951. Juan was waiting at the curb with the limousine to drive Katie home. The caterers would arrive at four o'clock, she reminded herself as Juan headed for Highland Park. An hour later Maura and Jeff would arrive. Maura would arrange the flowers.

She'd have plenty of time for a leisurely lunch, to

soak in a bubble bath, and to dress before the caterers appeared. They would take care of everything, she thought with pleasure. Even the liquor.

She ordered lunch to be served at a table in the sitting room of the master bedroom suite. Sunlight pouring into the area, belying the coldness of the day. She toyed with the thought of calling Joanne down in Palm Beach to wish her a happy new year. Wait until later—with all the partying down there Joanne might still be asleep. She'd phone later in the afternoon.

Most of the staff—with husbands or wives—would be at the party. She suspected several of the younger ones might have personal plans for the evening—but she'd made it clear she wouldn't be annoyed if they took off early. This was the first time she'd given a staff party in the house. She knew most of them were curious to see her home.

After lunch she went downstairs to wish the domestic staff a happy new year and to see them off.

"You're sure you won't be needing us?" Melinda asked solicitously.

"The caterers will handle everything," Katie assured her. "Enjoy the holiday, and I'll see you on January second, 1952!"

The caterers arrived on schedule, and right behind them came Maura and Jeff. The string quartet would arrive at seven.

"I brought my dress along," Maura said exuberantly. "I'll change later, after I've done the flowers. This is the dress I wore to the dinner you gave for George when he graduated from college," she said sentimentally, "and to your dinner when Willa graduated, and to Joanne's wedding. And each time it's harder for Jeff to zip me in. I know, I should be exercising," she sighed.

"The best exercise is closing the refrigerator door before you take out that nighttime slab of chocolate cake," Jeff said good-humoredly, swatting her across the rump.

"Oh, shut up," Maura ordered, unruffled by his husbandly reproach. "I know why Katie stays so slim. She doesn't walk around the office—she jogs. The way I'm going, in another five years I'll look like your mother," she told Katie. "For the rest of us, it's another birthday, another wrinkle, more sags, more padding. You never change."

Katie was grateful for the atmosphere of conviviality that invaded the house as the caterers moved about setting up a group of small tables, the bar, the party decorations. Jeff companionably followed Maura around the lower floor as she concentrated on arranging the flowers. The musicians arrived and set themselves up for the evening.

Katie stiffened in anguished recall as the string quartet began to play the poignant "The Last Time I Saw Paris." She had seen Paris only once—with Harry. Oh, how glad she was that she'd decided to have a big evening party here at the house instead of the usual Christmas party at the office. Holidays could be so painful.

The bartender took his place behind the improvised bar. Jeff dashed out to the kitchen for bags of ice cubes. Now the first guests began to trickle in, bringing with them holiday high spirits. In a pearl-gray gown by Dior—with a draped and wrapped neckline and a single sleeve, pearls at her throat and earlobes—Katie greeted each guest with an almost regal grace.

They were all impressed by the house, Katie noted with guilty pleasure. She knew that envy infiltrated their admiration. She saw it in furtive glances, in wistful glints. Most of her employees—except for a handful, like Terry and Irene—would never rise much higher than their present jobs.

Harry had never been able to understand, she thought involuntarily, that for most people small improvements in their lives were all they could expect in the years ahead. Men and women like Harry and Terry and Irene—enslaved by ambition—always had one hand out to reach the rung above. They couldn't conceive of a life that remained fairly stable, on one plane of existence. Circumstances had made her eager—impatient—to achieve.

The party was clearly a success, Katie told herself when the new year arrived amid a noisily convivial welcome and with most of the guests still present. She'd laid the foundation for success, she reminded herself with wry amusement, by handing out bonus checks to all employees yesterday. It had been a good year, but her accountant had been shocked at the size of the bonus checks.

He'd been shocked, too, by her gifts through the year to various cultural drives. She took pride in these. The Jews of Dallas were known for their contributions to the arts—whereas many a Christian Texas oil millionaire ignored support of the museums and the opera and the symphony. Her donations were tax-deductible, she'd pointed out to her accountant.

She was ever conscious that the Dallas Citizens' Council—a group of the most rich and powerful men who were responsible for major decisions in the city—had only one token Jew among its members. But then, to many people, Stanley Marcus of the Neiman-Marcus family was Mr. Dallas.

Maura and Jeff—along with Terry—remained after the other guests had left.

"It was a great party, Katie," Terry said as they settled in the library for a final round of coffee.

"I can't believe this is 1952." Maura's smile was whimsical. "The years run by so fast."

"I remember my first New Year's Eve in Texas," Katie said nostalgically, and turned to Terry. "I was sixteen and living with my husband on a farm without another house in sight—after growing up in New York City. I was enthralled with all the land around us—but on New Year's Eve it suddenly appeared bleak and desolate. If it weren't for Maura and Jeff, that would have been a grim holiday."

"We've been through a lot together, Katie." Jeff rose

from his chair to cross to the bottle of champagne Katie had brought into the library. "Remember our bootlegging days?" he asked humorously.

"I remember," Katie said. She remembered her terror that Harry would be jailed. She'd threatened to leave him if he didn't stop with the bootlegging. She hadn't meant it; she couldn't conceive—then—of a life without Harry. But he'd been afraid to take a chance of losing her. Where was Harry right this minute? Welcoming in 1952 with that blonde slut?

"We've got a long ride ahead of us." Maura finally broke into their stream of reminiscences—to which, Katie noticed, Terry listened with absorbed attention. He had a way of making other people seem important to him. A way of making others laugh. Everybody in the company liked him. Jeff didn't, she suspected. "Jeff, get our coats. Let's hit the road," Maura prodded.

"I'll help you clear up," Terry said, his smile ingratiatingly eager. "It's awful to wake up in the morning to look at the remains of a party. And you said you've given your domestic help tomorrow off."

"Thanks, Terry." Maura—incurable romantic, Katie thought with a mixture of irritation and affection—was deliberately leaving her alone with Terry. On other such occasions Maura and Jeff remained to help her with the cleaning-up. Tomorrow she'd scold Maura for this.

When would Maura understand she wasn't interested in Terry that way? That part of her life was over. She liked Terry. She liked him very much—as a trusted member of her team. Within such a short span of time—just six months—he'd made himself valuable.

Together Katie and Terry emptied ashtrays, transferred dishes and glassware to the kitchen sink for quick rinsing. They returned to the living room to retrieve party napkins, punctured balloons.

Terry talked with charming amusement about other New Year's Eves—during student days at Harvard, his years in New York.

"Do you ever miss New York?" he asked when their task was at last accomplished.

"I love Dallas. I think it's a wonderfully exciting city. I might not," she laughed, "if it was not the most air-conditioned city in the country."

"You've made it your town," he said with admiration. "It's incredible what you've accomplished here."

"Because I'm a woman?" she teased.

"Because you're a young and beautiful woman." The ardor in his eyes startled her.

"A forty-four-year-old woman who's worked like mad to build security for herself and her daughter. It's a tough world out there." Katie struggled to sound matter-of-fact—difficult, standing this close to Terry, feeling herself swept up in emotions she had kept submerged so many years.

"Katie, for a woman with all you have to offer, it's not enough to be a dramatic business success," he chided. "You're warm and beautiful and exciting." He reached for her hand. "When will you admit you need more from life than making tons of money? Not that I don't admire you for that," he said indulgently. "I have enormous respect for your talents. Your brains. That's the icing on a very luscious cake. . . ." He was pulling her into his arms, and she offered no rejection.

"Terry, this is insane," she murmured, but still she offered no resistance when he kissed her with unnerving thoroughness. "Happy New Year, Terry," she said shakily when his mouth released hers. *Pretend she believed that's all it was. A New Year's kiss.* "And now I think you'd better go."

"Happy New Year, Katie . . ." His voice was a caress, but his eyes told her of his disappointment. "See you tomorrow."

In the mocking silence of the house Katie walked up the curving staircase to the second floor . . . achingly aware that she need not have been alone in these early hours of the new year. The question in Terry's eyes had been eloquent. She had evaded that question because she was terrified by the knowledge that she had wished him to stay.

She had known since the day she married Harry that she would never love another man. But Joanne and the business had filled—consumed—the waking hours of her life. Now Joanne was off into a separate world of her own. Her magnificent house—bought to please Joanne but which she had come to enjoy as a symbol of her success—had become a prison. A velvet prison, she remembered labeling it months ago.

She would never marry again, Katie told herself—but that did not rule out masculine companionship. Socially. She saw Terry on a regular basis as part of their business relationship. Clearly he wished to extend that into their personal lives.

She and Harry had argued much during those last few years. Usually about his inflexible attitude toward the children. But in bed they had been perfect together. She didn't expect to find that again—ever. But she needed to be held with affection. To feel the comfort of a man's arms. She longed to be loved.

Her heart was pounding as she walked into her bedroom suite—her mind envisioning a new kind of life. She wouldn't be giving up any of her independence as a woman, she thought, if she began to see Terry outside the business. This wouldn't be a marriage. It would be good to have someone other than a designated escort to accompany her to social functions. Someone in her bed to remind her she was a woman—not just a business machine.

But she was almost forty-five years old, she taunted herself. There were a dozen years between Terry and her. *How could he be excited by a woman a dozen years older than he?*

In a sudden need for reassurance she crossed to her walk-in closet with its full-length mirror, pulled open the door, and began to undress with compulsive swiftness. Her eyes fastened to the reflection in the mirror. She tossed the exquisite gray Dior across her bed, dropped the silken underthings she cherished, her gossamer gray hose to the floor.

She stood nude before the mirror and inspected herself with merciless honesty. Not the body of a forty-five-year-old woman, she acknowledged at last. The woman staring back at her from the mirror might have been thirty.

She felt dizzy with exhilaration. She could give herself to a man—even a man as young as Terry—and not see revulsion in his eyes. For a little while, at least. *Let them have that little while.*

Chapter Thirty-six

KATIE WAS tense during her usual morning conference with Terry today. She was conscious of a new tenderness in his voice, yet he gave no indication that he meant to pursue that initial advance toward her. He was so sharp, she thought gratefully. He was waiting for some sign from her that she would be receptive.

She had not rejected him, she reminded herself. She had been too startled to reject or respond. But Terry was bright—he recognized that if she had been indignant, she would have made that clear. She might even have fired him. But she had given him to understand that she needed time to sort out her feelings.

Not until four days later—when they met in her office

to argue again over his proposal for the company to buy a private plane for the business—did Terry make a cautious overture.

"Look, it's been a long day. Why don't we discuss this more comfortably? Over dinner," he said with persuasive charm. "Not something unimaginative sent up from a neighborhood café."—A frequent habit when conferences ran late, Katie would later heat up a dinner left in the refrigerator by Melinda. "Not at one of those neon-lighted, jukebox-noisy downtown places. Over steaks at Arthur's or spaghetti at Mario's. When will the Big D come up with some real downtown restaurants?" He shook his head in indulgent reproach.

Katie hesitated.

"The Vieille Varsovie," she stipulated. She enjoyed its fine French cuisine, its perfect service, its Continental atmosphere. "It's a short drive."

"Call Juan and let him off the hook," Terry said casually. "I'll drive you home after dinner."

Katie phoned the house, instructed Melinda to forget about dinner for her and to tell Juan he was off for the night. Melinda and Juan lived in the two tiny apartments over the garage.

Katie and Terry left the company offices in the now near-deserted skyscraper and headed for Terry's car. Terry dropped an arm protectively about her shoulders as they walked out into the sharp cold of the night. The temperature had dropped 30 degrees in the last two hours, hovering just above the freezing point; but the icy winds of the "blue norther" sweeping down from Canada made the temperature seem far lower.

"You should be wearing a fur coat in this weather," Terry chided while they hurried toward his car.

"I never wear furs," Katie said with rare imperiousness. "They're beautiful—on the backs of animals, where they belong."

Terry squeezed her about the shoulders.

"Katie, you are a special lady."

He helped her into his Dodge Coronet—a company car—and hurried around to the other side.

"It'll be warm in a few minutes," he promised, reaching to turn on the heater.

"When I first came to Dallas," Katie said, "I was shocked that the weather could be so cold here. I imagined Dallas would be rather like southern California or Florida."

"Nine months of the year it's warm," he reminded her. "Or hot." He chuckled. "Brutally hot."

They drove in silence for a few minutes. Katie knew their ultimate destination. She longed for this, even while she was uneasy about it. Harry had been out of her life for over twelve years. There had been no one since except Sherwin.

"My first few months in Dallas," Terry said with a hint of laughter, "I was eating chili every night. It seems to be the local pastime. I used to think chili was Mexican. A waitress at one of those neon joints insisted chili was first made by some Texas cowhand."

"But you like Dallas?" Katie probed. She forced herself to make conversation. Instinct told her they would not linger long over dinner. She sensed that Terry, too, was impatient to be on their way back to her house. To the oversized bed in the master-bedroom suite—which she had never shared.

"I'm mad about this town," Terry conceded. "It's not like the rest of Texas. . . ."

"Spoken like a true Dallasite," Katie approved.

"I like the people. They may talk slow, but they think fast. Except, of course, for you," he teased. "You talk *and* think fast."

"That's my New York upbringing," she laughed.

In the restaurant they made a pretense of discussing business.

"I'll think about the plane," Katie promised when they'd decided to forego dessert and settle for coffee. "You're right—it would be very practical. Even though

393

non-Texans smirk at all the private planes in this town and call them part of our 'Cadillac-and-caviar culture.' "

"Sugar, don't you-all forget that this is still a city that dotes on chili," Terry drawled. "It's a steak-chili-beans—and bourbon—town. When the sun goes down, Dallasites figure it's time for drinkin'."

"I guess you know by now," Katie said humorously, "that most people in Dallas prefer to eat and to entertain in their homes. Or in their clubs." A certain acerbity crept involuntarily into her voice because she remembered the clubs where Jews were not welcome.

"The one thing I don't especially like about Dallas," Terry admitted, "are the B.O. families. Before Oil." He grinned at Katie's blank stare. "The 'old families' who kind of look down on everybody else, no matter how rich they are. The real 'Old South' attitude."

"Culturally Dallas is really 'Old South,' " Katie told him. "She's the end of the South, and Forth Worth—thirty miles west—is the beginning of the West."

The wind was still blowing sharply when they left the restaurant and returned to the car. Both were conscious of their ultimate destination tonight. For a moment—after he'd turned on the car heater—Terry allowed his hand to squeeze Katie's.

"The car will be warm in a few minutes," he promised—as he had on their drive out to the Vieille Varsovie.

Now they reminisced about New York, which Terry labeled cold and expensive. Katie remembered the theaters with special affection.

"I had no money in those days, but on special occasions we climbed to the top balcony seats and saw Ina Claire and Ethel Barrymore and Laurette Taylor." In truth, she thought subconsciously, she'd been to the theater only during the precious months with Harry.

"I hear that Margo Jones has done some exciting things at her theater-in-the-round. What's it called? Theater '51?"

"It's just become Theater '52," Katie pointed out. Now

the car was cozy with bursts of warmth from the heater. This new, unspoken intimacy with Terry was exhilarating. In some endearing ways Terry reminded her of Harry in their early years. He had Harry's drive, Harry's soaring ambition, Harry's affection for the finer things in life.

"We'll have to go to the theater this season, Katie. Life can't be all business," he scolded.

"What about the symphony?" she asked—caught up in his mood—and was all at once self-conscious. *He belonged more to Joanne's generation than to hers.* "Or do you hate the classics?"

"I think classical music is relaxing. I like it. I also like Miles Davis and Thelonious Monk—at intervals," he specified. "And the music from some Broadway shows. *South Pacific, The King and I, Kiss me, Kate.* I don't know anything about opera—except that Dallas is the only city west of the Mississippi that hears the Metropolitan Opera Company on a regular schedule." Back in 1939—with the Depression still not over—Arthur Kramer of the A. Harris department store, Katie recalled, had persuaded the Met to include Dallas in its tours. Harry had been proud that a member of the Jewish community had contrived this. When it came to cultural contributions, the Dallas Jews were always out front.

"We're a very aesthetic-minded city," Katie reminded Terry lightly. "Even the *Dallas Morning News* puts out its newspapers in a marble palace." She wasn't in love with Terry—she wasn't kidding herself about that. But she liked him a lot. She enjoyed being with him. He could fill a void in her life.

"Some of the most beautiful women in the world live in Dallas." A hand left the wheel again to grope for hers. "And I'm sitting beside one of them right now."

"Are you sure you're not southern by birth?" Katie teased. People knew Terry was in the business—they'd think it was natural that she was escorted by him on occasion. There had been important fund-raising dinners when Ed had filled this role—with his wife's consent. People wouldn't know that she and Terry were having an affair. They'd be discreet. "I can almost sniff the magnolias when you talk like that."

"Southern Ireland by descent," Terry laughed. "Is that in my favor?"

"You have much in your favor," Katie said candidly. "But you don't need me to tell you that." He must know what erotic thoughts he evoked among the girls on the staff. And in her.

"God, am I glad I chose Dallas rather than Fort Worth or Houston!" His voice exuded satisfaction. "I might never have met you."

When they drove up to the house, Katie saw that the lower floor had been left well-lighted. Melinda knew her dislike for coming into a darkened house alone, but she wasn't coming in alone tonight.

"Would you like a glass of wine? A drink?" She paused in the foyer. Uncertain about her next move.

"Just you," he murmured, and reached to kiss her.

When his mouth released hers, he dropped an arm about her waist and prodded her toward the stairs. No more wasting time, she thought exultantly. She was impatient to lie in his arms, to feel the masculine weight of him above her. To drown exuberantly in emotions she had sought to hide for so many years.

Katie stood at the window of her bedroom and watched Terry drive away from the house onto the public road. She wished that he could have stayed the night—as he'd pleaded—but she'd reminded him that discretion must be their rule. This was something between the two of them. No one else must ever know. People might suspect—but she and Terry would give them no reason to *know*.

Now she returned to the rumpled bed, with firelight invading the bedroom from the adjoining sitting room.

As usual on blustery nights Melinda had laid a fire for her. Without a word—when they arrived in the master bedroom suite—Terry had paused to light the fire. Then he walked arm in arm with her into the bedroom.

It had been great for both of them, she thought with pleasure. Neither was a wide-eyed teenager. Each had given fully, without reservations. She felt so *relaxed*. And there would be more nights like this. With Joanne involved in her own world, why shouldn't Katie move more often in the Dallas social scene? Terry was right. Life shouldn't be all business.

In the weeks ahead Katie relished the new relationship with Terry. It was like a small miracle, she told herself. As she had anticipated, he gave new meaning to her life. He looked for small ways to please her, in unexpected moments coaxed her into laughter. And the business was a bond between them, she acknowledged in contemplative moments. It was almost as though Harry were beside her again. Almost.

She tried not to be disturbed by Joanne and Gordie's recurrent financial crises, which she inevitably solved. They were a couple who might have been written by F. Scott Fitzgerald, she thought in pain. Then—with Dallas ablaze with the first April flowers—Joanne and Gordie talked about going to Paris.

"Gordie says we can borrow money on the house," she told Katie over a hastily arranged luncheon at Arthur's.

"Oh, Joanne, no," Katie protested. She recoiled from any liens on the house she had given them. The house must always be there for Joanne.

"But we want to go to Paris." Joanne stared at her mother in wide-eyed reproach.

"Joanne, it's time you and Gordie learned to live on your income," Katie said gently. His checks from his trust fund were impressive—though not sufficient to cover the lifestyle of Texas oil multimillionaires. "You should never mortgage your house. That's security for your future."

"But we want to go to Paris." All at once the atmosphere was hostile. "Gordie wants to show me Paris in the spring. I only saw it on that awful school tour, with that stupid chaperon at our heels every minute! But I should have known you wouldn't understand!"

Katie hesitated. This was the refrain that always sent shock waves of alarm through her.

"Don't borrow on the house," she said tautly. "I'll loan you the money. *Don't ever borrow on the house, darling.*"

Late in April Katie saw Joanne and Gordie off for two weeks in Paris. They were talking already about going to Spain in the fall. *"Mother, you wouldn't believe how far the American dollar goes in Madrid!"*

From the airport Katie returned to the office, fighting tiredness. She was always exhausted after time spent with Joanne and Gordie. Tired from anxiety, she told herself ruefully. When would they settle down to a normal life?

Back in her office Maura told her that Terry wanted to be notified the moment she returned.

"Have a mug of coffee first," Maura said. "Then I'll ring him up. You look beat, honey. All this socializing getting you down?" Maura clucked, but Katie saw a glint of approval in her eyes. "Did you see the photos in the *Morning News* from last night's benefit performance at the symphony? You and Terry are there, looking mighty smug."

"All right, show me," she ordered indulgently. "You know you're dying to."

Katie gazed at the flatteringly blurred photo of Terry and herself while Maura went off for a mug of coffee for her. Nobody would guess she was a dozen years older than Terry, she conceded with reluctant relief.

Did Harry make a habit of reading the Dallas newspapers, the way she did the Seattle papers? She'd had a subscription to the *Seattle Times* ever since she realized Harry was living there. He *must* be reading the Dallas newspapers, she told herself for the hundredth time. The dinnerware from Tiffany had to have come from him. But why had he made such a point of its not being traceable? Because he had a new life now—along with a new wife—and he wanted no intrusion, she taunted herself.

Five minutes later she told Maura to tell Terry she was back at the office. He came immediately.

"I've got all the figures for you," he said with a dazzling smile as he strode into the office. "On the planes," he amplified. "I've narrowed it down to our best bet."

"You have figures on operating costs?" Katie asked. "That's going to be major—"

"Katie, think of the man-hours that plane will save us. We'll get wherever we need to go without a waste of time. Any emergency arises in any area, we're there with no sweat. And it's a business write-off."

"Let's talk about it tonight," she stalled. "In about an hour we have a meeting with those TV people." Unlike Ed, Terry agreed with her that they ought to move into television advertising.

"Dinner at your house?" His eyes were amorous when they met hers.

"Right. We'll go over the plane project after dinner." Melinda would clear up and go to her own apartment over the garage. As far as the domestic staff knew, she was totally engrossed in business. There had been nights when Ed, too, had come for dinner and a business conference.

"An early dinner," Terry coaxed. "We have so little time for ourselves."

"An early dinner," she promised. "Tomorrow's a workday."

There were moments when she was tempted to allow Terry to stay overnight—as he constantly urged. Maura said she was neurotic about not wanting the domestic staff to know she was having an affair with Terry, yet she recoiled from any overt admission of this.

399

In truth, she thought with her usual candor, she preferred to wake up in the morning alone. No need to worry about how she looked, to wonder if Terry was conscious of the years that cosmetics hid by day. Only with Harry she would not have played such games.

She remembered a conversation she had overheard in the ladies' room at one of Dallas's most prestigious private clubs: *"Darling, I have special makeup for when I go to bed. I mean, after all, I don't want him to see my face totally naked."* The confidante had been a fifty-plus woman, recently remarried for the third time—to a man fifteen years her junior, according to local gossip.

She would never remarry, Katie reminded herself. Did Terry harbor such thoughts? There were moments, she admitted uneasily, when she thought he might be leading up to that. She had always managed to shift the conversation into another direction. It would not be the first time a younger man was eager to marry an older, *rich* woman.

Oh, this was ridiculous! Terry was dedicated to his career. What happened between them outside of the business was sweet and special—and transient. In time he'd turn to some attractive girl of his own age. But for now, she thought defiantly, she would enjoy what they shared.

Terry sat in the ultramodern office of the aircraft company executive who was handling the sale of the Gas Girls, Inc., plane. It had taken him weeks to pull this off—with Katie balking at some of the extras he wanted installed in the plane. But he'd won out, he gloated. Those extras added an additional two thousand to his personal settlement.

Terry glanced up with a smile as the executive strode into the office.

"Everything is all clear," he assured Terry as he settled himself behind his oversized desk. "You were in luck that we had that unfortunate last-minute cancellation. Somebody counting on an oil well that suddenly dried up." He shuffled through the invoices, handed them over to Terry.

Terry inspected the papers carefully, nodded approval.

"Everything seems shipshape." His eyes were appraising as they met those of the man behind the desk. "We have only to settle the matter of my consultation fee." Their way of covering the ten-thousand-dollar kickback, per prior arrangement.

"It's right here." The expensively garbed executive opened a middle drawer of his desk and brought out a check. "A pleasure doing business with you, sir."

Terry left the office in soaring high spirits. The check would go into an account in Fort Worth. Not that Katie was apt to discover his private deal, but he felt better depositing special commissions he acquired for himself in a bank outside of Dallas. Hell, Katie owed him shares in Gas Girls, Inc.—considering the way he'd helped build up profits in the year he'd been with the company.

He drove to the Fort Worth bank, made his deposit, and headed back for Dallas. When was Katie going to stop playing games and marry him? He'd dropped enough hints along the road. He hadn't come right out and asked her. He didn't want to kill off the deal he had now. Instinct told him she'd drop him like a hot potato if he pushed too hard. She was a tough cookie beneath that beautiful elegance.

Back at their headquarters he went directly to Katie's office. She was finishing up a meeting with the manager of their refinery. He waited outside—exchanging complaints about the June heat with Maura—until the man emerged.

"Tell the boss lady I need to talk to her," he said casually to Maura.

"Since when do you have to be announced?" Maura asked, and gestured him inside.

"Everything's all set," he told Katie with an air of triumph. "Now I'll arrange for a flight crew. We were lucky to get it so fast. It was supposed to be used as the honeymoon plane for some couple down in Houston—only they split before they said their 'I do's.'" He sat on the corner of Katie's desk. His eyes amorous. "A pity not to use it for such a romantic occasion."

"I'll never need it for anything like that. And that's a promise." Beneath Katie's playful words, Terry decoded a message. The little bitch! All she wanted from him was a great marketing manager and an unpaid stud!

"As soon as we have a crew on standby, I'll make a swing around the western half of the territory," he said offhandedly. "It'll be great for station morale to know we've moved into the aircraft age."

Katie had promised him a year-end bonus based on their increase in profits. Okay. *Watch those profits rise.* One way or another Katie would come across with big bucks for him. *And that was a promise.*

Chapter Thirty-seven

KATIE WAS pleased that Joanne and Gordie made a point of having dinner with her every week or two, yet she always left them with a feeling that their self-styled "perfect marriage" was on shaky ground. There were no outward signs, she probed. No bickering, no air of covert hostility—just an atmosphere of carefully concealed discontent.

"Gordie's mother is going on an around-the-world tour with a friend," Joanne reported on a hot July night—after a detailed report on the problems she and Gordie had been having with their swimming pool.

"They're sailing to Europe on that new ship. What's the name of it, Gordie?"

"The S.S. *United States*. It's supposed to be the fastest ship afloat," Gordie boasted. "One of her cocktail lounges is decorated with simulated Navajo sand paintings."

Katie listened with the expected smile of interest. Did the people in Joanne and Gordie's circle do nothing but travel? she asked herself with silent impatience.

"Mother, could we use the company plane to fly out to Acapulco?" Joanne asked with beguiling sweetness. Katie knew she was proud of this addition to the business. Especially since a family plane had been added to the Forbes entourage. "Just to fly us out on Friday afternoon and bring us home on Sunday evening."

"I'll have to clear it with Terry." Katie brushed aside her ruling that the plane was to be used only for business trips. "He may—"

"What would he be using it for on the weekend?" Joanne flared. The twice she had encountered Terry, Joanne had barely masked her dislike. She probably resented his replacing Ed, Katie had decided. Joanne had particularly liked Ed and his wife. "Really, Mother, he gives himself such airs."

"Joanne, that's ridiculous," Katie chided. "What weekend were you considering?"

"The last weekend of this month—we've been invited to stay at a gorgeous villa right on Acapulco Bay."

At Joanne's command Katie phoned Terry after dinner. She knew he meant to use the plane that Sunday, but she'd ask him to arrange an early Monday morning flight instead. She was surprised that he didn't answer the phone. He'd said he'd wait for her call. He'd come over to the house when Joanne and Gordie left. Probably, he was bored, had gone out for dinner, she decided. *Was he out with someone else?* That day would come, she forced herself to recognize. How much longer would he be interested in a woman so much older than himself?

"I'm sure it'll be all right," Katie told Joanne when she returned from the phone. "Usually when Terry or I are off on a business trip, we leave on Sunday so we can settle in at a hotel and be fresh for Monday morning conferences. But Terry won't mind if I ask him to schedule an early Monday morning flight."

"He's only your employee," Joanne reminded her with what Maura called her crown-princess air. "You make the rules. He follows them. It's not as though he's your husband or lover."

Katie froze for an instant. Did Joanne suspect there was something between Terry and her? But she relaxed. Joanne was just tossing off words.

"I try to be a good employer," Katie reproved. "And Terry is a terrific asset to the company."

"Thanks for letting us use the plane, Katie." Almost from the beginning she had been "Katie" to her son-in-law. Gordie liked her—she clung to this knowledge. "It'll be fun to fly in a private plane."

Immediately after Joanne and Gordie left, Katie phoned Terry again.

"I just got in," he told her. "I went out for chili. Have they gone?"

"Yes. Would you like to come over and go over the report from the refinery?"

"I'd like to come over and make love," he murmured provocatively. "Afterward we can go over the report."

The second quarterly report of the year had shown a small increase in profits for Gas Girls, Inc., which Katie noted with approval. Now the third quarterly report indicated an additional increase. Katie was impressed. She said as much to Terry after a meeting with the company accountant.

"That's my job," he said with the familiar charismatic smile. Yet lately she sensed a hint of covert hostility. He was irritated, she thought, because she kept refusing to let him stay over at the house. "Actually profits should be much higher. They're good, sure—but they ought to be sensational. Damn it, Katie, we should be at the top of the line profitwise."

"We've got something solid, Terry. Our profits are rising steadily." Why was it so important for Terry to stay over? Why must the domestic staff know she was having an affair with him? "That's more important than wild fluctuations."

"I'm working hard for that Christmas bonus," he said with charming levity. "I've got to show the boss lady how valuable I am."

Normally she would have laughed, but today she saw a cold, calculating glint in the eyes that could be passionate and tender and adoring. Involuntarily she remembered a conversation with Maura. She and Maura shared the kind of friendship—which few men could understand—in which there was nothing in their lives they didn't discuss. What was it Maura had said?

Spending the night with a man, waking up in the morning in his arms, and wanting to see him across your breakfast table is love. A couple of hours in bed together is lust.

She'd never pretended to be in love with Terry.

By early November Katie began her annual checking into company earnings. While the last quarterly report would not be in until late in January, the weekly figures thus far guided her in setting up bonuses. Employees would be happy this year, she thought with pleasure.

Then, a few days before Thanksgiving, she received a call at home from Irene in Seattle. Irene had risen swiftly in the Gas Girls, Inc., hierarchy. With the chain of stations burgeoning through the past five years, Katie had found it necessary to restructure their operation. Today Irene was in charge of the entire West Coast segment.

"Katie, I hope you don't mind my calling you at home this way?"

Despite Irene's obvious efforts to sound calm, Katie knew she was upset.

"Of course not, Irene." But she was instantly alert to trouble.

"I think it's important that you come out here as soon as possible."

"Irene, what's happened?"

"I don't think I should discuss it over the phone. And, please, say nothing of this to Terry."

"The plane is available," she said after a startled moment. "I'll alert the crew right now. I'll be in Seattle by lunchtime tomorrow." Terry was driving to Fort Worth first thing in the morning to set up a premium deal. He'd be there all day. "How's that?"

"Fine. I'm sorry to be so mysterious, but I know you'll agree this is important," Irene apologized.

"Make a luncheon reservation for one o'clock." Katie hesitated. Ever conscious that Harry lived in Seattle, she wasn't prepared just now for an unexpected encounter. "Some restaurant not favored by the business crowd. One of those places catering to 'the ladies who lunch,'" she said with an effort at humor. "We'll have privacy."

When Katie arrived at the Seattle airport, she found Irene waiting for her. By tacit agreement they didn't discuss business in the taxi. At the chic restaurant populated by expensively dressed women and an occasional male, they focused on ordering lunch.

"All right," Katie said briskly when the waiter had left their table, "what's happening?"

"Katie, I know this sounds bizarre," Irene cautioned, "but I've checked it out. First, Joe Hilton phoned me late yesterday afternoon." He was the area manager with offices in Tacoma. "He said he'd been struggling with himself for a week, but he couldn't follow Terry's instructions. He's resigning."

"What kind of instructions?" Katie was mystified.

"I told him not to jump so fast. I persuaded him to

drive up for a dinner meeting with me. Joe's always done a great job for us, Katie."

"I know." Katie nodded. "What kind of instructions did Terry give him?"

"Terry gave Joe a song and dance about how profits are slipping badly. That you were considering closing stations in his area. That his job was in jeopardy—"

"Joe's district is doing well!" Katie stared in disbelief. "Why did Terry tell him such a crazy thing?"

"It was a lead-in to a new routine," Irene said grimly. "When Terry was out here last week, he told Joe that to save the business he was issuing some tough rulings." Irene took a deep breath. "He told Joe that he expected him to go to the stations in his area, break the state seals on the gas pumps, and fix them so that they'll give seven inches less gasoline for every five gallons on the registers."

"Oh God!" Katie was white with shock. "That would make us guilty of a felony!"

"That's what Joe figured."

"He didn't go along with this?" Katie asked in alarm.

"He said he struggled in his mind with this, but he couldn't bring himself to do it. That's why he's resigning."

"How could Terry come up with such a ghastly thing?" That insane determination to make the profits soar, she realized. To make her believe the business couldn't survive without him. *How could he do that?*

"I told Joe to forget Terry's orders. Then I phoned Bill Logan down in San Diego. Terry gave Bill the same deal. Bill said he'd just sent me a letter of resignation. He said he wasn't committing a felony for any amount of money. I told him to stay put—you'd be in touch."

"After lunch we're going back to your office. I'm calling every area manager to tell them that Terry Faith is no longer employed by Gas Girls, Inc.—I'm firing him the minute I'm back at the Dallas office."

"That's what I figured." Irene brightened with relief. "But you understand why I didn't want to discuss this over the phone?"

"This company survived—well—without Terry." Katie's color was high—with anger and humiliation. *Terry had used her.* "We'll have ourselves a lovely lunch," she decreed. "And a luscious pastry from that dessert cart I see circulating. Then we'll go to the office and make phone calls. Nobody is placing Gas Girls, Inc., in that kind of position!"

When the plane landed at the Dallas airport. Katie found Juan waiting with the limousine as arranged. It was a clear, cool night. The sky was awash with stars, the moon spilling light on the earth below. Normally the kind of evening Katie relished. But not tonight. She was tense, exhausted, her head pounding.

As Juan turned into the driveway, she arrived at a sudden decision. She couldn't bear to wait until tomorrow to confront Terry. She'd drive over to his apartment now. It was just past ten o'clock. He'd be awake.

"Juan, will you please bring out my car and leave it before the house," she said.

"Miss Katie, don't you want me to drive you?" he asked anxiously.

"That won't be necessary, Juan. I'll just be gone a short while."

Juan parked before the house, carried her valise inside and up to her suite. Crazy, how cold and empty the house seemed tonight, she thought in distaste. Thank God nobody knew about Terry and her. Thank God she'd insisted on their being discreet.

In her bedroom she changed quickly into slacks, sweater, and loafers. No need to impress Terry anymore—she just wanted him out of her life. She reached for a jacket and hurried from her suite, down the stairs and out to the waiting car.

She gripped the wheel with unfamiliar tautness. On those rare occasions when she drove these days, she was usually relaxed—enjoying the experience. But tonight her mind churned with the knowledge of Terry's subterfuge, his felonious intent.

Her throat tightened as she approached the modest apartment building where Terry lived. Then—barely a hundred feet ahead—she spied Terry's car pulling up before the house. He emerged from the driver's side. A girl stepped out onto the curb from the other side. In the spill of the moonlight she saw the girl's face. *Donna from bookkeeping.* The one Maura called the company slut.

Her heart pounding, she slowed to a crawl. Terry was beside Donna now. He dropped an arm about her waist. For a moment they hung together in a passionate embrace. No need to worry that he had seen her, she mocked herself as she drove past. All they were concerned about was getting upstairs into Terry's apartment and into his bed.

She headed toward home. She had felt betrayed and defiled when she discovered what Terry had tried to do to her company. But *this* made her feel sick with humiliation. All the while he'd been playing games with her, he'd been carrying on with Donna. An employee in her own company. And with how many other women?

No man would ever put her in this position again. That part of her life was forever over. She had managed without a man in her life for a lot of years. It would be that way again. Never—*never*—would she expose herself to this kind of humiliation again.

Before 8:00 A.M.—fighting yawns because she had slept little last night—Katie sat at her desk and waited for Terry to appear, impatient to confront him.

At last—earlier than usual—Terry sauntered into her office for their customary morning conference. He carefully closed the door behind him. His eyes were guarded,

Katie noted. He seemed to sense the tension his appearance had escalated.

"Where were you yesterday?" he asked with an air of reproach. "You left no word for me."

"I flew out to Seattle," she said. Impersonal, cold—though she tingled with suppressed rage. "I didn't get back until late."

"What took you out to Seattle?" He lifted an eyebrow in surprise.

"Irene asked me to come out." Her heart was pounding. "Two area managers—Joe Hilton and Bill Logan—both were threatening to resign. How the hell did you have the gall to tell them to rig the pumps?" she lashed out at him.

"Did they say I did that?" he stalled, his eyes opaque now.

"Don't lie about it, Terry! You meant to make my company guilty of fraud!"

"Katie, don't be naive." He made a pretense of wry amusement. "Every company does that one time or another. As it suits their needs."

"Every company does not rig their pumps," Katie denied. "*My* company doesn't rig pumps. You're through here, Terry. I want you to clear out your desk and be out of here within an hour."

"You can't do that to me!" He was white with rage. "You can't prove I gave any such orders."

"I'm doing it," Katie said with sudden calm. "Either you're out of here within the hour, or I'm phoning the District Attorney's office to report what you've tried to do. If I do that, you'll spend time in prison."

For a heated moment their eyes clashed. Then Terry dropped his own.

"You're a bitch," he snarled. "I hope you rot in hell!"

Katie sat cold and trembling, watching Terry stalk from her office, past the receptionist and down the hall to his own office. He had put her whole empire at risk. She should have seen the warning signs. But she hadn't, she taunted herself, because she'd been blinded by misguided emotions. She didn't need a man in her bed. There was more to life than sexual satisfaction.

She reached to buzz Maura.

"Maura, would you come in, please?" Maura knew what was happening. They had talked for almost an hour last night.

"Be right there."

Maura came in bearing a mug of coffee.

"You need this," she guessed.

"I told him he was through. I threatened to go to the district attorney. Maura, how could I have been such a fool?"

"Katie, we all thought he was a young Greek god," Maura reminded her. "Like you said last night, he just got too greedy."

"I wanted to believe him, Maura," Katie said bitterly. "I wanted to believe I'd walked into a miracle."

"Honey, for a little while you had a great time with him," Maura reminded. "You never pretended this was a great love. It was great sex," she said bluntly. "And that's something most women never know."

"I was playing games with myself," Katie said slowly. "I was pretending Harry had come back into my life."

Again on Thanksgiving Katie entertained the Warrens—except for George, who went with his girlfriend to her parents' home for the holiday dinner. This year Joanne and Gordie had taken off for a week at the Homestead in Hot Springs, Virginia.

"If George isn't here, I assume he's serious about his girlfriend," Katie said affectionately, grateful that Maura and Jeff and Willa were here with her today. She still hurt from the ugliness with Terry—but having the Warrens here routed out some of the pain and self-recriminations—and helped compensate for the absence of Joanne and Gordie. But Joanne and Gordie always came for the first night of Chanukah, she remembered tenderly. That was Joanne's way of reaching back to the days when they had been a family and Chanukah gifts were eagerly anticipated.

"God, I can't believe it," Jeff said in mock dismay. "The conversation that goes on between those two. My staid, solid son and his down-to-earth girlfriend. He's here 'big, ole teddybear'—and she's his 'itty-bitty putty cat.' "

"They're sweet," Maura scolded. "Remember, for the moment"—she paused to gaze reproachfully at her daughter—"they're our only chance at becoming grandparents."

Katie thought of the women she encountered socially who were horrified at the prospect of becoming grandparents. *"Nothing makes you feel older, darling. It's terrifying."* She could be overbearingly sentimental, Katie told herself, about becoming a grandmother. She worried that Joanne and Gordie would forever avoid this situation, and at the same time worried how they would survive the rigors of becoming parents.

"Did you read Dad's article in that new Texas farm journal?" Willa asked Katie, her face alight with pride.

"I talk, but they don't listen," Jeff said gloomily.

"I have it on my night table," Katie confessed. "I'll read it over the weekend. But, Jeff, we know the situation has to change. Remember after the dust-bowl years, how the Soil Conservation Service came in and preached about strip-cropping and terracing and contouring farming and—"

"But the good years came in the forties, and they've pushed this aside." Jeff grunted in disgust. "All they're concerned about—most of them—is buying more land, more equipment. Not caring how they misuse the soil."

"I love what the American Indian chief—Chief Seattle, I think he was called—" Willa said softly, "told the white men who wanted to buy his land, back in 1854. 'Teach your children so that they will respect the land, that the earth is our mother. Whatever befalls the earth befalls the sons of the earth.' "

"Amen." But Jeff's eyes belied his smile.

"I put in a bid for that acreage I told you about down in the Lower Rio Grande Valley." Katie shrugged expressively. "I doubt they'll accept my offer. Everybody has such an inflated idea of what land is worth today."

"Keep your offer low," Jeff exhorted. "The way prices on farm products are dropping, they may be glad to unload. And we're about due for another dry spell. Once that happens, we'll see more dust storms. The price of land will go down for sure."

"No more pessimistic talk," Maura ordered. "Not on Thanksgiving Day. I know I'll hate myself for it tomorrow, Katie, but I want another slab of that terrific pumpkin pie. Even though I know Melinda makes it with heavy cream and brandy."

"That's all right," Jeff comforted her. "I love the extra pounds, too."

Thanksgiving night settled lovingly about the Homestead in Hot Springs, Virginia. The air was crisp and cool, fragrant with the last flowers of the year. In one of the two bedrooms of the cottage she and Gordie were occupying at the magnificent resort, Joanne lay sleepless far past midnight. As always, her bedroom door was open, with the embers in the sitting-room fireplace softening the darkness of the night.

In a white, pleated chiffon nightgown designed along Empire lines Joanne turned and twisted beneath a silken coverlet. Earlier she had pretended delight with the gourmet Thanksgiving dinner served in the elegant dining room. In truth she had felt a sense of desolation, of being in exile. But if she had stayed home for Thanksgiving dinner with Mother, she would have had to face Willa and Maura and Jeff.

Every Thanksgiving she remembered that first one

after Leo ran away from life. The Warrens were coming into town to have dinner with them. Leo had been gone just a few months, and Mother acted as though it was party time! She'd laughed and said Maura was bringing a Black Forest cake.

At today's Thanksgiving dinner she'd looked around at other guests—so festive and happy—and she had wanted to run and hide in a closet. Most of them were *families*. They'd been a family once. She'd loved Thanksgiving then. Everybody sitting around the table and having such fun. Why did everything have to go so crazy?

In a burst of restlessness she tossed aside the coverlet and rose from her bed. She'd go inside and sit by what was left of the fire. In bare feet she hurried toward the door, stumbled over the slippers she had left there earlier.

"Damn." She grunted in irritation and went into the sitting room.

"Jo?" Gordie called out.

"Yeah. It's okay," she soothed. Gordie said he hated all holidays. He'd spent a lot of them at boarding schools—with a handful of other rich kids whose parents were off at house parties or whatever.

"You got hit with insomnia?" He walked into the sitting room with a sympathetic smile and switched on a lamp.

"I don't think this was such a great idea," she admitted. "We should have pretended we were going away, but just stayed at home. We could have had Thanksgiving dinner by ourselves. You make terrific spaghetti," she remembered with an effort at humor. "And we could have bought a pumpkin pie at a bakery." On earlier Thanksgivings Mother had made a big turkey with great stuffing, and Maura always brought over two pies—one pumpkin and one a surprise.

"Jo, what's the matter with us?" Gordie asked, his voice a blend of exasperation and fear. "Why does everything always turn out so screwy?"

"Maybe because we're not really a family." She was

groping for an answer. For weeks now she'd been thinking about how it would be if they had a baby. She'd been thinking about how to talk to Gordie about that. Not their own baby. An adopted one. Maybe a boy first, then a girl. "Gordie, let's be a real family," she pleaded, breathless with anticipation. "Let's adopt a baby."

"Are you nuts?" His face was chalk-white. "That's like telling the whole world we can't have one."

"Gordie, millions of people adopt babies."

"Not us." His eyes were glazed with pain. "I can just hear my father and mother. 'What's the matter, Gordie? You're not man enough to have your own child?' Don't you know them, Jo? They'd make my life miserable." He crossed to a window and stared into the night. Then he swung around with a coaxing smile. "You know what we're going to do when we get back home? We're going out to a kennel and buy ourselves the greatest little puppy that ever lived. We'll spoil it to death, and it'll love us to death. I never had a dog of my own. Just my father's hunting dogs—and they were never allowed in the house. They were *his* dogs," Gordie remembered bitterly. "Did you ever have a dog?"

"No." But when they lived on the farm, she'd played with all the dogs on the Warrens' farm. She remembered how she'd loved the pups each time their dog had another litter, and how she and Willa had cried when Maura and Jeff found homes for each of them. That seemed a thousand years ago. "Let's get a dog, Gordie."

Then they would be almost like a family.

Chapter Thirty-eight

KATIE GLANCED anxiously at her watch as the plane neared the Dallas airport. Joanne and Gordie were coming for dinner this first night of Chanukah. She wanted to be home before they arrived.

"Katie, don't expect that piece of property to be suitable for growing decent oranges for at least six to eight years," Jeff warned, drawing her back to the moment. "Maybe even ten."

"I know. But it's worth the effort."

What had Jeff called it? A biological desert. The owners—hardworking people who couldn't understand why their trees were diseased and dying or dead—refused her offer to stay on as tenants, utilizing the new methods being urged by a few dedicated agricultural specialists. *"Miss Freeman, we did everything that was right. We fertilized, sprayed—and still those danged trees died on us. Newfangled ways ain't gonna make a difference."*

"When are you closing on the property?"

"The lawyer said in another three or four weeks. What's our first step, Jeff? After you arrange for tenants?"

"First we set up a chunk of acres for cover crops and another chunk for grain. . . ." Jeff outlined what he'd worked out in his head while they had walked most of the acreage earlier in the day. Now he paused. "Katie, you're tying up a lot of money these days in land that won't be paying its way for years."

"I'm like you and Maura," she said softly. "I feel it's a debt I owe."

"You know," Jeff said impatiently, "those folks down

416

there might have saved their land and been able to hold on financially if they hadn't kept throwing all that money to the chemical people. When are farmers going to wake up in this country? Willa keeps going back to stuff she's picked up in the classrooms. About how centuries ago the Chinese farmers brought in ants to control the insects that were eating their leaves." He paused to chuckle. "They even put up bamboo poles as bridges to help the ants travel from tree to tree. In India in 1762 farmers brought in mynah birds to get rid of the red locusts that were ruining their crops. We don't need all these chemicals. We have to work *with* nature, not against it."

Juan was waiting at the airport to drive Katie home and then to take Jeff back to the farm.

"Happy Chanukah," Jeff said, and leaned forward to kiss her on the cheek as Juan pulled up before the Highland Park house. "Remember how George and Willa always used to insist on sharing Chanukah with Leo and Joanne?"

"For the Chanukah loot." Her smile was tender. "In those days it was so easy to please them."

When Katie walked into the house, she spied a note by the phone in the foyer. Joanne had called. She wasn't going to beg off, was she? Fighting disappointment, Katie dialed Joanne's number.

"Mother, is it all right if we bring Tonto?" Joanne asked cajolingly. "He's giving us those sad looks again. He makes me feel so guilty about not taking him to Palm Beach when we go down there for New Year's week."

"Bring him," Katie agreed. Tonto was a beguiling pup. Instead of the pedigreed Doberman they had planned to buy, they had been adopted—they declared—by a half-starved wistfully affectionate mongrel, whose antecedents appeared to include collie and golden-retriever lineages.

"We'll be over in twenty minutes," Joanne said ebulliently.

Katie went out to the kitchen to check with Melinda

about dinner, then headed for the library to bring out the gift-wrapped packages tucked away in her desk. She was grateful that Joanne was so happy with Tonto. She wished that Joanne and Gordie would have a baby. That would give substance to their lives. But that was a decision that only Joanne and Gordie could make.

She would not allow herself even to think about the malicious gossip she'd overheard last week. People were so quick to spread vicious gossip. She prayed it would never reach Joanne. Not that she believed the accusations that Gordie was "a fairy."

Joanne told herself that she and Gordie were having a marvelous time this New Year's Eve. They'd come down to Palm Beach especially for Buffy's party. Then—just at midnight—Buffy had announced she was pregnant.

Why couldn't she and Gordie have a baby? They could, she thought defiantly, if Gordie *wanted* them to have one. Tyrone Power and Linda Christian had a baby. Lots of men who felt the way Gordie did had children.

All at once she was eager for the party to be over so she could talk to Gordie. But by the time they were back in their suite at the Breakers, Gordie was half-asleep. Why did he always have too much champagne at parties? But she'd talk to him tomorrow.

It was important to their marriage for them to have a baby. They'd only have to do it until she was pregnant, she told herself with sudden self-consciousness. Gordie could handle that.

It would be sweet to have a baby. They'd be a story-book family—she and Gordie and their baby and their dog. And nobody would ever again make those cracks about Gordie that she always pretended not to understand.

She waited until the following afternoon—when they

were having breakfast in their suite—to talk to Gordie about their having a baby. She faltered slightly when she saw his face turn ashen as her words sank into his brain.

"We could—if just for a little while we played at being really married. A baby would be the beginning of a whole new world for us." For a moment she faltered. *This was so important for both of them.* "It won't be for always," she reminded him, and was conscious of an odd excitement. She'd played a lot, she admitted—but nobody had ever persuaded her to "go all the way." She could—with Gordie. She suspected she would like it. Sometimes it scared her that she could feel that way about Gordie. "Gordie, don't you want to show your father you can have a child?"

"Jo, I don't know," he whispered with poignant humility. "I don't know if I can."

"Gordie, let's try," she pleaded. "Together we'll find a way."

"Let me think about it for a while," he hedged. But Joanne saw the glint of hope in his eyes that he could prove to those who talked behind his back that he was as much a man as his father.

Katie was conscious of a quiet desperation in Joanne and Gordie in the next few months. She was fearful of a rift in their marriage. They were like two lost children, she thought in anguish. What could she do to help them?

Then, early in July, Joanne called her at the office and asked if they could meet for lunch.

"Of course, darling," Katie agreed, fighting anxiety. Normally she saw Joanne and Gordie together. Was Joanne meeting her alone to talk about a divorce? "When?"

"Today?"

"Fine. Where would you like to have lunch?" She recalled a business lunch. She'd have to reschedule it. "And what time?"

Two hours later Katie sat in a secluded booth in her favorite of the new downtown restaurants and listened in a surge of euphoria to Joanne's news.

"I didn't want to tell you until we were absolutely sure," Joanne said earnestly. "Dr. Lenox says I'm about ten weeks pregnant. My waistline's already going!"

"Joanne, I'm so happy for you." Katie glowed. "Nothing could please me more." Yet already she worried that Joanne might have a rough pregnancy, that a difficult pregnancy and delivery might scar her emotionally. She was so fragile.

"Gordie is telling his parents tonight." Joanne's smile was cynical. "They probably couldn't care less."

"It doesn't matter, darling," Katie soothed. Her own smile luminous. She couldn't wait to hold Joanne's baby in her arms. "You and I and Gordie will love it enough to make up for his family. The day the baby is born I'm opening a bank account in its name. Fifty thousand dollars. And on every birthday," she said tenderly, "as long as I live, I'll add ten thousand. You'll never have to worry about the baby's security."

Joanne gazed quizzically at her mother.

"Did you worry about my security?"

"It was the major force in my life, Joanne," Katie told her. "I grew up poor. In some ways that stays with you forever. And then, after the '29 Crash, we had some rough years. Maura remembers, too—though that all seems far behind us now. Sometimes I worry that I spoiled you. You never knew what it was like to fight to keep food on the table. To know there'd be a roof overhead and fuel to keep the house warm in winter."

"I remember the farmhouse," Joanne said after a moment. Almost reluctantly, Katie thought. "It was so *little*."

"What is important now is that you take care of yourself." *Don't let Joanne's thoughts go rushing back to those last anguished days at the farm.* "This is a very precious time in your life. I remember. . . ." Sentimental tears clouded her vision. "I'm so happy for you and Gordie. And for *me*—because you're giving me the finest gift in the world."

Through Joanne's pregnancy Katie relived the months she'd carried Leo and then Joanne. She was grateful that now Joanne seemed to turn to her love and comfort. She showered Joanne with fine maternity clothes, new items for the layette.

Katie was upset when she realized Joanne was terrified of delivery.

"Darling, having a baby is the most natural thing in the world. You'll be fine," she promised, even while she flinched at the prospect of Joanne going into labor.

"You'll stay with me?" Joanne asked plaintively. Like a frightened little girl, Katie thought—wishing that, somehow, she could assume the pain of childbirth for her daughter.

Early in February—when she was fretful and prone to tears because she was already two weeks past the estimated due date—Joanne went into labor. Eight hours later she gave birth to a six-pound, seven-ounce daughter.

"I can't believe it!" Gordie was ecstatic as he gazed at the tiny bundle held up for their inspection behind the glass wall of the newborns' nursery. "Isn't she beautiful, Katie?"

"She's beautiful," Katie agreed. An incredible mass of near-black hair. Harry's hair, Katie thought involuntarily. His features but more delicate. "Miss Lisa Sharon Brooks." Lisa for Leo, she understood—though Joanne had not specified this. Sharon for the grandmother who had provided Gordie's trust fund. "Gordie, it's going to be so hard not to spoil her."

This was the beginning of a whole new life for Joanne, Katie told herself. At last the past was put to rest.

Harry arrived at his Seattle office early in the afternoon after a flight from Vancouver. Immediately he was swept up into another so-called crisis invented by Arnie. After a lengthy phone conference with Pierre in Minneapolis, the crisis was cleared up. How the hell did Pierre find the patience to deal with Arnie?

"Relax," Pierre ordered sympathetically, reading his mind. "Arnie is a necessary evil."

Off the phone Harry sought to unwind. On a corner table was a fresh batch of the Dallas newspapers—sent as always to the office rather than to the house. He brought the papers over to his desk and sat down to read.

All at once excitement shot through him. His hands tightened about the newspaper as he read an item on the society pages. Joanne had given birth to a daughter. *Oh God, he was a grandfather!* But he'd never see his grandchild. A little girl. Lisa. Named for Leo, he thought, his throat constricting with fresh anguish.

He sat motionless, trying to cope with this latest news. Katie must be out of her mind with joy. He remembered their happiness when Leo was born—and two years later Joanne. He remembered his silent vow to make a fine life for the four of them—and he'd created only grief.

He sat in his office long after the staff was gone for the night. Eileen hadn't bothered to call. She knew he'd be too tired after the flight from Vancouver and hectic hours in the office to go to that symphony performance tonight. And of course, when he flew in from a business trip, he always stayed late at the office to catch up on what had happened in his absence.

Whom was Eileen screwing this month? He'd long ago given up being upset over her affairs. She was a fixture in his life—someone to give the parties he demanded at regular intervals, to provide the aura of a happy, successful marriage. Thank God, she'd abandoned playing at being a member of his office staff. Probably it had interfered with her social life. At intervals—increasingly less frequent through the years because the business was so demanding—he availed himself of his marital privileges.

He always knew when Eileen started a new affair. There was a kind of defiant and arrogant glow about her. She seemed to understand that he recoiled from a second divorce. That he'd let her play around as long as she was fairly discreet.

How old was Eileen? He was apt to remember his own additional years, while Eileen remained a kid in his mind. She was about thirty, he pinpointed. *Young enough to give him a child.*

All at once his pulse was pounding. *Was* that just a wild fantasy? So he was forty-nine—plenty of men became fathers at that age and older. Hell, look at Charlie Chaplin and Leopold Stokowski.

Okay, it was a long shot, he reasoned. Eileen didn't want to have a baby—she had made that clear in the beginning. She was terrified a child might spoil that gorgeous body. Several times in the last three or four years they'd been careless—she'd been too lazy to get out of bed after they fucked—and nothing happened. Maybe he was over the hill.

He'd lost Joanne forever—and now this new grandchild was lost to him. Was it too late? Could he give Eileen a child? It would give new meaning to his life. So sex with them had degenerated into a fast, occasional exercise. He would revive it.

How could he be sure it was his kid? How could he get Eileen away from her weird circle of men? His mind leapt into high gear. There were ways to know, he decided at last in triumph.

Above all, he warned himself, he must remember that they had been careless and nothing happened. He may have run out of time. Or was it like Pierre liked to joke about—that you had to ring the gong at just the right moment? That there was only a forty-eight hour period each month when a woman could conceive.

He had always gone out and fought for what he wanted. He wanted this with a desperation that tore at his guts. Sure he could strike out—but for God's sake get out there and try to make it happen!

He sat and pondered over how to throw the odds in his favor. He would take Eileen with him on a month-long business trip, he plotted. They'd been talking for months about setting up a subsidiary in Europe. Cargill was doing it. He'd get together with Pierre to force Arnie to stop fighting this move. The accountants agreed it would be smart. He and Eileen would spend some time in Berne and Zurich, then focus on Geneva—where he'd set up their overseas subsidiary.

They'd leave at the time of the month when he knew Eileen couldn't be pregnant by one of those creeps who fawned over rich, idle women like her. During the next month he'd make sure they slept together every other night—so as not to miss her fertile period. Champagne by their bedside each time—Eileen would relish this. She wouldn't bother getting out of bed to take care of herself. *Make sure she didn't.*

Spring the trip on Eileen at the last moment, he cautioned himself. And start reviving their sex life now. Throw some crap about being sick of the business, wanting some pleasure in his life. Eileen might be surprised, but she'd respond. She knew there were other women who found him attractive—even at forty-nine. She'd be furious if he had an affair with somebody else.

At the right moment he'd concoct the sudden business trip. Eileen would love to talk to her Seattle friends about "our month in Switzerland." And with a slug of luck—and active sperm, he chuckled—he'd give Eileen a child.

She'd scream for an abortion, his mind warned. She'd be outraged to find herself pregnant after eleven years of marriage. But there would be no abortion, he promised himself. He'd make sure he had all the ammunition he needed to insure that.

He swung his chair around and reached for the Classified Directory. He'd find himself the smartest private investigator in Seattle. If Eileen insisted on an abortion, he'd threaten to divorce her. She'd leave his marriage with the clothes on her back and nothing else.

Though she was intrigued at visiting Switzerland, Eileen was sullen at having been given such short notice.

"Why couldn't we wait another couple of weeks so I could do some proper shopping?" she complained. "Who runs off for a month in Europe on five days notice? How the hell did you make reservations so quickly?" She knew he'd already arranged to have their passports renewed.

"Connections," he reminded her. "And you have enough clothes to open a shop. If you need anything else, you'll buy over there. Baby, you're going to be a sensational hit with those Swiss businessmen," he predicted. Not that he'd leave her alone even with a bell-hop. He'd plotted this campaign the way Eisenhower and his staff had plotted D-Day. "They love gorgeous blondes."

Eileen relished traveling. It made her feel important, Harry thought. A hangover from her dull, money-short childhood and adolescence. She was always envious of their jet-set friends—who popped in and out of their lives less frequently now that they were no longer based in Buenos Aires.

Early in June—before the annual tourist rush—Harry and Eileen flew to New York for a two-day layover before flying to Geneva. For Harry New York was always a traumatic experience—fraught with bittersweet memories of Katie and himself.

Pierre joined them for a lengthy business conference and a night on the town. Eileen enjoyed sitting in on company conferences. Again he thought, it makes her feel important. And she was sharp, he acknowledged.

More than once she had come up with a useful suggestion.

With Pierre they had an early dinner at Le Pavillon and went on to see the *Teahouse of the August Moon*. The following day—while Eileen shopped at Bergdorf's—Harry and Pierre settled in the Newhouses' suite at the Waldorf Towers for a final conference before Pierre headed for Washington, D.C., and he and Eileen left for Switzerland.

"By September we'll have our lobbyists set up in Washington," Pierre promised. "We have to get lower freight rates to the West Coast."

"My embassy contacts in Seattle tell me that the State Department is putting pressure on Japan to 'buy American'—to cut down their damn trade surplus with us. Thank God for PL 480." Public Law 480—just passed by Congress—was basically designed to combat hunger; but it was the perfect tool, Harry thought with approval, for disposing of the country's surplus grain. Of course, many conservatives and southern Democrats opposed so much foreign aid lest farmers in other countries cut back on their own production to produce crops for export, causing competition for American markets. "It couldn't have come at a better time."

Harry and Eileen left for Zurich that evening. Harry ever conscious of the schedule he had plotted for their nights together.

"Harry, where do you get the energy?" Eileen complained on their fourth evening in Zurich. "You've become a damn fucking machine."

"I told you—I've decided to live a little," he drawled.

With his business completed in Zurich, they moved on to Berne, then headed for Geneva. Here he'd already laid the groundwork for their new subsidiary. Involve Eileen, he ordered himself. Leave her no time on her own.

Neither of them had ever been in Switzerland before.

Eileen was disappointed that they had not arrived during the ski season. Still, Harry contrived to keep Eileen interested in Geneva. She was intrigued by stories of the world-famous Swiss banking corporations with billions of pounds hidden in the vaults, by tales of the great old families living in fortress-mansions in the rue des Granges. She was secretly triumphant at being entertained by one of these families, with whom Harry was doing business.

Eileen approved of their suite at the elegant Hotel des Bergues—favored by the jet set as well as visiting statesmen. She relished the chauffeur-driven gray Rolls-Royce put at their disposal for the length of their residence. She was impressed by the gourmet restaurants in Geneva and especially by Le Père Bise—one of France's best restaurants—fifty kilometers away, over the French border.

Bored though he was by nightclubs, Harry dutifully escorted Eileen to the best in and around Geneva. She was enjoying herself too much, he thought, to be suspicious of his motives. And he realized that she had abandoned any pretense of taking care of herself after their sexual encounters. She considered him an old man, he concluded with wry amusement—past the age when she had to worry about his making her pregnant.

Back in Seattle, Harry was in a constant state of anxiety and impatience, ever watchful of signs that his mission had been accomplished. Eileen was as regular as a clock, he reminded himself; but women could become irregular under stress of traveling and change in schedule. Maybe she was just late, he cautioned himself when he realized she had gone past her normal time for what she girlishly referred to as "the curse."

Then he came home after a late-night conference at the office to find Eileen waiting to confront him. Clutching a half-filled glass of champagne in one hand, she flipped off the television set with the other as he walked into the living room.

"Harry, you have to find a doctor fast!" She stared belligerently at him.

"Honey, what's the matter?" he asked with deceptive solicitude, excitement spiraling in him.

"I'm pregnant, that's what!" she screeched.

"Eileen, that's great," he soothed, and moved toward her.

"You keep away from me, you bastard! You know I never wanted this!"

"Eileen, you've always taken care of yourself," he said tentatively. "But what's wrong with our having a baby?"

"Why does it always have to be the woman who takes care of this?" she demanded. "You find a doctor, Harry. I'm not having a baby!"

"You'll have this baby, Eileen," he said with quiet conviction. "Our baby." Exhilaration lighted his face. No chance it could be anyone else's.

"You're out of your mind!" she blazed. "I'll find a doctor. And I'll divorce you. I'll—"

"If you don't have this baby—if you try to divorce me, you'll wind up with nothing but the clothes on your back." His eyes dueled with hers. He saw alarm taking root in her. He walked slowly to the Louis XV miniature bombe commode that sat between two tall, narrow windows and reached into the top drawer—where he kept fine Cuban cigars for special business associates. He reached beneath the cigar box and pulled out a collection of snapshots.

"What are you up to?" Eileen set her champagne glass on a nearby table. Her gaze fastened on the snapshots.

"My insurance policy." He strode toward her, holding out the sheaf of snapshots. She stared at the top photograph, flinched, turned her eyes away. "Unless you have this baby, I'll divorce you. You won't receive one cent of alimony. No settlement. As I said before," he said with devious coolness, "you'll walk out of the courtroom with nothing but the clothes on your back."

"You son of a bitch," she hissed. "You wanted this baby. You planned it."

"Darling, is that the way to talk to the father of your child?" he drawled. "Nothing's changed—except that for the next few months you'll be the beautiful, *pregnant* Eileen Newhouse. We'll go on with our normal lives as before."

"You'll never touch me again," she whispered, white-faced with shock. "My bedroom door will be forever locked to you."

"I can live with that."

Eileen was carrying his child. She wouldn't dare try for an abortion. And please, God, don't let her have a miscarriage, he prayed silently. Never in his life had he ever wanted anything as badly as he wanted this child.

In early February of 1955 Harry paced the reception area of the delivery floor in the posh private hospital where Eileen's obstetrician was on staff. Swearing like a dockhand, cursing the male sex in general, Eileen had gone into labor eight hours ago. Even the obstetrician had little patience with Eileen these last two months of her pregnancy. She had sulked, thrown tantrums, demanded a caesarean section as she approached full term.

"You're having a completely normal pregnancy," the obstetrician had told her sternly. "There's no reason for a C-section."

Now Harry paused to gaze out into the gray dawn. Ever since he had brought Eileen into the hospital, he had been caught up in memories of Katie. He remembered his terror when she had gone into labor with Leo. It had been a difficult labor—and he'd died a thousand deaths until the doctor came out and told him he had a son and that Katie was all right.

He had been afraid—again—when Katie gave birth to Joanne. Katie always seemed so small and fragile to go through the traumas of delivery. His throat tightened as he remembered how she had comforted *him* when she'd been moved into the delivery room.

"Harry—"

He spun around from the window to face Eileen's obstetrician.

"Yes?" His voice was hoarse with excitement, his heart pounding.

"Congratulations. You have a daughter. Seven pounds, two ounces."

"My wife?" he asked. Dizzy with the joyous news.

"Eileen's fine. Bitching, of course—but she had an easy time compared to most women."

"When can I see my daughter?" he asked shakily.

"In a few minutes." The obstetrician's smile was sympathetic. "She's a little beauty."

Later—reluctant to leave the hospital—Harry lingered at the glass-enclosed newborns nursery. There she lay. *His new daughter.* Samantha Newhouse. The name decreed by Eileen.

Such a long name for such a tiny little girl, he thought tenderly. They'd call her Sam.

Dark hair like his own. They wouldn't know for months whether she had his eyes or Eileen's. But gazing at her features, he recognized that Samantha Newhouse appeared remarkably like her father.

He would not make the mistakes he'd made before, he vowed. Everything must be right for Sam. But she would never know, he realized painfully, that she had a grown-up sister. She would never know Joanne—or Joanne's daughter. *Her niece.*

Already, he tormented himself, Sam was deprived of part of her birthright. But he would spend the rest of his life trying to make everything right for her. He would love her wisely. And his daughter, he thought humbly, would make his world whole again.

Yet deep inside, Harry knew, he would never be complete without Katie in his life.

Chapter Thirty-nine

DEEPLY ENGROSSED in the monthly reports sent in by the area managers, Katie glanced up with a start at the hesitant knock at her door.

"Yes?" Just now she realized that the day had officially begun. She relished the hour between 8:00 A.M. and 9.00 A.M., when the office floor was preternaturally quiet and deserted. Now the day would become chaotic.

"The Seattle newspapers just arrived, Miss Freeman," the mailroom clerk said, carrying the most recent week's editions.

"Thank you, Cal," she said with a smile. "Just put them on the table over there." It was not just the Seattle papers she read, she reminded herself, ever self-conscious about her compulsion to read the Seattle news, to look eagerly for word of Harry. Newspaper subscriptions came in from a dozen major cities. It was important to know what was happening in areas where she had stations.

Katie tried to focus again on the monthly reports. She had long ago decreed she must not desert everything else to skim the Seattle newspapers when they arrived. Yet she knew that the Seattle newspapers—unlike those of other cities—would not remain untouched for long.

"Coffee time," Maura intruded on her thoughts, strolling into her office with the morning mug. "And wish Miss Lisa a happy birthday for me."

"I can't believe she's a year old today." Katie leaned back, suffused with love. "I know it's ridiculous, but I told Joanne and Gordie to bring her over so we can be together for an early dinner and a birthday cake." Lisa's resemblance to Harry was uncanny, she thought with recurrent tenderness. It was like having part of Harry with her.

"Lisa may not understand about birthdays," Maura conceded, "but she'll love Melinda's birthday cake. Now have your coffee while it's hot," she ordered. "I have to get back to the salt mine."

Taking time out to savor the fragrant dark liquid, Katie thought how well bringing Maura into the office had worked out. Maura loved the daily hassle. She was bright and helpful in unexpected ways. There was Betsy plus the steno pool to take care of the dictation and routine business, but Maura was great at following through and reporting to her on various matters.

Katie drained the last of the coffee and set down the mug. Her eyes moved to the pileup of Seattle newspapers. Just holding them in her hands, she thought as she crossed to the table where Cal had left them, made her feel strangely close to Harry. She wished with a wistful intensity that he could know about Lisa.

She skimmed the first three days of the *Seattle Times* and laid them aside. She'd look at the others later. No, she decided. Look at them now. Then get on with the day's work. She flipped through the pages, scanning with practiced eyes. And then the Newhouse name rose up from the society page.

She read with disbelief, with a sense of unreality. *Harry's wife had given birth to a daughter.* Their first child after what she knew were years of marriage. Even now she could recall her shock when she saw the photograph of Harry and his second wife in that issue of *Town & Country*—when they were living in Buenos Aires.

Cold and trembling, she reread the brief item. Harry had a daughter, named Samantha Anne Newhouse. Joanne's half-sister. Born in the same month as Lisa—just one year later. Why was this such a shock? she rebuked herself. Men had children with second wives. Young second wives, she tormented herself.

She reached into a desk drawer and pulled out a small pair of scissors. She neatly cut out the item, held it in one hand, and reread its message yet again. Now she reached for the key that locked a private desk drawer. Here she kept the bits of information about Harry that she discovered from time to time. Seen by no eyes other than her own.

Fighting a poignant sense of loss, she pulled out the manila envelope that held all she knew of Harry's activities since he walked out of her life. Since she drove him out of her life, she taunted herself.

She had been stunned when she learned that he remarried. Somehow, she had never expected him to have another child. Maybe at forty-eight *she* was too old to have a child—though it wasn't unheard of, she thought defiantly. But it was not startling these days to hear of a man of fifty fathering a child. Men became distinguished with added years. Women became old.

She thrust the clipping into the envelope, returned it to the drawer, and locked the drawer again. Harry had been gone from her life for almost sixteen years, but the hurt had not gone away. In sudden decision she dialed Maura's extension. In moments of stress Maura was mother-sister-confidante.

"Lunch outside today?" she asked Maura. Normally they lunched at their desks or upstairs in the company cafeteria. "Expense-account luncheon," she added with an effort at levity.

"Who am I to turn that down?" Maura said gaily, yet Katie knew she understood this was not a celebration. Outside lunches meant personal problems—not to be discussed under the business roof.

By twelve-thirty they sat at a private table in Katie's favorite office-area restaurant.

"Maura, don't tell me I'm reacting like an emotional teenager," Katie warned. "I know that. It's absurd for me to feel betrayed because Harry has had a child with another woman. And don't bring up Terry. That was the most unreal time of my life. I was playing a role. And all the while I felt unfaithful to Harry."

"Katie," Maura protested. "You knew Harry remarried years ago."

"I was being unfaithful to the old Harry," Katie explained. "That young dreamer I married in a flat on Rivington Street. The Harry who was the boy wonder of Dallas before the Crash. The Harry who worked so hard to bring us through the Depression. And I keep asking myself, What would have happened if I had called out to him that day in the Seattle airport?"

"Katie, let go of the past."

"Don't you think I want to?" Katie's voice deepened in frustration. "Harry can do this. I can't. I tell myself that all I need is my daughter and my business. Do you suppose Harry knows how I've managed through the years?" At intervals she was curious about this.

"How can Harry not know? Gas Girls, Inc., is a major corporation. You've been profiled in the best magazines. He knows you've made it, darling."

"What have I made?" Katie demanded in contempt. "Money?"

"You have an enormously successful business. You're known nationally. You've raised Joanne on your own—and now you have Lisa. . . ."

"My darling Lisa." Katie's face was luminescent. "So precious, Maura. Such a happy baby." Now her eyes were wistful. "I wish that Harry could know about her. But she has *one* grandparent who adores her," Katie said defiantly. "Gordie's parents have seen her twice since she was born. But I know Lisa will never lack for love. I'll see to that."

"What are Joanne and Gordie doing these days?" Maura asked.

"Gordie's painting again. Usually portraits of Lisa. I don't think either Joanne or Gordie can really believe they're parents."

"Does it upset Lisa that her mother and father are dashing off so often on their little vacations?" Maura asked. Katie felt Maura's covert disapproval. Since Lisa's birth Joanne and Gordie had spent a week at Acapulco, three ski weekends in Colorado, and—most recently—ten days in Palm Beach.

"Maura, she's just a year old," Katie said defensively. "When Joanne and Gordie are away, she stays with me. You know that. And Nadine is there with her." She had personally chosen Lisa's nursemaid, paid Nadine's salary. Overpaid, Gordie said bluntly—but that was to be sure she wouldn't go running off to another job. It was important for Lisa to see familiar faces when her parents were away.

"And Melinda spoils her," Maura said with a reminiscent chuckle. "When I called you the other night and you hadn't got home from that orphanage benefit, Melinda talked for five minutes running about how wonderful Lisa is."

"And now Lisa has a new aunt." Katie tried to sound amused. "Samantha Anne Newhouse. Oh, Maura—" Katie's voice dropped to an anguished whisper. "I can't bear the thought of Harry's having a child with another woman. How awful to realize that Joanne will never know her baby sister—nor Lisa the aunt who's a year younger than herself."

At unwary intervals in the months ahead Katie's thoughts focused on Harry's new daughter. Did she look like Harry—or like his wife? How proud he would be if he knew Joanne's daughter was the image of himself. Holding Lisa in her arms, she was always conscious of the child's resemblance to her grandfather. Was Joanne aware of this? she asked herself in troubled moments.

Katie was disturbed by the aura of unhappiness that seemed to surround both Joanne and Gordie. *What was missing in their lives?* She had thought that Lisa's arrival would put an end to their perennial restlessness—but they were still dashing off on trips. Of course, she reminded herself conscientiously, they knew that Lisa would be all right with her.

She was convinced that Joanne was in love with Gordie. There was that special glow about her when she looked at him. And Gordie was solicitous always about Joanne. Were they upset because his parents were so cold and unfeeling toward them and Lisa? They both ran, she told herself, as though demons were forever on their trail.

With the arrival of the awesomely hot and dry Dallas summer, Katie rented a beach house for them in La Jolla.

"Lisa will have the biggest sandbox she's ever seen," Katie said laughingly to Maura on the morning that Joanne and Gordie and Lisa and their entourage left Dallas. "Poor baby, she couldn't spend every hour of the day and night inside an air-conditioned house."

"How did people in Dallas survive before air-conditioning?" Maura mused.

"We perspired a lot," Katie recalled. "I remember how impressed I was that the Centennial buildings were air-conditioned. And that was twenty years ago," she said with a burst of civic pride. "People had air-conditioning in their houses already by then."

"When we were dying of the heat," Maura reminded her, "we spent a quarter to sit through the same movie twice because the theaters were air-conditioned. And now," she teased, "you send your daughter and her family to a house sitting fifty feet from the Pacific."

Katie was simultaneously amused, irritated, and shocked when a major corporation seeking to extend its domain began to pursue her to sell Gas Girls, Inc.—at a startlingly high price. She rejected their overtures at regular intervals within the next few weeks.

"What would I do with myself if I sold?" she asked

Maura and Jeff over dinner at the Highland Park house. "I would be bored to death."

"You might learn to relax," Maura chided, but her smile was sympathetic.

Katie flew out to La Jolla on several weekends in the summer. Dallas seemed empty with both Joanne and Lisa away. Joanne insisted the three of them adored the beach house—yet Katie could not brush aside the nagging conviction that both Joanne and Gordie were unhappy.

Joanne came awake reluctantly, frowning in reproach. Her bedroom was clammy and overcool in the air-conditioning she normally relished. In the course of the night, yesterday's enervating heat had given way to an exhilarating October coolness. Hunching her shoulders in discomfort, she left her bed and crossed to turn off the air conditioner.

On the lush green grass below—acquired with such effort in Dallas—she saw Lisa playing ball with Nadine. Darting about with an elfin grace. Seeming so happy. Her sweet, darling baby, she thought with an overwhelming sense of love. But she wasn't a real mother, she taunted herself. She and Gordie played at being parents. Did Lisa know that? No, she comforted herself. Not yet. But one day she would.

All at once she felt a compulsion to prove to herself that she could be a good mother. *She could.* Bathed in the same warm glow that a glass of fine champagne elicited from her, she hurried from her bedroom and down the hall to Gordie's room.

"Gordie, wake up!" she called exuberantly, throwing open the door to his room.

"Joanne, I'm hung over," he protested. "Why did I drink so much last night?"

"You always drink too much when the party's dull,"

she laughed. And when it wasn't, she conceded to herself. "Gordie, I've just had a real brainstorm. When Nadine goes on her vacation next week, why don't we drive down to New Orleans—and take Lisa with us?"

"It won't be Mardi Gras time." He pulled himself up against the headboard. "Why go to New Orleans?"

"Because everybody says it's an exciting town—and I've never been there. We'll take Lisa with us. We've never gone away with her. It'll be fun."

"Who'll look after her?" Gordie asked. "We can't take her with us to the theater or to a nightclub. Not even to one of those great restaurants down there."

"Gordie, we'll look after Lisa. We don't have to go to nightclubs or the theater or great restaurants. We'll just sightsee and eat in restaurants where Lisa can go with us. We'll be parents, Gordie," she said softly. "We can't play games forever."

"Why not?" he challenged with a self-conscious laugh. "We've been having ourselves a ball."

"We'll go to New Orleans?" she coaxed. They had *not* been having themselves a ball, she thought in painful candor. They dressed their private torment in laughter—but it wouldn't go away. "And we'll take Lisa with us?" Maybe—just maybe—if they went down to New Orleans and took Lisa with them, they'd stop being make-believe characters and become real.

"All right, so the three of us will go to New Orleans." He shrugged good-humoredly. Gordie always gave in to her, she thought—but she wanted more than that. She wanted what he didn't have to give, she taunted herself. She didn't want to be Wendy to his Peter Pan. She wanted to be his wife. "Let's start out Saturday morning." Nadine was taking off for her vacation on Friday evening.

"Gordie, it'll be fun," she cajoled. "The weather is perfect this time of year. We'll stop off and have breakfast with Mother instead of having dinner with her the night before as we'd planned. We'll be busy packing Friday night. I'm just dying to see New Orleans. It's ridiculous that I've never been there!"

At 9:00 A.M. Saturday morning Joanne was jubilantly prodding Gordie—both of them carrying luggage—toward the white Jaguar, parked now in front of the house. Patrice—their maid, who doubled as nursemaid on Nadine's days off—had dressed Lisa in one of her doll-like ruffled dresses and given her breakfast and was playing with her now on the rambling veranda of the house.

"We've got enough luggage for a month's stay," Gordie grumbled, but Joanne sensed he was looking forward to their trip. Gordie was always happiest when they were traveling.

"Did you call your family and tell them we'll be away?" Joanne asked.

"Why bother?" Gordie shrugged. "They won't even know we're away."

A sumptuous buffet breakfast was waiting for them at Katie's house. Joanne and Gordie—holding Lisa—emerged from the car, and Tonto trailed happily behind them.

"Come on out to the breakfast room and eat while everything's hot," Katie encouraged them—when she had greeted Joanne and Gordie and patted Tonto. Now she reached to scoop Lisa up in her arms. "How's my precious this morning?"

"Nana!" Lisa threw her tiny arms about her grandmother with endearing approval.

"You made it a buffet breakfast because you figured we'd never be here this early," Gordie teased, "and you could keep things hot for a while, at least, in those chafing dishes."

"It entered my mind," Katie admitted with affectionate laughter. "Oh, bless you, darling." She inspected Lisa anxiously as her granddaughter sneezed twice. "Is she coming down with a cold?"

"Tonto's shedding like crazy," Joanne said. "It's probably just dog hair."

In the course of breakfast Lisa—content to be cuddled by her grandmother—sneezed again at regular intervals.

"I worry that Lisa's coming down with a cold," Katie said, touching her forehead. "No temperature, though." She hesitated. "Why don't you leave Lisa here with me? I'll be with her all weekend, and you know how Melinda adores her. Between us we'll take care of her."

"You don't think we should go to New Orleans," Joanne accused.

"Jo, she didn't say that," Gordie reproached her. "You always jump to conclusions."

"Darling, Lisa will be fine here. We've never had any problems when you've left her with me. I just think it would be wiser not to take her on a trip when she might be coming down with a cold."

Joanne hesitated. Gordie would be upset if they canceled the trip now. He'd be moody for days.

"Okay, we'll leave Lisa with you. But we'll phone every night to talk to her," Joanne promised. "Lisa, do you want to stay with Nana?" she asked.

"Stay with Nana!" Lisa approved.

"Then it's settled." Gordie sounded relieved. He'd been worried about how they'd manage with Lisa without Nadine, Joanne guessed. *That was so silly.*

In a flurry of conviviality Joanne and Gordie said extravagant good-byes to Lisa, to Tonto, to her mother. Joanne promised to bring Melinda and Juan pralines from New Orleans. With her mother holding Lisa and Tonto sprawled on the verandah, Joanne and Gordie hurried down the stairs to the car.

"Drive carefully," Katie called after them.

" 'Bye!" Joanne waved gaily when she had settled herself beside Gordie.

They drove away with a mutual show of pursuing adventure, the October sunlight providing a mantle of gold. But beneath their casual chatter Joanne felt a tension in Gordie that matched her own. *Nothing was ever really right with them.*

"We'll start making time as soon as we get on the highway," Gordie said. "I hate creeping along like this."

Joanne's eyes strayed to the speedometer. They weren't exactly creeping at fifty-five, but she understood. They both relished the exhilaration of passing every other car on the six-lane highway that led away from Dallas.

Twenty miles out of the city the dazzling sunlight gave way to clouds. Another five miles and huge droplets of rain pelted the roof of the car.

"It's going to storm." Joanne's smile was electric. "I love Texas storms."

"You know my secret fantasy?" Gordie asked with the insouciant smile that was less frequent these days. "Do you dare to hear it?"

"I dare." With Gordie it was always "follow the leader" for her. "What's your secret fantasy?"

"To gun the car as fast as it'll go on a wet stretch of road. It'll be almost like flying. Shall we?"

"Why not?" she countered. "Let's live dangerously!" What did it matter? Nobody needed them. Not even Lisa. Mother would always be there for Lisa. *Leo had needed her, but she'd failed him.*

"Hold on, Jo!" He leaned forward, gripping the wheel, excitement lighting his face. "Let's fly!"

Traffic on the highway was light this morning. The car zoomed ahead with soaring swiftness.

"Faster, Gordie," Joanne urged. "We can do it!"

"You bet we can!"

They passed the few cars on the road and moved onto an empty stretch.

"How do you feel, Jo?" Gordie demanded. "Great?"

"Great!" she assured him, dropping her head on his shoulder.

They didn't see the oil truck coming onto the highway until it was just ahead of them. Gordie swerved sharply. The car skidded. It was out of control.

"Gordie! Oh my God!" Joanne's scream froze in her throat as the car plunged off the road, down into a deep ravine.

Moments later the white Jaguar burst into a flaming inferno.

Part Four

Chapter Forty

KATIE STARED in disbelief as the pair of detectives uncomfortably reported the fatal accident several hours ago on the superhighway south of Dallas.

"I'm sorry, ma'am," one of the detectives said. "There were no survivors. All three died in the explosion." *They thought Lisa had been with Joanne and Gordie. Patrice must have told them that. Lisa was upstairs napping.*

"How do you know it was my daughter and son-in-law?" Katie challenged. She was ice-cold, her face drained of color. *The bodies cremated, one detective said.* "They don't own the only white Jaguar in Dallas."

"We checked the car's license plate," the older detective explained. Compassion seeped through his occupation-dictated calm. "The plate had been ripped off and thrown clear before the explosion. The maid at the Brooks house was very upset—she directed us to you."

"Are you alone here, Miss Freeman?" The other detective was solicitous.

"No." *Joanne and Gordie dead? It was happening all over again. First Leo, now Joanne. Her two babies.*

"Miss Freeman, would you like me to call someone to be with you?"

"I'm all right." She mustn't fall apart. "But how can you be sure it was my daughter and son-in-law in the

445

car? Perhaps the car had been stolen. . . ." She grasped at this fragile hope.

The younger detective cleared his throat.

"I'm sorry, ma'am. Just before we drove to the Brooks house, we heard from the team at the site of the accident. A woman's purse had been thrown clear of the car. It was Mrs. Brooks's purse."

"You'll—you'll want to report this to Gordie's parents." Katie was too numb to cry.

"That would be Mr. and Mrs. Gordon Brooks, Jr.?"

"Yes," Katie whispered. Everybody in Dallas knew the Brooks family. "Please notify them."

"We're sorry about your loss, ma'am."

"Thank you." She paused, straining for composure. "I'll be all right. Thank you."

For almost an hour she sat alone in the living room. Choking with muffled grief—because Lisa must not hear. Fighting to accept this devastating loss. Twilight darkening the lower floor of the house as though to clothe her in mourning. And then she heard the faint sounds of Lisa's voice and Melinda's. Thank God she had insisted that Lisa stay with her. Her precious Lisa—all that was left to her.

Now she left her chair and crossed to the phone. As always in grief, she reached out to Maura and Jeff.

Katie could hear Melinda singing softly to Lisa in the upstairs nursery. How would she explain to Lisa that she would never see her mother and father again? How could she accept this herself? She sat huddled on a corner of the sofa, one hand in Maura's, while Jeff made the necessary phone calls. There would be a memorial service for Joanne and Gordie at the synagogue. There would be a private burial of the charred remains.

"I wish you would eat something, Katie," Maura said anxiously. "You need your strength."

"I can't." Katie flinched at the thought of food.

"Thank God, you persuaded them to leave Lisa with you." Maura's voice was tender. "Lisa is going to need you."

"Oh, Maura!" Katie gasped in sudden comprehension. "The police think that Lisa was in the car. Patrice didn't know Lisa stayed with me. I'll have to call Gordie's parents and tell them."

Katie waited for one of Gordie's parents to respond to her call. At last his father was on the other end of the line.

"We're arranging private services for Gordon at our church," Gordie's father said tersely.

"I called to tell you that Lisa wasn't in the car," Katie said. "Lisa's alive. She's here with me. She—"

"Don't expect her to inherit Gordon's trust," Mr. Brooks interrupted. "The trust reverts to the family. Gordon had no assets to leave to her."

"My granddaughter wants nothing from your family!" Katie recoiled in shock. "She needs nothing from your family. I thought you would be grieving for her," she said scathingly. "I feel sorry for you and your wife, Mr. Brooks. You're beneath my contempt."

"We have never recognized Gordon's marriage. We've never recognized his child." His voice was cold as the Arctic winter.

"Your loss, Mr. Brooks. I thank God that I have this grandchild. And I mean to adopt her legally—so that she will be free of the Brooks name." Tears of rage filled her eyes. "She will be Lisa Freeman as soon as the courts can arrange this."

In the turbulent days ahead Katie thought constantly of Harry. She debated about contacting him, decided against this. She knew that Harry would mourn if he knew. But why intrude on his new life when it would mean only fresh pain?

She had Lisa, and Harry had his daughter. They would both survive—she to raise Lisa, Harry to raise

Samantha. She would sell the business, she resolved. She would devote the rest of her life to Lisa. But, oh, she needed Harry now! She needed him desperately.

Harry packed his valise, paused to gaze out of a window of his suite at the Château Frontenac—the huge, medieval castlelike hotel that overlooks the majestic St. Lawrence River and towers over centuries-old Quebec City. Thank God he was done with business and flying home this morning, he thought with relief. A stay of five days had extended to three weeks, but he was pleased with the results.

All arrangements were completed for the construction of a grain elevator at Baie Comeau, just north of Quebec City—where the company would have an ice-free port during the winter months. Once he'd learned that Cargill was building a huge elevator there, he knew that was their next major move. As usual he'd had to battle for months before Arnie agreed.

He glanced at his watch. Barely 6:30 A.M. He'd have time for a quick cup of coffee before the limousine arrived to drive him to the airport. The day was gray and cold. Dufferin Terrace below—the magnificent eighty-foot-wide boardwalk that travels for two-hundred feet above the St. Lawrence River—was deserted.

Over coffee he thought about Samantha. He'd called home every night to ask about her. He'd been unhappy at being away from her for this length of time. Every morning before he went to the office, he paused to visit with tiny Sam. His first stop at home in the evenings was the nursery. He was reliving—not without bittersweet recall—those early years with Leo and Joanne.

Everybody said Sam was the image of him, he thought with pleasure. How his mother would have adored her, he thought nostalgically. As he had thought when Leo and Joanne were born. He was grateful that Eileen never asked about his first family. It meant nothing to her that

448

Sam had a niece already. Lisa Sharon Brooks, he thought tenderly. Whom she would never know . . .

Harry went directly from the Seattle airport to their house—impatient to see Sam. Only now did he turn back his watch to reflect Pacific time. He'd spend some time with Sam, then go down to the office. While he talked regularly with Claire—his executive secretary—he liked to check into the office immediately after out-of-town trips.

He was delighted to find that Sam had just awakened from her afternoon nap and had not forgotten her father.

"Sam, I missed you," he crooned, tossing her up into the air. "Did you miss your old man?"

"I'm sure she did," Sam's nurse said diplomatically. "Didn't you see the way her eyes lighted up when she saw you?"

He had not expected Eileen to be home. She wasn't. The housekeeper reported she had gone to a benefit tea and fashion show at the Rainier—which meant, Harry thought with thinly veiled annoyance, that Sam would probably be sleeping by the time she came home.

Harry swept Sam away from the nursery and downstairs to the room set aside as his at-home office. Here was where Harry relaxed—away from the elaborate antiques decreed by Eileen. He'd recently ordered a playpen set up there so that he could have Sam close by when he worked at home over weekends.

With Sam playing happily in the playpen, Harry phoned the office and talked with Claire.

"Everything's under control, Mr. Newhouse," she said firmly. "No need for you to rush to the office now."

He hesitated a moment.

"You didn't allow anyone to throw out my out-of-town newspapers?" He'd never been away from the office more than four or five days—until this jaunt to Quebec.

"Everything's here," she reassured him. "In neat piles on their regular table." She knew his obsession to read out-of-town papers—without understanding the reason why.

"Good," he approved. "See you in the morning, Claire."

Harry waited for the nursemaid to reclaim Sam, then went out to the garage for his car. The limousine was not there. Eileen was still being chauffeured around town, he gathered. He slid behind the wheel of his Mercedes, and backed out of the garage. He'd told the housekeeper he'd be home for dinner—always served at 8:00 P.M., which Eileen considered the fashionable hour. Also practical, he conceded. He was rarely home from the office before seven-thirty.

The building that housed the two floors of Simon & Sinclair was mostly night-dark at this hour. He welcomed the silence that greeted him, went directly to his own suite of offices. He pulled off his Savile Row jacket, crossed to the table that held the out-of-town newspapers, and reached for the pile from Dallas. His other life, he thought with wry humor, as he settled himself at his desk.

Nothing in the first two copies of the Dallas newspapers captured his attention, though he was ever surprised at the way the city was expanding. Who would have expected this fifteen years ago?

He dumped the discarded newspapers atop a wastebasket and reached for another. His face suddenly drained of color, he read the headline: BEAUTIFUL YOUNG SOCIETY MATRON, HUSBAND, AND CHILD DIE IN HIGHWAY ACCIDENT. The photograph beneath the headline was of Joanne and Gordon at their wedding reception.

Dizzy with shock, he read the report of the accident. Three weeks ago, he realized—while he was in Quebec. Skid marks indicated the driver—believed to be Gordon Brooks—had been speeding. The highway had been wet.

His baby—his Joanne—was dead. Lisa—his grand-child was dead. *What crazy curse was on this family?* The one bond between Katie and himself—invisible though it might have been—had been destroyed. Their daughter, their son-in-law, and their grandchild were dead.

He dropped his head into his hands and wept. For Joanne. For Lisa, whose world was ended before it truly began. For the life he could never share again with Katie and Joanne and Lisa. And—again—he wept for Leo.

Now the image of Katie—alone in her grief—struck knives into his heart. He would go out to Dallas. He would try to comfort her. It was as though the past sixteen years had never happened. Their daughter was dead, and Katie was facing it alone.

He reached for the phone, called the airport. There was no flight to Dallas scheduled until morning. To hell with the expense, he thought impatiently, and arranged for a charter flight. He rushed home, relieved that Eileen was not there. He hastily packed a bag, told the house-keeper he had been called to Dallas.

"Ask Steve to pick up the Mercedes at the airport," he instructed. The chauffeur had spare keys to all three cars.

From the Dallas airport he tried to reach Katie by telephone. There was no response. She must have a housekeeper, a domestic staff, he thought. *Why didn't somebody reply?*

Reluctantly he left the airport to check into the Adolphus, and was immediately assaulted by memories. The first time he took Katie to dinner at the Adolphus, she had taken off her coat and folded it over her arm to hide its shabbiness. He'd just discovered the bucket shops and was making what in those days had been a killing. So many important moments of their lives had been celebrated in the dining room downstairs.

Where was Katie? And all at once he knew the answer. She couldn't bear staying in the house where Joanne and she had lived these last years. Tomorrow he'd call the office. She wouldn't refuse to see him. But now how was he going to tell her that he was married again? That he had another child?

He kicked off his shoes and stretched out on the bed—knowing he wouldn't sleep tonight. His mind haunted by images of Katie, devastated by this new tragedy in their lives. By visions of Joanne as a baby, as a little girl. So much like himself, he remembered—high-spirited, stubborn, rebellious. He'd lived with a covert hope that one day Joanne would accept him into her life again—but that life had been snuffed out.

Through the long hours of the night he relived his sixteen years with Katie—the high moments and the lows. She and Joanne had never been entirely absent through the blessing of the Dallas newspapers, which told him of important events. Katie's growing business success, Joanne's high school graduation, her college graduation, her engagement and marriage and the birth of her child. He had lived two lives in the years since he had walked out of the Dallas farmhouse.

At sunrise he forced himself to shower, changed into fresh clothes, and prepared for the day. Over breakfast—for which he had no appetite but instinct told him he must eat—he plotted his day. The office would open at nine o'clock. A few minutes later he would phone and ask to speak to Katie.

Shortly past 9:00 A.M. he called Gas Girls, Inc.—his heart pounding in anticipation. All these years later he could remember Katie's lilting voice. He could hear it in his mind.

"Gas Girls, Inc.," a crisp voice came to him.

"I'd like to speak to Katie Freeman, please." She never used the formal "Kate" in business, he knew from newspaper and magazine articles. "This is—"

"Oh, I'm sorry, sir," the switchboard operator interrupted. "Miss Freeman is out of town. Can someone else help you?"

"No!" He was startled. "Thank you, no. But can you tell me where I might reach her?"

"I'm sorry, sir. We're not allowed to give out that information."

Harry's hands were trembling when he put down the phone. How was he going to find Katie? Call Maura and Jeff—they would know.

But a call to the Warren house elicited no response. Then he would drive out there, he decided stubbornly. Rent a car and drive out. To reach their house, he reminded himself, he would have to drive past their old farmhouse. The prospect was unnerving—even all these years later. The last time he had seen Katie and Joanne was when he walked out of that house hours after they'd buried Leo.

The bright morning sun gave way to overcast skies as Harry drove out toward the Warrens' house in the rented car. God, how the city had developed in these last sixteen years! Endless tracts of suburban houses where once there had been farms. Then suburbia gave way to stretches of farmland. His heart began to pound at the approach to their old house. He slowed down, his throat constricting in fresh anguish.

That was their house? It had become a wing of a large, sprawling colonial ranch. Beautifully landscaped, with the same towering pecans and the mimosa that Katie had loved so much rising behind the expanded structure. He squinted at the rural mailbox. Smith, he noted the name. A family named Smith—obviously very prosperous—lived there now.

He saw a woman with a very little girl playing on the wide veranda, and he felt a wave of pain as he remembered Lisa—whom he had never seen. The age of that little girl, playing so happily with her nursemaid.

Drive on to Maura and Jeff's house, he exhorted himself. They would never give up the old farm, no matter how tempting developers' offers might be. Jeff was a stubborn cuss—he'd hang on.

Was that the house? He leaned forward in sudden excitement. Larger than he remembered. A three-car garage had been added. But yes, he told himself, this had to be it. He pulled up before the mailbox. Warren.

He got out of the car and started up the shrub-flanked flagstone path that led to the front steps. The shades were all drawn—as though everyone was away. Praying the shades were down against the morning sun, he rang the bell and waited. Rang again. Nobody was home.

He paused at the mailbox, pulled down the small door. Mail was piled up, as though untouched for several days. He had flown out to Dallas on a wild-goose chase, he taunted himself.

Knowing no other approach to finding Katie—suspecting that wherever she was, she was with Maura and Jeff—Harry sought out the cemetery where Leo was buried. He stood at the immaculate plot—where red geraniums grew—and cried in silence while he read the simple message on Leo's tombstone.

He would go back to the hotel, arrange for the first possible flight back to Seattle. It had been a mistake to come. With Joanne's death, he told himself again, there was nothing binding him to Katie. The best of his life lay behind him—with Katie, and Leo, and Joanne.

Chapter Forty-one

KATIE HOVERED lovingly over Lisa, sound asleep now in her crib in the newly set-up nursery at the long ago renovated and expanded farmhouse—and Katie's secret hideaway. It was sweet—and thoughtful—of Nadine to allow Lisa to stay up a little later tonight so that she could see her precious baby, Katie told herself. She'd missed Lisa those two days down in South Texas. She'd felt guilty at going away. But Lisa adored Nadine, and she loved Willa, too. Willa had stayed over at the house while she and Maura and Jeff were absent from the area.

"Sleep well, my darling," she whispered.

Thank God, Lisa was accepting Joanne and Gordie's absence from her life. She had asked about them for the first week, but accepted the explanation that they "will be back soon, Lisa." Joanne and Gordie had often disappeared for weeks at a time.

But for her, Katie thought in fresh anguish, there was no escaping from the knowledge that both of her children were gone forever from her life. But she was constantly aware that Lisa needed her. She must be both mother and father to Lisa.

Katie tiptoed from the nursery and down the hall toward the kitchen. Melinda was patiently waiting to serve them dinner. Bless Melinda and Nadine and Juan for their devotion these past four weeks. She had known she couldn't remain in the Highland Park house with Joanne gone. She had immediately transferred herself and Lisa, along with the staff, to the country house. Somehow, here she felt closer to Joanne and Leo—and to Harry.

"Lisa is asleep," Willa guessed when Katie appeared in the living room after instructing Melinda to serve dinner.

"She was tired but so triumphant at having been allowed to wait up for us." Katie's face was suffused with love. "When she puts those tiny hands about my neck and hugs me, I have the strength to go on with my life."

"Let's go into the dining room." Maura rose to her feet. "I know," she said with a sigh, gazing down at her spreading hips, "it would do me good to miss a meal. But I'm starving, and Melinda told me she has one of her great pot roasts just waiting to be brought to the table."

"How was the flight?" Willa asked Katie as she and her father followed the other two women into the country Chippendale dining room. "It must have seemed strange to be flying on a public airline after having your own plane." For the first time the company plane was laid up for repairs.

"Oh sure," Maura twitted affectionately, "the boss lady is spoiled."

"It's always the same when I fly," Katie confessed. "The way it is with you, Jeff," she guessed. "We look below and see how so many farmers are misusing the land."

"Not the land you own." Jeff's smile was smug.

"What I buy and we try to save is so little." Katie shook her head in frustration.

"Oh, that pot roast looks enticing," Maura said as Patrice walked into the dining room with a platter of succulent slabs of beef. "We could smell those wonderful aromas the minute we opened the front door."

"You eat, Miss Katie," Patrice ordered, pretending sternness, but her eyes were solicitous. "Everything Melinda made tonight you like."

"I will, Patrice," Katie promised.

"That land you bought down there can be a fine spread in a few years," Jeff told Katie and chuckled. "The auctioneer was shocked that anybody would lay out cash for it—the way it is now."

"I was doing a lot of thinking on the flight back," Katie began slowly. "Now don't jump and tell me I'm crazy. I've made up my mind to sell the company."

"Katie!" Maura stared in disbelief. "I don't believe it!"

"Let her talk, Maura," Jeff admonished. "Is it to the syndicate that's been after buying it for months now?"

"I'll make them raise the price again." Katie managed a wisp of a smile. Still thinking the way Harry taught her. "But don't worry about your job, Maura. One of the conditions of the sale will be that they agree to retain my full staff. I'll—"

"Katie, if you're not there, I'll resign," Maura said quickly.

"You love your job," Katie protested.

"I love working for you," Maura said bluntly. "Without

you there, it'll be just another dull office. But think about it, Katie. You've spent so many years building up the chain. What will you do without the business?"

"I'll raise Lisa. There'll be plenty of money," she reminded Maura. "I'll set up a trust fund for Lisa and another for myself. We'll never have to worry about finances. And I've always asked myself through the years," Katie said quietly, "if in my zeal to run the business I deprived Joanne of a mother. Perhaps if I'd been there for her all the time—"

"Bullshit," Maura interrupted. "You worked because you had a daughter to raise. *You had to work.* Don't ever think you weren't a good mother. You were the best, Katie."

"I want to be there every minute for Lisa. I want to know that I'm always there for her."

She hated the company now. She'd fought for riches for Joanne—to buy happiness for her surviving child. But there wasn't enough money in the world for that.

In the weeks ahead Katie was deeply involved in negotiations for the sale of the company. As she had anticipated, she was able to push up the sale price. But once the sale was consummated and she was no longer going into the office, Katie was restless, fighting against long, empty hours when grief usurped all other thoughts.

She made a point of spending part of each morning with Lisa. She was with her while Nadine gave her supper and prepared her for the night. Now she dismissed Nadine and took over, cherishing the new ritual of after-supper playtime, then reading Lisa to sleep. She was ever entranced by ecstatic pleas for "More, Nana! More stories!"

Lisa was so like Joanne had been in those early years. Affectionate, impulsive, with a bright, inquiring mind. And so like Harry, Katie was ever aware—in temperament and appearance. And why shouldn't she be? Katie asked herself. This was Harry's grandchild. Holding Lisa in her arms was holding part of Harry.

Yet the hours she spent with Lisa left too many other hours to brood over the consuming tragedy that had invaded her life again. By spring Katie knew that to maintain her sanity she must discover some new activity for herself. For Lisa's sake she couldn't allow herself to fall apart. And she was too young to sit on the sidelines and vegetate.

She searched her mind and arrived at a decision. She phoned Maura to ask her to come over with Jeff for dinner that evening.

"Something special?" Maura was instantly alert. Normally they had dinner together one night over the weekend. Rarely midweek.

"You know, Maura, you and Jeff are my board of directors. I want to move back into business. In a very small way," she clarified. "But I don't think I can handle it without you two."

"Katie, thank God! I'm dying of boredom. Can we talk about it now, or do I have to wait until tonight?"

"You'll survive until dinner," Katie laughed. "I have to sort out a few things in my mind."

Four hours later they sat in Katie's dining room and talked about the possibility of Adlai Stevenson becoming the Democratic presidential candidate again—until at last they were alone at the table.

"Katie, you spill your guts or Maura's going to split hers," Jeff ordered with wry amusement.

"This new venture depends on whether you and Maura will come in with me," Katie stipulated. "I have to do something or go out of my mind. I told myself it would be enough to take care of Lisa. . . ."

"Not you, Katie," Maura objected softly. "You've spent too many years out there running a business."

"Nadine has a warm, firm place in Lisa's life—I can't take that away. So I just sit around and think what a horror my life's become."

"What have you decided to do, Katie?" Jeff leaned forward in sympathy.

"I want to finance a new *small* company. A business that will allow me plenty of time to be with Lisa—and will give me personal satisfaction. American Farms Unlimited—with an office in downtown Dallas. Maura, you'll be office manager. I'm hoping you'll come in, Jeff—on a full-time basis now. Doing what you've done for me all along but on a larger scale. I want to search through Texas—through adjoining states—and buy up land that desperately needs reclaiming. I know it means bringing in a tenant farmer to handle your own land." Like herself, Jeff and Maura were the lone holdouts on their road against the enticements of suburban developers. "But don't you see, Jeff? We could do something important. In a small way—but important."

"You'll be tying up money that won't show a profit for years," Jeff warned.

"I can afford it." Katie impatiently brushed this aside. "You know what they paid me for the company. I'm setting up trust funds for Lisa and myself. We'll always be able to live well. But I want to put aside a large chunk of that money to improve land that's been almost destroyed. I know it's a slow process. . . ."

"You know, too," Jeff reminded grimly, "that tenants say one thing and then behave differently. We've had some rough times, even with the handful of farms you own now."

"If you buy in adjacent areas," Maura rationalized, "you can consolidate. Knowing you, Katie, I can see you with an agricultural empire in five years."

"Maura, no." Katie recoiled from this image. "I'm not going into this to make money. I want to restore these small farms and sell them back to farm families who'll care for the land."

"The future of agriculture lies with individual farm families," Jeff admonished Maura. "Not with huge corporations. That's the road to disaster."

"We'll buy a small plane and have a pilot on call," Katie picked up. "So that you can police these efforts. Any tenant who breaks our regulations about caring for the land won't be around for the next crop."

"I don't understand why some of them are so stubborn," Jeff said in frustration. "Why in hell can't they understand that insecticides are like heroin—they make great promises but they also make addicts. The more the farmers use, the more they need. The bloody insects develop an immunity to insecticides—and farmers pile up debts to the chemical companies. They—"

"Down, boy," Maura ordered. "Off the soapbox. We're on your side. We understand."

"So why—out of the six farms Katie owns—did four farming families sneak in insecticides behind our backs?" Jeff challenged.

"Because we haven't been able to educate them," Katie said somberly. "That's the big job ahead."

"It isn't because Jeff doesn't try," Maura reminded her. "God, the time he spends writing for farm journals that pay next to nothing. And the letters-to-the-editor he writes that pay nothing! I wish I could make him sit down at the typewriter and start a new novel."

"Knock it off, Maura," Jeff ordered, faintly testy. Their major fights were over this, Katie knew. "I spent too many fucking years writing novels and getting nowhere. It was the farm that kept us eating."

"All right." Maura's voice was determinedly cheerful. "So we're in business again. What's the next step, boss lady?"

Harry was upset that he had not been able to catch up with Katie in Dallas. The years since he had walked out of her life had seemed to evaporate with the news of Joanne's death. He was ever conscious of a need to hold Katie in his arms and comfort her. It haunted him that Joanne had died without reconciling with him. Yet back in Seattle he could not bring himself to try again to reach Katie. That moment was gone.

He was shocked when he read in the Dallas newspapers that Katie had sold Gas Girls, Inc., to a multinational corporation. In vain he searched the papers in the following months for some word of her activities. She had retired into her grief, he surmised. Word from him, he exhorted himself—and he was convinced she could be reached through Jeff and Maura—would only intensify her pain. In Katie's mind he was responsible for Leo's death.

He and Eileen were strangers living under one roof. Samantha was the one joy in his life. He rushed home from the office these days to spend an hour with her before bedtime, and often returned to the office after dinner to resume work. Weekends were devoted to Samantha.

He and Eileen attended social functions two or three times a week. He convinced himself that outsiders had no inkling that their marriage was a shambles. Their socializing—frequently with embassy staff—was important to business, a fact Eileen respected.

Harry scheduled an important European business trip for June. He insisted that Eileen and Samantha accompany him.

"Who dashes around Europe with a toddler?" Eileen demanded. "It's absurd."

"I do," he said grimly. "We'll take Rhoda with us." Rhoda—Sam's nursemaid—was a warm, easygoing, accommodating woman. "I won't leave Sam at home."

Harry remembered the trip to Europe—back in '29—with Katie and the children. One of the most glorious periods of their lives—until the news of the stock-market crash reached them aboard the *Île de France*.

How was Katie? How was she surviving this new tragedy?

In the first months of American Farms Unlimited, Katie went into the office twice a week, conferring regularly with Jeff at the house while Maura set up the Dallas office. The focal point of her life was Lisa. If Lisa sneezed, she called the pediatrician. If Lisa appeared less than her usual ebullient self, she worried. And then in October—on the anniversary of Joanne and Gordie's death—Katie was appalled when Lisa abandoned the familiar "Nana" for "Mommy."

"Katie, relax," Maura exhorted when Katie confided her anxiety about this. "If it makes Lisa happy, why not? She hears her little friends say 'Mommy' so it's natural for her to do the same. And let's face it, sweetie, you look more like her mother than her grandmother."

"I'm forty-nine years old!"

"And you look thirty or thirty-one," Maura pointed out. "I don't know how you do it. I ought to hate you for it," she laughed. "Nobody who doesn't know you would ever take you for more than early thirties. It's fine for Lisa to call you 'Mommy.' And legally, you are her mother. Legally she's Lisa Freeman."

Then Katie decided on an unexpected expansion for her new business. The company would circulate a small monthly publication, edited by Jeff, she decreed. A publication distributed to small farmers as "complimentary"—containing minuscule advertising—and aimed at spreading the latest information about saving the land.

By late autumn Katie was going into the Dallas office five days a week—though making sure to spend morning and early evening time with Lisa. Willa had joined the staff of American Farms, and George was a contributor to their publication.

Life was settling into a pattern that Katie could accept, though there were truant moments when grief threatened to overcome her. But always she remembered that she must be there for Lisa. Her whole world revolved around Joanne's child. Her precious granddaughter. As once she told herself she must survive for Joanne, now she knew she must survive for Lisa.

Chapter Forty-two

KATIE HAD BEEN crushed when Stevenson lost the presidency in 1952. She was equally disappointed when the man she most admired on the political scene was again defeated in November 1956. The Republicans, she was convinced, were on the side of big business. Not on the side of the farmers. It disturbed Katie that so many farm families were deserting their farms for town living. Especially now when the drought that had plagued the farmers since 1950 had been broken.

Like many Americans, she was drawn to the troubles in Cuba. She was repelled by Batista's police state—ruled by a dictator who utilized terrorists and corrupt bureaucrats. She was drawn to the seemingly idealistic, bearded young revolutionary named Fidel Castro, who headed a group of Cuban revolutionaries vowing to oust dictator Batista. This was a subject much discussed at dinners with the Warrens.

In Seattle Harry was fascinated by accounts of the young lawyer and revolutionary leader named Fidel Castro. He read the colorful accounts—particularly in *The New York Times*—of how Castro and his men hid out in the jungles of the Sierra Maestra range, awaiting the hour when they could wrest Cuba from Batista's grasp.

But not everybody, Harry discovered—despite the sympathetic American press—considered Fidel Castro and his *barbudos* as twentieth-century Robin Hoods out to give Cuba liberty and justice. Other interpretations came to him from foreign-embassy friends.

"Harry, don't be naive," one friend mocked. "Castro's

a smart operator. He's being financed by Cuban businessmen and landowners—all of whom hate Batista."

"So what's wrong with that?" Harry countered.

"The man's a Commie. He sees himself as a dictator—replacing Batista."

"Come on, are we still seeing Reds everywhere?" Harry scoffed.

"Vice President Nixon—according to the word in top circles—sent a twelve-page confidential memo to the White House, the State Department, and the CIA. He senses a Red tone in Castro's thinking. Of course, it got lost in the shuffle."

In the spring and summer of 1959—with more and more whispered warnings about Castro's true political affiliations—the romance between Castro and Americans began to fade. Castro was assuming dictatorial powers. But Harry was distracted now from his Castro-watching.

On one of those rare August mornings when Seattle temperature soared to 86 degrees, he received a phone call from Arnie Sinclair in Minneapolis.

"Pierre had a heart attack last night," Arnie reported. "He died two hours later. The funeral's scheduled for tomorrow afternoon. It's Jewish tradition to have a quick burial."

"I know," Harry said tersely. Shaken by the news. Pierre had talked for the past two years about retiring, but they'd both known this would never happen. "I'll fly out tonight." He hesitated. "What about his wife and daughters?"

"They won't be able to attend. Pierre's attorney has been in touch—he'll represent the family."

"I'll be in Minneapolis late tonight. I'll check with you on the details when I arrive."

They talked for another few moments, then Arnie was summoned to take an overseas phone call. Harry sat back, encased in shock. Pierre always seemed in top physical condition, one of those men who would still be at the helm of a major corporation at eighty—though he smoked too much and was a heavy drinker.

Harry's mind rushed back through the years to that first encounter with Pierre almost thirty years ago. From their first meeting he had been sure that somewhere along the line Pierre would one day play an important part in his life. Pierre was far more than a cherished business associate. He was his true and trusted friend. In all the dealings with Arnie—and Arnie was such a bastard—Pierre had always backed him up.

Later he'd worry about the business situation, Harry rebuked himself. Now was the time to cope with a painful personal loss. No man had ever been as close to him as Pierre. Nobody would ever fill Pierre's place in his life.

Harry glanced at his watch. No time to waste. He rang for his secretary, asked her to make arrangements for a flight to Minneapolis on the next available plane.

"I'll pick up my tickets at the airport," he told her. "I'm going home to pack. Call me there."

At anxious intervals on the flight to Minneapolis Harry considered his own situation. He owned only the shares he'd been able to buy through the years under the terms of his contract with Simon & Sinclair. Arnie and the syndicate owned a controlling interest. The remaining shares had belonged to Pierre.

Even if he was able to buy up Pierre's shares, he would still be the minority stockholder, Harry cautioned himself. Still, he would have to make the effort—though it would require heavy bank loans. Arnie might dislike him—but Arnie and the syndicate knew he and Pierre were the lifeblood of the company. And Pierre had always made it clear that *his* contributions were major.

All right, he'd have to make an offer to Pierre's estate to buy Pierre's stock in Simon & Sinclair. He'd borrow against his stock portfolio and the Seattle house. Pierre would want him to take over. He'd wait until a decent time after the funeral to make the offer. Pierre would leave his estate to his daughters and the grandchildren. He'd had only contempt for his wife.

Arnie was cold, plainly annoyed when Harry phoned him at close to midnight. He gave Harry details about the funeral services and the burial.

"I assume you'll be in town for a couple of days," Arnie wound up. "Let's schedule a meeting for ten A.M. day after tomorrow."

"Right. See you in the morning."

Harry slept little that night. In his mind he relived the crucial times he'd shared through the years with Pierre. Their escape from the Nazis during World War II, the establishment of Simon & Sinclair, the multitude of battles with Arnie.

Pierre had been popular in Minneapolis. His funeral was well-attended. Still, Harry was upset that Pierre's daughters were not present. They were represented, Arnie pointed out, by Pierre's personal Minneapolis attorney. Meaning, Harry interpreted, the attorney was representing the estate.

Call the attorney tomorrow, Harry ordered himself—after his meeting with Arnie. It was hardly likely that Pierre's daughters would want to hold on to his Simon & Sinclair stock. It wouldn't appear as pushing too hard to talk to the lawyer tomorrow, rather than waiting a respectable interval after the funeral. The lawyer would understand.

After another near-sleepless night Harry showered, dressed, forced himself to have a substantial breakfast in his room. He'd have his 10:00 A.M. meeting with Arnie, and then he'd try to see Pierre's lawyer later in the morning. With any luck at all he'd make the early afternoon flight out of Minneapolis—skipping lunch. Breakfast would see him through.

When he arrived at the Simon & Sinclair offices, Harry found Arnie waiting for him. Arnie was in unusual high spirits considering the situation. But Harry didn't expect

Arnie to mourn Pierre. Still, Arnie's mood alerted him to trouble. Arnie was forever trying to be in command. Hell, Arnie might be great at raising capital, but everybody knew *he* and Pierre ran the company.

"I can't believe that Pierre won't come charging in here, all excited about some new deal," Harry said with a rueful smile. "Or that—when I'm back in Seattle—he won't get on the phone to thrash out some new operation I've presented to him."

"Pierre won't be here—and *you* won't be in Seattle." Arnie grinned arrogantly at his startled state. "You may be in Seattle," Arnie amended. "But not at the offices of Simon & Sinclair. I want you off the premises by noon tomorrow."

"What are you talking about?" Harry's heart was suddenly pounding. He pretended low-keyed amusement.

"You're fired, Harry. Pierre isn't here to fight for you anymore. I'm buying Pierre's stock in the company. I've made a deal with Pierre's estate. Go back to Seattle, pack up your personal belongings, and vacate your office. Your replacement flew out yesterday. You're through."

Harry had waited up for Eileen. Tonight—knowing they would most likely be moving from Seattle—he felt a stranger in his own house. He had arrived home in time to spend an hour with Samantha, yet this had been tainted by the knowledge that once again he was afloat in an uncertain future.

Part of him still reeled from the brutal confrontation with Arnie. He had expected a hassle. He had not expected to be thrown out on his ear. And now he stood in their luxurious living room and reported the situation to Eileen.

Eileen stared at him in openmouthed shock.

"Arnie can't do that!" she shrieked. "The company will never survive without you!"

"He can do it, and he has." Harry felt a painful knot

between his shoulder blades. "Arnie is convinced he can handle the business. He has a terrible ego problem."

"Go to New York and talk to the syndicate." Eileen trembled with hostility. "All they care about is the bottom line. Make them understand the situation. Pierre gone and now you?"

"Elieen, it's all over for me with Simon and Sinclair," Harry interrupted tiredly. "Arnie's been waiting for this moment for nineteen years."

"We can't stay in Seattle." Eileen was on the edge of panic. "It'll be too embarrassing. And where are you going to get another job?" Her voice grew shrill. "You're going to be fifty-four years old!"

"I'm not ready for a wheelchair," he said dryly. "But we'll have to make some adjustments. We'll sell the house—there'll be a chunk of cash over the mortgage. I have a substantial stock portfolio." The market had been kind to them the last dozen years. "I'll look around and plot a new course."

"How can you be so fucking calm?" she demanded. "I won't live like a beggar again! I'm accustomed to—"

"Shut up, Eileen. We're not going to be starving."

"You should have worked out a deal with Pierre while he was alive," she reproached. "Pierre used you! Now the company's treating you like dirt. You—"

"Eileen, enough," he cut her off again. "I have to sit down and figure out our options." She was right, he conceded, about the meager possibilities of his walking into another high-salaried job, even with all his connections. "This might be the time to go into business on my own."

"Grain?" she scoffed. "Thirty years ago you could do it on our kind of capital. Not today." She was repeating what he'd said so often. The grain business had changed drastically through the years.

"I wasn't thinking of grain." What he'd been considering in a vague vein was crystallizing in his mind.

"Then what?"

"Sugar," he told her. "You're always talking about hating the cold weather. If I can buy a sugarcane plantation—plus a mill—in South Florida at a decent price, I figure we'd be in a great position. You know how Fidel Castro is acting up. It's a matter of time before the U.S. puts an embargo on Cuban sugar. The price of American-grown sugar will escalate like crazy."

"It's a gamble," Eileen said, but Harry saw a glint of interest in her eyes. Eileen had a sharp head for business. "Castro might backtrack to make Cuba's economy healthier."

"He won't," Harry predicted. "He's drunk with power. American sugar will become vital."

"What do you know about sugar?" Eileen challenged.

"Nothing much," he conceded, "but I'll learn. I know that the efficiency level in Hawaii and Louisiana is far higher than what it is in Cuba. I don't know about Florida."

"If you go into sugar, do it in Florida," Eileen ordered. "At least Palm Beach is civilized."

"Tomorrow we put the house on the market. You can handle the selling. I'll fly down to Florida and look around. Research the whole field. I can't go into a business until I understand every aspect of it."

"Don't make a year-long project of that," Eileen warned. She had grown to enjoy their Seattle lifestyle—though Harry knew that these days she was careful about her philandering. She had never forgotten their confrontation over the possibility of a divorce. "Money'll be going out and nothing coming in."

Two days later Harry left for Palm Beach. He knew there were several small towns close by where sugarcane was king. He knew, too, that August was off-season in Palm Beach, and he'd have no problems finding hotel accommodations.

In Palm Beach he rented a car and scouted the area within a hundred-mile radius during the daylight hours. He looked around for possible auctions. At night—after a telephone conversation with Sam about her day's activities—he pored over books on the raising of sugarcane and the production of sugar. Twice during his first ten days in Palm Beach he talked with Eileen about prospects for the house. She was appalled at the two offers their brokers had thus far received.

"We won't give the house away. We can afford to hold out for a decent price. Maybe you and Sam should come down here. . . ." He loathed being away from Sam this way. "I can find a rented furnished house with no sweat." A three-month rental this time of year would be available. Once the season opened, it would be a different story. "The house will bring a better price if we let it remain furnished until it's sold."

"What's it like down there this time of year?" Eileen hedged.

"I'll rent an air-conditioned house right on the water," he promised. Florida in August would be horrendous. "And see if Rhoda is willing to stay with us."

By the time Eileen arrived in Palm Beach with Sam and Rhoda, Harry was on the trail of a sugarcane plantation and mill that had recently been taken over by a Florida bank. A rather small plantation—no more than seven hundred acres, the banker advised Harry. Still, there was the possibility of annexing another plantation in the future.

Harry understood that most sugarcane plantations were huge because profits were small and volume was essential. The bank executive hinted that the adjoining plantation was in trouble because of mismanagement. Still, the bank was willing to extend Harry substantial loans on the basis of his business reputation.

To his astonishment Harry found Eileen eager to be active in the prospective new business. She was fascinated by the vast fields of sugarcane reaching ten to fifteen feet high—almost ready for harvest—and by the camp set up near the fields to accommodate the workers.

To Eileen, to own a sugar plantation was like ruling a private domain. Colonialism in the midst of America.

With heartening speed Harry was launched in business. The mill itself was located in West Grove—forty-some miles from Palm Beach. West Grove was a dreary town of less than one thousand, with the sugar mill the major employer. Harry found a house for his family several miles south. He recoiled from raising Sam in a mill town. He ignored Eileen's complaints that the house was too small and unattractive.

"We don't need a mansion, Eileen—a ten-room house is more than enough. You'll redecorate. We'll add a swimming pool. It'll be fine." Not the Breakers, he thought humorously, but the kind of house the average Florida corporate executive would be proud to own. Eileen was badly spoiled. "Rhoda will sleep in. The rest of the staff will come in by the day." Both he and Eileen were amazed by the low wages paid to local domestics.

Harry was able to retain the former owner's mill employees. Field crews and cutters were already contracted for the approaching season. This would be his apprenticeship. He would learn what was required of him. And he would watch for developments in Castro's Cuba. What happened with Cuban sugar would control their future.

At errant moments Eileen was terrified of the outcome of their investment. Of the bank loans that hung over them. Harry was convinced he was on a roll. It was a matter of time before the U.S. government lost patience with Castro. An embargo would go into effect. But he realized, too, that unless he was able to acquire the adjoining plantation and bring up his volume to help meet the bank loan payments, he could be in serious trouble.

Chapter Forty-three

LOVINGLY, KATIE tied the sash of the mint-green organdy dress Lisa was to wear as the flower girl at George's wedding this afternoon.

"Mommy, you'll watch?" Lisa asked for the dozenth time. She was simultaneously euphoric and nervous at being part of the wedding ceremony. "I won't be scared if you're watching."

"I'll be watching you every moment, darling," Katie promised.

Maura was so pleased that George—at long last—was marrying his longtime girlfriend, the only daughter of a farm couple who had finally capitulated and sold out to real estate developers. *"I can't wait to spoil my grandchildren!"* Maura crowed. *"Of course, I prefer that George and Nora be married first."*

"Mommy, is my hair all right?" Lisa demanded.

"It's perfect," Katie soothed, fondling the near waistlength dark hair. "You look beautiful." Katie checked her watch. "It's time for us to leave for the church."

Katie sat with George's family in the flower-bedecked church. As the wedding music began, Maura reached for her hand.

"Damn it, I'm not going to cry," Maura whispered ferociously. "I'm not losing a son—I'm acquiring grandchildren."

Thank God, Katie told herself, for Maura and Jeff and their kids. They made up Lisa's family. She and Lisa lived an almost cloistered life. Lisa, in time, of course, would learn about her parents' tragic death—but let her be sheltered from this for now.

It had become almost an obsession with her to avoid the public attention that had been part of her professional life as owner of Gas Girls, Inc., and as one of the wealthiest women in the Southwest. American Farms Unlimited was a small company that kept a low profile. And she'd insisted that her name not appear on the masthead of their monthly publication.

"Oh, Katie, Lisa looks adorable," Willa leaned forward to whisper as Lisa appeared at the head of the church aisle. "We must get snaps of her in that dress."

Katie watched Lisa walk down the aisle, her small face endearingly serious until her eyes spied Katie. All at once she was radiant. Tears of pride and love welled in Katie's eyes. *Her baby. Her precious baby.*

Now Katie's mind darted back through the years. She remembered Joanne's wedding—and how happy she had seemed that day. For a little while, Katie thought in poignant recall, Joanne had been happy.

The day after the wedding Lisa was to enter the first grade. Katie was as nervous and excited as Lisa as they prepared to leave the house for school.

"You'll come for me after school, Mommy?" Lisa asked as Juan drove up before the house with the car.

"I'll be there, darling," she promised. "Just like when you were in kindergarten."

Always at crucial moments like this she was attacked by *déjà vu*. She had gone through this with Leo and Joanne, felt these same emotions then. Only now she was alone. She couldn't run home and report to Harry how Lisa was reacting to this momentous occasion. *"Oh, Harry, Leo was so pleased and yet so solemn."* Joanne had been wildly delighted to start school. Leo was there, and she wanted to do whatever Leo did.

Katie left the school and returned to the car.

"To the office, Miss Katie?" Juan asked.

"Right, Juan."

Another milestone in Lisa's life had just been success-fully passed, Katie thought tenderly. It was Lisa who made life worth living. Yet with each landmark occasion in Lisa's life came painful memories. And the futile wish that Harry was here to savor the moment with her.

The first of the sugarcane was harvested in the fall. The cutting continued into the spring. On this late September evening—the weather still hot and humid—Harry and Eileen waited at the edge of one of the fields for the burning to begin. The day before its cutting, each field was to be burned.

"We just started burning about fifteen years ago," Harry's crew leader told him. "It makes the cutting a lot easier. It gets rid of the leaves and the tops."

"Why do we burn at night?" Eileen demanded. Harry was annoyed by her imperious tone. And in a corner of his mind he worried about the damage to the soil these annual burnings caused.

"It's easier to handle at night, ma'am." The crew leader was polite, though Harry suspected he disapproved of a woman being part of this scene. "With the dew on the ground the fire is easier to control. It's real exciting when the fire gets moving," he said with proprietary pride.

"How do you know how much to burn?" Eileen pursued.

"We burn what we need to keep the mill in operation twenty-four hours a day," the man explained. "What Mr. Newhouse orders."

"What's holding up the show?" Harry asked.

"We're ready to go, sir," the man told him. "The burners are carrying the pots into the field now."

There was a hell of a lot to learn, Harry warned himself—and little time in which to learn it. He had to figure out fast how to redirect a mismanaged business. He had done his customary intensive research—but sugarcane was a whole different ball game from wheat.

"Harry, look at that!" Eileen's voice was electric. Burners were lighting three sides of the field. The flames shooting upward and spreading.

"The wind's right today," the crew leader told them. "This will burn down to stalks."

In minutes, it seemed, the fire was spectacular. The field a raging furnace. The heat reached out to those watching. The air was filled with the aromas of the burning sugarcane.

"It smells like roasting corn," Harry said in astonishment. All at once he was back in the farmhouse and piling corncobs into the stove because they had no money to buy coal.

"Cane and corn are in the same family," the crew leader pointed out.

"What an awful noise!" Eileen covered her ears with her hands. "Like bombs falling!"

Harry and Eileen stayed to watch the burning—both mesmerized by the drama of the fire that rose into the night sky.

"I'll supervise the plantation operation," Eileen said with an air of exhilaration. "You can concentrate on the mill and selling, Harry."

"Eileen, the plantation is a big deal," Harry objected. "Without the cutting proceeding correctly, the mill can't operate around the clock. And that's essential if we're to pay off the bank loans."

"The plantation crew has to know the bosses have an eye on them," Eileen said calmly. "You can't be here and at the mill. That's what I'll be—a watchful eye on the plantation. The crew won't mess around if I'm there to see that nobody goofs off."

"We'll talk about it," Harry hedged.

Before the first week of the harvest was over, Harry was confronted by a crisis. The plant superintendent quit. With an absentee owner he had been able to line his own pockets—one reason for the company's financial situation, Harry comprehended now. In addition to his other responsibilities Harry was forced to settle into the role of plant superintendent. Eileen would oversee the plantation—as she was panting to do, Harry knew.

Now each morning Eileen drove from their house down to the fields, rising earlier each day until she was there when the cutters arrived in the fields at dawn.

Most of the cutters were Jamaicans. A cut foreman—in charge of the leadmen and the ticket writers, all of whom had once been cutters—told Eileen that for the past fifteen years American blacks had refused to cut sugarcane. Growers had been forced to look for workers in the West Indies.

Eileen was attracted to the handsome young Jamaicans. She was aroused by their tall, long-limbed bodies, by the way they moved—like dancers, she thought. Though the job of cutter was demeaning and tedious—as well as dangerous—she sensed a kind of arrogance in them.

She made a point of earning the reluctant respect of the cut foreman. *Let them know who was boss here.* She made them understand she knew when the work was not going well. She reviled cutters who dared to ask for replacement gloves.

"We issued gloves at the start of the season," she reminded them. "They're expensive—one pair to a cutter." Usually the gloves—canvas with leather palms—were worn out within a week or two. The cutters would work without them, she decreed. This was a common occurrence, she had learned by questioning leadmen who had worked for other growers—though without gloves the cutters' hands grew blistered and cramped.

By the beginning of the new year Eileen startled Harry with her insistence on having the cottage at the edge of the fields—in an earlier era the cutting-season residence of an owner—refurbished for her own use.

"It's ridiculous for me to leave home at dawn and not come back until well in the evening." For the past month the cutters had worked into the dark—by the headlights of cars—to fill the demands of the mill. "I can stay at the field cottage during the week and be home for the weekends."

"What about Sam?" Harry demanded. "You're her mother."

"I leave before she wakes in the morning. She's asleep when I come home. I'll have the whole weekend to spend with her," Eileen placated him. "We'll both spend all of the weekends with her." Harry, too, was working fourteen hours a day.

"I don't like it." He was upset. "Sam's being cheated of her parents."

"We're doing it for her," Eileen said coolly. "Besides, she's at that fancy school most of the day—she comes home and Rhoda fusses over her. Why don't you take off an hour or so and drive home to have dinner with her? Then go back to the mill." *All Harry gave a shit about was his daughter.* It was for her that he wanted the business to succeed.

"Okay." Harry brightened. "I'll do that."

Eileen arranged for two of the cutters to be diverted to work on the cottage. The ticket writer had been instructed to see that they would be paid above their normal earnings for the period she would use them. The two Jamaicans were delighted, she guessed, to be paid for this lighter, nonhazardous work.

When repairs had been made and the cottage painted, she dismissed one of the men. The other would handle some minor painting. Ostensibly that was why she kept him away from the fields.

She fought to conceal her anticipation as she issued orders. It had been a long time since a man had excited her the way this gorgeous Jamaican did.

"Be here tomorrow at the usual time, Thomas," she instructed him. She had been smugly aware of his furtive glances at her at regular intervals. She still had a great body, despite Samantha. "I want to put another coat of trim on the baseboards in the living room and my bedroom."

"Yes, ma'am," he said politely.

Dawn was creeping into her bedroom the following morning when she heard a furtive knock at the cottage door.

"Come in, Thomas," she called through the open window.

Already she felt a stirring deep within her. She visualized his excitement when he came into the house and saw her this way. Her skin white velvet beneath her black chiffon nightgown. The matching peignoir concealing nothing. *She was done living like a nun.* Harry would never know about this. How could he? she asked herself triumphantly.

She tossed aside the sheet and thrust her feet into black satin mules. With a secretive smile she rose to her feet.

"Miz Newhouse?" Thomas's deep, melodic voice sounded wary.

"Do you know how to make coffee, Thomas?" Eileen strolled out of the bedroom into view. She heard his sharp, startled intake of breath.

"Yes, ma'am," he said with the Caribbean accent she found erotic. His shirt was open at the throat, his trousers tight.

"Put up a pot for me. The small percolator," she ordered. "And bring it to me in the bedroom." Her maid—Rita—had been home sick for three days. Rita had instructions never to come to work when she had a cold. Eileen guarded her health as part of her beauty program. Nobody would come to the cottage today to disturb her—and Thomas.

Eileen settled herself on the bed again, her eyes aglow. Since before Sam was born, she'd lived in terror of Harry's divorcing her and turning her out into the cold. She knew he'd forever hold these snapshots over her head. But her life had acquired a new, enthralling dimension since she'd become active in the business and settled in the cottage. Here she could do whatever she liked—and Harry would never know. Here she was queen.

Lord, those Jamaicans were handsome! Those tall, muscular bodies—and the way they moved. All at once she didn't want to play the game she'd plotted.

"Thomas!" she called. "Forget about the coffee for now. I'll have it later. Come in here. . . ."

Moments later Thomas appeared in the doorway of her bedroom. She knew from the heated glint in his eyes that he understood what his primary duty would be today.

"You want me to start to paint now?" His eyes focused on the huge, dark nipples on display beneath the black chiffon. His tongue darted between sensuously full lips as though in anticipation of its destination.

"Later." She raised one leg so that the nightgown slid high on a white thigh. "Come here, Thomas."

With a grunt he moved toward the bed, then paused.

"First to close the drapes," he said and crossed to the window.

The area was deserted this time of day, Eileen thought impatiently. Nobody would see. Every muscle in her body was tense and demanding. She was conscious of a pulse going berserk low within her.

"Thomas, come here. . . ."

She murmured encouragement as he lowered himself above her. Large, muscular hands moving with tantalizing slowness, thrusting the straps of the nightgown away from her shoulders, down to her waist while his mouth sought a taut nipple.

Gasping in approval, she reached to his trousers, slid a hand to his hard, rising crotch.

"Hurry," she commanded. "Oh God, hurry!"

She waited, urging him in gutter language, while he stripped. She cried out in welcome as he sought his way between her thighs and found his destination, his mouth simultaneously nuzzling at a nipple. She didn't *need* that stupid Palm Beach whirl that had been eluding her. This was the life she'd been born to embrace.

"Don't leave, Thomas," she said huskily, tapered fingernails subconsciously digging into his shoulders when they at last lay exhausted. "We're just beginning the party."

Later—much later—she sprawled on a chaise before the window air conditioner and sipped the strong hot coffee that Thomas had brought to her. Now he sang some weird Caribbean song while he played at repainting the trim.

When the season was over, she plotted, she'd find a reason to keep Thomas here. Or an equally good-looking, equally passionate replacement. She could see the years moving ahead in waves of sensuous encounters.

Chapter Forty-four

WITH LISA starting school and her own involvement in American Farms Unlimited making increasing demands on her time, Katie bought a beautiful house in Highland Park again—to cut down on commuting time and to have more hours with Lisa on business days. Every Friday afternoon they traveled religiously to the farmhouse for the weekend. Through the years it had grown into a handsome residence. It delighted Katie that Lisa loved the farmhouse.

Like all Texans, Katie was proud that Lyndon Johnson was elected vice-president in November of 1960. Jeff kept assuring Katie that Lyndon Johnson would be for "the man in the street" and for the farmers. *"Hell, he was born in a Texas farmhouse. And he knows what it means to be poor."*

She was emotionally involved—and contributed financially—to the civil-rights movement. Like many other Dallasites, she was quick to point out that Dallas had long ago integrated workers in the city's postal staff, that there was less bitterness in Texas over "the colored question" than in any other southern state. She was aware—and troubled—that Dallas still had Jim Crow problems in housing and transportation. Still, Dallas Negroes ran their own businesses, had their own professionals, even their own debutante season.

In 1962 Katie was elated by the soaring success of Rachel Carson's controversial book *Silent Spring.* With her book Carson sought to make the world realize that the indiscriminate use of chemical pollutants, such as pesticides, could one day make the world uninhabitable.

Katie was horrified—as was most of the world—when John Kennedy was assassinated in downtown Dallas on November 22, 1963. For many Dallasites it was a blot on their city's fine name. It would be a long time, some warned, before Dallas could hold up its head again. Still, Texans were proud that one of their own—Lyndon Baines Johnson—was at the helm of the country.

A year later Texans rejoiced when LBJ defeated Barry Goldwater in the 1964 presidential election. On January 18 of the following year Katie flew with Jeff to Washington to attend the round of inaugural functions. Long before the rush for hotel accommodations began, Maura had reserved rooms for Katie and Jeff at the august Mayflower Hotel. They had seats for the Inauguration, tickets for the gala and the concert and the Inaugural Ball at the Mayflower. They meant to use the occasion to lobby congressmen and senators on behalf of the farm bloc.

Their Braniff DC-8 landed at Washington National Airport late in the afternoon. They were conscious of hordes of other Texans making this same pilgrimage. The accents, the men in the ten-gallon hats and the women in designer dresses from Neiman's, advertised this.

"I hear over three thousand are coming from Texas," Jeff said ebulliently as he prodded Katie through the crowds. "Remember what Marvin Watson said, though." Watson was the Texas State Democratic chairman. "It's up to us to 'show the world the moderate and warm temperament of the true Texans as we share our own LBJ with the world.'"

"I think most of us will abide by that," Katie said with mock solemnity. "Though I hear there's a lady from Fort Worth who's coming to town with a tiara that lights up and spells 'T-E-X-A-S.'"

After considerable hassle they arrived at the Mayflower and were assigned their rooms.

"We'll grab a fast dinner and head for the National Guard Armory," Katie told Jeff as they headed up in the packed-to-the-gills elevator. "That's where they're holding the Inaugural Gala."

"Yes, ma'am." Jeff grinned. "I tell you one thing. I wouldn't have faced this madness alone."

"Give me thirty minutes to unpack and change. Then come and get me," Katie ordered. "There are sure to be people we want to meet at the gala."

Katie and Jeff were immediately caught up in the excitement of the occasion as some ten thousand guests packed the cavernous District National Guard Armory. Hollywood personalities would preside over the function, they knew from the program. Johnny Carson, Carol Channing, Ann-Margret, Alfred Hitchcock. The highlight of the entertainment would be a performance by Margot Fonteyn and Rudolf Nureyev.

The excitement rose to a crescendo as President Johnson and his family entered their box. Drums rolled. Spotlights beamed on fourteen American flags, rippling in the breeze of twenty-eight electric fans. Then the show began. Hitchcock spoke. A sixty-piece band played a series of patriotic songs. Some of the nation's top performers entertained a delighted audience.

Afterward—as scheduled—Katie and Jeff attended a party given by a Texas group at the Statler Hilton, where "The Eyes of Texas" was sung with rebel yells. Katie and Jeff managed some earnest conversation with several congressmen, pressing their cause.

"Katie, we've got a long day ahead tomorrow," Jeff reminded her finally. "Let's get back to our hotel." He hesitated. "I suppose it's too late to call Maura. . . ."

"It's not too late," she said tenderly. "She'll be waiting to hear. And I'll talk to Lisa." Lisa was staying with Maura in her absence.

As prearranged, they slept late on Tuesday, met in the afternoon with the head of a professional lobbying group, and in the evening attended the Inaugural Concert at Constitution Hall. When a spotlight focused on the presidential box, the audience began to applaud. The applause was laced with laughter when LBJ joined in the applause.

"His mind's off on more important business than the concert," Jeff whispered—at the same moment that Lady Bird was whispering to her husband. The president grinned at his faux pas, stopped applauding, and joined in the laughter.

On Wednesday—Inauguration Day—Katie debated about what to wear. While the sun was out, the ground was covered with snow. Apt to be slush soon, she thought, gazing out onto the street. Warm boots, tweed slacks, a cashmere sweater, she decided—and her Russian-styled greatcoat. Boris Pasternak's best-selling novel

Doctor Zhivago had even influenced fashions. And she'd be warm.

Well before the scheduled time Katie and Jeff occupied their seats before the Capitol. Others had arrived even earlier, with blankets to protect them against the cold, Thermoses of coffee to keep them warm.

"It's going to be a different kind of Inauguration," Katie said whimsically. "No top hats, no tailcoats. And no military hardware in the parades. But I'll bet you the gowns at the Inaugural Balls will be as elegant as those at any Inauguration in history."

"Maura tells me Neiman's was doing a land-office business." Jeff chuckled. "Maybe it's just as well Maura insisted on not coming. You know how much an evening gown from Neiman's would have set us back?"

The wind was brisk, but a pale winter sun lent a sparkle to the scene. Still, Katie was relieved when at last the U.S. Marine Corps band played "Hail to the Chief" and the ceremony was launched. Mrs. Johnson sat between the president and the chief justice. Her American Beauty red coat a charming accent between her husband's Oxford gray business suit and the somber robe worn by Chief Justice Earl Warren.

At the appropriate moment Lady Bird held out a dog-eared family Bible. His head bare, without a coat despite the coldness of the day, her husband laid his left hand on it. At a cue from the Chief Justice he raised his right hand. Katie was totally involved in the swearing-in. For all Texans this was a special day. LBJ was beginning a term to which he had been duly elected. The Chief Justice's voice was loud and clear, LBJ's hushed, barely audible.

The ceremonies ran slightly more than an hour. Then the presidential party retired to the inaugural luncheon. Viewers hurried to try for advantageous places along the parade route, which would begin after the luncheon.

"Shall we head for the parade route?" Jeff asked Katie.

"Jeff, how can we go back and face the others if we

don't attend the parade?" Katie smiled. "Anyhow, it's warming up now."

Katie was glad they were attending the ball at the Mayflower. No problem about transportation, she thought gratefully. She wore a tiered turquoise crepe that lent her an air of fragile elegance. Her hair swept back to emphasize her delicate features. The reflection that gazed back from her mirror was that of a beautiful woman in her early forties, though Katie saw none of this.

She must remember to make a note of what the Johnson ladies wore, Katie told herself as she and Jeff mingled with the crowd at the Inaugural Ball. Lisa had given her strict instructions to report on their gowns.

LBJ and his party made the Mayflower ball their first stop. The band played "Hail to the Chief," and the president and Mrs. Johnson headed for their box. The guests applauded exuberantly. He surprised many by taking to the dance floor in person.

"Do you know," Jeff marveled, "he's one of the few presidents who's ever danced at his own Inauguration?"

"Look at him changing partners," Katie marveled. "Oh, there he goes again!"

The room was oppressively hot, but no one seemed to mind. The guests applauded wildly when President Johnson went over to Margaret Truman's box, helped her climb over the railing, and spun her around the floor to "I've Got the World on a String."

Not long after the presidential party left, Katie suggested that they head over to the Sheraton Park ballroom, where most Texans were staying.

"Let's," Jeff agreed. "If we can get in without tickets."

"We're Texans," Katie scoffed. "We'll get in."

At the Sheraton—at last gaining admittance—they met Steve Marcus, an eminent Texan based in Galveston. Katie and he knew each other by name, but their paths had never crossed. Blurred newspaper photos had not prepared Katie for his startling resemblance to Harry.

"No, I'm not related to the Dallas Marcuses," Steve said humorously, forestalling a question by Jeff. "My grandparents settled in New York. My parents, my two sisters, and I were all born there. I was the ne'er-do-well who ran off to southern Texas without even waiting to finish college."

"You managed to overcome that handicap," Katie said with a radiant smile. Steve Marcus had been a pioneer in the frozen-food field. Now he was head of one of the country's most successful processing firms. Her mind hurtled back through the years, and she remembered Harry's preoccupation back in the early thirties with the possibility of freezing garden-fresh vegetables.

"What led you into the frozen-food field?" Jeff asked curiously, and Katie thought, He remembers how Harry was fascinated by the possibility. "Research?"

"A visit to Georgia back in the early thirties," he said with a slow smile. "I gather the business never really got off the ground, but there was a man down there who had been freezing peaches and bananas. I ate one of those frozen bananas—covered with chocolate—and my mind was off to the races." His eyes traveled from Jeff to Katie. He was trying to pin down their relationship, Katie realized, suddenly self-conscious.

"My wife will be thrilled to hear that we met you," Jeff said casually. He had caught that glint of curiosity in Steve Marcus also, Katie understood. "She says you're the housewives' delight—you've cut down their kitchen time."

"Is she here in Washington with you?" Steve asked.

"No, she's minding the store back home," Jeff told him. "Katie and I came out here to do some lobbying."

"You run that farm magazine that's always warning us against pesticides," Steve recalled.

"You disagree with us?" Katie challenged, her eyes telling Marcus she would be quick with ammunition.

"No," Steve surprised her. "I'm with you."

They talked earnestly about the magazine and its efforts, as though they were a private island in the midst of all the celebrating. By the time the evening was over, he insisted they fly with him on his corporate jet to Texas.

"Hell, it's easy enough for me to drop you off in Dallas and then head on down to Galveston. You'll save me from being bored."

Aboard his private jet Katie learned that Steve Marcus was fifty-three, had been divorced eight years.

"The marriage was over long before then," he confided with a wry smile. "I came out to Texas, married when I was twenty-one and June was eighteen. I fought my way up the ladder—but June refused to grow with me. After a few years we had nothing in common except our two daughters. She was uncomfortable in our lifestyle. She divorced me to marry a man who drove tractor trailers. She left the girls with me—she was content to see them every now and then."

"Your daughters live in Galveston?" Jeff asked.

"One's in Oregon, the other in San Francisco. But we're close. They're both married and doing well. The younger should be making me a grandfather not too long from now."

He had a house in Galveston, an apartment in New York, and a home in the Bahamas.

"I'm restless," he admitted. "Business has been almost my whole life. Now I see sixty ahead, and I begin to ask myself—shouldn't there be more to life than being a workaholic?"

Before she and Jeff parted with Steve Marcus at the Dallas airport, Katie knew she'd be seeing more of him. He'd told her he flew his own plane—it was nothing for him to fly up from Galveston to take her out to dinner. She knew he was intrigued by her. And she was mesmerized by his physical resemblance to Harry.

It was more than a physical resemblance, Katie analyzed later. He had Harry's sharp, inventive mind,

Harry's way of becoming so eloquent over a cherished subject. And Harry's charm. Harry was almost sixty now—the figure that had brought Steve Marcus up short—but she guessed that Harry and Steve were both of a breed that changed little through the years.

Katie wasn't surprised when—ten days later—Steve phoned from Galveston to say he'd be in Dallas over the weekend.

"What about dinner Saturday night?" he asked casually. "We can bitch about what's happening in Vietnam."

"Not until after dessert and coffee," Katie stipulated with laughter. She brushed away warning signals, ignored her vow that there would never again be room in her life for a man. Steve Marcus was neither Sherwin nor Terry. He was astonishingly like Harry. "Let's enjoy dinner first."

Katie was eager for Saturday evening to arrive. Dressing for dinner with Steve, she discarded three dresses before she settled on a gray crepe by Yves Saint Laurent. She had never lost her love for exquisite clothes.

She enjoyed the evening with Steve. She knew that he, too, was reluctant to see it end. He said he'd arrange to fly up the following Saturday for dinner if she was free. Katie understood that business had not brought him to Dallas tonight. She had.

In mid-May—when they had seen each other once or twice a week for four months—Steve invited her to fly down with him on his private jet to his house in Nassau. The implication was clear.

"Do you know Nassau?" he asked.

"No." She had not expected this. Not yet. "None of the Caribbean islands." Why was her heart suddenly pounding this way? Steve made her feel as though she was a young girl again.

"You'll love Nassau," he promised. "Especially at this time of year. It's off-season for the jet-setters, too early for the summer tourists. And the weather in May is perfect."

"How long will you be down there?" she hedged. Why was she uneasy that he was pushing their relationship forward? They'd been seeing each other for months. "I'm rather bogged down in work."

"Just for four days. A long weekend."

"Hmm . . ." Lisa could stay with Maura and Jeff—she loved their farm.

"It's the perfect respite for workaholics like us," he pursued. "The house sits right on the beach. The couple who take care of it have this great way of never being underfoot. We'll spend our time walking beside the turquoise Caribbean, lying on chaises on one of the decks of the house. Maybe once," he said with a chuckle, "we'll go into town. You have to see it. And we'll probably have dinner at the Cat and Fiddle Club or Blackbeard's Tavern." His eyes and Katie's carried on another conversation. "It's where I go when I feel I have to escape the world."

"It sounds great." Katie dismissed caution. "When do we leave?"

Katie told herself it was ridiculous to be so elated about a long weekend in Nassau, but she spent a frenzied afternoon shopping in Neiman's. Feeling young and daring, she bought the new short shorts, two of the new nylon maillots—one in black and another in her favorite turquoise. In a gloriously defiant moment she bought a tiger-printed hooded beach cover-up that ended high on her still-perfect thighs.

Feeling a tidal wave of self-consciousness, she bought several long, pastel crepe nighties with square, lacy necklines plus matching chiffon peignoirs. Both she and Steve understood this trip marked the end of a platonic friendship that had never gone beyond a casual goodnight kiss. Being with Steve would be almost like being with Harry again.

At sight, Katie loved Nassau. Scarlet poinciana trees

were in flower everywhere. Lush gardens of exotic plants lent audacious color to pastel houses. Steve's villa—to call it less, Katie mused, would be a gross understatement—looked down not only upon the sea but upon much of the town.

At dusk Katie and Steve were served a gourmet dinner on the candlelighted deck that faced the water. Steve talked about his growing-up years in New York, and they marveled that they had inhabited the same city at the same period, Katie on the Lower East Side, Steve on the Concourse in the Bronx.

"That seems a million years away," he said as the dinner table was cleared. Soon, Katie knew, the couple who worked for him would leave for the night. "Sometimes it seems a different lifetime. We've both come a long way."

"That we have," she conceded with a bittersweet smile. She would give it all up to be able to go back and begin again—with Harry.

Katie and Steve remained on the deck even after they heard the domestic couple's car drive away from the house. Both were caught up in the loveliness of this quiet evening—silent except for their own voices and the sound of the waves lapping on the shore. Both were poignantly aware of their destination tonight.

"Shall we go inside?" Steve said at last, and held out a hand to Katie.

"Let's." Her smile was tremulous.

Steve walked with her to the master bedroom suite, kissed her gently as they paused at the entrance, then with a new passion.

"The occasion demands champagne," he said. "I told Claudia to chill a bottle of Château Lafite. I won't be long."

Earlier Claudia had unpacked for her. Ostensibly Katie was to occupy the master bedroom suite, Steve one of the four guest rooms. She walked into the bedroom and touched a wall switch, bringing subtle illumination into the room. A fire had been laid and lighted in the small, marble-faced fireplace. The nineteenth-century canopied bed—with a pineapple carved into each post—had been turned down. The pineapple was a symbol of welcome, Katie recalled. The other furniture was an eclectic collection of Early American and English miniatures.

Now she went to the closet to take down one of the nightie and peignoir sets that Claudia had hung on satin-quilted hangers. Enveloped in an aura of beautiful unreality, she quickly changed into the turquoise nightwear. She didn't feel fifty-seven years old. She felt young and desirable and passionate.

"Katie, you're beautiful." She whirled around at the sound of Steve's voice. In a forest-green silk dressing gown and slippers he walked toward her. "Let's drink to you." He held out a glass of champagne.

"Let's drink to *us*," she said with a dazzling smile. *It was almost as though she were talking to Harry.*

They sipped at the champagne. Then Steve took the glass from her hand and placed it on a table along with his own. Her throat was tight with expectancy. Oh, she wanted him to make love to her!

"I told myself I didn't need a woman in my life," he whispered, pulling away the chiffon peignoir. "But that was before I met you. . . ."

He left her for a moment to switch off the lamp. Now only rosy firelight intruded into the room. He came back to her and drew her close again. His mouth reached for hers. She felt herself grow limp in his arms.

She murmured a soft reproach when he drew his mouth away. But then he was leading her to the bed, an arm about her waist. A hand reaching to caress her breast. In moments the exquisite nightie lay on the floor beside the bed. Steve was evoking every erotic emotion of which her passionate body was capable.

"Oh, Katie, Katie . . ."

They moved together with one will, merging into an ecstatic climax, clung together.

It was almost like being with Harry.

On their last morning at the Nassau house Steve asked Katie to marry him.

"Not right away," he said quietly. "I know you need time to think about it. But when you're ready. I want to spend the rest of my life with you."

An hour later Steve received a phone call from his daughter in Oregon. Just past midnight she had given birth to his first grandchild, a boy.

"I can't believe it!" His face was suffused with pleasure as he told Katie the news. "Katie, I'm a grandfather!"

"Congratulations!" She leaned forward to kiss him.

"Andrea insists she's fine, and the baby's great." She saw the relief in his eyes. He'd been worried, she thought tenderly, and remembered her own feelings those last weeks before Joanne had given birth. "I'll fly right out there after I've taken you to Dallas."

"There'll be no talking to you for the next few days," Katie teased.

"This doesn't change anything about us," he reminded with a roguish grin. "Sex doesn't stop because you become a grandparent."

"The young never guess," she laughed. "Let's don't disillusion them."

Steve held her hand on the flight back to Texas and talked about the years when he'd struggled to be both father and mother to his daughters.

"They were good kids, but I never felt I was doing enough for them. Because they were growing up with one parent."

"I know," she sympathized. "But they've grown up just great." Not like Leo and Joanne, she remembered with fresh pain. But Lisa, bless her, was such a happy child. Despite the fact that her grandmother had to stand in for both mother and father.

When they landed at the Dallas airport, Steve seemed reluctant to leave her.

"Katie, come along with me to Oregon," he urged, his eyes amorous. "I won't say anything to the kids about us," he promised. "Not until you're ready."

"Lisa expects me home," she said apologetically. "She's staying with Maura and Jeff—but I know she misses me."

"I'll miss you," he murmured. "I'll call you from Oregon."

Three hours later—listening to the radio while she changed from traveling slacks and sweater to a dress because she was taking Lisa out for dinner to celebrate her return—Katie froze in shock. The classical-music program had been interrupted for a news flash. A private jet had crashed over the Rockies.

"The one passenger and the crew were killed instantly. Steve Marcus, CEO of—"

Katie heard nothing else. She stood motionless, trying to assimilate the news flash. Three hours ago they'd said good-bye at the airport. *Now Steve was dead.*

It was like losing Harry for a second time.

Chapter Forty-five

AGAIN, KATIE took refuge from grief in work. She was grateful for Lisa's sunny presence in her life, Lisa's need for her.

Now the years began to speed past as though weeks. Katie was disturbed by the Cold War, by the violence erupting in the civil-rights movement. By the unrest and growing rebellion on the campuses, the escalating American involvement in Vietnam. The assassination of Martin Luther King, Jr., in April of 1968 and the assassination of Robert Kennedy two months later made her fear for the future. Lisa was growing up in a world that was going berserk.

She watched for signs of aging—longing to stay young for Lisa. To be able to play the role of "Lisa's mother" rather than the grandmother she was. Though Maura vowed the years barely touched her, she saw the gray that crept into her still lushly thick honey-colored hair—but regular visits to the beauty salon took care of that. Maura said the tiny lines at her eyes were "laugh lines." *"You still look twenty years younger than you are."*

She bought a stationary bike for the house and used it regularly. She walked three miles a day, rain or shine. She was pleased that she never gained a pound. In this world where youth was such a premium, Katie thought whimsically, she was blessed.

As the years continued to rush past, she often asked herself where Harry was, how life was treating him. She had been shaken when she'd discovered he was no longer with Simon & Sinclair—and he seemed to vanish from the face of the earth. Yet knowing Harry, she suspected—she prayed—that he had landed on his feet yet again.

Lisa was the joy of her life. She reveled in Lisa's zest for living, which ever reminded her of the young Harry—and of Joanne in the years before Leo's death. There were moments—at Lisa's high school graduation, her college graduation, and just a few weeks ago when Lisa was awarded her degree in journalism from Columbia—that Katie felt as though Harry was hovering beside her in pride.

She'd been pleased when Lisa chose to go to a Texas school for her bachelor's degree. Her choosing Columbia for a degree in journalism was a poignant reminder of Harry's reverence for Columbia as a young man. He had looked forward to going to City College—before their trek to Dallas—but to attend Columbia would have been the height of happiness for him. Lisa was going to Columbia for her grandfather, Katie told herself in sentimental moments.

At times Katie was impatient with the progress of American Farms Unlimited and their monthly publication. She tried to be realistic. They were slowly reclaiming land and gaining a few converts among younger Texas farmers. There were groups all over the world now who were fighting for soil conservation. But greater efforts were necessary.

Sitting in her office on this torpid August morning, Katie listened while Jeff complained about the difficulty of reaching through to farmers about the urgency of protecting the soil.

"Damn it, Katie, why do the farmers try to squeeze as much as they can out of their land? After the dust-bowl years they worked at rotating crops, at contour-plowing and terracing. They were making a serious effort to fight soil erosion. But now they've swung back to the old ways. . . ."

"That and more and more of pesticides and chemical fertilizers," Katie added. "We didn't have those to worry about before World War Two."

"They're just making the chemical companies rich. Hell, they can't afford to pay those prices! We're seeing foreclosures again—and a lot of that because of mismanagement of their finances."

"And all those chemicals end up in our streams and lakes and rivers." Katie sighed. "I read a report that said agriculture is the single worst polluter in two thirds of our river basins."

Jeff nodded.

"Those chemicals are choking our streams, killing our fish, contaminating our water." His face softened. "George is working on an article for the next issue that's downright eloquent. And what do you hear from Lisa? When's she coming home?"

"I'm not sure. She'll get back from Europe early next

month." The trip was her birthday present. "She has something going with the editor of some small new weekly newspaper working out of New York. She's all excited about a possible assignment. If it comes through, she probably won't be home for another month. But she calls regularly, bless her."

"Your daughter the journalist," Jeff teased affectionately.

"My granddaughter," Katie corrected. Legally Lisa was her daughter—and that was how everybody, including Lisa—considered the relationship.

"She's a great kid," Jeff approved. "Remember how excited she was in her senior year at high school when we ran her article in the magazine? It was good," he said with satisfaction. "If it hadn't been, I wouldn't have run it."

"I've always tried not to spoil her," Katie said seriously. "But she has the income from her trust fund, so finding a steady job right away isn't urgent." Lisa would receive lump sums from the trust at thirty and again at thirty-five and forty. The remaining principal would be handed down to Lisa's heirs at her death. "She can afford to take low-paying assignments that excite her."

"But she means to join us here in time," Jeff pointed out. "That's what she always says."

"I want that so much." Katie's face was luminescent.

"When I retire, George and Lisa will take over the magazine," Jeff predicted. "I'm seventy-six, Katie."

"You're not retiring," Katie insisted vigorously. Maura was in semiretirement. She came into the office two or three days a week. "You'll die in the saddle at ninety-seven or ninety-eight."

"I feel young," he admitted with a grin. "Despite the grizzled farm face. But you, Katie," he twitted. "Nobody would ever believe we celebrated your seventieth birthday two months ago. You look a beautiful fifty."

"We're as young as we think," Katie said softly. "And you and I both think young. Of course, it helps," she laughed, "that L'Oréal keeps my hair the same color it was at twenty."

Her lush near-black hair tumbling about her shoulders, Lisa sat at a table with Paul Hecht amid the tantalizing aromas of fresh baking in the Hungarian Pastry shop on Amsterdam near 111th Street in Manhattan. She alternated between bites of hamantaschen and sips of coffee from a large, utilitarian mug. She'd arrived in New York from London two days ago, and after six weeks out of the country home seemed marvelous.

"Paul, do you think I'm crazy to take this assignment?" she asked. Her dark, richly lashed eyes pleaded for reassurance. It was an unimportant weekly—but she had enormous respect for the editor.

"Not when it excites you this way," he told her. "So the money is like nothing. It's something you want to do." His smile was encouraging.

"Yes!" Lisa's face was incandescent. The editor/publisher—Chuck Roberts—had heard grim stories about the migrant Caribbean workers who were brought into South Florida to harvest the sugarcane. Union organizers could get nowhere, despite conditions that were like slavery, he claimed. Chuck wanted to run an exposé—and he was willing to let her try to get it.

"If the situation gets rough, you cut out." All at once Paul was somber. "We get turned on by the possibilities of a great story, but don't take chances if you think there could be trouble."

"I'm a graduate student driving through Florida," Lisa said. "That's the way I'll play it. I'm working on a doctoral dissertation about the history of sugarcane. You know, the wide-eyed earnest student looking for local color. No sweat, Paul."

"I don't want you to get hurt."

"I won't get hurt. Now you're beginning to sound like my mother—and I didn't tell her I'm working on an

497

exposé," she laughed. "Just a story about sugarcane plantations."

"My father flipped when I dropped out of Columbia Law in my second year and transferred to journalism. All he thinks about is making money. So he's a successful lawyer—what does he have out of it? He thinks it's great because he owns a nine-room co-op on the West End and a house in East Hampton. But he's working fourteen hours a day, comes home to scream at my mother because of one petty annoyance or another at the apartment. The co-op's board of directors has its hand in the till, the handymen stink, the super is a lush. He can't understand it's the quality of life that matters to me."

"Mom puts in a lot of hours—but she loves it," Lisa said. "That makes it worthwhile."

"I know all the bickering between Dad and Mom doesn't mean anything," Paul acknowledged. "But I wish it wasn't there." Paul's social-worker mother had lost enthusiasm for the field after years of fighting in the urban ghetto and retired a year ago. She was finding it difficult to adjust to being just a housewife, Lisa gathered.

"Mom brought me up in a kind of sixties liberalism atmosphere. She's never lost that, thank God. I need to be able to be excited about causes."

"I'd thought all you were interested in was preserving the land," Paul challenged affectionately.

"It's my major cause. But I have other interests," she joshed. He must realize that by now. Wasn't she going up to East Hampton with him for the weekend? Nobody at the house except the two of them. His father was away on business. His mother had to stay in Manhattan for a wedding. "Haven't you noticed?"

"We need to talk," he said quietly. "About us."

"Up in East Hampton," she stalled.

She *thought* she was in love with Paul—but she was twenty-two and in no rush to marry. And according to statistics she was one of those rare women who reached the age of twenty-two without having had sex. It was just that nobody turned her on that way—until Paul. There'd be a minor change in those statistics this weekend. She was ready to take that step now.

They left the pastry shop and headed for their respective apartments to pack. Paul wanted to be on the road by 4:30 P.M. *"We'll see the sunset on the beach."* They'd have tonight and tomorrow night in East Hampton. On Sunday morning Paul would drive her to the airport for her flight to Palm Beach.

In Palm Beach she'd rent a car and drive to West Grove. This was the mill town the editor had chosen as her operating post. He'd told her to steer clear of the more publicized sugar plantations. The one he'd chosen as probably being more accessible was the plantation owned by the West Grove Sugar Company.

They were on the Long Island Expressway in the Cadillac Coupe DeVille that Paul had borrowed from his father for the weekend and headed for East Hampton right on schedule. Though the summer season had officially ended with Labor Day weekend, traffic was still heavy on this humid Friday afternoon. Lisa was content to sit back and listen to Paul talk with heated eloquence about his special cause—the rural poor. A Manhattanite born and bred, he'd spent the past two summers driving around in rural areas of the country.

"I know how you feel about the farmers and saving the land," he conceded, "but you can't not see all the people living in dire poverty in villages and small towns—some of them in shacks out in the country. Even in Texas," he kidded. "Some of them lost their farms way back during the Depression. Some in the postwar years because they couldn't handle the new technology. And nobody cares, Lisa!"

She had been listening to Paul's commitment to the rural poor—what he called "the forgotten poor"—for almost six months now, Lisa figured. They'd met at a concert at the Cathedral of St. John the Divine and gone from there for hamburgers and coffee at the West End bar. Right away she knew that she and Paul were on the same wavelength. Paul always laughed and said they were hangovers from the sixties.

Now—along with bursts of irritation about the jammed LIE—Paul switched to talking about his family. His older brother was finishing up his residency at Mount Sinai Hospital and marrying a med student in the fall.

"All they talk about is medicine. And how rich they'll be in ten years," Paul added grimly. "My sister and her husband are making a mint in real estate. I'm the pariah because I don't want to worry about how rich I'll be someday."

How was she going to handle *her* future? Lisa asked herself. She was almost sure she wanted Paul to be part of it. But how would he feel about living in Dallas? She couldn't imagine living anywhere else. That was home. She didn't have a large family like Paul—with aunts and uncles and cousins from both sides. But she had Aunt Maura and Uncle Jeff—and George and Willa and George's wife and their sweet kids. It wasn't a large family, she conceded wistfully—but they were all close. Mom had created a family for the two of them.

At intervals she wished she could know her grandfather. Mom would say little about him—just that he was a fine man, but circumstances demanded they divorce. She said she'd lost track of him years ago. What could have made them divorce, when she suspected they were still in love?

"Hey, you're awful quiet," Paul scolded. "What are you thinking about?"

Now they discussed her assignment down in Florida. Paul said he was going to loaf for a while before thinking about sending out résumés, looking for a job.

"If I'm broke, I'll go to work at the copy center." His customary refuge when he ran out of funds. "Heuston Copy's like a mecca for broke Columbia students and recent grads. John Heuston always finds a job for one of the clan."

They decided to wait until they arrived in East Hampton to have dinner.

"Did I ever tell you that the *Saturday Evening Post* ran a contest a lot of years ago to choose the most beautiful village or town in the country—and East Hampton won?" Paul boasted.

"I'll give you my decision when we get there," Lisa quipped.

"We've just passed Bridgehampton," he told her. The streets were already filling up with weekenders. "East Hampton coming up."

Lisa was enthralled by East Hampton's Main Street, where tall elms rose on both sides for the length of the street. The cobblestoned sidewalks were lined with flower boxes in extravagant bloom.

"Just look around," Paul urged. "No telephone wires, no electric wires. They're all underground. And no neon signs," he added triumphantly.

Would Paul want to live out here? It was beautiful—but it wasn't Dallas. She felt a surge of nostalgia for home. Why did families always seem to scatter these days? She wouldn't mind chasing around the country on journalism assignments—but she wanted roots in Dallas.

She'd always thought she'd fall in love with someone from Dallas, and he'd come into the business with Mom. Someday, Uncle Jeff kept predicting, she'd take over their magazine. But that was a little girl's fairy tale. Paul's big thing was rural poverty. He didn't say that, but she suspected he saw himself moving into politics and making changes.

"Hungry?" Paul intruded on her introspection.

"Yeah."

"We'll go to Sam's for dinner. We've been going there for everything from pizza to scampi since I was old enough to walk," Paul said humorously. "Everything's homemade. You'll like it."

After dinner they headed for the Hecht house. A long white frame contemporary with a window wall facing the Atlantic.

"We're in time for the sunset!" Lisa had the love for the ocean that infects so many raised far from the Atlantic or the Pacific. "Oh, Paul, it's going to be gorgeous. Look at that sky!"

They watched the sunset, then walked along the beach until dusk closed in about them. In the house Paul brought in wood to start a fire in the living-room fireplace while Lisa went out to the kitchen to make coffee. They sat on the floor before the blazing fire and sipped from tall mugs of strong black coffee. When Paul reached for her, Lisa knew tonight there would be no stopping.

The only sounds in the living room were the crackling of the wood and the rising symphony of their passion.

"Oh, Lisa, love!" he said as they clung together, satiated. "I wish we could stay here forever!"

The following day Lisa and Paul swam in the morning—early, before others emerged from their houses. Conscious that tomorrow morning they would be en route to New York and Lisa's flight to Palm Beach, Paul was determined to show Lisa as much as possible of the area. He *did* want to live out here, Lisa thought in a surge of alarm.

After last night she knew she'd have to live wherever Paul wished. How could she bear not to be with him? They both agreed that their lives would be spent together—but neither was in a rush to marry. Right now it was enough to be together.

"We'll have lunch in Amagansett," Paul decreed, "and dinner in Montauk. This is where I come alive. I figure eventually Mom and Dad will retire out here. If they ever decide to give up the rat race."

Today she'd forsake the jeans and T-shirt that were

practically her uniform. She'd wear the bubbly little dress by Marc Bohan, cut off just above the knees, that Mom had bought her in New York. It was making a statement, she thought sentimentally. She and Paul were entering into a solid relationship.

In Amagansett they parked the car and explored the village, lunched, and drove on to Montauk. Paul showed her the lighthouse, then drove her back into town to roam about the business section. Lisa paused before a charming white clapboard store with a small antique one-seater carriage laden with appealing stuffed animals gracing the wide, sunlit window.

"Claudia's Carriage House," she read with pleasure. Obviously a new—intriguing—addition to the town. "Paul, let me go in and buy a little memento for Mom."

"I'll buy her a present, too," he said ebulliently.

"Why?" she laughed.

"Because without her I wouldn't have you." He reached for her hand. "When do I meet her?"

"Soon," she promised. "Real soon."

Chapter Forty-six

SAMANTHA NEWHOUSE—dressing in her bedroom in the overly air-conditioned house near West Grove for a luncheon with her father—paused to increase the volume of the radio. She hoped to block out the sound of her parents screaming at each other on the lower floor. She focused on piling her mane of blond hair—reminiscent of Farrah Fawcett's—into a seductively simple cluster atop her head. One more comb, she decided—that would do it.

Sam inspected her reflection with approval. Of course,

Dad hated her bleaching her hair this way—but she liked the look for a change. The outfit was sexy. Black moiré corselet bodice and white cotton Bermuda shorts—with a black lace, multicolored-fringed mantilla to protect her against the air-conditioning that was omnipresent in South Florida.

Dad might lift his eyebrows at the shorts for lunch, but the restaurant wouldn't mind. Not when it was what Saint Laurent called his "Spanish" day ensemble. She'd bought it at Saint Laurent's Rive Gauche boutique in Saks on a weekend down from Vassar. Dad never guessed she'd chosen Vassar over Radcliffe because it was close enough to New York to come down for weekends. All that partying had been great—for a while.

Dad was so thrilled that his daughter had graduated from Vassar *magna cum laude*. Eileen couldn't have cared less. What had impressed Eileen was that she had been invited for a long weekend after graduation at her roommate's beach house in stuffy Osterville on the Cape. These people might be jet-setters the rest of the year, but at Osterville they were dull.

But after the week at Osterville she and Kitty had taken off for Monte Carlo and then Cap-Martin. It should have been a great summer—but most of the time she'd been bored out of her skull.

Eileen wasn't going to lunch with her and Dad. She said she wouldn't be caught dead in Palm Beach off-season. *Damn, why didn't they shut up down there?* Why had Dad put up with Eileen's craziness all these years?

Her mother had been "Eileen" to her since she was fourteen. It was a sign of rebellion, but her mother hadn't seen it that way. She'd been delighted. She was forever hoping people would take them for sisters.

"Harry, you're going senile" Eileen shrieked. "The whole sugar industry is in chaos—and that conglomerate is offering far more than anybody else would consider paying for the company!"

"The company is not for sale," Harry said with ominous calm. "Knock it off."

"Listen to me, Harry." Eileen was clearly fighting for calm. Determined to reason with him. "Prices are in one hell of a slump. We've got to compete with the damn fructose market. We—"

"I've heard this crap from you for months. Sure, prices have dropped way down. But they were unrealistically high. Between January and November of '74 the price jumped from sixteen cents a pound to sixty-five cents. That's fifteen times what it was ten years ago."

"We're losing like crazy," Eileen warned, "and it'll get worse. We all know the sugar consumption is down. The Sugar Act is dead—we have no more government protection!"

"This is not the time to sell." Harry's voice was harsh with impatience. "That's my decision to make."

Dad was so bloody proud of her when he came up for graduation, Sam remembered tenderly. He'd never got over the fact that *he* hadn't gone to college. It hadn't stopped him from becoming one of the most successful men in the country.

Every time he got kicked in the face, he came back, she thought with satisfaction. She knew about his rise and fall on the stock market, about his manipulations with international wheat, and how he'd moved into sugar at just the crucial moment.

What was she going to do with *her* life? The B.A. with a major in political science had been just to please Dad. He'd always been so good to her, spoiled her so—she'd wanted to do something to make him proud of her. But as close as she and Dad were, she felt sometimes as though she didn't really know him at all. Sometimes she wondered about that other life he'd led before she was born. When he'd had another wife and two children who'd died tragically. Though he said little about his first family, she sensed they were always there deep in his heart and mind. But she *knew* she was loved. When Eileen fought with him, she'd yell, "Damn you—all you care about is Sam!"

Enough of this shit, she scolded herself. Go on downstairs, take Dad off to lunch. On Monday cutting started at the plantation. The mill would be running twenty-four hours a day. Dad would be caught up again in the rat race. And September in Florida was not the time for soul-searching.

Sam took a final glance at herself in the mirror. Ten to one Eileen would make some crack about the outfit. So she wasn't clothes-model flat-chested. No male ever complained about her cleavage. Sometimes she thought Eileen was anorexic, the way she carried on about staying thin. *"I'm five-seven, just like Gloria Vanderbilt and Cyd Charisse. Gloria weighs one-hundred-seventeen. Cyd weighs one-hundred-sixteen. I never let myself go over one-hundred-fifteen."* Couldn't Eileen understand that at her age a few extra pounds were *friends*?

Sam headed downstairs. Her father was reading *The Wall Street Journal*. Her mother had disappeared. They'd be seeing little of Eileen with the harvest about to start. She'd come to the house for the weekend, but she'd just sleep.

Dad had cut back on his fifteen-hour days during the season. Still, it would be a rare day when he wasn't at the mill at least ten hours—six days a week. He allowed himself Sunday off, he said, in deference to his age. But he didn't look or act like a man of seventy-two.

"Sam, let's go eat," her father said briskly as she strolled into the living room. His face lighted up at the sight of her. "Missed you all those weeks you were chasing around in Europe." Those years she'd been at Vassar he'd kept making business trips to New York—half of them invented so they could spend a weekend together in the city. Always in the same suite at the Waldorf Towers.

"I gather Eileen isn't going with us," said Sam, her smile ironic. Eileen only went with them when she felt it was to her advantage to be seen with family.

He shrugged. "She's peeved at me." Didn't it bother him the way Eileen chased around with other men? Sam wondered. Of course, nobody knew for sure—Eileen was cagey about that. But everybody whispered. Even as a little kid, Sam had known.

"So what else is new?" Sam drawled.

They settled themselves in the Mercedes that was waiting in the driveway. Her father never drove anything except a Mercedes, though at times he made dark threats not to buy any more foreign cars.

"You aren't thinking of selling, are you, Dad?" she asked curiously as they headed toward Palm Beach. He was so proud of the mill and the housing he'd built for his mill workers—and the loyalty of his employees. The West Grove Mill was one of the first to be unionized—with Dad's cooperation. The mill was his life. Eileen ruled the plantation. Neither she nor Dad ever set foot on the plantation except occasionally off-season. "I can't see you spending your days on the golf course," she laughed.

"This is the wrong time to sell," he told her. "When the time is ripe, I just might. Not to sit back and play golf," he said with a slow smile. "That's not my style. I'd like to head back Texas way. Buy a big spread, do some serious farming. My roots are back there, Sam. . . ."

"Come on, your roots are in the Lower East Side," she kidded. "How many times have I heard about how you went to night school back there and wanted to be a lawyer?"

"But Texas was home." His voice was reverent. "Everything else has always been exile."

"I'd like to see Texas sometime. It's the one place I've missed." Eileen would hate it, she guessed. Unless she latched onto some young and willing cowboys. Sam's face tightened as she remembered the article in *Vogue* Eileen had been reading when she came home for the spring break. An article by Erica Jong: "Take a Young Lover."

Tense with anticipation of her first professional assignment, Lisa checked into a comfortable but unostentatious Palm Beach hotel. If anyone asked questions—and that was unlikely, she assured herself—she was a graduate student researching her dissertation. At Paul's urging, she had chosen a hotel in Palm Beach rather than trying for accommodations in West Grove. *"You'd probably have to settle for a fleabag. Anyhow, this will be more the graduate-student scene."*

She unpacked, went downstairs for dinner, then returned to her room to go over her notes. Chuck had chosen West Grove Plantation because it was a thirty-five-minute drive from Palm Beach and because its owners had managed to maintain a low profile through the years. They wouldn't be suspicious the way other companies who'd been involved in battles with the United Farm Workers might be.

There had been trouble organizing some of the Florida sugar mills, Chuck indicated. The West Grove Mill had been unionized without any incidents. But he suspected this was just a front for their slavery-style plantation operations.

"The word has come through that all the work on all the Florida plantations is done by migrants from the West Indies. It's the kind of work that nobody in this country will accept. Hard and low-paying—and the most dangerous in this country. Back in 1942 the U.S. Sugar Corporation was indicted by a federal grand jury on grounds they were conspiring to commit slavery. After that the growers started bringing in workers from the Caribbean. According to my contact, they're being exploited brutally—and nobody outside of the industry is aware of this."

Lisa awoke early the next morning, had breakfast, and drove to West Grove. It was a small town. Main Street appeared to stretch for about three blocks. There was a bank, a café, a furniture store, a clothing store, and a church to her left. On the right—the most substantial and largest building in town—was the West Grove Mill. It was a red-brick building that appeared well-maintained.

Okay, Lisa prodded herself, go into the mill and make contact. Explain her mission. She opened the door of the air-conditioned car and stepped out into the torpid morning heat. It would be a scorcher by noon, she guessed.

Did she look the part? she asked herself, all at once aware of trepidation. The Calvin Klein natural handkerchief linen blouse and the silk-knit dirndl skirt in pale tobacco made a smart but casual outfit. Her Coach shoulder bag identified her as well-heeled enough to have come from an important university. The loose-leaf notebook said she was here to do research.

Frowning involuntarily at the noise that emerged from the mill, she crossed the street to the neat white entrance. The atmosphere in the reception room seemed pleasant enough. The voices that drifted out from the mill area were jocular. The mill was unionized, she remembered—no labor problems in the *mill*.

The receptionist seemed vague about whom she was to see about permission to visit the West Grove plantation—somewhere in this area.

"I have all my information about sugarcane plantations in Hawaii and Louisiana and Texas," Lisa rattled off with a show of confidence. "I just need the Florida plantations to start the actual writing on my dissertation."

"I guess maybe Mr. Newhouse's private secretary could help you," she said after a moment. "Wait here. I'll go talk to her."

Lisa sat on one of the wicker chairs in the reception room. Chuck said they'd probably refuse to let her see the plantation officially, but that it was worth a try.

Lisa glanced up with a smile when the receptionist returned, accompanied by an older woman.

"We don't usually allow visitors during harvest time," the woman told her, "but Mr. Newhouse said you could go over to the plantation office and talk to his wife. She handles the plantation. The office is in the house there, about a hundred yards before Field Number One." The woman reached for a piece of notepaper and a pencil from the reception desk. "I'll draw you a diagram."

Delighted at this unexpected cooperation, Lisa expressed her gratitude and left the mill. She sat at the wheel of the car and studied the directions to the plantation. The fields were close by—a few minutes' drive.

She'd explain she was looking for local color. Little details about the appearance of the fields, the look of the sugarcane ready for harvest. The specific operations of cutting the cane and getting it to the mill. *Make it sound plausible.*

They'd been running this exploitation of migrant workers in South Florida so long—since the early forties, Chuck said—that they probably didn't even think of it as that. Chuck said that sugarcane first became a commercial deal in Florida back in 1931. Originally the companies brought blacks hungry for work in from other towns. But word of the slaverylike hardships circulated, and the number of workers willing to come down to cut sugarcane dwindled to nothing. That's when they started bringing in help from the Caribbean.

That must be the house, Lisa decided, and drew up before a freshly painted cottage. She paused to stare at men working in the field beyond, observed cut-up stalks of cane being piled into field wagons. It appeared a harmless situation. Tall, dark-skinned men cutting sugarcane. *Had Chuck made a terrible mistake?*

Fighting self-consciousness Lisa left the car and walked to the cottage. A small sign read WEST GROVE PLANTATION. *Okay, West Grove Plantation, let's see if Chuck is off his rocker.* She hesitated on the porch, gazed through the screen door into the small foyer, then knocked lightly.

"Come in," an imperious male voice ordered.

She opened the door and walked inside. The door to the right was closed. The one to the left was open. A youngish man sat behind the desk. If he had not appeared so arrogant, Lisa thought, he would have been handsome. He leaned forward, his eyes wary.

"What are you doing here?"

"Mr. Newhouse's secretary sent me," said Lisa, trying to sound casual. "I told her that I was doing research for my doctoral dissertation. On the raising of sugarcane."

"Mr. Newhouse's secretary should not have sent you here. We're in the harvest season—we have no time for such nonsense."

"I won't ask a lot of questions," she said ingratiatingly. "I'd just like to look around and observe. I—"

"What the hell is going on here, Clive?" A tall, thin blonde in a ridiculously short white eyelet dress with a camisole top strode into the room. Fifty-five trying to look like twenty-five, Lisa thought in distaste.

"She wants to visit the fields," he told the blonde. Lisa intercepted a guarded exchange between them. "She's writing a doctoral dissertation," he said derisively.

"No one's allowed in the fields." The woman tried to appear amused. Lisa sensed she was furious. "Our workers dislike being questioned. And my assistant and I have no time for that. Please leave. This is private property."

Driving away from the cottage, Lisa dissected the situation. There was something going on in those fields that the two in the cottage didn't want her to see. *Chuck was right.* But where did she go from here?

Eager to get a feel for the town, she stopped off at the café for coffee and a muffin. It was deserted except for a pair of elderly men at a rear table, arguing over how Governor Dukakis of Massachusetts had declared the Sacco-Vanzetti trial unfair and had proclaimed the fiftieth anniversary of their execution as Sacco and Vanzetti Memorial Day.

Lisa sat at the counter and exchanged a few words about the weather with the waitress after the woman had taken her order.

"I'll bet you get tired of hearing the noise from the mill all day," Lisa said sympathetically when the waitress returned with her coffee and muffin.

"All day and all night in season, seven days a week." The waitress sighed. "I don't know why I stay in this town. I don't know why anybody does."

"I suppose the mill keeps everybody working. And the plantation."

"The mill's good enough—if you have to live in this town," the waitress conceded. "Decent wages, good working conditions. The folks here don't work in the fields. That's for animals," she said contemptuously.

"Just cutting sugarcane?"

"Honey, you wouldn't believe the way those cutters have to work." She grimaced. "The stories that come out of those camps make you sick." She chuckled. "Enough to make you go off sugar."

"Like what?" Lisa asked ingenuously.

"They're out there in the fields when the stars are still out—and never quit until sundown. Sometimes they'll work by the light of the car headlights. All the time doing backbreaking work. And that goes on for four to five months of harvest-time."

"Nobody ever said farming was easy," Lisa said with a whimsical smile.

"This ain't like farming." The woman was emphatic. "They can't get no Americans—white or black—to work out in that hot sun, take the chances cutters take every day. Just the Jamaicans they bring up from the Islands. Somebody's always getting cut bad from them swinging machetes or getting heatstroke or a crippled back or puncturing an eardrum or an eye because he missed seeing a stalk of cane in the way."

"Doesn't sound like much fun," Lisa agreed. Her heart was pounding. *She had to get a look at the fields. She had to see for herself.*

"You just passing through?" All at once the waitress seemed wary.

"I'm a graduate student up at Columbia in New York," Lisa said casually. "I'm doing my dissertation on sugar plantations. I've been through the ones in Texas and Louisiana and—"

"Don't mess around with the ones in Florida. If you're smart, you'll clear out of town fast. What goes on here you don't want to know about." She whipped out her book. "Will you be wanting anything else?" Her voice was terse now, her eyes opaque. Lisa understood—she figured she'd talked too much.

"That's all, thanks. And maybe you're right. It's so bloody hot down here I think I'll stick to library research for Florida. I can do that back home."

Lisa comprehended that whatever she did must be undercover. She drove back to Palm Beach. Chafing at idleness, she swam in the hotel pool, had lunch. Instinct told her the West Grove plantation was the basis for a desperately needed exposé of the sugar industry. Maybe the story wouldn't make a lot of difference—considering the newspaper's light circulation—but it would be a start.

Rejecting the thought of an afternoon of shopping in the glitzy boutiques on Worth Avenue, Lisa drove to the local library to scout back issues of the *Palm Beach Times*. At the library she found brief articles about efforts to organize the sugarcane-plantation workers. As Chuck had told her, these efforts had failed.

She discovered a number of detailed articles dealing with the unionizing at the mills, but these held no interest for her. How was she to get to the migrant workers—talk to them—without being caught? There had to be a way. She would find it.

Before dawn the following morning Lisa drove away from her hotel. The temperature had dropped. Fog hung low on every side. She drove slowly, squinting at the strip of road ahead. Visibility was close to zero. That was good, she congratulated herself.

Driving into West Grove, she heard the whir of the mill machinery. Main Street was otherwise deserted. Now she reached into the pocket of her slacks for the diagram Newhouse's secretary had given her. She'd park a quarter-mile from the fields, walk the rest of the way. In this fog—wearing black slacks, black sweatshirt, and black sneakers—nobody would notice her.

She parked, began to walk in the eerie, fog-shrouded stillness. She skirted the cottage that was also the plantation office. The windows were dark. She sighed with relief, moved on toward the fields. The first hints of dawn crept into the sky now, but the fog remained a protective shield.

Her heart pounding, she approached the first field. Quickly she realized there was no chance she could move in close enough to talk to any of the cutters. Through the fog she saw the tall, stooped figures of the Jamaicans slashing at the stalks of cane with their machetes. She saw other men—and from their voices she understood they were the cut foremen, the leadmen, the ticket writers—all part of the harvest crew, as Chuck had described them.

"Hey, you, back there!" a harsh voice yelled. For an instant Lisa froze, fearful she'd been discovered—but she realized the leadman was calling to a cutter. "You ain't gettin' off with that kinda slop. Come back and clean up!"

Conscious that the fog was beginning to lift, Lisa retreated from the field. Fighting frustration. She paused to inspect a long, low, corrugated-metal-roofed cement structure close by the field. That must be the camp where the cutters lived. Maybe some of them were not out in the fields today. Check it out.

She walked swiftly toward the dilapidated building. Trash was scattered about the outside. A dog searched for scraps. At the door she hesitated, then pushed it wide and walked inside. The large room she entered was lined on both sides by double-decker bunk beds. The air was fetid and hot.

Four men lay snoring in bunks to her left, their clothes dark with grime, the sheets of the bunks soiled and wrinkled. To her left another man sat at the edge of his bunk and gingerly attended to a blood-soaked bandage on his arm.

"Excuse me," Lisa called out uncertainly, and he turned to her in shock.

"Missy, not good you be here," he said in the soft, charming accent of the islands. "Best you go quick."

"Please," she asked ingratiatingly, "may I ask you a few questions about your work?" The others, she guessed, were out cold. They couldn't be awakened by anything less than a bomb.

"The boss lady find out, me be fired." But he seemed intrigued by her presence.

Taking advantage of this, Lisa moved forward and began to question him. Softly and with obvious sympathy. All the while—as he stammered out answers—his eyes clung to the door. Lisa didn't dare make notes, but she knew his words were etched on her brain.

They worked at piece rates—and were sure they were cheated. The pay per row of cane was too low. If they were sick or hurt, they were not paid. Accidents happened daily—it was a dangerous job.

"Nobody care us cut up. Nobody care us die."

The sticky gum from the stalks blackened their clothes, clung to their scalps. Over the course of the season their hands became blistered, callused, causing arms to cramp all the way to the shoulders—useless for weeks after the harvest.

"Us get one pair gloves when us come. No more. Boss lady say cost too much money."

"The gloves don't last?" Lisa probed.

"Maybe week. That's all. Now go," he ordered with sudden intensity. "Me lose day's work because me cut arm. Them find you here, me lose job. Go."

Back in her hotel room in Palm Beach, Lisa set up her portable typewriter, wrote about the tortured lives of the sugarcane cutters. Their incredibly long working day, the flood of accidents that beset them, their brutal living conditions, their loneliness for home and family.

But there was too much here for one article, she thought with messianic fervor. It should be a three-part exposé. She needed more information. Photographs. Fly back to New York and confront Chuck, she told herself.

Before checking out of the hotel, she phoned Chuck. He agreed to wait at the office until she arrived.

"You're okay?" he asked anxiously.

"I'm okay, but there's more to be done," she told him. "We'll talk when I get there."

On the third try she reached Paul.

"I'll be at the airport to meet you," he promised.

By shortly past 7:00 P.M. Lisa and Paul sat with Chuck in his tiny, overcrowded office—its dimensions limited by his working capital—and discussed what she had learned about the conditions of the migrant workers in the sugarcane fields.

"I want to go back, Chuck. I can see this as a three-parter that'll hit people right between the eyes," Lisa said earnestly.

"It could get nasty," Chuck warned. "Especially once the first part hit the stands." He grinned. "I know—our circulation is small. But it'll reach the sugar people."

"I'll go with her," Paul offered. "Get backup photos. I'm not a professional photographer, but it's been a hobby for years."

"He's good," Lisa told Chuck. "I've seen his photos."

"I can't invest much in this," Chuck hedged.

"Pay my airfare," Paul said. "I'll take it from there."

"Deal," Chuck agreed. "I don't like Lisa down there alone."

"When does the first installment appear?" Lisa asked.

"I'm pulling the lead story on the next edition and replacing it with yours," Chuck said. "It'll be on the stands Thursday morning."

"We'll be a pair of grad students doing research." Paul chuckled. "And presumably we're grabbing a vacation at the same time. Nobody will be suspicious. West Grove, Florida, here we come!"

Chapter Forty-seven

HARRY DIALED Eileen's number at the cottage. Simultaneously he reread the front-page article of the new weekly newspaper his New York office had rushed to him. *Sleazy* rag, he thought with contempt. Going after the supermarket checkout-counter circulation.

"West Grove Plantation." The voice of Eileen's newest "assistant"—they were always young and male—was aloof, as though chiding the caller for this interruption.

"Clive, you tell Eileen I want to see her at the house right away. I don't care if she's busy—I want to see her now." Harry slammed the phone down without waiting for a reply.

What was this newspaper shit about their running a slave deal on the plantation? Accidents every day in the fields—often bad ones. Cutters living in degrading, dismal conditions, cheated on their wages. *Find out what was going on.* Muckraking journalism—or Eileen playing a bad scene?

He was oddly unnerved that the byline belonged to a

reporter named Freeman. Katie's maiden name. The same surname as that sweet young coed—dedicated to doing good—who'd been killed five years ago in some incident during a strike at the Talisman mill.

"Juanita!" he called to his secretary in the adjoining office. "I'll be out of the office for a while. Anything urgent comes up, buzz me at my house." He wanted to confront Eileen in privacy.

He hurried from the mill to his Mercedes, parked beneath a live oak to protect it from the hot morning sun. He'd been among the first in the industry to unionize his mill. He was proud of his relationship with his employees. What was going on out there on the plantation that he didn't know about? Or *was* it just a muckraker at work?

Driving toward the house, he reran in his mind the ugly story reported by Lisa Freeman. He was assaulted by guilt now that he had allowed Eileen such leeway. Damn it, he should have checked on how she was running the operation! *But don't jump to conclusions.*

He knew vaguely that there had been some efforts to organize the agricultural workers. That had been going on for years in other areas. But everybody down here insisted it was impossible when dealing with migrant workers from out of the country.

All his life he'd made a practice of giving a square deal to everybody who worked for him. Even when he was with Simon & Sinclair, he had fought Arnie, taking the side of his employees when problems arose. *What the hell was Eileen doing out there on the plantation?*

He was pacing in the library with a tall, frosted glass of iced coffee in his hand when he heard Eileen's car pull into the driveway. He stalked to the entrance, waiting for her to appear in the hall.

"Harry, what do you mean summoning me this way?" Eileen demanded as she walked toward him. "You know how busy I am this time of year."

"The New York office just sent me this little billet-doux," he said sarcastically and extended the folded-back newspaper. "Read it."

Eileen took the newspaper, frowned at the headline, and swore under her breath as she read.

"Some cheap rag trying to start something up," she said with contempt. "Why are you wasting my time on this garbage?"

"I don't like my good name being dragged through the mud," he shot back. "I don't—"

"Who reads this rag?" Eileen interrupted, and handed it back to him. "It's put out by some dumb small-time operator with illusions of its becoming another *National Enquirer*."

"Is it true that we—"

"Harry, stop being naive," she interrupted impatiently. "We do just what other sugarcane plantations in Florida do. No more—no less. We're not running a rest home. We have a rough job to get done. We—" She paused as Harry suddenly clutched at his chest with one hand and grunted in pain. His face drained of color as he dropped the newspaper on his desk.

"Call Freddie," he gasped. "I think I'm having a heart attack."

Sam drove into the hospital parking area, came to a screeching halt. Terrified of what she would find, she hurried from the car into the hospital. Eileen had left word for her to come here as soon as possible. *"Your father's had a heart attack."*

She found Eileen slouched in a chair in the reception area, flipping through a magazine.

"What happened?" Sam asked, her throat tight with alarm. "How is he?"

"There's a whole crew working over him now," Eileen said. "I've been waiting out here almost an hour. . . ."

How could this be happening to Dad? He was strong as a horse. He was nineteen years older than Eileen, and looked the same age. There'd been no hint of anything like this!

"Tell me everything that happened," Sam ordered shakily.

"There's Freddie." Eileen rose to her feet. Dr. Fred Weston was the family internist.

"Harry's going to be all right," Dr. Weston soothed as he approached them. "I've been telling him for a year now to start getting more exercise and to take off twenty pounds."

"He will," Sam promised grimly while relief surged through her. *Dad was all right.* "Can we see him now?"

"As soon as we get him transferred to a private room," Dr. Weston said briskly. "It was a very mild heart attack, but we want to do some tests just to be on the safe side. We'll keep him here a couple of days or so."

"You'd better make it a few days, Freddie," Eileen said. "You know Harry. If you let him out of here, he'll be back at the mill the next day. Make him stay a week—that's the only way he'll ever slow down."

"You're probably right," Dr. Weston agreed with a chuckle. "I never saw a man of his age with so much energy. You'd think he was about thirty. I'll arrange to schedule the tests so we can keep him here. He'll bitch, but he'll listen to me."

Eileen left Harry's hospital room—with Sam apparently planning to stay all evening, she guessed. But perhaps that was just as well. She had a job to do. A job that required Harry's continuing presence in the hospital—and Sam out of her hair.

She drove directly to the mill and went to Harry's private office. The mill, of course, was in operation, the office staff long gone for the day.

She went through his desk and his files, searching for all the correspondence she could find from the conglomerate that was so eager to buy the mill and the plantation. Certain that she had gathered together every letter that had passed between Kramer Enterprises and West Grove, she phoned Ray Duggan at his home.

"Ray, I have to see you," she told him when he was on the phone. "Tonight."

"Eileen, my wife's in town," he said, faintly testy. Last year—when his wife had been in Europe—they'd had a mad weekend together. Neither had cared to prolong it. Ray was nervous about his wife finding out, and Eileen preferred younger men. "What is it?"

"I need your services as a lawyer," she said coldly. "This is an emergency. Come over to the mill office. Not to my field cottage. Harry's in the hospital," she added.

"What happened?" Ray was immediately solicitous.

"He's had a heart attack."

"I'm sorry to hear that, Eileen."

"He'll recover, Freddie Weston assured us. But he says Harry has to take it easy. I need papers drawn up so I can carry on at the mill."

"I'll be right over."

Eileen put down the phone with a triumphant smile. She'd waited over twenty years for this moment. *Everything was going to work out great.*

"What the hell does Freddie Weston mean?" Harry demanded of Eileen. "Why do I have to stay here for a week? I feel fine now."

"Harry, you had a heart attack. Freddie's careful—he's ordered a lot of tests. You don't have to worry—I'll carry on at the mill." She concealed her irritation that he hadn't signed the power of attorney yet.

"Why do I have to sign this?" Harry grumbled.

"Because the mill has to meet its payroll," she pointed out. "I'll have to sign the checks. Freddie says you're to stay here in the hospital and relax. You're not to think about business." She handed him the pen again. "Harry, sign it and let me get over to the bank and explain I have to sign the payroll checks."

"Freddie's crazy to keep me holed up here." But Harry took the pen, signed the power of attorney while Eileen braced it on a clipboard she'd dug out of her briefcase. "Who's in charge at the plantation? Not that stupid Clive?"

"Tim. He's the best supervisor we've ever had. He's got everything under control. Relax, Harry."

"Where's Sam today?" Harry asked, scowling.

"It's eight o'clock in the morning, Harry." She sighed in exasperation. "She's probably still asleep."

Eileen left the hospital, drove back to the mill. Later she'd go to the bank. First she had a phone call to put through to Ted Carson at Kramer Enterprises. He was the kind of executive who'd be at his desk by 8:00 A.M.—no need to wait to call. They wanted to buy the West Grove Mill and plantation? She wanted to sell. She had Harry's power of attorney. They could do business.

At La Guardia Lisa and Paul learned their early-morning flight would be delayed forty minutes.

"Let's go for coffee," said Paul, grinning at her grunt of frustration. "So we'll be late coming into town. We can't do anything tonight about the story."

"I'll call Mom," Lisa decided. "If she tries to reach me at the hotel down in Florida and she learns I've checked out, she'll be worried. I didn't know how long I'd be on this story—I said I might be down there three weeks."

"You struck pay dirt on the first dig. Beginner's luck," he teased.

Lisa reached Katie at the office, as she'd expected.

"I flew up to New York for a conference with my boss," she said lightly. "And now I'm headed back to Florida. I'll call from there to let you know where we're staying."

"We?" Katie asked.

"Paul's flying down with me to get photos. You know, Paul Hecht." Was Mom going to get uptight about this?

"Yes, you mentioned him." A lilt in her voice now. "Am I going to meet him one of these days?"

"Most likely. Paul's asking, too." There, that pleased Mom.

"Lisa, this assignment isn't something dangerous, is it?" Lisa guessed she'd been fretting about this all along. But Mom was never one to play the anxious mother.

"Just a story on the sugarcane industry down in South Florida. Like I told you."

"I remember reading about troubles with the unionizing of the sugar mills," Katie said. "Of course, that was a while back."

"We're doing the sugarcane plantations," Lisa told her.

"An exposé?" An involuntary sharpness in her voice now.

"You could call it that," Lisa acknowledged. "But I'll be all right. Don't worry, Mom."

"Lisa, don't take chances," Katie urged.

"I'll be fine, Mom," Lisa reassured her. "No problems."

"Dad, are you supposed to be floating around like this?" Sam scolded when she had finally located him and was walking with him back to his room. Four days after a heart attack he was a dynamo again.

"I've been here too long," he grumbled. "I don't know why Freddie insists on my staying. I'm great—I never felt better."

"He says you're to start a regular exercise regimen when you get out of here. And no more rich desserts and Texas steaks—you're taking off twenty pounds."

"Yes, ma'am," he said with mock-deference, and grinned. "I guess the waistline has been getting out of shape."

"Shall I bring you some magazines?"

"I'd rather you brought me a thick porterhouse and a

chunk of strawberry shortcake. You wouldn't believe what I just had for breakfast. I know—" He put up a hand to forestall her reproach. "I'm on a diet. Bring me *The Wall Street Journal* and *The New York Times*."

"Can't stay away from the business even in the hospital?" Sam shook her head with a mixture of affection and exasperation as they settled themselves in a pair of chairs in the flower-filled room.

"Business is what put me here." All at once his face was grim. "I have to get out of here, Sam. That damn Freddie keeps stalling me with these tests. I told him—he's just trying to build up a fancy bill to help pay for those machines the hospital keeps buying."

"You'll leave when Dr. Weston says you can," Sam said. How was she going to get him to take time out to recuperate? She'd talk to Dr. Weston about that.

"Eileen hasn't been around since the day before yesterday. I suppose she's busting her butt at the mill?"

"She loves it," Sam dismissed this. "The lady tycoon. Maybe you ought to let her take over at the mill for a few weeks," she tried hopefully. "You shouldn't go right back into that madhouse."

"I've given her too much leeway already. I think," he amended. "Of course, the story in that cheap newspaper could be a pack of lies. You know me, quick to fly off the handle." But he seemed apprehensive. "How could we have stayed in business all these years if all that shit was true?"

"What shit?" Sam demanded. "What's this about a newspaper story?"

"The New York office airmailed a copy down to me. It made some damning accusations about how we run our plantation."

"Where is it?" Anger spiraled in Sam. He'd got all worked up over that story. *That was what brought on the heart attack.* "Where's that newspaper?"

"Where I dropped it on my desk when I had the attack," Harry said slowly.

"Freddie says you're doing well." Harry and Sam whirled about to face Eileen. "Another three days and you can go home."

"Why three more days?" Harry challenged.

"To finish up the tests," Eileen reminded him. "But there's no problem. Freddie says you'll outlive him."

"I'll come back to see you after dinner, Dad." Sam kissed him, waved a casual farewell to her mother, and left the room.

"What's happening at the mill?" Harry asked Eileen.

"The usual craziness. It'll survive." She paused, her eyes opaque. "Harry, we have to talk."

He pounced. "Something *is* wrong at the mill."

"Not at all. It's never been better. We have to talk about us."

"Yeah?" Harry was guarded.

"You know we haven't had a marriage since Sam was born. These years have been rotten for me. I'm still young enough to have needs. . . ."

"I gather you've been having your needs filled," Harry said caustically.

Eileen ignored the dig. "I'm sick of the plantation. I'm sick of Florida. This is as good a time as any for me to get out. I want to fly to Mexico City for a divorce, Harry. I want to live down there." Her eyes dared him to refuse her.

"I won't stop you." He was startled but not unhappy. He'd have to find somebody to run the plantation.

"I'm using Ray Duggan as my lawyer. He's made a contact for me in Mexico City. He drew up papers for you to sign, stating you're not contesting the divorce." She opened her crocodile briefcase and pulled out a sheaf of papers. "There are four copies. One for you." She handed him the papers and a pen.

"You want me to sign it now?"

"Is there any reason not to sign now?" Her smile was supercilious. Her brows furrowed in impatience.

"None," he conceded. If the conditions were acceptable. He paused to read the brief statement. *Nothing here about a financial settlement.* What the devil was going on? This wasn't like Eileen. When it came to money, nobody was sharper. "Okay, it's signed." He handed three copies back to her. "When is all this taking place?"

"I'm flying out tonight. As soon as I have my divorce, I'm marrying Clive. You can work out our financial settlement with Ray."

"Who's in charge at the mill?" Harry's mind was in chaos. This was all happening too fast. What was Eileen up to? *She was trusting him to work out a financial settlement with her lawyer?* "I'll have to make Freddie agree to my leaving here in the morning. . . ."

"No problem, Harry. You've trained Bud Jackson well. He can handle everything for now." She slid the papers into her briefcase and snapped it shut. "Good-bye, Harry. I'll drop you a line sometime from Mexico City."

Chapter Forty-eight

SAM SAT hunched over her father's desk in the library and read the searing article about the West Grove Plantation. That stupid bitch! Probably sitting up there in New York and dreaming up this whole rotten deal! She grunted in fresh outrage when she read that this was the first of a the three-part series.

Sam searched out the masthead for the address of the newspaper's office. She'd call up to New York and warn this Lisa Freeman that Dad would file a libel suit if she dared to write one more word about the plantation. And she'd demand a retraction.

When she'd acquired the phone number of the newspaper, Sam called the office and asked for Lisa Freeman.

"Lisa Freeman isn't in town right now. Can somebody else help you?" the receptionist asked breezily.

"Oh, I'm a friend of hers from college," Sam improvised. *Freeman was down in Florida, to try to dig up more dirt.* "I've been living in Switzerland for two years, and I'm just in this country for a few days. Could you tell me where she's staying so I can phone?"

"I really shouldn't give out that information," the girl said doubtfully.

"Oh, Lisa will kill you if she finds out I was in New York and you wouldn't give me her phone number. Overseas calls are so damned expensive. . . ." Sam waited, praying for a little luck.

"Well, all right," the receptionist agreed after a moment's hesitation. "Since you're a friend of Lisa's from college. She's in this small town called West Grove, in Florida. At least, she's staying at the Wilmington Motel, about seven miles north of West Grove. Just hold and I'll dig up the phone number."

Sam called the Wilmington Motel and asked for Lisa.

"She doesn't answer," the switchboard operator reported. "Would you like to leave a message?"

"No. No message, thank you," she said. Seething as particularly brutal phrases in the article flashed across her mind.

She sat motionless by the phone for a moment, searching for her next move. *Okay. Drive over to the motel and sit in the car until Lisa Freeman returns. No matter how long it takes. She* had to stop the follow-up stories—and demand a retraction. Sam reached for the newspaper, folded it over, stuffed it into her purse. Now she headed out of the house and to the white Jaguar her father had bought as her college graduation present.

How could they do this to Dad? Everybody in this state knew his sense of fairness, his reputation as a model employer. A job at West Grove was considered a prize. Almost everybody at the mill had been there at least fifteen years.

That bitchy reporter couldn't hit the mill, Sam fumed, so she went after the plantation with its migrant workers. But even there, she remembered Eileen's boasting, the same bunch came back regularly. Did that sound like the workers were being exploited?

Sam left the house and drove over to the Wilmington Motel. A row of charming, red-brick and white clapboard units designed to appeal to the more affluent motorists. In-season every unit was probably rented. In September only a handful of cars occupied the parking wedges. On the off-chance that Lisa Freeman had returned, Sam inquired at the office.

"No ma'am, she ain't back yet," the elderly desk clerk reported with an admiring smile.

"I don't know her by sight," Sam said ingratiatingly. "What does she look like?"

"Well," he said after a moment, "she looks a lot like you. About your age." Okay, so physically they were the same type. "Except she's got black hair that she wears hanging about her shoulders—and you're a little bit taller," he gauged. "A real good-looking young lady."

"Thank you." At least she'd know to look for someone dark-haired, slim, and about her own height.

She returned to her car, parked beneath a towering live oak. The builder had the good sense not to chop down those trees, she thought with approval. Restless at this waiting, she flipped on the radio and leaned over to the backseat to pick up the copy of *Vogue* she'd thrown back there earlier. After almost an hour—with not one car turning off the road into the parking area—she decided to drive to the nearest Howard Johnson's for a quick lunch. She was famished.

Returning from lunch thirty minutes later, Sam saw a car swing into the Wilmington parking area. Her hands tightened on the wheel. Already furious words were forming in her mind. How dare they malign Dad that way!

Sam followed the car into the parking area at a slow

pace. A man and a woman on the front seat, she noted. Nobody in the back. The other car pulled into a wedge. A man emerged. Then a woman. About her age and size—with black hair that fell to her shoulders. Lisa Freeman, Sam guessed, her jaw tightening in anticipation of a momentary confrontation.

She dug the newspaper from her purse, waited until the two had let themselves into a motel unit, then left the car—the newspaper clutched in one hand—and walked to their door. She wished Lisa Freeman had been alone, but nobody was going to stand in her way at this point. She wanted to go back to the hospital and tell Dad there would not be two more installments of that lurid article—and that the newspaper would carry a retraction.

She paused at the door for an instant, gearing herself for what she had to say. Then she knocked. Almost immediately the door swung partially open. A handsome man in his mid-twenties stood there.

"Yes?" he asked, polite but wary.

"I'd like to talk to Lisa Freeman." They'd anticipated repercussions, Sam guessed.

"What's it about?" He was making a point of keeping the door half-closed.

"I'd prefer to tell her." Sam fought to sound casual.

"It's all right, Paul," a feminine voice called. A moment later a slim brunette appeared. "I'm Lisa Freeman."

"You wrote this scurrilous article?" Despite her determination to be cool, Sam radiated fury. "It drove my father into a heart attack!"

"I wrote it," Lisa agreed. For a moment she seemed unnerved. "But it isn't scurrilous. I researched carefully. I—"

"Everybody in this state knows my father would never resort to anything like you wrote about!" Sam's eyes were ablaze. "He's one of the most respected businessmen in the South. I want to know that there'll be no more such articles—and I want a retraction and an apology for my father."

"When was the last time you were on the West Grove plantation?" Lisa challenged.

Sam felt suddenly defensive.

"Well, I—I haven't been there lately. But—" She'd never been there during the harvest. Never in the camp.

"*I* was there a few days ago. I saw what I wrote about. I talked with the cutter—"

"I don't believe you!" Sam interrupted, her color high.

"You haven't seen it!" Lisa lashed back. "Go with us at dawn tomorrow morning. Let us show you the kind of plantation your father runs. We'll have to creep around because Mrs. Newhouse set up guards the day after we asked to visit the plantation."

"My father doesn't run the plantation." All at once Sam was attacked by doubts. Dad never went to the plantation. That was Eileen's territory. What Dad called—in moments of derision—"Eileen's domain." *What had she perpetrated behind his back?* "My mother has complete charge of the plantation." Sam struggled to keep her voice even. "My Dad runs the mill and the sales office."

"Then maybe you owe it to yourself to see," Paul said quietly. "Let us show you, Miss Newhouse."

"Samantha," she said shakily, "but everybody calls me Sam."

"If the plantation bosses know you're coming, they'll try to clean up their act," Lisa warned. "Don't say anything to anybody. Let us show you the way it is. The guards stay out front—we know how to get into the camp from the rear without being seen. We—"

"Why should I believe you?" Sam tried again, but her defiance was weak.

"Don't believe us," Paul said. "Believe what you see. And with you there we'll get to see the fields—unless your mother tries to stop us."

"My mother flew to Mexico City last night. We'll see the fields." Sam hesitated. "When?"

"Tomorrow morning, just after dawn," Lisa said. "By then the men are in the fields. You'll see the camp first.

You can talk with the men who're there. There are injuries every day—if they can't use a machete, they have to stay back in the camp. And they don't get paid when they're not in the fields."

"Where do we meet?" Sam asked. *For Dad she had to know the truth.* "Tell me, and I'll be there."

Sam drove about aimlessly for hours. Maybe she was crazy to believe what Lisa Freeman and her friend Paul insisted were the real conditions on the plantation, but instinct told her they were not lying.

At last she returned to the house. She was grateful that Eileen was not around. She had dinner on a tray in her room, then drove to the hospital for her nightly visit with her father. Should she tell Dad what was happening tomorrow morning at dawn? No, she decided. How could she do that when he was just recovering from a heart attack? But soon he would have to know—if what Lisa and Paul said was true.

Sam arrived at the hospital with a wedge of Black Forest cake. Rhoda—who had been her nurse when she was a child—had graduated to family housekeeper-cook, and there was nothing Dad liked better than Rhoda's Black Forest cake. She'd cleared it with Dr. Weston. *"With what they're giving your father at the hospital, he can have a treat. A small treat."*

"Guess what I brought you, Dad!" She managed a festive smile.

"Did you see your mother?" he asked brusquely. "Before she left for Mexico City?"

"No. Why?"

"She's divorcing me, Sam. Didn't she say good-bye to you?"

"I haven't seen her except here at the hospital." Sam hesitated. "Dad, you're not unhappy about the divorce?" Her voice deepened with sarcasm. "It's long past due." Was it because of that article? Was Eileen afraid Dad would make mincemeat of her when he found out it was true?

"I'm not unhappy about it," he admitted. "But the hackles at the back of my neck tell me there's something weird going on. I signed papers so that the divorce would go through uncontested. Ray Duggan is her lawyer. You know how sharp he is. You know how conniving Eileen is," he added meaningfully. "So why haven't I been asked to sign a financial settlement?"

"I don't know." She put the wedge of cake, carefully wrapped in aluminum foil, on the table at the foot of his bed. "Did you talk to Ray?"

"I can't get through to him, damn it! I've called half a dozen times, and I get conflicting statements. The maid said one thing, his wife something else. He's dodging me, Sam."

"You want me to try to track him down?"

"He'll stall until he's ready to talk. I just want to know what kind of settlement she's going to ask for. I can't remember if there's a community-property law in Florida—"

"She's going for a Mexican divorce. Can she ask for a settlement?"

"I'll call Rick Bernstein," Harry decided. Bernstein had been his personal and business attorney for seventeen years. "He'll grab hold of Ray."

"She flew off to Mexico without even saying a word to me." Sam's smile blended cynicism with hurt. "But I shouldn't have expected anything different." From habit she hurt a little, Sam analyzed. Time the habit was broken.

"Sam, we don't need her." Harry reached out for his daughter. "We have each other."

"Eileen has never been there for us," Sam mocked. "And we've done all right. But it's kind of hard to admit that your own mother doesn't give a damn about you."

She couldn't tell Dad tonight that she believed the

article Lisa Freeman had written. Later she'd tell him—because the situation had to change.

"Oh, one more little goodie." Harry's smile was twisted. "Eileen's giving you a stepfather—of sorts. She's marrying Clive after the divorce."

"That creep?" Sam stared at him in disbelief, then unexpectedly broke into laughter. "Oh, Dad, talk about justice! She's getting just what she deserves!"

As arranged, Sam stood in front of the silent house and waited for Lisa and Paul to pick her up. The gray early-morning sky was touched by flecks of pink, the sun still beneath the horizon. She was glad she'd worn the long-sleeved blue cotton turtleneck along with her jeans instead of a sleeveless T-shirt. There was an unexpected chill in the air.

Last night—before going to bed—she'd forced herself to go into her mother's room. Eileen kept most of her clothes at the cottage—the spillover was at the house. She had stripped the closets. The only signs of her presence here was a near-empty bottle of Chanel No. 5 and several back issues of *Town & Country* that lay on the floor. In the morning one of the maids would come in and put the bedroom in order.

Sam tensed as she saw a car approach. She dreaded what she would see at the plantation. But it was something she must do. She didn't hate Lisa Freeman anymore. She was afraid Lisa was right.

"We'll park about a quarter-mile from the camp," Lisa told her, "and walk the rest of the way."

"Sure. I'm wearing sneakers." Sam held up one foot with an air of bravado.

"How's your father?" Lisa asked somberly.

"Carrying on about staying in the hospital," Sam told her as she climbed into the car. "But the doctor has ordered a load of tests. He'll be there at least another three days."

They were silent until they arrived at their destination. Paul parked, and the three of them emerged and began to walk.

"We'll circle around and go into the camp first," Lisa said.

"Let's move," Sam said tensely.

Even before they walked into the barrackslike camp, Sam was sure she'd find exactly what Lisa had said. Several men lay asleep in the bunks. A pair was gathered around a hot plate, watching the contents of a saucepan. They flinched in alarm when they saw the intruders.

"They're not allowed to cook," Lisa whispered.

"Please don't stop what you're doing," Sam said with confidence—though even at first glance she felt sick. The bunks were so close together there was hardly room for a man to stand. The air stank. While the morning was cooler than normal, the huge room still suffered from yesterday's heat. "My father is worried that the camp is not properly run. He's concerned about accidents in the fields. He's sent me to hear your feelings about these things."

The pair at the hot plate hurried forward, their faces glistening with hope. Words tumbled over one another in their rush to explain their anguish. *Oh yes*, Sam thought, *Lisa Freeman had been right*.

Chapter Forty-nine

HARRY FINISHED his hospital breakfast—with cryptic remarks to a sympathetic nurse—and crossed to a window to gaze out into the sunlight. How long did it take for a Mexican divorce to go through? Twenty-four hours? When would Eileen be his ex-wife? It had been a long time since he had regarded her as a woman. She was the person who ran his plantation. But he owed her a certain gratitude—she'd given him Sam.

"Harry, I hope I haven't come too early. . . ." He swung around to face the mill superintendent. "They gave me some flak about how visiting hours hadn't started yet."

"It's never too early, Bud." Harry frowned. "What's up?"

"I'm hurt," Bud said frankly. "How could you sell out and not tell me? I'm not sure I want to stay with the new people. . . ."

"What do you mean—sell out?" Harry bristled. "I told those people at Kramer Enterprises I'd never sell. So we've had some slowdown in profits, that doesn't mean that—"

"Harry, their team showed up at seven A.M. this morning! They're taking over!"

"That's insane!" Harry's mind shot into high gear. Suddenly he understood. *That stupid power of attorney he'd signed so Eileen could meet the payroll.* He hadn't bothered to read it—he'd just glanced at it. When Eileen came in with it, he was still groggy from the sleeping pills he'd been given the night before. "Oh Christ, Bud! My bitch of a wife has cut my throat!"

"I don't understand." Bud waited for an explanation.

"Eileen brought a power of attorney for me to sign so she could handle the payroll checks. She was after me for months to sell out to Kramer. I told her no deal. She went behind my back and sold. I have to get to my office!"

"Harry, calm down." Bud was upset. "Don't push yourself into another heart attack. I'll go back and—"

"What's that?" Harry demanded. Just now aware that Bud carried an envelope in one hand. "For me?"

"Yeah. Juanita said she found it on her desk this morning with a note. She was supposed to bring it over to you. She's practically hysterical about the takeover. She asked me to bring it over."

Before Harry ripped open the envelope, he knew the letter was from Eileen. She told him bluntly that she had sold the business and had the funds deposited in a Mexico City bank in her name.

"You keep the house. I never liked it anyway."

Harry sat down at the edge of the bed, dizzy with shock. The bitch had taken everything except the house and his small stock portfolio. He couldn't keep up the mortgage payments on his Texas parcels! Even if he sold the house and the stock, he couldn't pay off the mortgages. He'd done what Katie always warned him against—low down payments and big mortgages. *But he hadn't expected this.* He was down at the bottom again. Seventy-two and almost broke.

"Harry, you okay?"

"I will be." Silently he handed the letter to Bud. How the hell had Eileen managed to push the sale through so fast? But she was always a conniver. This was her big payoff, and she'd let nothing stand in her way.

"Harry, you can't do anything about it?" Bud lifted his eyes from the letter.

"Nothing. The mill and the plantation belong to Kramer Enterprises as of yesterday morning." He shook his head in disbelief. "Both sides must have set a record in pushing through the sale so fast."

"What'll you do now?" Bud—a friend as well as business associate for over fifteen years—was solicitous.

"Sell the house and go back out to Texas," Harry said after a moment. "That's always really been home." Never Paris. Never Minneapolis—where the newly titled Sinclair Associates fell into bankruptcy six years after he was kicked out. Never Seattle or West Grove. Only Texas.

What about Sam? How was he going to tell her that everything was gone but the house and some piddling stocks? He'd let down his daughter. Christ, he'd had no right to have another child. *He only brought disaster to his children.*

* * *

Lisa and Paul returned to the motel after a long, somber breakfast with Sam to assess the situation. At her own instigation Sam would sit down later in the week with Lisa and discuss—for use in Lisa's two follow-up articles—what she had seen at the West Grove plantation. She would place the blame where it belonged: with her mother. Her father's name would be cleared. Paul had taken many snapshots so there would be photos to accompany the follow-ups.

"Maybe I ought to drive up to Palm Beach and have these rolls of film processed there," said Paul, lingering behind the wheel of the car.

"Good thinking," Lisa approved. "It might take forever to get them back in West Grove. And people in town *like* Harry Newhouse. You saw their loyalty when we tried to talk to the locals." They knew the fine working conditions at the mill. They didn't know about Eileen Newhouse's despotic rule on the plantation, only that life on the sugar plantation was too harsh to hold American workers. "There's just a chance the film might get destroyed." She was troubled that Sam's father had suffered a heart attack when he'd read her article. She'd meant to help remedy a terrible situation. She hadn't meant to land Harry Newhouse in the hospital.

"Do you want to go with me to Palm Beach?" Paul asked gently.

"You go on. I'll call Chuck in New York."

"Sure." He leaned forward to brush his mouth lightly against hers. "See you in about an hour."

Lisa let herself into their unit and settled down at her typewriter to make notes. But she couldn't dismiss from her mind the realization that a *good* man had suffered a heart attack because of something she wrote. She abandoned her typing and reached for the phone. At moments like this she needed to talk to Mom.

537

In her Dallas office—studying the report on their latest farm acquisition—Katie frowned at the intrusion of the phone. This was one of the days when Maura didn't come in, and the secretary she shared with Jeff and George was out on an errand.

"Hello." Katie was terse, annoyed at this interruption.

"Am I calling at a bad time, Mom?" Lisa asked.

"Darling, no time is bad for you to call," Katie said quickly, her voice tender. "What's happening down in Florida?"

Katie listened absorbedly while Lisa reported on the situation at the West Grove plantation.

"We're getting full cooperation now," Lisa summed up. "Only I feel so rotten. I mean, Sam's father had a heart attack because he was so upset over the article. And Mom, he's a fine man. It's his wife who's a monster."

"But Sam—his son, I gather—told you his father is recovering nicely," Katie comforted.

"Sam's his daughter," Lisa explained. "And yes, Mr. Newhouse is doing well. Sam said—"

"Newhouse?" Katie's heart began to pound. "She's Samantha Newhouse? Her father is Harry Newhouse?"

"Yes. Do you know him?"

"You said he had a heart attack," Katie pinned down. Her throat tightening in anxiety. "The doctors are sure he's going to be all right?"

"Well, he has to stay in the hospital for more tests—"

"Lisa, I'm flying to Florida immediately!" Harry mustn't die! She had to go to him! "I'll arrange for a charter flight to Palm Beach. I'll—"

"Mom, who is Harry Newhouse to you?" Lisa was bewildered.

"Oh, Lisa, how can I tell you?" Katie's voice broke. Here was the third terrible crisis of her life. "Harry Newhouse, my darling, is your grandfather."

Lisa was shocked into silence for an agonizing moment. "Mom, why did you divorce him? Why was I never

538

told about him?" She knew there was a grandfather somewhere, Lisa remembered. That was all she knew.

With fresh anguish, Katie explained about Leo's suicide and Joanne's traumatic reaction. She told Lisa how she had been able to follow Harry's tracks—though she didn't dare even to think about reconciliation—until he'd left Seattle.

"Since then I knew nothing of his whereabouts. But he was always in my thoughts, Lisa. Always in my heart. Fate took you down to West Grove. Fate brought you together with him, Lisa."

"He walked out on you," Lisa said defiantly. "He didn't want us in his life."

"I drove him away," Katie whispered painfully. "For your mother's sanity I had to do that. And then he married again. He had another child. Samantha. I told myself there was no room in his life for us."

"His wife just left him," Lisa told her. "It was not a happy marriage."

"Harry had a heart attack, and she left him?" Katie's voice soared in scorn. "But enough talk—I have to go to Harry. I can't let him die thinking I haven't forgiven him."

"Call me when you have your flight schedule. Paul and I will pick you up at the Palm Beach airport."

Katie was trembling as she walked toward the door of Harry's hospital room. The others had been ordered to say nothing of her arrival.

"Wait out here for a while," Katie whispered to Lisa and Sam. Paul sat in the reception area near the bank of elevators. "I'd like to see him alone first."

She approached the door of his room. Her heart hammering. Her throat tightening. Would Harry recognize her? Did anything of what they'd felt for each other remain in him? It was so many years, she thought in terror, and paused.

She turned around to look at Lisa and Sam. The family resemblance was amazingly obvious. Both had tears in their eyes. She smiled tremulously and walked with swift steps the remaining distance to the door.

He was standing at the window, gazing out into the sunlight. Harry always loved the sun—except in Texas summers.

"Harry—" She felt a surge of love as he turned around. It was incredible. Except for that fleeting glance in the Seattle airport, she had not seen him in thirty-eight years—but it was Harry as she remembered him. Slightly heavier. His hair speckled with gray. Lines here and there. *But Harry*.

"Katie!" He gasped in recognition. "Oh my God, Katie!"

He moved toward her with outstretched arms. They weren't two very well preserved oldsters, she thought with joy—they were Katie and Harry, as they'd been that morning they left New York and headed for Texas.

"I've missed you so, Katie," he whispered, holding her face between his hands. "You've never been out of my heart."

"Nor you out of mine."

His mouth came down on hers with the passion of eighteen. Harry still loved her, she rejoiced. The terrible empty years were over.

"How did you know I was here?" Harry asked. "What brought you to me?"

"Our granddaughter, Harry," Katie said softly. "Lisa came down here to do a story about the sugar plantations—"

"Lisa Freeman? Our granddaughter?" Harry clutched at her shoulders. "But our Lisa died. I read it in the Dallas newspapers!"

"The police thought Lisa was with Joanne and Gordie. She was with me. There was a last-minute change because Lisa had a cold, and I thought she shouldn't be traveling. You didn't see the newspaper retraction. . . ."

"When will I meet her?" Harry's voice broke. "Joanne's child. I can't believe it. I can't believe any of this."

"I'll call Lisa. She's waiting outside. Harry, she's the image of you. She and Sam look like two sisters instead of aunt and niece." Katie laughed. "The aunt is a year younger." She crossed to the door and leaned forward. "Lisa, come meet your grandfather."

Later Katie sat alone with Harry, her hand in his. Both were exhausted from this traumatic reconciliation, their faces luminous with newfound happiness.

"Katie, you have no luck," he jibed. "You've come into my life just when I've lost everything again." He'd told her about losing the company, that he was left with only the house and a few stocks. "I had such great plans. . . ."

"Harry, you've always had great plans." She squeezed his hand in approval.

"I'd been buying up farmland all over Texas. With mortgages on each," he said ruefully. "In four or five months I'll have lost all of it. I bought in Texas because it made me feel closer to you. And I prophesy that Texas real estate is in for one sensational boom."

"You won't lose one acre," Katie promised. "Together we'll meet the payments. Everything I've earned, Harry, I earned because part of you was in my mind and heart—telling me how to operate. We were never totally apart."

"I won't be a kept man," he kidded. "You'll have to marry me."

"I'll consider it," she said lightly.

"Let the young kids live in sin. I want to stand under the *chuppa* with you again."

"I want that, too, Harry."

"You know, Katie, it's downright indecent for a woman your age to look so sexy."

"Are you complaining?"

"Hell no! Boasting. Just being close to you this way,

I'm getting horny. I can't wait to get out of this hospital room and into some privacy."

"Harry, it's been a long time," she said tenderly.

"Don't worry, Katie." He pulled her close. "It's like learning to ride a bike. Once you've the knack, you never forget. We have a lot of years ahead of us—and I mean to take advantage of every beautiful moment."

"But we'll allot some time to business," Katie joshed. "Remember that land empire you always wanted? Between the two of us we'll have it. But we'll be 'stewards of the land.'" Her face was radiant. "We'll be part of the new generation that wants to save the earth. All of us together. A family again," she said softly. It was like a benediction.

Epilogue

THIS OCTOBER Sunday afternoon was Dallas at its best, Katie thought with pleasure as she scrutinized her reflection in the floor-to-ceiling mirror on her dressing-room door. The air was balmy, fragrant with the scent of late-blooming roses. Here in the master suite—in its own wing of the house she still called "the farmhouse" —she was isolated from the exuberant activities in the main wing. Alone here to savor her happiness.

Harry had gone with her to Neiman's to choose her "second wedding" dress. Both of them drawn instantly to this turquoise silk shift that was reminiscent of the dress she wore at their first wedding in the Hirsches' flat on Rivington Street. Today she would become Katie Newhouse again.

Enveloped in poignant nostalgia, Katie walked into the sitting room, crossed to gaze out a window. Her eyes were tender as they focused on the *chuppa*—already set up in the picturesque gardens behind the house, with mimosas and towering pecans as a backdrop.

Delicious aromas from the kitchen—where Melinda was, as Lisa phrased it, cooking up a storm—drifted through the house. Katie heard Harry in conversation with the string quartet that would play for the wedding ceremony and the small dinner party afterward. She heard Maura greeting guests. There was Irene, arriving from Seattle!

She started at the light knock on her door.

"Everybody is here, Mom." Lisa glowed as she came into the sitting room. "We'll start on schedule."

"We'd better." Katie reached forward to hug Lisa. "Harry and I have flights to catch." First, a few days in New York, then a week each in London and Paris. "This time we can afford a honeymoon."

Arm in arm, Katie and Lisa walked from the master suite down the hall and into the living room. Through the tall, lace-paneled French doors Katie saw the cluster of wedding guests seated on the small gold chairs rented for the occasion. Everyone dear to her gathered here today. Maura and Jeff, George and Nora, and their two children. Willa and a friend Maura hoped would become a son-in-law. Paul was being attentive to the cluster of friends close to her at Gas Girls, Inc.

Involuntarily Katie's eyes swung to the crystal-framed snapshots that dominated the elegant fireplace mantel. Snapshots of Leo and Joanne. Forever they lived in a corner of her heart—and in Harry's heart. For a poignant moment she felt as though they were here with her—willing her to be happy.

The string quartet began to play. Harry was walking to the *chuppa* with Sam. Her new—precious—daughter, Katie thought with a rush of affection, again finding such pleasure in the strong resemblance between the two young women. So happy that Sam had moved to Dallas, meant to be active—like Harry—in the business.

"Mom, it's our turn," Lisa whispered, her face alight with love. "Take my arm."

Katie stood beneath the *chuppa* with Harry. They went through the small ritual they had enacted all those years ago. The rabbi said the words that once more made them husband and wife.

"Harry, we're a family again," she whispered, her face luminous. "Harry and Katie Newhouse and their children."